For Annie

The Seventh Ceiling

Fondest
wishes !

Lucienne

Selena Di Angelo kept a secret diary.

In it she recorded her stunning rise from the slums of Naples to the heights of the international cosmetic world.

In it is the story of how she gets there-opposed by a murderous Chinese Tong, threatened by powerful New York bankers, rescued by the Mafia, and betrayed by one of her inner circle.

In it she tells of teachers, friends and lovers who impact on her life, and where she meets them-Naples, Cairo, the Big Sur, Greenwich Village, Rome, London, Paris.

In it are the challenges and victories, the losses and hurts, death, and a vicious corporate takeover.

And how finally, she finds her Seventh Ceiling.

The Seventh Ceiling

Lucienne Countess von Doz
with M.E. Hecht

Pen-y-Bryn Ltd.

Printed in the United States of America.
10 9 8 7 6 5 4 3 2 1

Pen-y-Bryn Ltd.
240 Central Park South
New York, NY, 10019.

We would like to thank Lisa Hagan of Paraview Literary Agency for her patience and belief. Christine Bullin for her encouragement. Gloria Guerrero, long time secretary and friend. Baron Paul Pourbaix for historical accuracy. Alicija Ziecina for her willing help. Ralph Rucci my designer and friend. Kristin Doney for her artistic and technical expertise. Estée Lauder Companies for their encouragement and support. And in memoriam Max Huber, whose cosmetic inspiration founded my own. Marina Crispo for all her help. Martina Arroyo and Jackie Horne, friends from the world of opera. For encouraging in the beginning, Venanzio Ciampa. For restoring a previous memory, Laurent Bruyére and Bertrand Lémont. Love and thanks to my sister, Valentina.

Profits from sales of this book will be contributed to The Singers Development Foundation.

ISBN: 0-9702-942-0-4

Library of Congress Number: 00-134127

DEDICATION

To the two Marilyns in my life:

To Marilyn Berger, a loyal friend and creative soul.
and
Marilyn (Jackie) Horne, an inspiration and musical genie.

INTRODUCTION

Chapter: 1   New York 1980

'In twenty years if it comes to a choice between laughter and tears, I have chosen laughter. I have learned to laugh when those who would eat you alive gather to do so. One must show them laughter or indifference, one must dominate and rule, or be swallowed whole.'

Selena was a small figure, etched in silhouette on the floor to ceiling doubled paned window brilliant with a late Fall sun, many floors above New York's Fifth Avenue. She wore a severe-cut black Valentino suit. My suit of armor she thought. It was almost un-feminine she mused created in the manner of so many of the top fashion designers-men who had reservations about the sex of the women they dressed, and yet perfect for the woman who must use it, especially on this occasion.

The strong light pouring through the windows as if to melt them, might have been cruel to some, but limned her style and beauty as if drawn in fine by a bold master.

Despite the cool of her outward look and the control exerted over the sequence of her thoughts, she boiled with rage. And something else, she admitted to herself, fear, yes fear.

'Today may end in tears for me. But for now I could cut the tension "a dull butter knife." Now there's something to laugh at. I know now what that stale expression means, although I wouldn't have had the faintest idea twenty years ago.'

Selena actually laughed aloud at the joke no one but she would ever hear.

'Somehow I find it possible to laugh at the silly, common words which come into my mind to cover the ugliness of betrayal and greed. And even wonder at my enemies within and without the company. I know the enemies I expect, is it possible there are some I don't ? And how many millions are they willing to put into hazard, how much of the future?

Well, we'll just have to see.

In the next hour I'll know whether I, Selena Di Angelo, still have and run my beloved Selena Ltd, or whether others will take my ideas and company for their own.'

She looked around at the space that served as her executive boardroom on the thirtieth floor of New York's Mansard Building. She had designed it with a very specific idea in mind-the idea that energy flowed, and the imagination was loosed, if one thought and worked in extraordinary and beautiful surroundings. Especially if one's business was Beauty.

The boardroom of Selena Ltd, now a successful international cosmetic company, was one of a kind. A small cosmos meant to engender creativity-all subtly colored and irregularly shaped Carara marble, brazed chrome, and focused columns of cool light around the large oval table; light that equalized yet identified the executives who sat around it each centered in their own unit of candescense.

The walls were carpeted with the same thick silken grey as the floor. It was a room meant for intense concentration. Every detail of its furnishing was chosen with this in mind. Meetings that were held within its walls structured major corporate ideas and goals. The people who were invited to attend meetings here, were deliberately isolated and cocooned for this specific purpose. So they could focus without interference, in an abstract setting about problems that were worldly and sensory in the extreme. Ironic, but it worked brilliantly as many of Selena's impulses did. She called them impulses, underlying them was a reasoning, that was apparent often only after they were "fleshed out". It was the one of the bases for the success of the company.

Had anyone, however unlikely, had the nerve to intrude upon this moment in the antechamber to the boardroom, they would have seen a striking woman in her mid thirties. Standing still in front of the window, if still was a term could ever be used about Selena.

She was five feet five inches tall, in her adored Beltrami stiletto heels. Her long legs made her seem much taller.

A source of energy, seemed always coiled and ready within her small frame, available at a moment's notice to work on any task set before her. It seemed to radiate from her, almost as an invisible magnetic field radiates hidden energy seen only when evoked by opposing steel.

Dark brilliant eyes, dark enough to be thought 'black' lighted with intelligence, keenness, or delight, by turn.

No one could mistake her for anything but Italian. The raven's wing hair, worn short, framing the head like a helmet. Her skin faintly blushed with the sun of her native shores, translucent. As glowing as if she were an ad for her own products. Her nose long but straight and fine, and a sensuous mouth completed the picture she presented.

No one who ever met her forgot the wonderfully live face and manner. Her hands seemed to sculpt in three-dimension the ideas, the images she wished to convey. Hands that were an extension of speech as only the those born Latin seem to be able to effect.

Selena had a way of moving that made one think of a trained classical dancer. Sometimes quicksilver, sometimes tantalizingly slow, but always graceful even athletic.

Somewhere in the streets below, Selena knew ordinary city activities were being pursued by ordinary New Yorkers, and even reluctant commuters. From this height they seemed entirely mechanical, entirely unreal.

'Real' crouched waiting to destroy in the board meeting to come; real was in the threat to break her that she would have to face within the hour

As she waited these last minutes, she felt restless. She had to pace about, and so entered the boardroom, 'walking' the center table-checking the minutes and figures contained in the papers she herself had aligned at each place an hour ago. Everything was there. Then as if magnetized, left to return to the windows.

This time she looked up. Up to the space caught now in the light arching above the city. 'Ah yes', She thought- 'that is the Ceiling of God.'

When she was a child in Napoli, she had seen the same high beauty and endless space above her. In those long off days she barely had time to breath much less look up, but some how had snatched moments early in the morning when dawn began to touch the clouds halo-bright, or sometimes late at night when the golden stars of southern Italy blazed in the night sky.

In those days there were hours of "Work." Her father's run-down "Trattoria" opened at six each morning, its broken-faced stone at one with the slum buildings it leant against.

She served thick mud-like Neapolitan coffee and pannini left over from the evening before to the surly, barely wakened laboring men of the neighborhood. Work through the day-bringing mid-day stacks of thick, chipped dishes of heavy pasta, to be quickly scoured in the courtyard. Later heaped dinner trays to be brought round to the common wooden tables for the same work-soiled "patrons". And then still later, after the dinner was served work behind the bar.

Hour after hour of heavy, mind-numbing work that left no time for thoughts of who she was, or what it all meant, or how to soothe adolescent muscles not yet ready for hours of lifting and fetching burdens of this weight.

But that long ago Ceiling of God was her solace when she needed it, the glimpse of all that was beautiful and serene, in the hard days that were her childhood. Now again she needed its wide sense of space to give her perspective and coolness in the fight to come. To curb anger, make it serve. In a very real sense, it would be her weapon for survival in a business world often cold, and even more often hard. Well, she had known "hard" and survived.

The next hour or so would tell. She would finish what she started-or be out. Yesterday's Wunderkind. Bones for the gossip columns of the business journals to pick, meat for the Paparazzi of the scandal sheets. Finished! Done and over!... But not yet.

Again she looked skyward. Her thoughts drifting back.

She had traveled so far. So far from those days and nights as a child in Napoli, and yet that time in the meanest slum section of Via Roma in the Quartiere Spagnoli was still startlingly clear.

The last night she had ever spent in the house where she was born came sweeping into her mind-each detail as sharp as the night it had happened.

CEILING I

Chapter: 1

Late night found the crumbling taverna, emptied of the last patrons, drunk on Mama's cheap home-brewed wine. "Vino Urbino" they called it mocking the crass, raw taste. The echoes of their loud laughter and horseplay had died in the neighborhood streets. Their cobbles released the last of the scuds of work boots dragged along by legs made stupid and clumsy with drink, scattered the shouts and local humor, echoed and mocked the drunken songs and laughter.

Finally quiet set in. The taverna stank of cheap cigarettes, carelessly stubbed in clay ashtrays compounded by the stale smell of worker's sweat, re-newed each evening. The odors of old cooking oil and past meals hung always as a permanent fug in the closed space. The deserted and shuttered hours after closing never served to dilute the smell. It was as permanent and identifying as the lead-lined bar, irreparably dented and scarred over the years.

Fridays the men of the Quartiere came in, pockets holding small packets of lira, a week's pay for rough labor, looking for a pasta or a ragout, and lots of the wine made and bottled in the cellar. Or sometimes a 'special'-spit-turned roast of coniglio-a young rabbit or pollo, fresh-killed chicken. Mama kept them penned up in the courtyard. Most days Uncle Peppino, Mama's favorite younger brother, came just before lunch to slaughter the rabbits, and wring the necks of the fowl she needed that day.

Fridays most regulars stayed on drinking until just able to stagger the few streets to their own beds. It was a night of noise, and hoarse talk, of quarrels, and useless bets on Tombola, the local lotto. Young as she was,

Selena knew the Tombola was a fool's game. Money soon come, and sooner gone.

It was after one when she'd finally been able to clear the tables of wineglasses, and thick chipped bowls still holding leftover pasta and small bones. Papa had long since closed the cash box, and gone upstairs to his bed. Mama always left the kitchen at eleven.

Selena scrubbed down the tabletops, and the bar, upended the worn wooden chairs and stools onto the tables, swept and mopped the stone floor.

She was aching with weariness. At sixteen Selena had lots of energy. But come Friday nights she was tired. The seven out of seven days, morning to late night was grinding, and painful even for her wiry young strength.

She looked around carefully to see if she had missed anything. In the morning, when Mama came down, if she found anything undone or unready for the next day's use, she would scream at Selena. And slap the back of her head as hard as she could, to 'help put in that brain what was important to be in there'. No. It was all finished. Everything. Mama would find nothing to complain of in the morning.

She washed and hung her apron to dry, left the bar, moved quietly across the inner court yard, deliberately ignoring the small night sounds and rustlings that came from the wooden chicken and rabbit cages. She couldn't afford to think about the animals or care, knowing the kitchen's routine.

Uncle Peppino understood her feelings, and had laughed until tears streamed from his eyes when she had refused to collect the few eggs the hens laid. It was one of the few refusals she had ever offered her family. Her Mama had shouted at her, but surprisingly her Papa had said "Basta", and adverted the punishment he had seen coming in Mama's eyes. Had he understood or was he just not in the mood for one of Mama's tantrums? Selena never knew.

She climbed the worn stairs leading to the small attic under the eaves of the five-story house on Via Roma. She lifted the wooden door-latch and went into her room.

Shedding her clothes, with the quickness and efficiency of long practice in the unlit room, she hung them to air on a wall peg. The smells of Mama's heavy cooking, and the patron's smoke trapped in their folds would be less by morning if they were left to air.

Exhausted, she slipped on the cotton shift she used for a nightgown, washed her face with the water in her nightstand bowl, and climbed into bed. Almost instantly she slept.

A shaft of moonlight and a stream of cold air reached her from the dormer window but she was oblivious, deep asleep.

She didn't hear the door open, or see the huge form of her uncle Peppino stoop, enter, and carefully bolt the door. She was wakened when he shook her by the shoulder, one knee on her bed.

"Bambola", he rasped in what was meant to be an affectionate whisper. He turned her head towards him, for a moment she was aware of the overpowering odor of dirt and stale sweat which surged from him, and then his mouth fell on hers covering it in a rough slobbering kiss.

His tongue forced its way into her mouth. She could barely breathe. His breath smelled of rotten teeth and garlic.

When she tried to twist her head away under his mouth. He stopped for a moment, as if pleased by her resistance. Smiled. And grasped her face in one huge hand, forcing her to look as he slipped his tongue rapidly in and out of his mouth in the lewd way she had seen several of the bar customers do.

"Carina, Stai zitta. Zio Peppi a qualcosa speciale per te." She didn't know what he meant when he said he had something special to give her. But his heavy forefinger laid across her mouth made it clear she was not to speak.

Still more than half asleep, accustomed to obey familial orders, and drugged from physical exhaustion, she could only comply.

He grunted as he rose, from the bed, turning his body away from her. When he turned back he had taken off his pants, and was standing at her side between the bed and the door. Again the rancid odor coming from his lower body was nauseating. She was aware of his nakedness amid the immense quantity of coarse black curling hair, which enveloped him from his genitals to his belly.

"Guarda," look, he said, and took his half erect penis in his own hand as he again knelt down near her head. "Tocca!" Feel. He reached for her hand, put the weight of his scrotum in it. She looked at him with revulsion and fear. He smiled, the idea of her fear and reluctance aphrodisiac to his growing erection.

"Guarda" he said with satisfaction, "Questo bel cazzo é per te." He manipulated her hand so that it could grasp his huge genitals. In horror she saw the thickly-veined, empurpled penis rise up to his belly, and throb with the suffusion of blood being pumped into its thick shaft.

She tried to rise from the bed, but he trapped her quickly up against the head of the bed. He dropped his penis, seeking to part her legs. Propelled by an instinct too deep and ancient to question, she had drawn them up tight together. But Selena was trapped up against railings of the head board. He was able to straighten her legs, and pull her body down flat under his. She continued to twist, trying to escape.

"Basta" he said. And when she continued to writhe, he hit her a heavy blow across the face. Her head rang with it and tears leapt to her eyes. "Basta". He hit her again. And now she knew he would continue to strike if she moved.

"Ah, Bene." He pushed his heavy body in between her legs, forcing them wide apart. " É adesso, ".

She was pinned to the bed by his weight, as he put his huge member to the opening of her vagina and began to ram her. The battering was, intense and painful. She took a breath and finally, hoping to stop him before he did anything more cried "Zio Peppi, ti prego, no, no!"

He slapped her mouth, then clamped it with a hand strong from the habit of wringing the necks of the trattoria's fowl, and holding shoats for the butchering blade. "Silenzio. Ho detto, Silenzio." There was nothing else she could do, crushed beneath his weight.

Realizing as a sixteen year old virgin, he would have to enlarge her in order to shaft her, he took first two fingers, then three and shoved them brutally up into her, stifling her screams with his mouth. He was elated by the quantity of blood he caused to flow onto his hand and then over the sheets. A true virgin!

Then he replaced his fingers with his member, now thoroughly stiff and erect. He pushed and pushed until he was able to shaft most of his penis, and worked enough to friction himself into orgasm. For Selena the pain and shock were so intense, for the first time in her life, she fainted.

When she came to, she saw him arousing himself with his own hand, as he licked at the blood on her pudendum. He knew she had been unconscious, and was taking advantage of her passive form to get himself ready again.

"Adesso, mia piccola. Encore, eh?! Que felicitá. He talked as if he felt she would not be able to resist the pleasure to come, now she had had her first taste.

Once again she tried to rise from the bed, crying out-"Mama, Mama! Mama!" He cuffed her brutally snapping her head back against the iron of the bedpost. The room blacked out in spinning lights.

He was insatiable. Time and again penetrating her vagina or rectum at will. She hadn't the strength to prevent it. She lost count of the hours, where she was and exactly what he was doing,

She was wrapped in such pain and fear, that only the ceiling of her room had any reality for her. Over his massively fat body as he raped her repeatedly, she caught glimpses of the rough stucco, and slanted eaves of her room. The sole space that was hers alone. Her only thought was survival. She had to continue to breathe when his mass settled on her. She had to deaden her mind to the pain, the fresh battering each time he entered her. Somehow she knew if she could count the beams on the ceiling, and see the repeat rough pattern of the workman's strokes in the gesso, enter dim shadows cast in the night light, if she could center up there on the ceiling she would endure.

When he had had enough, when his penis would respond no more, Peppino rose. Wiped his slack member on the bedclothes.

"Era fantastico, No? Forse domani? It was great, but then there's always tomorrow. Now that you know how to do it Eh? Dio!" he commented as he did up the buttons of his workman's pants and buckled his belt.

He must have crept out of the room Selena never knew. She lost consciousness once again.

Chapter: 2

She had no idea exactly how much time had passed since Peppino left her room. She knew the roosters in the courtyard had not yet begun to crow, and there was no light showing in the window. But her attic bedroom, her own beloved room as familiar as a part of her body confounded her. The outlines of the walls and windows and nightstand had become charged with strangeness, and as memory returned fully, polluted with violence.

As to herself she lay akimbo on torn bed sheets-the linens crushed and stained with sweat and blood. Finger nails torn where she'd tried to resist. She stared at the blood smeared over her thighs. Her body felt beaten. Battered. No longer intact. She couldn't tell how badly she was hurt.

She looked around quickly full of fear. No one! For a moment it was enough that she could see there was nothing in the room with her. The taste of blood was in her mouth, and another taste, a foul taste that had to be spent semen.

And then it hit. Pain. Pain washing over her. Surging from her violated parts. Overwhelming pain. Slowly, she willed her arms to move. She braced them behind her and levered up from the bed to a sitting position. Thank God the pain didn't increase. A wave of nausea swept her. She retched again and again. She knew she had to had to do something, had to get off the bed.

She got her legs together, and slid them over the side of the bed. Dizziness hit immediately. She had to pant for breath, wait for the room which canted crazily around to become solid and upright and the violent shaking to stop.

I have to know, how bad it is, she thought, and

looked down between her legs. No fresh spurts of blood. That was good. Just the tackiness of blood already congealed. Whatever damage Peppino had done was finished. Nausea rose flooding the back of her throat. She knew with dead certainty, she could not afford to give in to it again. Breathe. Just breathe she told herself. You have to control it. Finally the nausea subsided.

She reached up to the iron bedpost, grasped it and pulled herself to her feet clinging to its metal strength. Again the pain and dizziness. She bit her lips fearing any involuntary cry, and found them swollen and split. She'd started up fresh bleeding. She grasped a loose corner of linen and pressed it against the split.

Now she thought, I must get water and the stracci-scraps of cloth Mama had taught her to use. Discarded strips and old rags of cloth useless for any other purpose except to staunch "the monthly flows".

Leaning against the bed for support she forced herself to move. She reached the nightstand. Poured some water into the basin, washed her hands and face. Again had to wait for new faintness to pass. Then cleansed her thighs. And finally, ignoring the pain, her pudendum, and the creases between her buttocks. She washed her anus free of feces and blood. The area was so raw, she came near dropping to the floor with fresh pain. But it had to be cleansed. That much she knew even though she risked more oozing.

She felt herself. There were tears in her vagina and anus. She used the stracci to dress them as best she could. They were all she had. She wished she had some Mama's aloe made in the pharmacy down the street but knew it an impossibility even as she longed for its easement.

She took a sip of clean water from the pitcher. Stared for a moment at its familiar cracked pattern.

And thought, what now? What will I do now?

Her world had changed completely, and it had to be dealt with. But she would have to know what was to be done before dawn...have to sort things out.

As she stood some of the strength of her legs came back. The awful trembling that had started as she regained consciousness lessened. Traces of ideas and images of what the morning would bring began to form into coherent thoughts.

If she told Mama what had happened, Mama would not believe that Peppino, darling Peppino, her youngest brother would do such a thing. Or if she had the least trickle of suspicion, would think it could only have happened if Selena had provoked it. No. There lay neither help nor protection.

Well then, Papa. But if she told Papa, and if he believed her, he would feel obliged to 'kill' Peppino. Peppino twice his size, younger and stronger-the fight would be lost before it began. Papa would know this; it would stop him cold. In frustration he'd be furious not with Peppino, but with Selena for causing a loss of Figura, loss of pride, loss of face and status.

On the other hand, if he thought to send Peppino away, Mama would be outraged by the upset in the order of the household-where would they get another butcher, especially so cheap, whose services cost no more than-a few glasses of wine, a plate of pasta, and a place to gossip with his friends. Papa's anger would again fall on Selena as the root of the trouble. Girls should not make such problems.

As for Peppino, he had promised her more of the same, and Selena knew he meant exactly that. There was nothing and no one to stop him.

Dear God. What was the answer? What was to be done? Here eyes traveled the room, as if the answer might come from the old whitewashed walls-survivors of the centuries, solid and cool with the scars of endurance they bore.

There were the pegs that held her few skirts and blouses and her aprons. The washstand with its bloody water. The painted wooden crucifix on the wall. Today the suffering the artist had scribed on the flaking face of the Savior seemed all too real. Finally she looked at the bed with its torn and stained linen. She had wept futilely, no one had heard. Her child's body seemed to have wept bloody tears-no one heeded, no one would heed.

Selena knew in that moment she had no choice but to go. Leave the Trattoria. Leave Napoli. And immediately. But where? How? She had no idea-but she must go where the famiglia wouldn't dream of finding her.

Once decided, she wrapped her clothes in one of the voluminous skirts handed down from her Mama and not yet re-cut for her size, and left the room silently, without a backward look.

Now to get out without rousing anyone.

The trip down the stairs was a matter of creeping down a few treads, waiting for the strength in her legs to come back, checking for tell-tale blood spotting then going on. She thought of a caterpillar she had once seen desperate to cross a pane of a large window, inching along, using all its body, impelled to travel what must have seemed like an immense distance. She had no choice. Crawl then rest, crawl then rest until the three steep flights finished in the courtyard.

The animals were still sleeping. Their morning calls would not betray her presence at this hour. She crossed the yard, clinging to its walls for support, and entered the bar. Once more she had to sit down at a table to rest a moment. She knew nobody would be up but still listened in case.

Some how the shattering of her body made her fear the normal household the pattern wouldn't hold. She found she'd been holding her breath, as if breathing in this place at this time would wake an animal or some way rouse Papa or even Peppino. She knew it wasn't rational, but fear batted her back and forth like an broken shell on the shore with the tide incoming. She had to stop this panic. So she deliberately took a deep rasping breath. Nothing stirred.

She sat quietly for a moment. Images of the night past swept her. She felt a rush of shame and humiliation. Then as she continued to think, anger replaced the shame and frustration. Blazing anger. She knew instinctively that she should leave other feelings for now and trust the anger. It carried her over to the bar. She knew what she had to do next. She listened. Nothing.

She went to where Papa kept the tin cash box. The key was not in it. But she found a knife, and sprung the lock. Again listened. No one had heard the sounds she made breaking it. Inside she found several hundred lira. These she took, shut the box and replaced it.

She had worked from dawn to dusk for as long as she could remember without thanks, and without pay. But even so, when she could she'd return the money.

She lifted the wooden bar from the front door, opened it just enough to get through, then eased it shut.

It was done. She'd left behind the only home she'd ever known. And she recognized she'd left her childhood with it.

Chapter: 3

Darkness was beginning to lift in the eastern sky. No moon shone, but masses of brilliant stars sparked in the fastness of space. The sky never slept, Selena thought. Just the people below it. She looked up. There at the edge of the heavens was the faintest hint of the dawn to come, but down here there were still only, muffled sounds of sleep, the brief surcease from the grinding struggle for those who lived in the quartiere-the opium that drugged them to the mean drudgery of each day.

As she crept across the blocks, she almost felt the ever-present smells of sewage from the open gutters in alleys that ran off the main streets, from the refuse that was often as not left raw in them. She saw the silent scurrying forms of rats- the oldest and best-fed citizens of the neighborhood as she passed from street to street.

Fearful, she stopped to look over her shoulder. No one followed. She stumbled over one of the old broken slabs of paving stone. The huge, round-edged blocks which surfaced many of the city's main streets. Some of them dated back to the times when Pax Romana was visited on most of the known world, and Imperial Rome ruled. Now the stones were irregular, pitted, and worn by centuries of constant traffic. Never replaced. Many were slime covered, others had sprouted a slippery kind of moss. They made footage difficult.

She stumbled repeatedly. There was so little light she couldn't see many of the mounds and holes to be avoided, and in any case, there was little spring in her knees to accommodate them.

She heard the flapping of laundry forgotten and left out overnight on the lines stretched between the small windows of neighboring tenements in the old Via

Sanitá. The walls of the buildings oozed sourness, old age, and decay. They always felt wet to the touch in the dampness of the night air. The "night airs" that so frightened the inhabitants of the Quartiere that drunk or sober, early or late, their windows were shut and barred against them. Of equal importance to the knowing Napolitani was the thought they afforded protection against thieves, as common as rats in the dilapidated neighborhoods.

She managed the length of Via Caracciola, leading away from the Quartiere. And as she turned without conscious thought in the direction of the harbor, she passed the dilapidated stands covered by rusting tin. By day, from their shelves overripe fruit, cheap souvenirs, and pornographic postcards were peddled to tourists and sailors. Now they lay shuttered. Just cheap, shabby landmarks of the approach to the harbor.

She stopped and looked before entering each new block. Napoli was infested with thieves and druggies, who never slept. She must be careful. In her present state she couldn't handle an encounter with either. If she met one of them, her lira would be gone as surely as if they had never existed. She kept on. One block, two blocks, the way seemed unending.

Selena looked up at the next street sign. Mola Carmina. Blessed Mary! She had made it to the beginning of the port section. Mola Carmina. Here were the oldest wharves of the city.

As dawn was breaking she arrived at the waters of the harbor. Not the glorious curve of the Bay of Naples painted by so many Italian period painters, but the rotting wharves at the farthest part of the harbor where the meanest and smallest freighters docked.

Everything seemed still. No hint of activity from any of the boats save one. All the way down at the end of the wharf, wisps of steam came from the funnels of a boat which looked as if it was readying for an early departure.

The deep bells of the Madonna del Carmine began calling people to six o'clock Matins, the first mass of the day. She had to hurry. Blocks of paving stone gave way to the thick wooden planks of the wharves.

When she got to the ship she saw through the chipped, weathered paint on its bow the name "Victoria". What an odd name, she thought for a ship that looked so tired and used. But still she looked the ship over-up and down the length of its decks. Rivers of discolored paint and rust streaked down its hull. Dents from rough docking encounters were everywhere. Patches of crusted old oil or tar showed at the anchor hawse, and slime stained brown in a cascade where the bilge had been pumped out over the years.

As a Napolitano, Selena knew of the small older freighters that took unscheduled cargoes from port to port, and that these ships were called "Trampers". This one looked beaten and neglected even for a "Tramper". Her condition made Selena wonder about the men who sailed her, and the Captain who ran her.

Perhaps they wouldn't accept a passenger. Then the decrepitude of the boat, its forlorn look of neglect and hard use, reassured her that an offer of money might well get her aboard to the next port of call.

Yes, I must take my chances that they will take money to get me away. I must get on this ship, wherever it's to go, and leave. I'll ask for the next stop. No matter where. Anywhere away from Napoli.

She saw the gangplank resting unguarded on the pier, and hurried to it. Clutching her small pack of clothing in one hand, and the rope that served as railing in the other, she managed her way up the steep cant of the gangway. Many of its slats were broken and made irregular by careless repair.

Arriving breathless at the top she was stopped abruptly by a large slovenly deckhand. He was dirty, unshaven and slouched directly in front of her, blocking her way. The image of his broken-nailed bare feet, threadbare overalls filthy with grease, and an equally filthy duck-billed hat pegged him as a low-ranking member of the crew.

Smoke curled up from the limp end of a cigarette in his hand. A suggestive smile showed a few rotting stumps of teeth. He scratched at his chest through a grey torn shirt with his free hand, as he looked her up and down. Whores had been known to be smuggled aboard in ports for those of the crew who were not given liberty. Maybe he'd lucked out. She could feel his eyes undressing her. Without moving he asked,"Eh ragazza. Che vuoi?" Hey girl, what do you want here? Selena never knew where the authority in her manner and posture came from, but she straightened up to her tallest and looking directly at him, with command in her voice she said, "Il Commandante. E subito!" I wish to see your Captain, immediately.

Instinctively, and to his own surprise, the sailor responded to her tone and manner. He too straightened up as he found himself responding without further challenge.

"Si, vado cercare il Commandante." Yes, I'll go find the Captain. Leaving Selena to look after him, he turned directly toward the bridge.

She set her belongings at her feet. Inwardly collected her purpose and determination. Drew herself up to her full height and waited for the man whose response would determine her immediate future.

CEILINGS II

Chapter: 1

The porthole to John Harvey's deckside cabin was laid open to catch whatever harbor breeze could be caught in its small opening. So in spite of the early hour, he couldn't fail to hear the sharp exchange taking place on the main deck not far away. It sounded like one of the deckhands and a young female, if he could judge from her voice. A voice rather deep and husky. The dialect unmistakably Neapolitan. The tone commanding. And what was in essence a demand to see the Captain. This intrigued him. It was a definite break in the normal routine of port departure.

Actually he had been wakened an hour earlier by the startup of familiar vibrations traveling the hull. The ship's engine room was getting up steam. He knew it took the best part of an hour to get the coal-fired engines ready to obey the command for half power that would overcome the inertia of the berthing. So whatever the resolution with the girl, it would happen quickly.

He was curious how the Captain would handle this intrusion. And, he had to face it, he was just plain curious.

He rose from his narrow bunk, and turned the sheets back to air, while he dressed in a clean shirt and sea-faded jeans. His movements were quick, well coordinated, with more than a hint of the athlete, though it had been many years since he'd seen competition or been in formal training for it. Three years ago the pants had fit him. Now, they hung loose about his hips, kept up by a pair of sun-faded black braces.

He splashed his face with water, and took a quick look. Jesus, he was getting to look like one of the crew.

He had sprouted a three-day beard, and being as it was starting to grey, it gave him, in a word, a definitely scruffy look. His eyes which were surrounded now by 'crows feet' were a deep grey. He thought the lines around his mouth seemed ruled almost like two parenthses. Elsa might have said he looked like one of those monochromatic studies by Shawn or one of the lesser modernists. And talk of haircuts... The ship's cook had given him his last aided by a hand clipper. It had grown out. Now ragged only began to describe what it looked like. Later he would tend to it all.

His cabin, about 12 by 14 feet, was considered the luxury accommodation aboard the Victoria for its space, and private "head" which provided a fresh water shower. For John Harvey, it was "Home", or had been for the last six months.

He thought idly, "I wonder what the date is today?" The wanderings of the ship had robbed him of an accurate sense of time. Sometimes it seemed a few weeks since he had boarded at Newark port and engaged quarters, other times the ship seemed like a carapace inside of which he'd always lived. Actually it made little difference either way-months or days. No wonder he looked as if he fit right in with the boat-a shoddy reject of a ship.

Still, compelled by an old habit, he opened one of the slim grey logbooks in which he kept notes of days, and places, and wrote March 25, 1962. Thursday. Napoli. Weather clear. 55 degrees. In port.

He'd known when he'd bought passage for an indetermined length, that tramp steamers picked up cargoes and ladings no larger or faster ship would carry, and took them without specific scheduling to wherever they were consigned. Days and weeks of repeated sound and activities, the harbor to harbor pattern following the calls of small portage, suited him just fine.

The Victoria had minimal mechanical assists to load and unload, balance, store and retrieve at each port. But she carried a shouting, swearing lading crew, who maneuvered her cargoes of crates and barrels in nets that dipped into the hold to be guided up and over the side to waiting wagons and trucks in port after port.

He'd learned too, that the men who labored aboard were rough saltwater merchant mariners, unacceptable or unsuitable to a better class of ship for any number of reasons, most of which didn't bear close investigation. They were a motley crew speaking diverse native tongues. Some bore frightful scars on their face or arms, souvenirs of violent encounters in bars, or streets, or jails around the world-ill sutured, if sutured at all. A grim, sullen group of men, but all familiar with the universal language of a tramp steamer, and responsive to the commands of the Captain, a man even tougher and colder, who ran the ship at all times with mechanical, merciless discipline.

The crew obeyed his orders without question and on the instant. Theirs was a precarious existence at best. Anyone of them could be discharged at the nearest port without notice or cause other than the Captain's will, and without back pay. Wages and passports locked securely in the Captain's quarters were given out to the men solely at his whim.

Every soul aboard knew that as recently as the port at Ostia, just outside Rome, he had thrown two Nigerian crewmen off the boat in just this manner.

"Too slow! Too stupid! You verdamt schwartzen. Get gone!"

Stauger's voice had carried easily the length of the upper deck. The two men were stranded on the wharf, without funds, and worse without work-papers or passport. As the gangway was pulled up, they were seen weeping and begging in their native language, terrified.

At the last minute, Stauger laughed uproariously at the sight of the two men crumpled on their knees, and flung their passports towards the dock. One landed on the pier, the other sank beneath the harbor waters.

"Dive, Monkey man, Dive!" He shouted, and laughed even harder as the document was lost to sight.\

Captain Stauger was a large, physically imposing man, not reluctant to use his size and brute strength. His head and hands were outsized. His face would have graced a cathedral, along with the gargoyles found there. And like they, it was a face frightening and meant to frighten. His voice was invariably loud, its language the foulest. He made no attempt to modify either knowing he intimidated most men he met. But if he expected to impress John, he was mistaken.

The Captain's obvious manipulations of sailing 'terms' had been both unimportant and meaningless to him. He was neither fazed nor intimidated. Harvey understood exactly that the Captain was habitual in his need for dominance not to mention money. And these flaws he would accept, as he accepted most of the other conditions of sailing with the ship with indifference. Particularly as the planless itinerary of the Victoria suited him so perfectly. The ship had sailed at the vagaries of her capacity to haul the cargoes offered. The matter of his passageway fees, he set on a continuing basis.

He was looking for isolation, and escape. For time without obligations. And something that could put distance between himself and the last three years of his existence.

Therefore, he simply informed the man that he would leave ship, when it came to that, at a port of his choosing. The Captain accepted this condition as well as his cash. And so interpersonal matters between them were left.

Well part of it had worked. The ship with its unchanging routine had produced a certain calm and also distance from life in New York. Neither the Captain nor any of the crew asked anything of him other than to appear in the mess hall on time if he wanted to eat, and to keep out from underfoot when they were taking on or off-loading cargo.

When they got to a harbor, he could go ashore for whatever small necessities, or books, or supplies he wanted. Then tour the port city until called back by the blast of the ship's horn that summoned all hands. After six months he had seen a fair part of the world, at least its harbor cities.

Each morning he worked out hard for two hours forward in the ship's bows. A life long habit. Keeping his body in reasonable shape. Almost done without willing it. A shower and breakfast usually followed this routine. Then he returned to his cabin and sat down at the tiny wall-hung counter that served him as a desk. Its scratched vinyl surface secured his old portable Remington and reams of paper.

He noted time and place in his logbook. And for the next three hours did what he could to write. Sometimes he would get the beginnings of an idea, and write a few words or if lucky a few paragraphs before nothing more came. He tried the old writer's trick of turning the mind blank, like a tabula rasa, to let images or ideas flow spontaneously without direction or guidance on his part. Well, the tabula rasa part of the exercise he could manage, but as to ideas, only unwanted images from the last year floated by, sometimes not even that. Sometimes, he had the odd idea, that the grey-painted bulkhead walls of the cabin, its watertight steel enclosure, held him numb, powerless to create, caught and frustrated in its small space. But more often he knew that the trap lay in his mind, coiled by the past.

And at these times he had to settle for reading or studying.

The engine revolutions had increased to the point that he knew the ship would be departing within less than a half-hour. He went up on deck to see how Captain Stauger would settle matters with the girl.

The Captain appeared as he normally did, in the early morning light heavily bearded, truculent, ready to shout at the men or the mates, quick to blame, quick to anger. He spoke a little English and Italian, both with a heavy German accent. Mornings, when he was often hung over from what passed for a type of cheap, generic local gin he picked up in each port, were times he was to be avoided. This morning was no exception. He rubbed at his eyes with his knuckles as if that might help clear the blear of the night before.

As he approached the bridge, John could see him taking in the very young girl waiting for him. She seemed little more than a child. The threadbare skirt and outsized sweater she wore against the morning cold in the clear morning light was rusty black, the traditional color of the poor. A skirt, and a scarf of the same color completed the picture, Even her shoes must once have had black lasts to the thin soles. He could see even from the distance the details of darning at shoulder and elbow.

Her face appeared noticeably swollen and discolored, as if recently battered. It was obvious from the postures of both, that she was asking something of the Captain, as she held out money in her hand.

He could imagine how frightening the man must seem to the slight girl, who nevertheless stood before him with dignity, displaying no fear, no matter what she might be feeling. Stauger's expression showed what passed for a smile, as he shook his head.

John heard him say, "Cinque mille fino a Messina"

Five thousand lira to go to Messina Sicily. Messina, John knew, lay overnight but less than sixty miles down the western coast of Italy.

Selena looked at the Captain appalled by the amount of money being asked. It was an impossible sum-she had nothing like that. What she had no way of knowing was, that it was an outrageous fare for a such short passage. She did know instinctively that if she showed anything but calm, at this point, it would go poorly for her. Like showing fear to a guarding dog it would provoke attack. Or with this man, denial.

She tried to think what would strengthen her appeal. Perhaps he would accept her passage if she were to work for the lacking money.

"Signor Commandante," she offered politely, " La prego." Sir I beg you. I haven't got five thousand, but I am willing to give you what I've got, and work on the ship to pay the rest. I can clean, and iron, and cook and

"And?" Strauger grinned, "The boat does not need someone to cook or clean."

He raked her with his eyes. "But perhaps a little daily attention to the Captain's quarters..." Again he grinned. It was not a pretty sight. His eyes roving her body left no doubt as to the kind of cabin care he had in mind. Selena had seen this kind of look before and knew what it meant.

Before she could respond, he caught at the few hundred lira she held out. Counted. Then quickly, apparently thinking to seal the bargain he said,
" Eight hundred lira. Good. I will take it towards your passage, Eh? And the rest..."

Selena, for the first time uncertain, shrank away from him, and looked back toward the pier from which she'd come. The Captain scowled. It was clear she was loath to consider his proposal. It turned him sullen. Why shouldn't this "Scunizza", this little tramp, pay her way with pleasure if not lira?

He continued in his broken Italian, knowing that almost surely she had offered all she had,

"Well then, give me another four thousand, and we'll consider it done."

The rumble coming from the engine sounded stronger now, as departure time was minutes away. The ship's horn gave two blasts, signaling the deckhands to take their places for leaving, and the men dockside to man the stanchions holding the hawses securing the ship.

Selena, not knowing what to do turned in appeal to this terrible man, involuntary tears forming in her eyes despite her efforts to control them.

"É tutto!" This is all I have. I haven't anymore.

John refused to watch anymore of the Captain's cat and mouse game played with all the cards in his favor. Catching his eye, he beckoned him over.

The American was an important person on the ship; Stauger couldn't afford to ignore him. Even though it was with reluctance, made clear by the slowness of his response, he turned from the girl and sauntered over.

"It would seem the Signorina doesn't have the full fare in hand, Captain, but I do."

John went into his pocket counted out 4,000 lira, holding it just out of the grasp of the Captain, almost as the Captain had done to Selena. It was John's way of saying unmistakably-enough is enough.

A moment passed in which the Captain turned almost purple with anger. It was clear, he wanted to strike out at this presumptuous American.

Selena had no insight into what lay between them. She recognized the surge of violence coming from the Captain, and what had to be, from its tone defiance from the other man. The tension on deck palpable. An explosion imminent.

Had John been anyone else a blow would have followed. In that moment, thinking about his pocket, Stauger mastered himself. He started to reach for the money, John held it just out of his grasp, adding,

"I couldn't help overhearing that this is the proposed "fare to Messina". It seems a little steep, don't you think?"

The tone was lightly sarcastic. He wanted the Captain to know that he was aware of the outlandish amount of the fee, but didn't want him to dig his heels in.

Dio, I can't believe, he's provoking that monster, Selena thought.

" It is my ship, my decision. I set the price", the Captain said in a voice meant to carry.

"Of course it is", John said, shrewdly going with the show of authority. Then speaking softly so only the Captain could hear, "But let me suggest the fare include a cabin for the Signorina, and cover the transportation to the port of her choosing within the next few weeks."

Stauger loathed the interference. The effrontery, and considered for a moment casting the girl off the ship. On second thought, he felt he couldn't afford to challenge this source of continuing money, and made up his mind that he had to accept what the American was proposing for the moment. He would find a way to get at the girl, who had evidently evoked Harvey's sympathy. But later. After all she was only a passenger, passive, and helpless on board. She was evidently also poor, without resource or connections. The American would lose interest, retreat back into the isolated routine he had pursued ever since he had come on board. It only made sense.

Then the perfect solution came to him. With a show of acceptance, he took the money John held out, and called one of the hands over.

" Take the girl to the forward crew cabin" he growled in German.

The seaman looked at the captain and repeated, "The forward crew Cabin?"

"Yes. It's empty now, no?"

Both captain and seaman knew the two Nigerians had occupied this isolated, least desirable of ship's cabins given over to crew accommodation. They both knew the cabin, isolated in the in the extreme forward hold, had neither lock nor bar to secure it against entry. John failed to catch the wink that passed from the Captain to the hand.

"Aye, Aye, Sir." The seaman beckoned to Selena.

She hadn't been able to follow all of the exchange between the Captain and the man who had appeared suddenly, but she understood that the tall authoritative figure who had come to the bridge from out of nowhere, changed the nature of her exchange with the Captain, and made it possible to leave the city. Made it possible to survive, free of the Captain's conditions. In a choked voice she said to him,

"Grazie, signor, Grazie tanto." Thank you, thank you so much.

John responded simply "Prego". You are welcome. Selena would have said more but the Captain interrupted to indicate she should follow the seaman who would lead her below. As she left the bridge, she thought, later. Later I will sort it all out.

The sun began its climb into the morning sky, the gulls wheeled and screamed over the littered harbor waters, the stevedores on shore loosed the cables, and the ship edged away from the pier.

Selena walking painfully toward the hold of the ship stopped to look at the sky over Napoli once more. She was leaving all that was familiar, all that she had known. What lay before her? Who knew? For now she needed to sleep, to let rest heal her body.

The Molla drew back slowly. Selena turned away from the shore, from the hills of the city now falling behind the departing freighter. Finally she nodded, and followed the deck hand into the hold of the ship. It was done. She left her childhood behind in the taverna on Via Roma.

Chapter: 2

Having settled the girl's passage, John put it out of his mind for the time being. Later that morning, he sat down at his desk. Pulled out a thin manilla folder, and shook several sheets of paper from it. They each held a number of lines of text, but still more lines scratched out or overwritten. He sighed. Paragraph captions identified an essay on travel.

He read a few lines. Frowned. Tore the sheets across, and tossed them away. It was a practiced action. And why not? He hadn't written anything half acceptable since leaving Newark, and in fact nothing for the last two years.

Jesus! Had it been two? It seemed more like an eternity, although the exact time was two years, five months, twenty days, and he stopped before he got to the hours realizing how obsessive he was being.

At three in the morning, while he held her in his arms, gasping for the last breath of air, no longer able to utter screams against the agony beating at her body, Elsa, his wife of ten years gave up, and in less than an instant, died. John was left with the memory, the hollow shell of their life for the last year. A year of bootless, frightful chemotherapy and irradiation. A year centered only on trying to arrest breast cancer, with less and less effect, but ever increasing pain and disability. By the time of Elsa's last hospitalization, morphine proved useless against the pain of a malignancy spread to the bones of her spine.

From the beginning he felt useless. He could only watch as Elsa became gripped by her disease, helpless to aid. And then she died.

The days that followed her funeral stretched into

weeks of unreality, of not understanding why Elsa died, her life unspent. Weeks of anger at her desertion, framed by his awareness of the futility, the irrationality of his emotions. And of a paralyzing drift into inertia. Weeks turned into months.

Friends came and called, then gradually stopped when he couldn't respond to their sympathy or return their calls. His agent picked up on what was happening after several deadlines went by unheeded by one of the most reliable of his clients. And when he came to the apartment the unanswered mail and bills piled unattended on a table in the hallway, the untended rooms, and John's appearance spoke for themselves.

Upset for him, he called these things roughly to his attention. John finally realized that some things, day to day things, he simply had to take care of, as a matter of practicality. The agent sent an assistant over to help sort out the mess, and a cleaning service to go through the apartment.

Over the following weeks, by day John sat at his desk, looking at the half-finished life of Samuel Morse, nineteenth century inventor of the telegraph, long since promised to his publisher, unable to write a word. Afternoons he shopped mostly for frozen dinners he could heat in the microwave.

At night his life played over and over in his head. The precious ten years he had with Elsa. The desolation of his earlier life, which she had changed with her warmth, her humor, her love.

John was born in Bridgewater Connecticut, his father a janitor of one of the local High Schools. Life in the Harvey household was one of unremitting struggle to keep ahead of the landlord and the grocer. It left little room for close family life. But the public school he attended had, oddly, the combined distinction of a high academic level and a swimming team which practiced in an unheated pool in the school basement.

At seventeen, he had been spotted as a medley swimmer of outstanding promise by one of the senior swimming coaches of Yale University, which prided itself on its swimming teams, and a man who was also Bridgewater born. The coach, excited by the rarity of John's swimming ability, and further encouraged by his academic standing, was able to arrange a full board and tuition scholarship at the University-outstanding medley swimmers who had to be accomplished in three strokes, being hard to come by.

John met Elsa when she was not many years older than the young girl he'd seen this morning. He was twenty-one, in his senior year at Yale. She was nineteen. He remembered perfectly their first meeting.

He'd just won his heat at the Yale-Harvard swimming meet, and sat dripping wet and shivering visibly, having misplaced his towel. She came out of the spectator section to congratulate him on his race, and saw his condition. In typical fashion, cast about, spotted a stack of towels, picked one up, and brought it to him as she introduced herself, and then congratulated him on his race.

He had a typical swimmer's lanky, smooth-muscled body, with over-developed shoulders, lithe hips and highly defined calves and thighs. This was topped by an undistinguished face, and thick blonde unruly straight hair, held back by his swimming goggles. He was well over six feet, although crouched over as he presently was, it was hard to appreciate his height.

Without thinking, he wrapped himself in the towel, rubbed hard at his legs and arms, then looked up gratefully to see a tiny, copper-headed beauty laughing a little at his discomfort.

Her hazel eyes danced. "I'm Elsa Danfort", she said, and offered her hand.

" John Harvey".

"Yes I know." She laughed again holding up a program listing his name. This time he joined her.

It was the beginning for them. Elsa was a sophomore at Yale University, an art major, lucky enough to find work in one of the more prosperous art galleries in New Haven. He was by then, still on full scholarship.

By the end of the year they were married. Both worked part time to pay for a small apartment on Elm street. It was a marvelous time of goals set, achieved, and new goals set. Of laughter, and pride, and intoxication with one another.

John was accepted into the combined M.A. / Ph.D. program in the history department. He applied for, and got a grant which helped support his studies. Life, for the first time for him, was complete and full of joy and when not joy, contentment.

Most autumn weekends they went out into the glorious Connecticut countryside, of riotous fall colors, Seckel pears, and heritage varieties of local apples. They often slept outdoors cuddled in GI surplus sleeping bags, cooking their own food over an outdoor wood fire, and eating the fruits they had found in small roadside stands beside the country fields.

Winters they found inexpensive bed and breakfast inns, and went for long cross-country ski treks, bundled in impossibly bulky layers of clothing which set them laughing often as not.

One day, John recalled, it had snowed hard during the night. When they woke and looked out, eight inches had fallen making the Berkshire mountains exquisite, with the dark green stands of fir trees, breaking into the glistening white expanses, feathering the rolling foot hills of the icy crags.

Elsa put on her scarlet snowsuit, mittens and boots.

John, whose ski jacket and pants were the khaki offered by the surplus store, had asked her why this color.

"So no one, not even the biggest idiot hunter could mistake me for a deer."

"Fair enough, sweetheart. Mission accomplished", John teased her, but thought she looked adorable, head to toe in red.

They'd come to a meadow, edged with red-berried Hawthorne bushes, and shadowed by the old mountain range just beyond. John took out his camera, and had Elsa pose with this scene behind her. He'd taken several shots, when Elsa said, "Enough. My turn. I want some photos of you."

They'd switched places. Elsa looked at the camera, uncertain of exactly what to do.

"Come here. I need you." John abandoned his place in front of the camera to come to her side.

"It looks complicated, Johnny. What do I do?"

"Elsa, it's a P.H.D. camera. Look here. You aim, there." He indicated the small shutter lever. "You shoot. It's as simple as that. P!H!D!" He gave her back the camera and returned to the field, laughing under his breath.

Elsa knew he was making a joke at her expense. But even so couldn't help herself. "Okay Professor, what's a P.H.D. Camera?"

"The initials stand for Push Here Dummy", he answered. Which set them both laughing. It was a silly age-worn joke, but the frame of their love and appreciation for each other made it funny.

John invariably carried with him his Remington portable typewriter, source books for his work, and lots of paper. Elsa painted. She was a skilled water colorist, who had begun to sell some of her landscapes. She wanted to go to Japan one day, to study their ancient graphic techniques. John thought it would be a wonderful graduation gift, if he could save up enough to make her dream a reality.

At the end of his first year in the graduate program, he had written a paper on Cotton Mather, an early New England Protestant evangelist. It was submitted at the suggestion of his university advisor, and accepted for publication in a popular magazine devoted to Americana.

With its acceptance had come a good check with a note from the editor stating that the magazine would be interested in any other short papers John could produce on similar subjects. John did a two-part follow-up study on Mather's parish for the magazine, and found he had made almost enough to realize his dream for Elsa.

Two years later, John was hard at work on his Ph.D. thesis on the early Governors of the Colony of Massachusetts. Elsa, now painting full-time, had celebrated a successful showing at the gallery where she used to work. They got news from his advisor that the preliminary script of his thesis had been accepted by Macmillan and company for national publication. The accompanying check represented a substantial advance.

They took six months off. Kyoto, Mt Fuji, Osaka, the tiny primitive northern islands. Everywhere they went, the incredible artistry of the master water-colorists, the beauty of the Japanese stringed instruments, the wooden flutes, and the formal courtesy of the people overwhelming.

When they returned, they put a down payment on a small house. John was offered a job as a research assistant, which would leave time for his own writing. He started a detailed biography of an early and colorful Governor of Massachusetts, John Lodge of Massachusetts. When his publisher read the synopsis, he accepted it on the spot. When published, to John's astonishment and Elsa's delight, it became a runaway bestseller. It was the first of several.

Five years later, they had moved to an old farm in the Berkshire Mountains of northern Connecticut, whose ancient apple and pear orchards still bore.

Elsa was showing in New York once a year and was happily installed in the old icehouse that had been converted into a studio for her. John's latest biography on Aaron Burr was selling well and he was into the beginning phases of research for the life of the clock maker Seth Thomas. They needed to keep a small studio apartment for days when either had to be in the city late.

They talked of children. In Elsa's mind, now was the time to start a family.

They were doing well, she was in perfect health. Her work and commissions would allow it without problem.

She went to her obstetrician for a routine check up. It had been a year since she had seen him. She wanted to find out how long after being regularly on birth-control pills, she would be able to conceive. During his examination he discovered a small lump in her left breast. He felt, at her age, it was simply a cyst. But to be on the safe side, he ordered a mammogram, a diagnostic technique just beginning to come into use.

To his uneasiness, reading the films, the small mass was solid, and solid tumors had a serious propensity for being malignant. He followed the mammogram with a needle biopsy, which indicated to his horror, not only was the mass malignant, but populated with an aggressive cell type. Elsa asked the doctor for a straightforward prognosis, all the treatment possibilities, and what difference each would make.

The prognosis was bleak given the cell type. At her age, with a mastectomy, the five-year survival rate was less than 30%! And no one even discussed the percentage of women cured permanently.

Elsa had courage. She also had the ability to face what was a virtual death sentence. She wanted John to have something of her love to keep and remember. She wanted to give him a child.

When she talked of getting pregnant, her obstetrician was dumfounded! He told her unmistakably, that the hormones which pregnancy evoked would nurture and spread her malignancy, despite a mastectomy.

Elsa knew this was one decision she couldn't share with anyone. Not even John. So she didn't. As things were, he would almost certainly be left alone in five years or less. That it would be an end to their life. Their love. And there was no option about it. No choice. No second chance. But if he had a child, their child, it would be as if part of her, part of them continued beyond the brief years they had had together.

Her decision was made. She scheduled a lumpectomy with the obstetrician, and would promise no more. That evening and the next week were ones of passionate lovemaking. John, unaware of her condition was thrilled when the next month she missed her menstrual period, and began feeling queasy in the morning. Her obstetrician could only confirm her pregnancy, and book the lumpectomy.

John had to be told. When he got over the shock of the significance of the breast mass and planned surgery, he nearly went insane." How could you get pregnant, knowing what it would mean", he asked Elsa again and again. "No child is worth it. It's you I care about, not some infant, I don't know."

Elsa was adamant. She refused to consider the abortion both John and the doctor wanted for her. As she reassured both of them she knew what she wanted.

And secretly she felt she knew what was best for John in the long run.

Eight weeks after the lumpectomy her obstetrician picked up a swollen lymph node in her left axilla. Six weeks later he found swollen nodes under her right arm. John was beside himself with anxiety. But Elsa thought only of the child to come. Her pregnancy was beginning to show.

In the middle of her second trimester, months after she had become pregnant, Elsa miscarried. She was devastated. The doctor was then able to start x-ray treatment. It was too late to be effective. Within the next two months, she had a radical mastectomy of the left breast, but by then it was obvious the cancer had spread to her spine.

The rest of the year was hell for them both. There was so little to do for her, for the most part John could only watch. Love her, hate what was happening, and watch. And then the agony of the last month of her life!...

He was glad for her release from a year of unimaginable torment, but left desolate. Emotionally and physically bankrupt. At thirty-three, paralyzed. He knew what it must have been for a musician to become suddenly deaf, or an artist blind. He was totally unable to use the one thing that might have helped him to recover. His writing. It was not a new project. This last year with Elsa he'd been unable to write. He'd had to cover up when she asked him how the Seth Thomas work was coming. She'd thought it contained some of his best work, and would have a wonderful impact on the reading public which was in the midst of a vogue of several years of bashing American historical figures.

After her death, he thought of it as his memorial to her. But, desperately as he wanted to finish it, he wasn't able to write worth a damn. Not only the biography, but even the lesser magazine articles he was contracted to do.

"97-98-99-100." John counted out loud the last push-ups, then let his body ease down onto the old beach towel he had spread out on the forward deck. He turned onto his back, still panting. The sun now fully above the horizon was beginning to give warmth as well as light. The ship slipped through the last of the waters of the Bay of Naples. He could see Vesuvio to port side. This day emitting only faint traces of smoke.

As he started to towel off before leaving the bow, an odd thought came to him. Odd only in the force with which it struck him-He'd not been able to help his wife, but perhaps this young girl, so desperate to leave Naples, so courageous, perhaps here he could make the difference. At least he would have a damn good try.

Chapter: 3

The Victoria pushed her stubby bows through the waters of the Italian coast, riding the seas like an over-the-hill middleweight, with many of the old tricks of punching and sliding, but executed within a sluggish, weary motion.

The sun rose up to warm the metal plates of the deck. Breakfast then lunch had been served. The men were at their usual sea-going tasks.

Selena woke mid-afternoon with a start. For a moment she had no idea where she was. Then the motion of the ship brought the morning back to her. She had made it aboard! Left behind her the Taverna! La Famiglia! She felt like laughing with relief at her escape, but at the same time saddened by all she had known and left behind in Napoli. Enough! There was the new day, and a new life to be coped with.

She rose, looked about the small cabin taking in the grime gathered everywhere-in age-old accretions on the floor and corners of the cabin. The sheets on which she'd slept were gray, untended and unwashed. Something would have to be done. She changed her shirt, and went off to find what she needed to put the cabin to rights.

Coming on deck she saw the sun was well up in an afternoon sky. The hold covers were open to permit air to circulate to the dunnage below. But no one seemed to be on deck. She had no idea where to find anybody to ask about cleaning materials. And so, for a moment, simply stood wondering what to do next. As her eyes searched the ship's bow, she saw the figure of the man who had come to her aid earlier.

He was lying in an old folding deck chair, a battered

straw hat protecting his face from the sun, to all intents and purposes asleep. It looked as if he had abandoned the book, which lay spine up, at the ends of his fingertips. She hesitated a moment then went quietly toward him. Actually John was drifting between sleep and wakefulness.

As she came within the last few feet, he raised his head, twisted around in his chair, recognized who it was, in spite of the sun directly behind her.

" Come over. I'm not really sleeping".

When the only response was a sudden and silent arrest, he knew she hadn't understood a word he'd said. As he levered himself upright, he continued, " Non parlo bene Italiano" I don't speak Italian very well. "Ma venga qui, la prego." But do come on over, You won't disturb me.

"Grazie, Signore."

Selena came around to stand by his chair. It was the first time he had had a chance to really study her. God, he thought, she's so young! And yet the face reminded him of a beautiful baby hawk. The eyes so fierce and quick. At the moment they showed a decided wariness. And why not. There was nothing on board to produce anything of reassurance.

"Do you speak any English", he asked. "Parla Inglese?"

"No", Selena responded.

"Well I will do my best in Italian." John smiled, "Although I have to warn you it is both rusty, and never that grammatical in the first place." All she got from this was the kindly tone of voice, a deep baritono. As Selena looked at him quizzically, trying to decipher his meaning, he went on, " But then, you'll need to learn English. It is after all, the Lingua Franca." He laughed gently at his own pun.

Again, Selena had to be satisfied with a humorous

tone of voice, and the attempt to create a common language, so she responded, "Va bene. Noi parliamo Inglese." Very well we'll try to talk in English. She had her doubts about the present but knew he was right about learning the language as soon as possible.

"Actually since I knew the ship would be in and around Italy for a while, I bought a pocket Italian/English dictionary. I think, to begin, you should have it." He rose to his feet.

Selena found he was offering her his dictionary to get started in English. Her first impression of him colored by the overwhelming anxiety of trying to get on the ship, was that he was somewhat elderly. Now she saw that she had been misled by the grey which shot through his blonde hair, making it a kind of non-color, and the worn look about his dark grey eyes. His carriage was straight, upright showing none of the slump of a middle-aged man. He was slim, and angular but hadn't the skeletal look that age brought to some. Actually, she thought he was probably in his late thirties. Later she found she'd guessed right.

"Grazie" she said. "Thank you" he immediately replied, indicating they should start speaking English right away.

"Thank you", she echoed, in a more than passable imitation of his words.

" Good", he approved with a smile.

Selena explained she needed to clean her cabin as soon as possible. John rose asking whether she could show him her quarters, so he could help sort out supplies.

When he saw the interior of her cabin, he was appalled. But she assured him it would be quite different once she had the chance fix it. Neither one of them picked up on the missing lock to the door.

They went below to the lower decks where the

engine and storage rooms lay, and found the cook's helper. From his shelves Selena chose liquids and polish-mostly by smell. She picked brushes, steel wool, rags and finally, a chamois. The helper loaded them into a basket.

When they regained the deck, they parted-John to return to his reading, Selena to start on her cleanup. He reminded her that dinner was served punctually at six. She nodded.

Looking after her, it struck John again how young she was, and yet her self-possession caught at him. This morning she'd seemed a vulnerable child. Now it was plain she had a competence and purpose that showed up unmistakably in the face of the unfamiliar.

"I'll meet you in the common room just before and take you in", he said. "Thank you Signor 'Arvey. A presto." I'll see you soon, Selena responded.

As she went toward her cabin she thought, what a nice man, with such a nice smile. She wondered what made it seem almost sad. But before she could speculate further, she arrived at her cabin. Speculation about Signor 'Arvey had to await attention to her living quarters. She set to work.

Dinner that night in the mess room, like so many to follow, was basically a silent, utilitarian affair. The food was plentiful and cheap, served in large plastic bowls set down before the Captain who passed them along only after he had taken his fill. None of the ship's officers spoke to one another, and none to Selena or John in the grim presence of the Captain who seemed intent on consuming the most food he could in the least amount of time, with no interruptions for talk. Selena and John ate quickly, excused themselves, and escaped as soon as possible to the deck.

The moon shone down on the restless waters of the straits of Messina. The night air at sea was clean and not in the least cold. As they leaned over the railing at the stern, watching the play of the ships wake, they shared that part of the day they had spent separately, and made plans for the beginning of the English lessons John would give Selena starting the next day. She could barely contain her excitement and a kind of disbelief at the prospect.

It was so beautiful-the light from the half-moon in the sky, the scattered millions of stars, and now the odd flickering sea light below. Pointing, she asked him, what caused it? John explained the bioluminescence of the tiny primitive sea creatures churned by the ship's way, as she listened intently. They stood side by side leaning on the railing. A tall man and a slight girl at his side, in the simple enjoyment of watching in silence with another person equally caught by the display.

John noticed Selena wore the same clothing as when she had boarded, and wondered not so much why, but whether she had anything other than these obviously worn-out clothes. He wondered too about the bruises showing even in the changing light of the moon. But the time was not ripe to ask her about these. He resolved in the next port to see whether she would accept a few necessities, perhaps a scarf, or a blouse, or sweater.

Selena thought, this is the first night I have had time and peace to watch, just watch, as things go by. And this is the first man I have felt cared what I think or feel about them. I will not, not even think about what is past. It is just that. Past. It must be. I closed a door somehow I must keep it shut.

She was tired. Even though she wanted to stay in the stern with this gentle man, her body still craved sleep. John saw her to her cabin.

It was the first day of a patterned existence, mornings given to study, afternoons to whatever interested them. It was the first day of a new life for Selena, much of it she felt she owed to John

Chapter: 4

The next morning the Victoria arrived at Messina. It was a rough looking town which served as the principal port of the island of Sicily.

Through out the centuries, since the Phoenicians first visited its harbor, the city had been ravaged over and over again. Disasters, natural or man-made, and repeated invasions had fallen hard upon it. The last devastation, more remote and mechanical than the earlier ones, fell from the skies with the intensive Allied bombing during the war. Some of the City's center had now been rebuilt with hastily thrown up box-like buildings which would likely crumble with the next serious earthquake.

It had always been a sailor's town, serviced by them with ladings of supplies, and returning the favor with taverns, bars, and women sailors could afford. It was not a city for tourists, innocents or a young girl seeking a new life.

Knowing this, John talked briefly with Selena.

"I don't think this is a good city to begin a new life". John pointed out the obvious roughness and filth of much of what could be seen of the city from the deck of the Victoria. "It's rough, and tough and not especially kind to pretty young women without protection." His concern rang through his voice. His opinion about the dangers waiting her should she debark evident.

Selena had no reason to question his judgment. "Do you think the Captain will let me stay on"

"If you'll leave it to me, I think I can persuade him that you shouldn't get off here."

"Sicuramente?" Are you sure? Selena was worried. The Captain was such a beast, and of all things, she didn't wish to make trouble for John.

" Non preoccuparti!" Don't worry Selena.

John left to talk to Stauger.

" What do you mean, the girl is not leaving ship here?! The Captain's response was predictably irate. He gritted his teeth, letting John see his annoyance.

"We both know Captain, this is not the port for an innocent young girl."

Stauger could not disagree. Messina was notorious.

With poor grace, he said, "In less than three days, the ship will put in to Trieste. Do you think that port will suit la Signorina?" Sarcasm made the question ugly, even threatening.

His passenger didn't feel a verbal response called for, and simply nodded.

Later, John settled Selena down with the grammar at the beginning of the dictionary he had given her, told her he would be back in a matter of a few hours, and took off for the harborside shops.

The men were busy off-loading crates of machinery when John returned with his purchases. He was not thrilled by the selection but had managed to find a hand-dyed scarf, and a simple heavy red cardigan which he thought would suit Selena's coloring. He had the stores gift wrap them, remembering how he had felt when he was Selena's age about presents-half the joy in the unwrapping.

When he gave her the gifts, she turned them over and over in her hands, looking at their shapes, and feeling their weight, before carefully opening each. She tried on the sweater, which was a little big, stroking the red wool, then wound the scarf around her neck. There were tears in her eyes, as she half reached out to him saying

"Ah Signore, grazie tante grazie. Sono bellissimi." Thank you they are so beautiful. They are truly for me?"

John nodded. Pleased.

" I've never had anything like them. But never."

"They will keep you warm in the evenings. We're headed north to Trieste. The nights will get a little cooler."

Selena didn't know how to express her joy with the things he had bought her, nor how to tell him it was a first for her. She felt warmth and gratitude towards this man who had been a total stranger a day ago. She had not known this type of person existed. She felt as if she'd like to throw her arms around him, but nothing in her past, nothing with her family made such an expression possible. She had no idea, he could read her intense pleasure.

Her reaction gave John an idea. If they could drum up a mirror for her cabin, however small, it would complete his gift to her.

Half an hour later, they had located, and mounted a very small sea-speckled mirror in her cabin. Selena placed it in front of a ladder-back chair, the only furniture in the cabin other than the berth, and right over a pull-down ledge similar to the one in John's cabin. He saw it gave her real pleasure. She sat in the chair smiling at her image, moving one way and another to see around the mirror's defects, as she adjusted the scarf to her liking. John watched, fascinated-this child-woman with her masses of shining black hair falling to her shoulders, and a wondrous smile on her face.

At dinner that evening Stauger made an announcement. Its stentorian tones startled the crew. The steward who had started in with the main course quickly retreated to the galley.

'Dio' Selena thought, 'what now?' His manner was frightening. The crew stopped eating, soup ignored every eye trained on the captain.

" You think to be clever, Eh? That the Captain, he is a dumkopf?"

Selena stared at him still uncertain what was to come. I must not let this man see my hands tremble, she told herself and tucked them out of sight beneath the table. I must keep a calm face.

"This mirror.. This mirror you found, Herr Harvey," He now included John in his anger, "Did I give permission to borrow?"

"No" John admitted tonelessly.

"Nein. Or to have?"

"No." John was again forced to answer, He was prepared to pay for the tiny object if necessary.

" Nein. I know everything on my ship. What happens, what does not happen. Alles. Verstandt?!, He wanted to make clear his absolute control and their stupidity in thinking he might miss any occurrence aboard the Victoria, however trivial.

Selena nodded, hoping to stem the tirade.

The Captain saw her capitulation. "Gutt. Now, it is my pleasure you keep your little toy." He grinned pleased with the humiliation he had imposed. He felt he'd diminished their dignity.

Manners forced Selena to thank him.

John seethed, but realized anything he might say would prolong the hectoring, so kept silent. He knew Selena had done the right thing in defusing the Captain's bullying. It was a singularly mature act. He'd tell Selena later she could take pride in how she handled the man.

Dinner resumed. The only sound the scrape of flatware against the thick boat's plates.

As to the Captain, he was far from pleased with the John's concentration on the Italian girl. It was much better when the American stayed in his cabin, or exercised unobtrusively by himself. Well, his plans for this particular night might give the American something to think about. Many matters would soon be put in perspective. Let them moon about on deck for the while, he would bring them to hand.

Again as yesterday, John and Selena excused themselves from the table before the captain was finished eating. As they left, Stauger smiled after them mocking them with a gross gesture. And muttered, "Das ist der nicht mein Herr und Fraulein". Until tonight, then.

Chapter: 5

Standing in the ship's stern, John watched Selena, fascinated by the ease with which she balanced without thought against the decided sea roll. She stood, frowning slightly in concentration, her back to the railing, his dictionary held before her. There was enough light for her young eyes to see the text she was studying. The whole picture held him-the sky, the sea, the girl.

Unaware of anything but the book before her, she tucked a strand of hair caught by the breeze behind her ear, as she held the book with care, but already with the familiarity of use. Then pointing to the text as she went along, she reviewed aloud the grammar and words she had learned that day.

John listened carefully gently correcting her pronunciation where needed. There were few mistakes in the recital.

It was a magical time for both pupil and teacher. John thought what an odd class room-this tramp steamer, chugging its way around the boot of Italy, through the Tyrrhenian sea. Selena for her part, was discovering the love of learning that was to capture her all her life.

He laid out the material for the next day. Amazingly, she had mastered what was needed to get into the use of the past and future tenses. He bent towards her showing her where to find the verb forms. Selena felt protected by him and by the tool he was teaching her to use.

She felt the beginnings of control, in the strange world in which she found herself. It was a matter of knowledge. The more one had, the more secure. It was the unforeseen and the unknown which could destroy. That lesson she had learned at the Trattoria. It was an error she would not repeat.

After several turns on deck, they parted. John impressed with Selena's progress, Selena trying to cover a yawn as she made her way to her cabin. It had been full, day.

For a huge man, Captain Stauger could move with total silence when he wished, and right now that was exactly what he wanted. The darkness was intense, the moon having set more than an hour ago. It would not be long before dawn, would lighten the end of the dogwatch. He knew the skeletal crew standing watch would be somnolent, paying little attention to non-existent hazards in the calm coastal swells.

He went along the deck, easing himself down the stairs of the forward hold. Moving still noiselessly he came to the Nigerians' old cabin, now given over to the girl. He could barely control his impatience. He wanted sex now, and now willing or no, he would have it. No one to hear or disturb. Stooping close to her door, he reached out, and began to turn the handle.

Night had captured the day's heat, and trapped it in the forward hold. The dented brass knob was stiff to move, requiring enough force to make the muscles of his forearm clench. But slowly, it began to ease into a turn. Stauger had to work hard to control all sound as the handle moved. It would be easiest if he could surprise the whore. Turning his wrist very slowly, twisting the knob, he began to sweat in the musty heat and darkness of the hold. His breath issue hoarsely through his throat with his efforts. It was intensely hot in the tiny space.

Heavy drops of perspiration started to roll down his cheeks and into his eyes. "Scheiss". He could barely see what he was doing with the "verdammt" handle. As sweat ran from his armpits down his arm, the handle became slick.

All of a sudden the knob slipped in his hand, screeching as it snapped back to its original position.

The noise penetrated Selena' s sleep. She came suddenly awake, hearing the sharp metallic sound, and the noise of heavy breathing outside her door. Without conscious thought, she rose, seized the chair and jammed it tight between her berth and the door. It would bar whoever was trying to get in. But not completely. The door had been forced open a half inch.

On the outside the man now ignoring the sounds he made, heaved at the door. Selena held the chair in place, praying that its wood would withstand the battering it was receiving. Thank God for the strength in her wrists and arms that years of work had given her.

Again and again Stauger shoved at the door trying to get more than a crack open. The half inch that was all he could get half an inch and a lot of sweat and frustration.

He finally realized that the girl had braced something against the door. Something she had to be holding in place, that much was sure, nothing else could prevent its opening.

He stopped for the moment, wiping the sweat from his face and hands with a filthy handkerchief. The thing to do was to trick her. If she felt safe she would ease up on her brace, and then...

He let go of the handle, and said in a voice meant to be heard " Damn door. It won't move. I'll go get a jimmy, that 'll do it."

He walked away from the door, making his steps as loud as possible. After several paces, he spun noiselessly, and crept back, again grasping the door handle.

Inside the cabin Selena felt her heart pounding with

fear. She had no doubt she had to continue to hold the chair in place. It was her only chance. She recognized the voice of the Captain. And knew he would try again. The only question in her mind was whether he was really going after a tool or whether it was a ruse.

Her arms began to tremble from the effort of clenching the chair in place. But she knew, from the quality of the little light coming in through the porthole, that if she could just hold on, morning would come soon, and with it he would have to stop.

Stauger tried the door once again, rattling at the handle, and swearing when he could get no further.
Selena watched the chair bow with each push. She had no idea how long it would continue to stand up. She thought she had to say something, anything to make the intruder stop and think about what he was doing. But she knew Stauger would make her life on board impossible if he realized he had been identified.

She took a deep breath, steadying her voice, and said "Basta"! You must stop this. I have the door held shut. You won't get in. If you don't stop, I'll report you to the Captain in the morning." Part of what she said was in Italian, part English, but she was sure she was understood.

The rattling stopped. For a moment all was silent. Then she heard her attacker leave. But she remained wide-eyed, on her knees, holding the chair with all her strength, watching the door throughout what was left of the night.

Chapter: 6

When Selena didn't appear at breakfast, John knew he must find her something felt wrong. He was sure something had happened. But he'd only know what after he found her. He must find her now. He looked quickly in the likely places on deck, then ran down to the forward hold. His glance shot around the corridor outside her cabin door. Nothing. He got no clue from its emptiness. He became tense, and yet had nothing concrete to center on. He crossed over to her cabin and knocked on the door.

For a moment there was only silence, then he heard Selena ask in a barely audible voice, "Chi é?" Who's there?

"Selena," He said relieved to hear her answer, "It's John."

"Grazie Dio." Thank God, the words spilled out as she opened the door, drew him in to the cabin, and sat abruptly on the berth. John looked at her. There were dark circles under her eyes. She was white, breathless and shaking badly.

"What on earth", he began.

"No, no, not yet. Just come and sit beside me."

John went to her, took her in his arms, without further questions, knowing she would have to regain some calm, some distance from whatever had happened before she could tell him about it.

They sat for several minutes, neither speaking. Then Selena told him in a quiet voice, trembling with emotion.

"Durante la notte", Late, late last night, early this morning, I saw the door to the cabin start to open. I was frightened. I knew, it was not good. Someone wanted..." a shudder cut into her voice. She had to wait for a moment before she was able to continue. John just held her. Waiting until she could go on.

" I used the chair to stop the door. When I heard the voice, I knew it was the Captain. That voice! You can't mistake it, again she shuddered, her hair falling over her eyes hid in part the fear caught in them.

" I didn't know what to do except to keep holding the door. Just keep holding. If I could just last til morning, I knew you would come for me."

" Si, Amore mio," Yes, my love, "of course I would come for you", John murmured. He stroked her hair trying to still her trembling.

After a while, when she had calmed a little, he said, "I want you to come to my cabin. Now. And have a shower. That'll help. When you finish, I'll have a cup of hot tea for you. Don't talk anymore now. Viene", just come.

Selena looked at him in wonder. Somehow he had offered the very thing she knew she needed. The problem of the Captain and the door could wait. She rose, shakily and went with him to his cabin. He showed her how the shower worked, laid out towels, and told her to take her time.

The hot water beating down on her shoulders and back loosened the tension in her muscles. It felt good, as if some of her troubles and fear washed away with the swirl of water going down the drain. She washed from head to toe, once and then once again. Then got out to wrap herself in the largest of the towels, and use another to dry then turban her hair.

She looked around the cabin. It had the scent and feel of John stamped all over, from the shelves of books to the old straw hat on the peg near the bulkhead, and the sheaves of paper lined so carefully next to a typewriter. A distinctive trace of Atkinson after shave lotion, pervaded the small room, overcoming the native metallic odor. His presence was unmistakable. It was as if his room extended the protective power of the man himself. She felt safe and cared for.

John used the time it took to get a cup of tea and some toast to control his reaction to the attack on Selena. He felt he'd like to confront Stauger, and beat the man to a pulp. His feelings startled him. He was not, never had been, a violent man. Believing that violence bred violence in a non-ending, senseless cycle. And that the ugliness of anger or hate came to rest with a vengeance on the person who let these feelings take over. Squeezing and distorting character and being. It was not something he ever wanted to experience, having seen too frequently what it did to others, including some of the men he wrote about. But now, with the threat to Selena, with the thought of the power wielded by any Captain of a ship, much less this one, and the vulnerability of the girl, anger rose up.

He knew he must stop it. Use his mind to solve the problem of what to do, and how to protect Selena for as long as she needed to be on the ship. Confrontation was not the way. It would only make for more trouble, and might prod Stauger into other means of attack or retribution.

They were days from the nearest port, so he couldn't get her off the ship-the ideal solution. To get the lock repaired would be countered by the Captain. Somehow the repair would be botched or found impossible to do. To guard Selena twenty-four hours a day was not only impracticable, but he was almost sure, she would reject such a plan. Yet he had to come up with something which would prevent anything further happening.

Then it came to him. Of course. Something entirely practical, and publicly demonstrable. Something that would prevent anyone on board, from the Captain to the lowest-life from making another attempt.

He went back to his cabin. Selena was sleeping, wrapped in towels on his bunk. Good, John thought. She needed the sleep.

He went to his locker. From the top shelf he removed a small carton carefully tied and wrapped with tough brown paper. He sat at his 'desk', unwrapped, and opened the box, took out a .32 caliber automatic pistol, with several dozen smaller boxes of ammunition, and set them down on the shelf.

The gun was a beautifully crafted weapon. The machine-tooled ridging prevented grip slippage. The stock and barrel were balanced perfectly. A small centered notch at the gun's tip made for augmented accuracy.

Over the next hours, he disassembled, checked, oiled the gun, loaded it, and set it back in its box. Selena slept on. Wishing her to sleep as long as possible, John picked up the book he had been reading and went on with it.

When Selena awoke. John handed her her clothes, and stepped outside the cabin to give her a chance to dress. After a few minutes she called to him. Youth erased much of the physical traces of her night. Only the haunted look in her eyes, gave way anything of her inner thoughts. He wondered if the bruises he'd seen on her face when she first boarded could have anything to do with this. But thought it best to deal in practicalities for the moment.

"Selena," he said, "I've had time to think about what to do." His manner was calm, even grave. His look held naked determination. It was an expression Selena was not familiar with, though she had often studied his face in the time they'd been together. It gave weight to what followed.

" I want you to sleep in this cabin. I can sleep in yours, or if you prefer, I can use a sleeping bag on the floor here."

Normally, Selena would have refused such an offer, but both she and John knew this was a time for basics. And so she nodded.

"Good. It's agreed then."

"Yes. Thank you, it is."

" There's something else I want you to do", he said, opening the box and withdrawing the weapon. " I'm going to teach you how to use this pistol. And I'm going to do it in a very public way."

Selena understood immediately what he had in mind. The next half-hour, he spent showing her the gun's mechanism, having her dry run shooting it, letting her get the feel of the resistance of the trigger, and how to squeeze rather than pull it.

She knew something of weapons, from the frequent fights in the Quartiere, but those she knew were hand-held knives. No one could afford a pistol on her street. The gun fascinated her, yet she was repelled by the violence which lay at the heart of its function. It was intended to maim or kill at a distance. Cold, and quick, efficient.

John broke into her thoughts. "Now, andiamo mangiare", we're going to lunch. "Right after you'll do your first target practice."

"Va bene," all right, she responded.

They went into the mess hall. John making a point of laying the box down on the table, in plain sight of the Captain and the ship's officers. He offered no explanation when the Stauger looked at it pointedly.

As soon as lunch was finished, to the surprise of the officers, John picked the box up, and left with Selena for the Galley. Stauger looked after them puzzled, with obvious curiosity, but said nothing.

From the Galley they went directly to Victoria's stern, John carrying several large empty crates. Just before they arrived there, John threw one of them overboard.

The crate bobbed up and down in the waters by the side of the boat. As the ship moved forward, the crate found its way to the sternway, then tumbled over the wake and into the calm between the twin turbulences. For the next few minutes it remained, within range of the automatic-a relatively stable target.

Wood splintered up from the crate as John shot several rounds at it. He hit the target each time he fired. It was an apt demonstration.

The sound attracted much of the crew, the officer on watch and the Captain. John then transferred the gun to Selena's grasp, showing her again how to brace into a two-handed shooting position. Checking that she released the safety, and reminding her to wait until the crate centered and settled. He threw another crate over the side.

Selena shot raggedly several times, missing. John reassured her, and threw the next crate over. This time her shots came more evenly spaced. When he threw the third over, one of her shots hit the target. John smiled. He kept her at target practice for a full hour, until he could see her arms were tired from the gun's recoil. Then they stopped. Several times Selena had hit one of the crates. Considering the size of the target, and the motion of the boat, she was a "natural".

Finally he informed her in a voice meant to be heard all along the deck, that although she had done well for the day, they would have their second session after lunch tomorrow.

There was complete silence on board, but several of the men glanced at one another. Without a word, the Captain who had watched the entire session, grimaced, then returned to his bridge.

Watching him, John smiled again. It was check, counter check.

Chapter: 7

The weeks after Trieste flew by, patterned for Selena by English lessons and gun practice; for John by workouts and reading, by the unvarying intensity of the blue skies above, and the chugging of the ship's engine. Selena was not disturbed by further "visits".

She had become quite expert with the automatic, and now took a certain pride in her mastery of a weapon which frightened her at first. John was impressed with her quickness with this, as he was with her new language. They talked often of the geography and history of the Mediterranean through which they made passage. Days were peaceful.

In Trieste John had found several books on the countries that bordered the sea, and others which dealt with America. Selena was fascinated by all of them, but particularly those which written about her own country and John's. As her reading skills grew, she spent more of her time reading of the United States. She was enthralled by its leaders, men of industry and government, or as John put it, the movers and shakers of the country. So many of them arrived at the top from the humblest beginnings, even poverty.

It was a shock one day, where the Adriatic flowed into the Mediterranean, when the ship's engines stopped without warning. The chief engineer covered in oil and soot emerged from his engine room, hurrying to the bridge. Shortly thereafter the Captain accompanied him back below deck. The crew seemed to be drawn to the stern railing, where they peered down.

After a half-hour the Captain came up on deck, his face red with anger and frustration. He slammed past Selena and John making for his quarters.

John and Selena were intrigued to see the engineer and several of his crew organize a small platform and lower it over the stern, all the way to the waterline, heavy tools secured to the ropes suspending it. They could hear the ringing of metal on metal as a repair took place.

Ten hours later, the platform was hauled back on board and the ship resumed sailing, at quarter speed.

John went to the bridge to find out exactly what had happened, only to see the first mate, standing behind the ship's wheel struggling with a "jury rigged" rudder. The system governing the steering had broken down completely, presumably from the wear and tear of ages of ocean going without much attention. The officer said, it would take twenty-four hours or so at the speed the Victoria could manage, but they would make for Port Said, the nearest harbor, for repairs. When asked if he had any idea how long the repair would take, he answered likely ten days or more.

John thought, ten days? Talk of luck! He and Selena would get the chance for a real visit to Egypt. She would love it, he was sure, with its ancient history and monuments, its current day bazaars and color.

His mind went to Husseine El Alamein, his old classmate, who'd, made him promise so many times, that should he ever arrive in Egypt...

He remembered with warmth his young friend, enormously talented, bright-eyed, laughing, always up for some sort of fun, but a member of one of Egypt's oldest, most prominent families. Hospitality, Hussein said always- no people really understood it except the people from poor or desert lands. It was the tradition of virtually endless protection, comfort, and generosity.

John arranged for the first mate to leave word at the Palace Hotel in Cairo as soon as he could calculate the ship's repair would finish.

When the ship berthed, Selena and John debarked.

Chapter: 8

Almost before the gangplank was secured to the dock, Selena had jumped off. John laughed at her eagerness as she looked about her at the scene taking place at the wharf.

How odd she thought, the men all in white, the women in black, and almost no other color to be seen in their clothing. The sun gave off intense uninterrupted heat, but its blare was colorless in the noonday sky. All color came from the animals and cars, the bales and containers, that spilled over from small shops containing copper and carpets and all kinds of odd brightly hued goods. Dust and noise and confusion were everywhere. It was noisy and exciting. Selena turned back towards John, beckoning him to hurry off the ship.

He came, but paused at the nearest telephone kiosk. He wanted to reach his old friend here in Egypt. There were things to get out of the way before he and Selena would be free to go where they wished.

John's friend Hussein El Alamein came from one of the most influential families in Egypt. They had been advisors to the kings, Bashaws, and Pashas of the country for centuries, whoever held the scepter of power. More important, they had survived the fall of Farouk, and the rise of Colonel Nasser with fortune and position intact. They were among the foreign-educated economic specialists whose talents emerging political powers ignored at the peril of failure. Egypt was now a democratic country, at least that's what the news releases of the new government insisted. No more king, no more king's court, a people's government. More accurately, perhaps, a military government. Whatever regent prevailed, the El Alameins pervaded most of the ministries.

Selena had heard John say over and over, it was always a relative matter, the idea of democracy. Thousands of years of monarchist history lay buried in the kingdoms along the Nile. Hundreds of years of desert monarchs ruled absolutely from Cairo, or Memphis or Alexandria. And only the last few years gain-said these traditions.

Hussein had been such a good friend that until the last two years, they'd maintained steady ties. At Yale, they studied, and swam, and larked together. Elsa had accepted him as a brother into their household. He was always in and out, always welcome, bringing laughter, and a love of the extravagant with him.

When Nassser took over, Hussein's Father called him back to Egypt to assume the responsibilities for which he was trained. Here he'd shouldered with enormous success, the burdens required of him. He'd returned for Elsa's funeral, when he learned of her death, but just at that time things at home were in turmoil. It had been a turn around stay with no real personal time before he'd had to return. Later his letters with all others had gone unanswered.

When John he gave his name and that of Hussein, the layers of in-built telephone resistance in the Ministry of Economics peeled away.

Hussein came on the phone. His voice exuberant.

"John! My God! Is it really you?

"Yep." was the answer he got.

Hussein started to laugh. In the old days, it was a game between them. Who could get the most conveyed, or done, for that matter, with the fewest words.

" So where are you?"

"Port Said. I need some help, if possible."

"Port Said?" Let me get a pen." there was slight

pause "Okay, shoot."

John explained he would need a passport for Selena, then advice as to Cairo hotels. He told Hussein they had at least ten days in Egypt while their ship was being repaired, assuming they went back to the Victoria.

Knowing they would have to catch up on lots later, Hussein asked nothing about Selena or who she might be, but asked John to have passport control call his number as soon as they arrived there.

He also wanted to send a limo to the port. John thanked him but asked if it could be arranged for el Quantara el-Gharbiya, a half days journey down the Suez Canal. He wanted a chance to let Selena see something of that marvel of De Lessup's engineering.

"Of course. The car will meet you right by the lock. See you in Cairo this evening."

"Yep." Laughing again, Hussein rang off.

With the promised telephone call, the formalities of custom and passport clearances disappeared quickly. John thought for a Middle East country, with some political turmoil in its immediate past, it was nothing short of a minor miracle.

They got on the narrow gage railway that paralleled the Suez Canal. The sights and activities of ships, and men, using the canal, the local bazaars, and animals, the women covered all but their eyes, the sound and smells were at once shocking and Lucullan after the isolation of the Victoria. It was hard to get used to. Also, Selena thought, the sights were like something out of a fantasy. So strange, but at the same time more than real and alive.

They ate Kebobs and Pita filled with eggplant which they bought from one of the rail station vendors, washed it down with hot sweet tea. The ships, and locks, the portage from water level to water level all went by.

Shapes and movement seen against a background of desert and village. As John thought, Selena was fascinated.

About four that afternoon, they reached El Qantra. Waiting for them a long black Mercedes sat idling in the late afternoon sun. As they approached, a uniformed chauffeur jumped out, salaamed, put their bags in the boot, and installed them in the comfort of the back seat, asking them to help themselves to beverages ranked behind railings.

In the air conditioned darkness Selena fell asleep. As he sipped an ice-cold mint tea, John watched the small desert villages flash by.

Chapter: 9

The limo drove up to a pair of dusty old wooden gates, set in what looked to be a rough stone wall, high and very long. The driver paused long enough to code a series of numbers into a scanner. The doors swung back to reveal a glimpse of a huge tiled courtyard beyond and an internal portecochere off which stables, and garages put an end to the incursion of visiting cars, animals and people, until inspected by several large watchful "attendants".

Once they had gotten out, the limo disappeared into one of the garage structures. They were offered slippers and a soft cotton burnoose, to replace the discomfort and dust of their outerwear, that was taken away for care.

One ancient Arab indicated they should follow him through the courtyard, and proceeded as escort. Selena gasped, the tiled court was a marvel of intricate design in blues and greens. The perimeter off which many doors could be seen, was a colonnaded, covered walk extending along three walls. Designs of vines and fruits, and mythical stylized lions and leopards in small mosaic tesserae wound around these columns from base to capital. At the center of the court, a mammoth fountain ornamented in lapis lazuli spouted crystalline waters toward the intensity of the sapphire sky. The whole effect was one of richness, beauty, and repose.

Hussein rose, as they entered one of the reception rooms off the courtyard, came over and hugged John, then releasing him administered welcoming bear-like backslaps saying over and over, "I can't believe you're really here." Then as he turned to her, " And you must be Selena. Welcome." He bowed.

Hussein was well over six feet of heavy muscle. His face was round and huge, his mouth surrounded by a heavy mustache, which moved constantly, almost comically, Selena thought, as he talked. Just as his hands were never still, filling out details which he felt he hadn't managed to convey verbally. His bonhomie was infectious, and yet under it, you couldn't help knowing that it was the good-natured manner of one accustomed to possessing immense power, rather than the usual social tool. He wore a burnoose over his business suit, and a tarboosh angled slightly over one ear. He gestured to the pillows centered around a marble table.

" Come. Sit", Hussein commanded, and folded himself into a low chair. "Tell me everything".

Selena dropped gracefully onto a pile of embroidered pillows, opposite him. John followed a little more awkward. Tea, and sweets appeared on the instant set out on the gold veined blue marble table between them.

John told him about the Victoria, his decision to go with the ship, and the ports they had visited. Then he explained Selena's presence, and their desire to stay in Egypt at least until the ships repairs were completed.

Hussein listened carefully. Seeing the changes tragedy had rung on the face of his old friend. Seeing the youth, and energy of the young beauty at his side. He didn't speculate as to whether they were lovers, but an obviously close, relationship had developed between them. "Ha!" Good," he thought, "this girl may be just what is wanted for my friend", and silently acknowledged to himself the old saying about Egyptian Arabs, they were born tent, monument, and matchmakers.

When tea was over, Hussein clapped his hands to summon attendants. John was taken off to quarters not far from Hussein's own, Selena to the women's part of the palace. Dinner would be served at ten, when the Cairo heat had finished with her sons, and all commerce and affairs would come to an end, and be laid aside for the day.

Her room was immense as was the tub of steaming rose-scented water into which Selena was helped. Her clothes were taken off for repairs. She soaked luxuriously in the scented warmth half drowsing. Then one of the attendants returned with shampoo, washed and rinsed her hair. When she emerged she had a choice of many attars and oils. She chose something light and also rose-scented. Then had to endure a light massage, from the bath attendant before accepting an undergarment of the softest cotton from still another. She was given full pants, gathered in at the ankle, she later learned these were called saroud and were traditional for women. Over these was draped a loose white caftan, with a single narrow line of blue silk that went from shoulder to hem. A silken scarf which covered her hair, and soft slippers of camels wool tipped up at the toe. And finally, with infinite tact a white silken kerchief that could be used as a chador veil or simply held in the hand. Then she was escorted to the dining area.

Later when he joined them for dinner, she saw Hussein in a Djalaba and traditional headdress. John had been similarly dressed, in native robes, but his head was uncovered.

Dinner was many small courses of meats, and fruits, most of which could be eaten without implements. Dessert was baklavah a light pastry of honey and ground nuts. There followed coffee mud-thick, sweet and black, served in tiny gold cups. Hussein, knowing the first time for Egyptian coffee could be a shock, looked over to see what Selena would make of his native coffee.

Selena used to Neapolitan style espresso, was still surprised by the strength of the brew, but liked it.

During dinner Hussein told them that several generations of his family shared quarters within the palace.

"It is a somewhat odd household. My Father observes the old Islamic ways, he has four wives, my Mother being the first wife, and the head of his household."

Her eyes widened slightly, as Selena asked in a carefully neutral tone "Four?"

"All four get along splendidly. They have arranged a division of labor-really a time/motion paradigm, that many of our businesses could well afford to study. They live in the west wing."

With just detectable awkwardness-she being left-handed-Selena reached for a fresh date from the large gold epergne in the center of the table with her right. In one of the few specific commands John ever issued to her, he told her she was never to use her left hand at table. It was a fast rule among all Arabs that the left hand was reserved exclusively for personal sanitary needs-most notably urinating and defecating. If one ate with, or offered the left hand in greeting, one gave the ultimate insult. Among men it could occasion a duel to the death, among Princes, a war.

A huge platter of eastern sweetmeats was served, as Hussein continued, "The women live in strictly guarded female quarters, isolated from all grown males except my Father".

It was a simple statement of fact, given as information with no judgment attached. "When my younger brother married, times had changed. He has but one wife, and they live together with all his children in the main sleeping quarters."

Popping several sweets in his mouth, Hussein

insisted that they try a taste of each of the lukoum pistacchio and honey cakes issuing from the kitchen. He smacked his lips with relish.

"I myself live, as befits an old bachelor, in my own wing. On holy days and every Wednesday, we all feast together in peace and harmony, thanks be to Allah." He smiled affectionately at the thought of these occasions with all generations brought together.

As an old friend who had seen some of his early struggles, Hussein inquired delicately how John's latest book was coming. John turned to him, able to say to an old friend, "Not well." I really haven't been able to buckle down, since Elsa died." Hussein face wrinkled with concern.

"It's all right, my old son. It will come when it comes." To his amazement, John was able to reassure Hussein and go on to express the essence of his last year, without tearing guilt, and pain. It came out as a simple statement. Both Selena and Hussein could hear the undertones of suffering, but very much overlaid with acceptance, and a sort of newfound strength.

"And what about your plans to go on with the boat?"

"Well we know the repairs will be extensive, and we really hadn't thought beyond wanting to see something of the land. Selena, has read about Luxor, the Valley of the Kings, and Kharnak. I think she wants to see it all, as well as Cairo and Alexandria."

"You're planning several years, in my beautiful country then?", Hussein asked Selena with an expansive welcoming gesture.

Understanding he was teasing, Selena answered, "Well , perhaps not quite that, but..."

" But let me suggest a way to start. Not in Cairo, but out in the desert where so much of the history of our country lies sleeping. Giza, Luxor, Kharnak... Those.

After you have seen something of them-Cairo, perhaps even Alexandria, will make more sense."

"That sounds just right. Selena what do you think?"

"Oh, Yes", she breathed.

"All right then. Let me arrange that you use our oasis, it is very near Giza. You will be safe, and comfortable, and able to make trips to the ancient monuments from this base. Our people will see to your keep and transportation for as long as you want."

"Hussein, that's wonderful. How will we be able to thank you?"

"The expression on Signorina Selena's face is thanks enough. And recently there have been some rough events with tourists. I do not want you exposed to these. I shall send several of our best men with you, the rest you will find already there near the Bawiti gardens."

Selena and John were overwhelmed, with the offer, but accepted.

"I have much to do at the ministry in the morning, but I'll arrange to get you kitted up and ready, so you can leave just after lunch. That way you should arrive at Bawiti in time for the setting of the sun-not to be missed."

Dinner finished leisurely. Hussein rose from his cushions gracefully for such a large man. He had calls to make to set in motion the plans for their journey. John and Selena left for their quarters. tomorrow promised to be a long day.

Chapter: 10

Just as Hussein had suggested, they arrived at the foot of the Bawiti cliffs, and entered the oasis created by the spring in the declivity which lay at their feet. The trees shading the oasis, the towering royal palms, the date and smaller palms dipped their roots in sand fed gently by the waters of the spring "Ayn Bishmu".

The spring in turn created a small lake, surrounded by tall bulrushes, and flowering water plants which John thought might be papyrus. Shadows were falling, filling the oasis with purples and greys of the coming twilight, while the sun lingering over the desert around Ayn Bismu still blazed with royal reds and oranges. Selena though it breathtaking. There were a few things that were so beautiful no words could capture them. You simply had to be there and see or hear. This oasis in the sands of Egypt, had to be one of them.

Hakim, senior of the El Alamein attendants came to greet them and show them around the campsite. It consisted of several tents of various sizes, the form of each , the size, location and height, dictated by its function. They were introduced the to the main tent, the living and dining room of the camp, the supply tents, and bathing tents. Then the main male and female sleeping quarters. The men and animals slept as they always had in the desert out in the open. Selena curious, asked Hakim, what happened if the weather turned bad.

The ancient camp chief replied, "Well, Maam Hiya , it is rare, that Allah sends such. But should he forget his desert children for a moment, he will know that man looks after beast, and beast looks after man, and so they endure."

Selena looked at some of the camels-large and furred, kneeling in groups, draped with quantities of blankets and rugs, being fed their evening meal. And the small cook fires of the men not far from them, and understood that for both there was little need of more. Earlier that day, robes, and lingerie had appeared magically in Selena's size at the downtown shops to which she was taken. She was told that a riding habit, jodhpurs and boots were mandatory for daytime in the desert. And as a last thought, several gowns suitable for dining out were added to her wardrobe. The accompanying shoes, scent, and light makeup were marvels of subtlety. She did not then know, that much of the style and makeup created for her was French in concept.

If Napoleon had devastated the country, and taken hundreds of Egyptian shibboleths and monuments as souvenirs back to his native shores; De Lessops with his French polytechnique administrators and engineers, who stayed far longer in creating the Suez canal, left Egypt with French habits of life, cuisine and dress. Much of the country's so called upper classes had a definite penchant for things Parisian, which made many of the Cairean women, with their enormous black eyes and lush good looks, among the most stylish in the world.

The tent in which their dinner was served was of a black felt, and very large, its floor heaped with silk carpets, its front flaps laid wide open facing the spring. In the far distance, the peaks of Giza's three great pyramids could just be seen. The soft sound of the men tending to their animals, blended with the palm leaves stirring in a slight evening breeze. Both were interrupted briefly by a muezzin's call to prayer, and the men's intoned responses.

A table covered with white damask linen, and full

silver service, lit by candles shielded by glass "wind shields" was set for them in the opening of the tent. Roast kid, eggplant, stuffed grape leafs, and fruits, were followed by coffee and honeyed dates. Everything perfectly served. When the table was cleared, they continued to sit gazing out into the desert night.

"John, how can I thank you for all this...I don't begin to have the words to describe it. If I said it was like one of my dreams, that would be only part true. Because before now I could not have made such a dream. I could not have imagined such things."

John didn't answer her directly, but said after a moment," Hussein is in his way an old soul. I think he understands, and wanted us to have this time out here."

" Old soul? What does that mean?"

"He was born knowing things it takes many of us years to understand. He reminded me yesterday, after you went to your room, always to remember to 'stay in the moment'. He meant you must live, within each moment, not try to dissect it, or on the other hand be thinking of other things while you are in it. It's a formula for contentment. Matter of fact it's probably a whole philosophy. Simple sounding, but not always easy to do. I've been guilty of not staying in the moment, these last few years. And I think failing to do this has made many problems for me. And so this is Hussein's way of extending a hand to me. Actually to us."

John leaned forward in his chair persuasively, he wanted Selena to understand how important this was for him. He reached for her hand, and held it lightly in his.

" Selena, teaching you, being with you has made me start to be able to stay in the moment, in the present. Begin to see beauty, and want to see more of it, begin to live, and do something with my life. Before you came the past captured me, holding me prisoner, unable to get on with life. Now I think I can."

"Oh, John, sono felice per te," I'm so happy for you,
Selena responded, placing her hand over his for a
moment, assuring him she understood the importance
of what he was saying, and what it cost him to do so.
Simple joy shone in her eyes.

They said little more, but relaxed back into the
canvas folding chairs and watched the velvet skies
above, and the winking fires below for a long while.
Time passed in comfortable silence.

Selena was aware that his hand on her was really a
caress. She thought, Dio, he really cares for me. He
looked young, at peace with himself. The moonlight
picked out the strong bones of his forehead and cheeks,
the fine line of his mouth. Something within her
responded to his warmth. The more she learned of him,
the more she felt as if she could spend many days, with
this man.

John discovered, to his amazement, he was falling in
love. It was not just that Selena was a beautiful, bright
young girl, but something of her joie de vivre, her
courage, her spirit, drew him to her. But my God. She
was still just a child, what had she said sixteen years
old? He felt all of his thirty-three years. He felt
alienated from her not so much by the years but the
separation that experience alone thrust between them.

He would have to very careful not to violate the
relationship they had formed, not to destroy the nature
of their being together. He must remember they were
essentially pupil and teacher. He must remember that
his role was to guard her, keep her from harm. And so
he knew at whatever cost he must never become a
burden to her, or part of things that might cause harm
to her.

"Selena", he said at last, Hakim says that the
approach to the pyramids is most beautiful at dawn.

And that he thinks we can go to them on Camelback if we wish."

" I would love to see them that way."

" Then I think we should sleep now", John rose.

" Si, you're probably right." Selena smiled, stretched, and lightly touched John's hand on her way to her tent.

Chapter: 11

Neither John nor Selena had any way of knowing that this day spent around the great pyramids, would be caught, held sharp in memory, and incidentally on camera. They could have anticipated the excitement and the novelty, but never the odd combination of beauty and humor they were to find there.

Many years later, and unknown to one another, a grainy black and white Kodak photograph was always to be found on the mantle or bureau of any bedroom either occupied. That slightly out of focus "candid" picture was to travel the world with each of them, the first thing to be packed or unpacked.

The sun was just rising when Hakkim took them over to the circle of waiting guides and camels. As they approached, Hakkim asked politely about the depth of their past experience with these animals.

"We've had absolutely none." John answered a little nervous. Selena was excited by the unique expression and long lashed look of the kneeling camels. She had not realized they were cud chewing much as the goats of Italy. They appeared somnolent, ageless, benevolent.

"By day's end, In' cha Allah, you will know something of our Ships of the Desert. They are patient, they are strong. Since the beginning of time, they have been with us, not servants but companions of our land. "Hakkim spoke with a marked degree of respect. Then went on,"Your guide will stay by you always, sir and maam Hiya, but I think that their English may be hard. And so, remember only this, that around the animals one must move with calm, quiet and always very slow, so they will know you do not threaten."

"Thank you Hakkim." The old Egyptian bowed.

The camels were saddled and kneeling as John and Selena came to them. Selena's guide showed her the stirrup and reins, then indicated she should mount the camel, while it was still kneeling, and hold tight as it got first to its front knees then to its back feet, a violent rocking motion, which threw many first timers about like rag dolls.

When her camel got all the way up, Selena thought the ground looked awfully far away, and she contemplated the trek with some grimness, until she saw John go through the same maneuvers on his animal. It was comical to watch. She started to get the giggles, but quickly got them under control, realizing the guides might interpret her response as disrespectful.

The caravan formed up, getting underway-Selena, then John, each with a guide, then two camels with supplies.

In the beginning, they were lead by their guides, until they got the feeling of control with reins, and leather wrapped "bats". John thought the rocking, gliding gait of the camels did indeed remind him of a ship's motion.

A few miles brought them within full view of the great pyramid of Khufu, and its lesser companion of Khafre, on which much of the original limestone casing remained intact towards the top. So too, they came onto the complex surrounding the Sphinx. And as they got still nearer, they saw the lion figure, with its disfigured face and beard said to be Khafre himself.

John's guide told them the story of the granite stele set up in the front of the Sphinx by order of Tutmosis.

A thousand years after the Sphinx was erected, while yet a minor prince, Tutmosis had a dream. His hunting party had come to a rest in the shade of that great beast statue. Over scores of years, the desert sands had piled up around its feet and flanks. The prince, who slept in the noon day as his men guarded the royal presence, dreamed the Sphinx came to him and promised him the rule of Egypt, if he would clear away the sands which had grown high around it.

The sand was cleared, the stele built to indicate a promise kept, and Tuthmosis became Pharaoh of the upper and lower kingdoms.

They hadn't appreciated that there were actually scores of lesser tombs and pyramids, oriented on a north-south axis. The smallest of the great pyramids, begun by Menkaure, completed by his son, showed traces of the red granite which was intended as its finish.

As their camels bore them closer, the majesty and power of the structures, impressed a silence on the whole group. They stopped a half-mile from the pyramid of Khufu, just at the feet of the Sphinx. John's guide said quietly that they followed the footsteps of thousand upon thousands of pilgrims, who came over the centuries, drawn by the wonders about them. Then with a roguish expression he pointed out the rude Greek drinking song, scratched on one of the toes of the sphinx sometime during the Ptolemaic period. But made no offer to translate.

It was near two in the afternoon, the massive form of the Sphinx cast enough shade for them to dismount for food, and drink. Hakkim had prepared light fare-cold chicken, fruits, and minted tea. Selena and John dismounted, had their lunch, and told the men to take their time, as they would wander about on foot. The walking was rock-strewn and difficult at times. They found that hand in hand was the surest way around.

Selena, became aware more and more of John's strength and coordination. He had still, the grace of motion, that spoke of his early athleticism. She herself, was accustomed to long hours on foot, but had never dealt with hazards of uneven, and large rocks, thrown in the way of walking.

It was hot, even the stirring wind which lifted curls of fine sand about their feet and off the battered corners of the statues was hot. The whites of their riding clothes has become stained with sweat and the dust of the desert. But the ruins held their attention. They wandered content with their own company, whispering and pointing to objects or vistas that interested them.

Hakkim had told them mighty as they appeared, the the stone blocks of the Pyramids were fragile. And so the government asked guides to discourage clients from climbing on their massive steps. Although everyone knew if " the price was right" the guides would take them up. Being a professional historian, and very much an environmentalist, John responded they had no desire to mount the stones.

It was about four in the afternoon when John and Selena returned to their guides. The sun was still hot, but its rays fell more kindly, outlining the camels against the Sphinx. The picture it made was superb. John felt he wanted a snapshot of Selena on her camel with the ageless monument as background. So he asked Selena's guide to help her mount her camel.

Selena and the guide set up about twenty feet in front of John's camel, who knelt, chewing his cud, and blinking contentedly in the sun. John got his box camera from a pack on his camel's back.

"All right", he said setting up the shot, "now, turn the camel's profile to me."

Selena relayed what John wanted in soft tones. The Arab obliging, grasped the animal's reins and began coaxing him around.

"Good, good. More." John urged.

The Camel, Selena, and the guide, were slow and

somewhat awkward as they tried to execute his directions.

"A little to the left. Good. Again." John wasn't quite satisfied. "Turn the camel's head more to me!"

What he wanted to capture was Selena in full face, the camel in profile, against the heads and paws of the great beast within the perspective of desert sands. Having failed to explain specifically what he was after, neither Selena nor her guide understood completely. As to her camel, not only was it confused, but also rapidly becoming obdurate at the strange manipulations visited on him.

Frustrated, John decided he had to demonstrate what he wanted. He pulled quickly on his camel's reins, getting him up, and tugging him along, as he approached Selena on foot. Trying to make things clear, he made the mistake many do when not understood, he raised his voice and tried broader gestures, as he insisted, "Go! Go on! More to the left!"

With the last of these directions, his arm swept rapidly in front of his camel, who rudely interrupted from his nap, finally took offense at the excessive noise and activity going on right in front of his nose.

As John snapped the picture, he promptly received a large wad of camel cud delivered over his head and shoulders with total accuracy. He gasped and leapt out of range, but too late. He was head to toe by showered a mass of first rumen stomach contents. Selena later assured John that she was sure he had been assigned to a beady-eyed, malevolent monster, not at all the usual limpid eyed, long lashed, placid transporter of man. Which would explain what happened.

Whatever the explanation, John and the camera were thoroughly covered with thick green brown camel juice. Selena began to laugh, as did the guides who witnessed the shot. John was first startled and upset, but then had to see the funny side.

" Oh my God," Selena gasped with laughter, holding on with dear life to her perch, trying to recover. Then immediately "John, you must give me the camera,"

John handed it to a driver who in turn handed it up to Selena. It was the simple box made famous by Kodak in the early part of the century-having only a knob for film advancement, and a small lever for shutter control. She focused, and took a perfect picture of John, covered from head to waist, in camel slime, standing beside his "mount" who had reverted to its normal sleepy eyed, contented look. When he saw the developed photo, John swore that she managed to capture the camel with a look of the complacency which followed a totally satisfactory revenge.

The guides brought cloths and did the best they could with the surplus juice. Back in camp, Selena said with affection, despite their best efforts, John looked like a perfectly camouflaged desert warfare soldier. An interesting look. However, John noticed she managed to keep a considerable distance between the two of them.

When they arrived back at the oasis, John departed immediately for the shower. Selena told Hakkim how wonderful the day had been and thanked all the guides for their help.

Chapter: 12

The night had become colder than usual in the desert. Hakkim had a large fire built up outside the dinner tent. It's flames reflected off the whiteness of their dress, as they finished dinner.

John looked over at Selena, who sat with her legs tucked under her, contentedly finishing grapes which somehow Hakkim had managed to present chilled.

"You look wonderful. White suits you. Especially as it catches the color of the firelight." She looked graceful, and very much at home under the soft night skies.

" Now that you're cleaned up, you are very, Come si dice, what is the word I want, ah yes, 'handsome' in your burnoose and boots. Perhaps the picture should have waited until now." They started to laugh.

"If I were a professional, I would do a photograph of you as you sit, this evening. Portrait of beauty in the desert, we could call it. The professionals are able to do good photos at night using a strong flashlight, but the box camera Hussein lent me is from another era. As matter of fact, it's so old the image in the viewer is upside down"

Selena looked down at her hands, her eyes focused on them as she spoke softly. "In Napoli, we could not afford a camera, there has never been one in my family. But we all learned to catch "picture" images of those we loved, frozen in our minds, which we could call on again and again. Many of the people in our Quartiere could do this. No, that is wrong, Had to do this."

John listened intrigued. It was the first she had spoken of her family or Naples. She didn't continue. But sat silent for a moment. Then gave a little shiver.

"You're cold, Selena?" John rose from his chair,

taking his jacket off and placing it around her slim shoulders. She looked up gratefully.

"Why don't we wander nearer the fire for a moment. Come, we can take our drinks." As a very special consideration Hussein had sent along a reserve Armagnac from his cellar. The Muslims of Egypt were forbidden alcohol by their religion, although the same proscription didn't apply to their guests.

The men were gathered far away around their own fire. Selena and John had the warmth of the main fire to themselves. They stood, sipping their drinks, looking into the changing shapes for a long while, "Warmer?" John put his arm lightly around her shoulders.

"Yes. I'm quite comfortable now." Selena looked at him, "You take such care of me John. It's still so strange, so difficult to get used to."

The factual tone she used to say the words, not as many women would in invitation, or to arouse further commitment or even as part of man/woman flirtation, struck John forcefully. Recently, he didn't know how to handle his increasing feelings for Selena. It seemed so much of what she did, often without intent or self-consciousness was irresistible.

As to Selena, she was aware that day by day the relationship between them was becoming fuller, closer, especially on his part. She seemed to crave the care he gave her so spontaneously, so generously. She had a lifetime behind her of its absence, and was now reveling in it.

They finished their drinks. John took Selena's glass, and they headed back to the tent.

" Another?"

"No, No thank you."

" Buona notte, amore." John took Selena lightly in his arms. As he leant down to kiss her cheek, he found she'd turned her head. In stead his mouth found her lips. They were soft, soft and warm, with just a trace of the flavor of Armagnac still left upon them.

Selena put her arms around his neck. It was a breathless moment for each. Neither moved, but their lips clung almost without conscious thought, tenderly.

Selena moved back a little in his arms and sighed. She looked deep into his eyes, to seek, she didn't know exactly what. What she saw was love, tenderness, and unmistakable passion. The passion of a man for a woman. She understood instinctively the tenderness, and passion were made one by the love which shone there. She trusted it. Here, at last was a way to tell John how much she cared for him, how deep her gratitude.

"John", she said softly, " Vieni stai con me, amore mio", I want you to stay with me tonight, my love.

"Oh, Selena. You're sure?" He whispered.

"Tesore Mio, I am sure."

They turned slowly toward her quarters.

Chapter: 13

A flickering oil lamp gave the only light in the soft dark folds of the tent. Layers of silken coverlets lay on the opened bed. Selena's robe and nightclothes had been neatly laid out at its foot awaiting her.

Selena drew John into to her quarters, fastening the tent behind him as he entered. Then turning once again to embrace him.

John felt the soft giving of her breasts crushed lightly against him. He took her face between his hands, looking deeply in her eyes, again seeking her consent. The mounds of her ebony hair smelled of the desert and a wonderful light flower scent. and were silken soft where they fell over his hands, and surrounded her head.

He stroked her hair over and over. Murmuring "Selena, Selena."

She lifted her lips to his. He took them, let his hands slip to her waist, and began to kiss her from one corner of her mouth to the other, brushing and pressing her lips, until he felt her open to him. Slowly, with infinite gentleness, his tongue met, and began to caress hers.

She gasped, and felt warmth creep up from her limbs to her face, melting her body.

John lifted and, carried her easily to the bed, without removing his lips. There he put her down, laid beside her in the silken drapes, and began stroking her arms and face.

Selena turned towards him so that she had the entire length of his body against hers. It felt hard, strange, unlike her own, but his touch was so gentle. Her breathing was becoming uneven with excitement. Something within melted, something centered deep within. She knew she wanted to give herself to him, to abandon her own center for his.

"John, stop. I want to feel you tight against me," she whispered as she turned away for a moment, and started to shed her clothes.

"Let me." John took off her robe, then her blouse letting them fall as they might, kissing each part of her body, her neck, her shoulders and her breasts as they came free. Her skin was velvet to his touch, and lightly bronzed where the desert sun had found it.

"My God. You're so lovely" John looked at her, then softly touched each breast. Selena felt as if his fingertips were molten, enchanting her wherever his fingers rested.

Then quickly he took her back in his arms, lowered his head to her nipples and began to kiss them.

Fire shot from her nipples up into her face and down to her lower body. Her whole body turned liquid. And she knew then that what she felt was desire.

John stopped for a moment to take off his own clothes. Selena looked at him, he was beautiful with carved masculine planes, his forearms and legs powerful, and lightly covered with blond hair, which glinted in the light of the oil lamp. His need for her evident in his erection. She felt none of the revulsion she had known before, when she saw his readiness, on the contrary her own heat and melting seemed right, seemed to match his, to welcome his desire.

She reached for him. John reclaimed her mouth and with light long strokes roamed the length of her body kissing and mouthing more insistently as he went. Her legs fell apart under his tenderness.

As he reached her mound, seeing her wet, glistening and ready for him, he parted her lips and began to tongue her clitoris, Selena gasped, then caught his head to her. It seemed as if her very being was afire.

"John, ho besogna di te," John, I need you inside of me, I need to feel you deep inside.

Gently he touched the tip of his organ to her vagina. Finding her open and ready he slid gently into her. She gasped as she felt him enter her. Caught him around his buttocks as she whispered, "All, John. Give me all of you.'

He hesitated for a moment. He knew he was large, and she unused to penetration. Then entered her fully. Selena began to rock with the rhythm she didn't even know she was setting. It became faster and faster, more and more intense, until she cried out as a series of spasms grasped her body leaving it limp. His own orgasm was set off by hers.

So it was as if they'd both passed through a turbulent sea, that seized and held them until it relented, and set them free as if on a lone beach on the other side. Only they knew the sea was of their making.

John lay back, took Selena into his arms, kissing her over and over without words. Then he stopped. Something was wrong, he felt her shaking violently. He turned quickly to see what was the matter.

Selena hid her face from him. But he saw she was weeping uncontrollably, in utter silence.

"Oh, my love, what is it? He asked anxiously, afraid something in their lovemaking had upset her. He took her in his arms again asking, "What is it?"

Selena was unable to answer him. Tears coursed down her face. He held her, making inarticulate reassuring sounds. Finally the sobbing subsided.

In a voice so low, he wasn't sure he'd heard all she was saying, Selena finally said, "I was thinking of Napoli. I thought this was for animals. I thought it was only to relieve the man, to pleasure him. I thought it was only pain and ugliness. But you, you have taken that away. I know now. I know how it should be with a man and a woman."

"Yes Selena." He reached for a scarf which lay on the bedside table, and wiped her tears away. Then kissed her eyelids, he wanted to soothe her.

" I read once the children of Tibet are taught that this is how butterflies kiss."

Then he softly rubbed noses with her. "And this, I read, is how Eskimos kiss."

Selena looked at him through tear filled eyes, and smiled, at his gentleness, knowing he was softening the moment of her grief as one would a wounded child.

" John, not even as a child have I cried before now. Now I don't cry for what was, but for the joy of you."

"Selena, you are so beautiful, I can't begin to tell you...."

"No. No words now", she said softly. "No words, tesoro mio. But possiamo, can we...?" She wasn't sure that she could ask directly.

John laughed with relief, and playing lightly with her shyness, simply said "Of course. Subito." Yes, right away.

The moon was setting in the Eastern sky when they finally slept, limbs entwined on the silken bed.

Hakkim came to their tent after morning prayer rugs had been stored, he saw the tent flaps closed. Smiled, made a blessing for them and told his men to spend the morning currying their beasts and polishing their equipment, but without a sound. The man who made noise would answer to him.

Chapter: 14

The Days went by in a golden haze of intoxication for John. Selena seemed to blossom before his eyes from a child into a bronze young goddess. A goddess whose eyes met his with unfailing warmth. He could barely believe her love. But there it was-his to evoke.

By day they talked of many things, some monumentally important, some daily trivia. John was able to tell Selena of Elsa, and what their life had meant to him. She listened intent. This was something she could give him. Something to repay his kindness and protection. She knew, despite her lack of years and experiemce, he had to relive the days of his marriage and loss, so that he might recover from them.

Ironically, though she couldn't speak of it, John recognized that Selena needed much the same to get over the filth and ugliness that rape had visited on her.

It was one of those times that John gave her one of his unused "journals". One of the thin grey accountant's books, he used for preliminary notes for his work. He suggested gently she keep a diary of her thoughts and feelings, wanting to give her this way to rid her mind of the past. But also explaining the relevance of the American phrase, "You only go around once."

Selena listened to his explanation solemnly, took the book, thanked him as she did for all his gifts, put it carefully away with the things he had given her without specifically responding. John never knew, and never felt he should ask how or even if she used it. He always thought of her past much as the ancient map makers thought of what lay outside the boundaries of the known world- 'Take care, beyond these seas be dragons.'

One day Selena marveled at the scarabs carved in the tombs they visited. She thought how strange it was that these small carved insects should carry a mantle of holiness, until John told her of the essential part the dung beetle played along the thin corridor of cultivation by Nile side.

"John, can it possibly be true, that they made so much of these strange looking bugs?"

"Not only could but did. You see, without the millions upon millions of these small creatures, all active, all swarming, fertilization of crops as the ancients knew it, would not have happened."

Selena continued to look at him, waiting for what she was sure was more of the story of this extraordinary life. John was full of the most wonderful bits of knowledge.

He went on, "It was the difference between starvation and plenty. Pharaohs, or conquerors in their chariots could triumph, priests and scholars opine in their hieroglyphics the history and religion of the country, armies conquer or surrender, the Gods themselves weigh souls and rule the living as the walls of the temples tell us-but the scarab, the dung beetle was the real arbiter of life and death in the kingdom of ancient Egypt."

"What a thought. But then why not? The farmers della campagna, the men who grow the grapes and make the wine always talk of 'il bel sole', the sun. But under their feet the women look for the worms who turn the soil, who make the earth yield, who seem to disappear with the crops in a rainless season."

" That's about the same sort of thing."

" Yes. But they never sainted the worms, not even the women who should have known to do it."

" Let us say only, that some men are more appreciative than others. The soil of your native country is volcanic, rich, not desert sand. Perhaps its richness made the men less grateful."

"I think you must be right. I will try always to remember the dung beetle, the enchanting scarab of old Egypt."

Another day they walked in the canyons created by the columns and statues at Kharnak, hearing the echoes of their pilgrim steps . Speaking softly to one another in hushed tones. Feeling the shadows, the ghosts of ancient rulers follow the hollow sound of their passage, imagining what it would be like to live in those long gone times.

Night fell. The cinders of the fire glowed. Occasional sparks few up to the moon and clouds above. The daytime heat was effaced with sundown, replaced by the surprising low temperatures of evening. It was a typical night in 'their desert'.

"Are you warm enough, my dearest?" John asked concerned.

"You always worry, mio caro. Sto benissimo", I'm perfect. "I could stay here with you an eternity."
Selena nestled against his side as they watched the flames dying down.

John put his arm around her slender waist, drawing her close. He could never get enough of her, her scent, the feel of her hair, the softness of her skin, her wonderfully curved body, the low husky voice, the lilting accent as she spoke.

"If I were a cat, I would be purring."

John smiled, and stroked her hair and neck playfully.

"Cats who purr invite caresses." He turned her face to his and gently kissed her mouth.

She returned his kiss. Intoxicating, he thought. She is intoxicating.

As their kiss deepened, Selena's breath quickened.

"John…" It was half question, half-command. Captivated, he turned, lifted her in his arms. Quickly and easily, he carried her to their tent.

Much later, the embers of the fire died down, gentle wind blew off the hills, strengthening the chill curling in the desert valleys. But the folds of the tent protected her, the layers of soft camel's wool blankets warmed her from shoulder to toe, and John slept peacefully at her side. Selena was wakeful, reliving the days and nights, her present existence. She was happy.

Dawn came. She rose and went to talk over the coming day with Hakkim-where they should go, what they should do.

As the sun mounted higher, John lazed for a time in their bed. It still carried the imprint of her body, the faintest trace of her warmth. He visualized Selena adoringly. She would be out planning the new day with Hakkim.

Her knowledge, her vision of the world had grown quickly, so quickly John felt hard pressed to keep up with her, and more and more had to think carefully before answering her questioning mind.

Unexpectedly, John found She had the gift of joy and even laughter, which she was able to share with him. So that for him too, life changed.

It was time to rise.

They gave up the oasis and all but two attendants as they traveled to the ruins of Memphis. Hakkim saw to their comfort and accommodation. The camels were replaced by a Land Rover which could cover the distances they traveled in little time.

Nights were ardent. As they learned each other's bodies and desires. Selena discovered she could initiate, even control their lovemaking on occasion. John found that to surrender control, could bring out passion, and generosity he hadn't thought possible.

He would watch the play of light on her body, the grace with which she moved, a turn of the head or the expression on her face after they made love. A look of absolute peace and repose.

Selena found the pleasure of evoking a range of responses, sometimes with blatancy, sometimes suggestion. She knew ultimately that women were better at expanding the world of lovemaking, they were more instinctive.

She found there were times when she could tease lingeringly, as only a woman can tease the man she cares for, and other times when her desire to please and be pleased was so intense, she became almost awkward in her haste.

Each loved and was loved in return without stint. Neither had a sense of time passing. It was as if time was of no importance whatever. Place-the desert with its monuments under the Egyptian skies was no more than a background to their love.

One night, after John had fallen asleep, Selena wrote of the skies above the desert, remote, eternal in their watch over the sands. And then of the black felt of the tent above her head the first night they had made love. The warmth and intimacy that its dark folds lent.

It took several hours to write the few words which she felt just held the experience she wanted to catch forever. But in the end, she thought, yes, with these words I shall be able to come back whenever I want, and know again how it was.

When it came to their actual lovemaking she found she couldn't capture it in words. She thought perhaps actual physical pleasure much as actual physical pain couldn't be caught, nor the sensation relived.

But she wanted at least the mnemonic of when, and where, and perhaps why things happened. At least the essence. Many years later she would think, it was as if one opened the stopper of an old perfume bottle, catching the hint of what had been, enough to satisfy memory.

Accepting the obliqueness, the limitations, but the intensely personal quality she was able to garner, she decided to call her journal "Ceilings". She remembered then and wrote of her childhood 'Ceiling of God'. These things she knew she could describe in detail, and with an accuracy made intense by her feelings. She opened the ledger John had given her. On the first page, where the publisher had printed Ledger, she blacked out the printed word, and wrote in a clear hand "Ceilings" and underlined it.

It was three weeks almost to the day, after they had arrived at the oasis, that Hussein sent word to them. The Victoria had completed her repairs and would be ready to sail from Port Said within 48 hours. They went to the nearest telegraph office and wired back that they would return to Cairo immediately.

They had no intention of sailing on with the ship.

Chapter: 15

As they sat down to a traditional welcome-home dinner of couscous and lamb, Hussein couldn't help notice the change in their relationship. It showed in quick glances between them, the not infrequent brushing of hands, the affectionate tone they used to one another.

Both were brown and rosy with health. Joy shone unmistakably in John's face, and Selena appeared content with his solicitude, and his obvious pleasure in her, so that Hussein finally said aloud, " It seemed to him that happiness sat as a fourth guest at the table"

To which John responded, " In' cha Allah."

"So our desert has taught you...."

John used the cadence of the language of the desert to thank his friend, "Many things. Eternal thanks to you."

Hussein said nothing more, but continued to beam at his young friends." 'Well done', he thought to himself John told him of their experiences, and the guides. Selena, for her part, promised him a copy of the picture of John and the camel. She glanced slyly at John. Catching her glance, he made a mock-grim face, then laughed. He thought-since he would have to live with this experience for as long as he knew her. It might as well be gracefully. She thought, as she continued to regard him, a sense of humor is a prize above pearls!

When Hussein asked them to stay on in the El Alamein quarters, Selena responded, " How wonderful of you to ask us."

"Absolutely", John agreed, "If you're sure it's convenient?"

"Absolutely", Hussein grinned. "We'll fix up a car

for you, so you'll be mobile. Tomorrow, you may want to add something to your wardrobe. Desert outfits are fine for the desert." He indicated his own beautifully tailored corpulence, "but we Caireans, are a little more dressy."

"Granted", John acknowledged his friend's sartorial splendor.

And so the next day, after the morning's shopping John remained behind to 'work', while Selena explored the Museum of Egyptian Civilization, known for the extent of its collection of ancient artifacts. Selena was delighted that he was once again eager to write, and went off with a light heart.

When she arrived at the room dedicated to Nefertiti, and saw the many, statues, and friezes depicting that Queen, she was overwhelmed by her beauty. It was obvious that the artists who painted or sculpted the monarch were possessed by her, looks and grace. The cosmesis the Queen used to enhance her appearance was as faithfully rendered, as her jewelry which seemed immensely heavy for her long slender neck.

Selena noted the use of kohl, and the shading of the upper eyelids, the painting of the mouth, and the ecru color of the skin. She wasn't certain whether or not the translucence was the invention of the artists or a faithful rendering of Nefertiti's own complexion.

She continued on through room after room of the old museum illumined by clerestory windows. The dust-moted light fell on statues of past regents with kindness, lending encouragement to those who wished to remember past life, and attainment-children and Gods of the Nile, spawned in the glory of river's flow, and cradled by the lotus lining its banks.

When she came upon the rooms dedicated to later periods, she entered one given over to Cleopatra. There were busts and portraits of that renowned beauty, many from the year that Caesar first conquered the kingdom of the Nile.

At that time, Egypt was ruinously ruled by Cleopatra's young brother-wastrel, pederast, and puppet of the priests, who made his every decision. Cleopatra, needed Caesar to wrest power away from him, and give rule of the kingdom over to her. There were several reasons that this might be desirable from her point of view-she was brilliantly educated, ambitious, and handled power with surpassing skill. But most important, from her point of view, she was in imminent danger of annihilation as the single living challenge to her brother.

The legend of how she reached Caesar, in spite of his Praetorian legions, personal guards, and those of her brother, was told larger than life on the walls of the room.

She was fourteen, and knew she must convince Caesar, that she was far more able to rule, under Roman aegis than her sibling. But her brother, at the time more powerful than she, managed to see to it that his sister was given no possible access to the Roman general. Thus seeking to obviate any possible threat to his reign.

Cleopatra had herself perfumed, anointed, and decked in a single diaphanous robe, barely disguising the nubile body beneath it. Her hair was elaborately coiffed-the work of hours by her most skilled dressers, her eyes, and lips dusted with gold.

She had herself laid in the most precious silken rug of her palace, wrapped in its folds, and carried off by six beautiful, muscled male slaves, similarly decked out in gold. They delivered her to Caesar's quarters, a rich 'gift' ostensibly offered by the young Pharaoh-to-be.

Thus as the carpet was unrolled before him,

Cleopatra appeared literally at the feet of Caesar.

Enthralled by her live young beauty, appreciative of both the ruse and cleverness needed to gain his presence, Caesar made her at once his mistress, and that of both kingdoms of Egypt.

Within days, she had her brother killed with more dispatch and much less notoriety than the later assassination of Caesar by his fellow Romans. And kept her kingdom after he returned to Rome, as foretold, to the noisome murder on the Senate steps on the Ides of March.

Selena saw some of the later portraits, done when Cleopatra was in her thirties, the cynosure of most of the most stylish matrons of Rome, who envied the repute of her beauty and seductiveness. And another done when she was almost forty, old age in those days of short lives, which showed the skillful use of cosmetics to maintain the appearance of youth. It was, of course, the year of her death after the defeat of the fleet commanded by her then lover, Marc Anthony. The victor at the battle of Actium, later crowned as 'Augustus', wished to troop her beauty in chains as a trophy in the triumphal march he was granted through the streets of Rome.

The texts surrounding this statue made clear that Cleopatra chose suicide rather than submit to this indignity for herself, and for Egypt.

Selena studied her face. She noted the exaggerated kohl lines carried out to the temple to elongate the eyes, the green coloration of the lower and upper lid, which made for a fresh doe-like appearance. The carefully defined and rouged lips, drawn fuller than the actual lip line underneath for sensuous effect.

She read of the oils perfumed by teak and acacia to soften the skin, and bathing solutions of asses milk and honey, refined turpentines and oliban to efface body odors and exudates, and finally the chignons and elaborate knots and loops Cleopatra used in dressing her hair.

She was fascinated, and had to be reminded by the guards that the museum was closing. She left then, realizing that she could come back as often as she wished.

Her return to the palace passed in a daze. Staggered by the richness, the skill, and the ingenuity which enhanced these beauties, who lived so many, many centuries ago.

When she arrived home, she tried to express the wonder she felt, and the magic of these women. It simply wasn't possible. John always paid attention to what she had to say, but she could tell from his expression, that she failed utterly to convey her marvel, or if truth be known engage his serious interest.

Disconcerted by his lack of response, she thought if only he could see what I saw in person..."John, would you come and see for yourself?"

"Of course, as soon as I can. Right now I'm on a roll. The book is finally coming on so fast, I can hardly keep up with my notes." He barely looked up from the papers in his hand.

"That's wonderful. Just wonderful." Selena said as she sank into a soft chair, and put her feet up on an ottoman, tired from all she had seen. Then still thinking she'd like him to visit the museum she asked, "Do you think you could take a break soon?"

John, his mind still on his work, echoed absently,

"Yes of course, as soon as a break comes."

Selena saw his distraction as well as his effort at attention. She knew at some point he would come, just because she asked him to. But she read his face too easily to be fooled into thinking the subject would ever hold any interest for him. In a sense it put a little damper on her excitement, but after a moment the thrill of the afternoon returned.

They parted to bathe and dress for dinner. Hussein had left on an embassy matter, so they dined alone, and retired early to make love, and sleep.

The next day, when asked, Selena's chauffeur took her to the heart of the chic shopping area. As yesterday, she was followed, although at a discreet distance by a body guard, who when not shadowing her, sat in front with the driver.

She wandered leisurely through boutiques, showing the latest Paris fashions, jewelry, and cosmetics, becoming more aware, and more impatient with the presence of a guardian as the day went on. There were no encounters, no threats that she could see. On the contrary, the people on the street seemed courteous, and pleasant but kept distant by the guard. She felt Hussein was being overprotective.

That afternoon, having seen most of the central shopping district, she decided to see another part of the city. She had her driver take her to the Souk, in the Bab al-Bahr quarter, which held the old native market. It was large, bustling, full of color and noise. It made the more European parts of the city seem sterile, and contrived. People jostled against people, and the shopkeepers did not confine themselves to their tiny stores with their dark interiors and wildly colorful goods, but spilled out into the street calling, selling, showing.

When she stepped out of the limousine, she told the driver she would meet him back just where he let her off. Her guard made disapproving sounds and followed her into the maze of streets and shops. It was so crowded, that she knew she could lose him, and before she explored the market, proceeded to do just that.

She passed sellers of incense, carvings, brassware

and countless other objects, in small shop after shop. Shops that were dark carpeted miniature Alibaba's caverns containing treasures and the promise of still more.

On and on she went, lured by the variety until, drawn by the subtle music of beaded curtains moving to the current of a gentle breeze, she focused on a doorway. There she was caught by a pair of dark hypnotic eyes set deeply in the wrinkled face of a tiny and ancient woman, swathed in saffron silk from head to toe. Wisdom and power sat unmistakably in her face; the world seen and learned written in her eyes. Unable to resist, Selena approached with a deep sense of the inevitable. She knew, and recognized that the other knew they were meant to meet.

Selena stopped before her as the woman answered her unspoken question.

" My name is Fatimah. This is my shop."

And then without pause, or thought of refusal, " Won't you take tea with me?"

"Of course", Selena responded, and entered a world of colored boxes and bottles, of scarves and veils, of brushes and jars, of the scent of spices and exotic blooms.

"It has been mine, and my mother's before, and her mother's before her."

" And you do...?"

" I deal in appearances. In the ways of the faces and bodies of women."

Selena was later to learn that there was not a fashionable woman of the city, who didn't seek out Fatimah's attention and ministrations. Or who thought twice about coming to her tiny shop in this old dusty section of the city.

And then she found there were those who came brutally scarred or deformed who were treated for nothing. Of these women, Fatimah said later, only Allah could erase their scourging, but then Allah had given her hands and eyes their skill, and she used both for these, his creatures.

Those who wished to enhance their looks, those who wished to create them, those who sought to be desirable, those who wished to disguise age, anyone seeking attraction came to Fatimah, who dealt in the beauty secrets of the past, and in techniques of the present with equal ease.

" It is this that I seek to learn."

" For yourself, my dear?" The old woman asked. " You have so little need."

" No, I think to give to others." Selena found herself answering.

"Ah, I thought so. Good. That is what I saw in your beautiful eyes." It was as if Fatimah confirmed what Selena just discovered with certainty-what she wanted to do with her life.

"Come. Sit. We will take an infusion and begin."

Selena entered into the soft twilight of the shop, filled with intoxicating smells, whose shelves were neatly lined with odd flacons and containers of lotions and solutions, powders and potions, herbs and oils.

Fatimah poured steaming water from an old dented brass kettle over the leaves she had carefully placed in a small net suspended within a china pot. After a few moments, when the scent of the tea, just began to escape, she removed the net and poured the tea into two small cups.

Selena sipped her tea. It was the most delicious brew she had ever tasted. She had no idea then what it was, and at that moment didn't wish to try to analyze. It was a luxury Fatimah never again permitted.

" Drink, my little one. Then we will begin."

Chapter: 16

With John's whole-hearted approval, Hussein had assigned a bodyguard permanently for Selena's safety.

"John, I absolutely refuse to have a keeper, hung around my neck, to follow me about, or frighten people I want to talk to. It's completely unnecessary and very cumbersome." John was impressed with her command of English on this level. But nonetheless convinced that she needed the protection.

Selena was not finished her objections. "I feel caged in, on a leash, like an unthinking child, and I will not have it!" Hussein wasn't spared her indignation, perhaps I should be confined to the Oda with your Father's wives!"

"But, Selena, you don't know the hazards of Cairo. Our beggars are actually highly trained professionals. The very least they do is persist and confront. Our pickpockets are second to none. And our shopkeepers will follow you in the street right into the car. They'll pester and cheat you." Hussein did his best to convince her.

"There is nothing in your streets I haven't seen before in Napoli. Believe me. And in any case, I just won't have it."

"Selena…" John started, exasperated.

She simply shook her head, refusing to argue further.

In spite of the continuing attempts of both men, especially John's, she got her way. They knew if they sent a man along in spite of her wishes, she would simply give him the slip.

Hussein threw up his hands in concerned but good-natured surrender. As to John, who was angry, it was the first real disagreement he'd had with Selena. And it made a small rift in the continuum of their existence.

In the time that followed, Selena returned day after day to the little shop in the Souk. Once there she'd change into the same dress as that of Fatimah, thus becoming, her "assistant". The customers never questioned the presence of the younger woman, as they never questioned any of Fatimah's ways and wares. The place was magical, and its practices and advice were taken whole. It was well known that if both were followed assiduously, success too followed.

Selena first watched, then began to apply some of the simpler cosmetics and lotions. Fatimah saw her pupil had skillful, caring hands with long gentle fingers. Hands which were supple, yet strong, soothing but very precise in their movements, at once lovely and powerful. Often Fatimah would smile as she looked at her own gnarled, arthritic fingers, saying to her clients, "It is good to have beautiful things done by beautiful hands, and mine are no longer things of beauty."

She watched as Selena, following her example carefully inspected and analyzed the face and form of every woman who came to the shop, listening to their requests and how they were put.

After this first 'look', Fatimah would call Selena into the back room, and question her in the softest tones as to what she saw. What might be done for the client. And how to achieve it.

Selena learned more and more each day of the potential that lay behind each face and body, and how to build on this base. In the beginning, she was bewildered by the variety of faces, of bodies, of problems and desires, all come to seek help. But later she looked forward to the spectrum and what must be done for each.

Soon if, any differences came up in the back room,

Fatimah would return to the customer for a second look. Selena was surprised the first time this happened. But her friend said, "Look carefully into my eyes. You see a light ring around my pupils?"

Selena placed her hands on either side of her friend's face, drawing it close to hers. "Why yes. It is a light blue, so light it's almost white."

" Yes, my dear. Exactly. It has a name this ring-it's called Arcis senilis. It is the mark of years passed, just as those years are stamped on my fingers. But your eyes are bright, sharp, without flaw, And I begin to trust them more than my own. I must have total light to see, where you see plainly in shadow as well as light. And too your eyes are beginning to see that beauty is only partly achieved by cosmetics but these, of course, must be pure. "

" I understand."

"Yes, ma Cherie, I think you do." Fatimah smiled at her young protégé with affection.

Later in the day, as dusk approached, and their clients had gone, they took time for their "tea". These teas brought talk of the nature of cosmetics-concealment of flaws, or emphasis of desired feature. What could be altered by cosmesis, what could not. How the health of the body was reflected in the face. What age did to some and what could be done about it. Their talks where sometimes profound, sometimes technical, and sometimes an exploration of esthetics themselves. But always Selena learned.

One day, many weeks after she started coming to Fatimah, and they had finished for the day, Selena went into the back room, stripped naked, and stood in front of the full-length mirror. She called Fatimah to her. And both women looked intently at the image seen in the mirror, as Selena moved, sat, and moved again. First at a distance then close up. Selena had become for the moment her own client.

They talked for a short time. Fatimah brought a very light gray-blue eye shadow, a kohl-based mascara, and a very subtle rose color for the lips, enhancing their natural color. Selena looked them over, nodded, and slowly applied them, still sitting naked in front of the mirror.

" So much for the face", she said, after she inspected her work carefully from all angles. "Now for the body..."

"I think as little as possible, at most a trace of refinement about the hair. You have the wonderful glow of youth, and an almost perfect body. So nearly perfect, that as the ancients used to say, 'Do not tempt the Gods with perfection, for they will surely visit destruction.' We must not do too much."

"Agreed", Selena responded. "A touch of rouge to the nipples."

"Yes. That's lovely."

"And the mons veneris, too full. It should be easier to keep fresh." Selena took scissors, and trimmed down the edges, then sheared the length of her pubic hair, until it formed an attractive, shadowed triangle between her legs. "I think this is better."

Then she said, "I think my coif could be shorter, closer to the head."

"Yes. Let me." Fatimah worked for a time with comb and scissors. Then finished with a light pomade.

Looking at the overall effect, the face with the body, Fatimah said simply, "You are enchanting." She was fearful to say aloud that she really felt-that Selena closely resembled one of the sculptured deities of her beloved museum.

Then the older woman walked slowly to a small round table in the darkness at the back of the room, and sat down on one side of it. Overhead a beam of light came on, illumining its surface, leaving her face in shadow.

" Come Selena", she said quietly. "Sit here. Just opposite me."

Selena came over and sat.

"Now, give me your hand."

As Selena reached forward Fatimah turned her hand palm up. For several minutes she looked at it, occasionally touching an area, or tracing her finger across a line or crease.

After a short silence, Fatimah closed her eyes and spoke, "Yes. Far away from here, you will be an Empress ruling a vast world. Not the world you have known. But a new world you will create. I have taught you all I can, now you will be the teacher. The voice of the past and the voice of the future as one. Now go, my darling girl."

Selena returned to the palace, excited, anticipating John's admiration. She made sure that their room was softly lit that evening. She wanted the perfect background for her new look.

When they undressed, she came over to John who was propped up in bed awaiting her, Slowly she dropped her robe, letting the light fall full on her body, as she walked towards him, pausing to let him take her in, sure his arousal would be complete by the time she reached his side.

To her shock she heard him say, "Selena, what in God's name have you done to yourself?" He looked at her face and then her breasts, "What is this all over your breasts?" He reached up and wiped his hand over one nipple. "And your bush? What has happened to it? It's, it's... unnatural!"

For a moment Selena had no idea how to react. Then without a word, she turned, went back to her dressing room, and removed everything. She sat for a few moments staring at the image of her cast by the mirror. John's reaction was so vehement! So unexpected! What was it all about? Then it came to her, he thought of her as a girl essentially, despite their affair he saw her as a girl. It was as a woman she had presented herself tonight. And it seriously disrupted the teacher/pupil interaction which still made up a large part of their relationship.

She knew in some way she must have reminded him that she, like his wife, and had an independent streak, was capable of doing things on her own. And in another way this went along with her refusal to have a guard. Tonight was tonight, and there wasn't much to do, nor say for the moment. But Selena recognized a serious break in the relationship with the man she loved, and a dawning realization that they were truly different. They loved and cared as one, but were none-the-less two.

As she sat before her mirror removing the offending cosmetics. Selena looked hard to see whether the image showed that she felt much older than she had earlier in the day. Nothing she could see, at least on the surface. Tears came to her eyes. She dashed them away impatiently, put her robe on and went back to the bedroom. Change came when it would, and often at a price.

Chapter :17

When John awoke in the morning he knew things between them were off-key. Although each had come to full orgasm last night, for the first time their lovemaking, had an almost, detached quality. They'd made love not as strangers certainly, but not with the closeness, not with the total communion that lay at the heart of their passion. Their differences had begun to rag at their oneness, their world.

He looked over at Selena, still asleep apparently, curled on her side facing away from him. And knew, their relationship was about to change in some basic way.

He'd not mentioned it yesterday, but his agent had telexed him in the late afternoon that his publisher needed him back in the states within the week to review proposed changes in his manuscript. It was an imperative that couldn't be put off. He waited for Selena to wake.

Selena was not sleeping, but lying quietly thinking about last night. She wondered if there was always a moment, a critical moment when things between people changed so fundamentally, that they couldn't recapture what was, no matter hard they tried, or wanted to. She was no longer a girl but had in just a few weeks become a woman. With a woman's mind and insight.

She stirred. Turned over and stretched.

" Selena, you slept well?" John ventured, not quite knowing how to approach her this morning.

" Yes, very well." She answered, reaching over to stroke his cheek.

At this point, their breakfast was brought in on a

table, and set up in a window overlooking the courtyard, through which the early morning sun was streaming. They rose, got their robes and went to the table. Selena poured coffee, adding four lumps of sugar, as she knew John liked.

Usually breakfast was a time of talk between them. The plans and activities of the coming day were lightly exchanged, shared and mutually enjoyed.

This morning came with a fragile silence which both were reluctant to break lest the distance between them be made concrete by words or irreversible reactions.

The room was filled with a kind of ache, with hurt unresolved and unexpiated.

Finally, when they'd finished, John looked directly at Selena as he said, "Selena, I'm wanted back in New York as soon as possible for manuscript revisions. The book is moving along quickly. We've got just a few months if we want to have it out in time for the holidays, and the Frankfurt book mart."

His announcement caused Selena's thoughts to tumble. It wasn't that she hadn't anticipated this, it was just that coming when it did struck her with such force, and yet....

For herself, she had known for weeks that she had to go to New York and as one of the guide books said of many who came there, 'try her fortunes in the big city'. Now she felt propelled toward this huge metropolis, with its teeming people. It was a challenge she could not deny, a challenge that was fearful, and yet one, she knew she had to accept.

"John, I too, want to go to New York." Her voice held deep conviction. It is where I must go now. And I know what I must do."

John looked across at her, startled by the commitment he heard. He had not been privy to her experiences in Cairo, and most especially with Fatimah, so for him her decision came from the blue. He watched as Selena rose and began to pace up and down the room, her silken peignoir rustling behind almost as if it too were impatient with any hindrance.

"What is it?" He asked, feeling the waves of excitement coming from her.

"I am going to open a cosmetic shop, a cosmetic shop which will offer clients, all that I have learned about helping appearance."

"Selena," John said, still not understanding what the concept of cosmesis meant to her, or was capable of meaning to many women, "Are you sure that that is what you want to do? I mean, I think I could get you into an academic program full time. You could get your degree and then decide what you want to do. Or I could get you a good job perhaps in a gallery. "

Selena came to a full stop in front of him. "Do you really want to help me, John?"

"Of course I do."

"Pay for my passage to America, and lend me, oh... 5,000 lira."

"Eight hundred dollars?"

"Yes, yes exactly."

Knowing Selena could leap before she looked, John began to become anxious for her. "What will you do exactly?"

Selena came over, sat in his lap and stroked his hair, then she gave a little sigh, kissed him and explained almost as if to a child, or at least to some one who had no way of knowing the importance of what she was going to say, " I am going to find a small room in the part of New York that is called "Little Italy". There language will be easy for me, and also finding work with one of my compatriots. I will use it as my base. And when I have, I think the word is 'tested the waters' I will know how to open my shop."

The absolute quality of her decision left little room for argument.

John thought with a touch of irony, it was as if she was the more assured and mature of the two of them, almost as if she were reassuring him. And he could use it. He knew that a chapter in his life was closing, and what he was losing was the exclusivity in their relationship. It hurt. He knew there would be days and nights of missing her.

Something of what he felt must have come through to Selena. She turned in his arms, kissing him gently on the mouth. Later she was not sure whose lips were trembling. He put his arms around her, and held her tight to him.

"Come to bed with me, John."

He lifted and carried her to the bed. Their lovemaking was warm and ardent. Each wanting to give themself unstinting to the other, trying to erase the void which had come between them. To some extent they succeeded.

But later that day, John went to the Pan American office and bought two tickets on the Clipper leaving from London for New York the next day.

CEILINGS III

Chapter: 1

The fourteen-hour flight was broken only for refueling at Gander airport in Greenland. Then it continued on down the eastern coastline of New England, making the required circle just south of New York City in approach to Idlewild airfield.

Selena had perfect vision of the Statue of Liberty as the airship descended to five thousand feet over New York harbor. Then in quick order, John pointed out the spires of the Empire State building, the Chrysler building, and an oblong patch of green surrounded by tall structures-Central Park.

Within minutes their plane touched down. They cleared customs, found a cab in the waiting ranks, were driven mid-town to the Beresford, a large well-built apartment house on Central Park West, and followed the luggage up to John's rooms.

Selena sat in the living room, while he made them coffee. It was lived-in and spacious, with well-worn leather furniture, a working fireplace, and a large oak desk mostly covered by John's journals and books. A comfortable room meant for work rather than entertaining. The windows looked out over the Park from the twelfth floor. She scanned it briefly with admiration, and a certain wistfulness. She knew John's home would have this kind of casual but inviting character. But she also knew she would only visit it as an outsider.

Before John had gone to the kitchen, he'd put a Schubert quartet on the record player. Its haunting themes played softly as he came back in and sat close beside her on the couch.

For a while they drank their coffee and listened in

an unaccustomed, uneasy silence, each thinking of what the next hours would bring, and the separate ways they would have to go.

John held on to the thought that he must honor the commitment to contact his editor. Despite a strong desire to simply take her in his arms, make love to her and somehow get her to change her mind, he refrained-sitting beside her with tight control.

Selena focused on the thought she would only take what she could carry easily in one suitcase as she made her way to 'Little Italy. The rest of her beautiful Egyptian things would rest here. She felt that it might not be wise to carry the past into the future.

But before that, she must try to let John know, in spite of what she had to do, how deeply she cared about him. She didn't have the experience to do this with any sort of grace, much less tact. She knew he was having trouble accepting her plans, and that she was causing him pain, which she had never wanted to do.

She felt awkward, inept and as if tears were not far away. But if she broke down, it would destroy the dignity both were fighting to maintain. She knew she must leave John with his intact.

In the end when she finished her coffee, she could do no more then kiss him, tell him she would telephone as soon as she got set, take up her suitcase, kiss him once more and bolt for the door.

She asked the doorman for the nearest subway, plunged down its steps, and got a map of the Metropolitan transportation system when she paid her fare. Advised to take the local so not to have to transfer, she clutched the map studying it street by street, silently forming the names like a mantra so as not to think of what had just passed, as she rode the swaying train grinding its way downtown. The noise of its passage, with shuddering stops, the confusion of crowds of people pushing at each other as they struggled for seats, shoving through doors which threatened to close them out as they got on or off, the garish advertising posters lining overhead slots provided further distraction.

She rose as the subway stopped at Houston Street. The next station would be Mott Street. She could hardly wait. The doors opened onto the platform. Selena left the train, found the exit stairs, and mounted into fresh air.

The scene she saw around her held a lot that was familiar, certainly the smells of the small salumerie, selling dried meats and sausage, and the laticceria with their cheeses and milk, the vegetable and fruit stalls, the run down tenement buildings-it all seemed to hold much in common with her old Quartiere in Napoli.

She puzzled for a short time over the hand-written price signs, working on the translation of dollars and cents into lira. But soon realized that if careful, much would be within her means.

As she went from street to street, exploring the neighborhood, she saw buildings, with common decayed brickwork crowded one on top of the other giving them the look of a transmissable disease. Originally erected with fresh brownstone, now defaced with the grime coal-fired furnaces lent, and stained by the fumes and grit the city produced twenty-four out of twenty-fours hours; eight and ten-story buildings whose fronts were slashed from ground to roof by rusting fire escapes, there only because building codes required them to be; bearing clothes-lines, pots of herbs, cheap baby carriages, and odds and ends of scrap furniture. She knew from experience that the rooms inside would be dark, small and of uncertain cleanliness, and that bathrooms would be one to a floor at best.

When her wanderings took her to Hester Street, she

saw a vacancy sign in the first floor window of just such a building. She knocked, on the door tucked under the front stairs, and was shown a sixth floor walk-up room which contained a single bed, a night-stand, clothes line, two-burner electric plate, one table and a chair-all worn from countless years of use, but, surprisingly, clean. And it was this as much as anything that made her want to take it.

Selena turned to the landlady, an ancient crone who fit perfectly with the condition of the quarters she was showing, and asked simply, "Quanto?"

The old woman looked her over carefully- Selena could see wheels turning as she assessed what she could ask from this young 'Greenhorn'.

"Venti dollari la settimana." It will be twenty dollars a week.

Selena knew this was an outrageous demand, based on what the old woman thought was her naiveté. She laughed, without the least rancor or resentment, countered with a straight face, and discovered in herself an unsuspected talent. An instinct which would later develop into a 'feel' for business.

"Sette dollari." Seven dollars. It was an equally outrageous offer.

" Cosa! Che Diece?" What??! That's crazy! The old woman saw she had misjudged the younger. But, times were not good and the room had been vacant for several weeks. "Eh bene, Quindici". Well then, fifteen.

As if there had been no previous exchange, Selena looked directly at the landlady and said, "Dieci", ten. For her the discussion was closed.

Recognizing the finality when she heard it, the old woman agreed, "Dieci," and Selena had her new home. She wasted little time arranging her few clothes. She had still to supply her room with food and cleaning things, and although it was now well past three, she intended to start looking for work.

Finding work, was not as simple as finding quarters. There was very little on offer in little Italy. A few restaurants seemed to need dishwashers, or cleaning women, and she knew if it came to that she might have to take this work for the time being, but that time was not yet.

She went slowly through the streets, looking at the shops, selling small items of housewares, or clothes especially work clothes, dingy drugstores which sold Italian homeopathic products, and stores with third hand furniture on unfavorable time terms. It was several cuts above her native Quartiere, but still spoke of borderline living, far from the prosperity that many thought was universal in America with its fabled 'streets of gold'.

Sometime after eight o'clock, she saw a hairdressing shop, advertising for a helper. It was shut for the night. But she peered into its windows. It held three barber chairs, what looked like an elaborate electrical device, two standing beehive hair dryers, and a rank of tall mirrors.

Sun-faded color photographs illustrating several styles of coiffures lay in the windows, along with some bottles of 'hair preparation', and advertisements for other beauty products, all presumably available for its customers.

She looked at the name shown in foot high letters on the window. Maria Parruchiere, Maria's Beauty Salon. Under the name and just slightly smaller the address-163 Mott street.

Here, Selena thought, here is where I will start. She returned to her room for the night. Excited. Tomorrow, one way or the other, tomorrow she would be a part of Maria's Beauty Salon.

Chapter: 2

At 7:30 the next morning Selena stood waiting outside of Maria's. Mott Street was still shimmering from the water sprayed on its narrow width by the street cleaners even earlier. But the vendors were up and setting out their wares for the day. There were the familiar sounds of store shutters being opened, sidewalks being swept, and chatter of helper to helper as produce was laid out in ranks for the day.

She became aware of a kind of minor disturbance coming from the beginning of the block. Curious she craned on tiptoe to see what was causing such a change in the character of the early morning scene.

Approaching was one of the shortest, fattest women she ever remembered seeing, greeting and being in turn greeted by all the vendors as well as the least of their assistants, receiving a flower here, a canole, or a roll or small sausage, there. Pausing to exchange words or laughter with everyone, as if time were of no consequence whatever. She was later to learn, that indeed for Maria Gemignani, time had no meaning unless well spent, and she spent it lavishly on affection and care for others. Her extended family was much of Mott Street and its immediate vicinity.

"Buon Giorno", this lively creature shouted as she came close to where Selena waited outside the shop. Several women, obviously her first customers, followed in her train like so many super-annuated chicks after their mother hen. Looking at the sign Selena had removed from the door and now held in her hands, she saw that this young woman wished to apply for the open 'assistant position'.

" Venga", come she said, broadly indicating her

customers as well as Selena. She leaned over toward an old-fashioned brass keyhole, with some difficulty, squinting at the opening over a bosom which largely obscured direct vision. The front door on closer look bore the scars of numberless previous, probes.

"Posso?" May I? Selena gently took the key from her hand and opened the lock with one easy twist. Then held the door for the others to enter.

"Brava!"

Maria dropped her packages, as she flipped the light switches on. Her three clients like so many homing pigeons, scuttled for their 'usual' chair, chattering to each other and Maria while awaiting their 'turn'.

She beckoned Selena into the back supply room and looked her over. What she saw was an immaculately clean, quietly dressed, eager young woman, whose bright black eyes in turn missed nothing of the smallness, and neighborhood quality of the salon.

"I've come about the Job..."

"Ma si." Maria had a busy day before her, her former assistant, had gotten engaged yesterday, and given notice the same day. As an affianced woman, she had no further desire to work, leaving Maria to cope as best she could. Another might have been irritated, by the pomposity of the sentiment, and the abrupt resignation, but Maria had simply said, "Ah , it is good to be fidanzata, and a Bride, and a Wife and a Mother. It is all good!" And figured tomorrow would take care of itself as indeed, looking at the girl who was able to open the front door with no difficulty, it seemed it had.

"You will hang the coats. You will drape the customer with the sheet, wash and rinse the hair, comb out the snarls. You will also sweep the floor, see that the scissors are sharp, the combs washed, and the bottles of solutions always full. You will fetch espressos and biscotti for those who wish. Sunday and Monday the shop is closed. We start at eight each morning and finish when we finish. I pay forty dollars the week. That is the job if you wish it, and it will start now."

Selena realized that when Maria wanted to organize her thoughts, and move matters along she could. It just, by and large, was not the way she enjoyed or wished to do things.

" That will be fine, Signora."

"Va bene, and I am not Signora, I'm Maria, piccola." Now get a clean uniform there behind you. Here is a dollar, go get three espressi. I will start. You will watch the first time when you get back, then you will begin." Selena went off. She spotted a tiny café down the street, thought this was probably the supplier she was seeking, got four expressi from the huge, gold and steel imported coffee maker and hurried back.

By this time, Maria had her three clients enveloped in large striped cloths, each had a towel draped around the neck, the one in front of Maria had sopping wet hair, and a well used beauty trade magazine in hand. A voluble discussion in an execrable Italian dialect was underway as to just what she would like done with her hair-do. The remaining two clients having heard her choice, who asked to see and were shown the chosen ' pittora', were offering comments and advise equally to Maria and their 'goomba'.

The salon atmosphere was club-like. Alive with sounds-running water, the rush of heated blown air, the women's voices, but given the sartorial equipment lying in wait, it was unmistakably professional.

"Che Brava!" With a huge smile Maria saw at once that Selena had had the insight to bring her new 'boss' a coffee without instruction. She congratulated herself on acquiring such an assistant.

As both customers and beautician sipped the scalding hot liquid, Selena had her first chance to inspect the clients and the work done for them. She had to bite her lip. All three middle aged women, had identical dyed shoepolish-black, hair, relentlessly and identically crimped by the electric permanent wave machine set over in the corner, and worn long, either with or without pompador. True, all three were uniformly Italianate in looks, but the faces unlike the hair style were quite individual.

The process for each client became obvious. She would consult with Maria, about a style published in one of the magazines. They would agree on a choice, after looking at several. Maria would then proceed to duplicate her own patented hairstyle for each. It was hard to characterize exactly the private response of each lady to the resultant look, but it was obvious they were so devoted to Maria, that it didn't make the critical difference.

Maria, for her part, bustled about as quickly as she could, servicing her customers, with the equipment and technique she had been taught in trade school when she first came to America.

However, no matter what the final look, the shampooing and massage that each client received was tops Selena found, as she watched Maria shampoo her second customer. She copied the technique exactly on the third customer, as Maria looked on with approval at the strong, skillful hands of her new assistant.

New clients came in as the first were being finished. And so it went that day, with Selena working almost as hard as she had at the taverna, but with a much lighter heart. At nine o'clock, when the last customer was done. Maria helped her neaten and clean shop.

"Sono contenta", she said, I'm happy with your work, as they locked up for the night. It was to become her invariable way of thanking Selena after each day.

"Anch' Io", I am too, Maria, she would answer

warmed by the other woman's courtesy and kindness.

Still later that evening, Selena telephoned John to let him know what her day had brought. It was the first of once a week calls to him.

My darling John, she thought. I must never leave him feeling.. what were the exact words Verdi used?... Solo e abondonato, Alone and forsaken.

Chapter: 3

In the days that followed Selena continued to work long hours. Especially busy were the mornings and early evenings. Maria's clientele was not one whose days were measured by mid-day leisure.

She began little by little to change the routine at the shop. No longer did shorn locks accumulate on the linoleum floor until the black and white checkered pattern couldn't be seen. Maria never went to a container to find it less than filled. The sloping rubber drain boards in front of the sinks weren't wet with the water of a previous shampoo. Fashion magazines with curled edges or creased pages more than a year old, no longer cluttered small tables. Ashtrays, used by a few of the more adventurous customers were invariably emptied. Selena had found a lightly pine-scented room spray, which countered the acrid ammoniac smell of the solution used for permanent waving.

Each client was promptly prepared, whether combed or washed, or combed and gowned ready for Maria as she finished with the last, without any feeling of being rushed or part of a routine.

Maria noticed each change with approval, and often could be heard praising the 'smarts' of her new assistant. Inwardly, she wondered how she had managed to function before Selena came along.

Selena found that she began, much as Maria had, to become a repository of confidence and confidences. The women relied on the shop to bolster egos too often battered by the wanderings of spouses or lovers, disprized by their children as being 'old country', or burdened by the awareness they carried of the short, stocky, unglamorous figure that was their heritage-mirrors didn't lie. Their lives so often demanded courage, and 'figura' putting a good face on things, little noticed and even less remarked. Selena's heart went out to them. She knew that Maria felt this too. And that the shop represented a deliberate oasis of care and attention in the neighborhood controlled by the mafia-Little Italy.

Evenings she often stopped for an espresso on the way home. Always curious about her surroundings she learned there something of the social tectonics of the neighborhood.

For scores of years the area had been neatly divided by ethnic groups. The stores, places of worship, whole blocks of buildings had been Jewish east of Third Avenue, and from Houston south. Just to the west and north of Canal Street the Italians lived. And south of Canal was Oriental. Traveling from area to area had been as distinct as traveling from country to country.

Then the second generation of Jews prospered and moved out, often to the suburbs. Some Italians followed suit, but to a much lesser extent territorial roots no matter how modest, being a more basic part of their tradition. But the Orientals who seemed to multiply by the dozens overnight, took over the eastern area and spilled upwards from Canal street. The Italians cosseted by their Cosa Nostro, felt this presence more invasive and alien with each passing year. They were also aware of the growing power and reach of their counterpart-the Chinese Tongs. But still held to their ground with determination. Selena took this history in with interest, but doubted it would ever effect her.

For several weeks Selena kept silent about how Maria handled the business part of the salon. Customers, when they were done, would amble over to a tin box kept on a shelf near the front door, call out to Maria to ask how much they owed, put in the cash, make change, and leave. Occasionally when they had had more than the usual wash and set, or if Maria were busy, she would say without looking up, "Whatever", essentially leaving it to the client. And again on occasion, she forgot what she had done for whom, laugh and wave vaguely at the cash box, figuring it would all work out in the end.

Suppliers, were paid cash for deliveries which were stored in the back room without further ado or invoicing.

The lack of system drove Selena wild. She knew how many hours Maria put in, and how little she charged. And so one day she asked in a carefully neutral tone of voice if she could not take on the responsibility to see to this part of things. It was something she didn't want Maria to dismiss as not worth the bother, or fall back on 'how it had always been done'.

With her consent, she began to take payments in hand. Also she increased the charges a little. At the end of each day, she emptied the cash box, handed the money to Maria, and entered the sum in a notebook she had bought to keep records of what they had paid out, and what they took in.

Once having gotten part of the finances regularized, she opened two accounts at the Immigrant Savings Bank situated on Grand Street, two blocks away. One for her wages, and the other for the shop. As she left each night with Maria, she insisted putting in the night deposit drop most of the moneys they had taken in for the day. Maria grumbled, but was thrilled when she got her first end of the month statement from the bank. Both women watched with satisfaction as the accounts begin to grow from week to week.

One Saturday after a particularly hectic day, Maria waddled over as they were closing for the evening, drew

Selena into her short arms, kissed her resoundingly on both cheeks and issued an invitation.

"Eh, ragazza, vuoi mangiare con me stasera?" Come, have dinner with me this evening. I know a little restaurant where you will eat like royalty.

"Ma si, con piacere." But of course, with pleasure, Maria.

It was the first, of what was to become the regular dinner in celebration of the close of business for the week, and the beginning of a lifelong bond. For Selena, Maria became the mother she had never really had. Maria had no children or husband of her own, and took Selena to her heart in their stead.

That first dinner over pasta with calamari, whole baby octopus in their 'ink', veal piccata, insalata verde, formaggio, and a Bruscanti wine, they talked easily of the shop and the neighborhood. Then later of their lives, or at least Maria did. Selena still couldn't talk of the life she had left, and Maria, knew that when the child was ready and needed to talk about it would be soon enough, so didn't pry.

Maria had come to this country from Puglia, a harsh, poor section of southern Italy as a girl little older than Selena, with her Father and two older brothers.

They settled on Greene Street. Her father was a cobbler, and opened a street booth repairing shoes. In the old European way of things, the two boys were apprenticed to the trade, and she young as she was, kept house for them. It was a matter of intense pleasure to her father, who was never able to master the language of his new country, that his children became U.S. citizens.

After he had saved enough to open a tiny indoor store, the two boys came to work with him. And all was well.

World War II broke out. The U.S. was attacked at

Pearl Harbor. The boys volunteered for army service. Her father took great pride in their enlistment. They all felt the privilege granted them of defending their adopted country.

Having only one to care for then, Maria was able to take a beautician's course. On graduation, she dedicated her diploma embossed with gold lettering and ribbons to her Father, who looked over each inscribed line, never admitting he was unable to read any of the words other than her name.

Letters arrived from her brothers, at first regularly, but as the war went on, and difficulties of communication in wartime mounted, they came less frequently, until weeks would go by when they heard nothing other than the official news over the radio each night.

The first time Maria saw a gold star in the window of a neighbor, she didn't know what it was, until associated with the darkened house and rending grief.

On one Sunday, when they'd just come back from mass, they too received an official telegram from the army. The government regretted it must inform the family of the death of private Gemignani killed in action in Okinawa. Her father and she were staggered. That evening, surrounded by consoling friends and neighbors, a second telegram arrived. Until she read it word for word, Maria thought it a mistaken duplication of the first notice. Then she realized that it was really her second brother who had been killed within hours of his elder.

When two gold stars arrived, her father burned them, never spoke, or left the house again. Maria found work as a hair dresser, and ultimately, started her own shop in addition to caring for her father, who lived only two years after his sons, who gave their young lives for their new country.

It took Maria many months to regain her balance, to go on with a solitary life, emptied of caring for and feeding a family. She never married. Never could deal with one-on-one intimacy of any kind, until Selena came into her life. And now whether she chose or not she had found the recipient of all her stored love and warmth.

Chapter: 4

Selena was out getting sandwiches midday, when Carla Silvestri one of their oldest clients, caught fire. She had been washed, and colored, and at the time was sitting half asleep having her monthly permanent, attached to the machine by dozens of electrical coils each wrapped in conducting foil.

Maria was setting one of the customers, when one of the others noticed a curl of smoke rising steadily from the apparatus. And started to scream.

"Guarda! Jesu Maria! Guarda", look, oh my God, look! She jumped from her chair, still wrapped in a cover sheet.

"Ai! Ai! Ai!", the panic continued among the women as wisps of smoke continued to rise. Everyone was up and out of her chair. Gesturing. No one knew what to do.

"Maria! Maria!" The shouts rose.

Maria heard the shouts and confusion but didn't yet understand what was happening.

"Il fuoco! Guarda il fuoco!" Look. Fire! Maria hurry! The smoke-see the smoke! One of the women pointed to Carla attached to the permanent wave machine spitting flames. Carla bolted up screaming, batting futilely at her head –a frantic Medusa.

Then Maria grasped what they meant. She rushed to Carla, but seeing the smoke rising hideously from the trapped woman, she panicked.

"Dio! Dio!" Aiutami!" Help me, God!

She did the only thing she could think of. She reached out, and began to separate the hair from the machine coil by coil. She succeeded in detaching half before her hands were so badly burned by the heat and the chemicals that she could no longer touch the machine.

Just at this time Selena returned. Took in the scene with one glance, ran to the wall, and ripped the plug out of the outlet. Moving with blurring speed, she went to the sink, soaked a large towel in cold water, and wrapped it around Carla's head which stopped the burning. By the time she got to Maria, both her handshad suffered severe burns.

One of the other customers who nursed at Beekman Downtown Hospital, took a quick look, realized the gravity of the injury, told Selena Maria would have to go to the hospital for treatment, and volunteered to accompany her.

Selena realized that both women needed help. She nodded assent to the nurse, who promised to call as soon as a doctor saw Maria, then calmed the other clients, and turned to Carla who was weeping quietly still partly attached to the machine.

As she unraveled her from the coils. What was left of her hair was a ragged mess. Part of the hair was short, part long and all the ends were thoroughly singed.

Selena lead the woman to one of the chairs, sat her down, inspected the hair left, picked up a comb and a pair of scissors, and began. When she was done, Carla had a soft, feathered cut which waved naturally around her face. She took the mirror handed her, as Selena turned the chair first this way and then that, so she could see from all angles. At first there was no sound, not from Carla, not from any of the others.

Then one of the older clients breathed "Che Bella." How beautiful. Carla catching Selena's eyes in the mirror said simply, "Si."

At the end of the day, although she had only sought to control damage, several of the other regular clients had asked for Selena's 'new hair style.' She gave them each something different, either changing the way the hair was set and combed, or the cut.

The day seemed endless, with no word from the hospital. When she closed, Selena went there, asked after Maria, and was told to have a seat, one of the doctors would be with her shortly. Actually it was over an hour before a young man in rumpled green surgical garb walked tiredly over to where she sat waiting.

"Maria Gemignani, you are her....?"

"Niece," Selena was not about to be denied information on a technicality.

"She has suffered third degree burns to both hands. The metal paper was imbedded in many of her fingers. We have debrided them as best we can. But the prognosis is very guarded."

" Doctor, what does this mean? And please, my English is not at the top level, so can you explain this to me?"

The young man saw the terrible fear and concern written large over the face of this beautiful young girl, who fought to keep the tone of her voice quiet and her mind open so she could fully understand anything he could tell her.

"Well, it's too soon to be able to say exactly, but your Aunt has been badly burned. Much of the damage to her hands will be permanent. We can't tell you at this time how much use she will lose, but certainly a significant part."

"Oh, Dio mio, Santa Maria" Selena moaned softly. She sank back into the wooden bench, unable to say more. Swaying slightly in her shock, and grief.

"Let me get you some water." The young man went to a nearby fountain finally grasping the degree of her concern and brought her a cup. Selena sipped a little, took several deep breaths, looked up and said, "Grazie Dottore."

"Will you be all right now?" he said manners taking precedence over his need to get back to the countless tasks awaiting him.

"Ma si." Yes, I will. Thank you for your kindness. When can I see my Aunt?"

Moved by the effort to gain control of her emotions, and the courtesy despite her distress, he took one more minute.

"She will be down soon from the operating room. You can wait in her room, I'll write you a pass."

Selena took the hand written note to the desk, was told the number, and went to Maria's room.

It was close to eleven when the door opened and Maria, just conscious was transferred from a gurney. The assigned nurse attached a blood pressure cuff to her arm, and settled her in the high bed, made several notes, and hung the chart on the foot of the bed. A dim light over head was turned on. Selena saw Maria's hands, resting on her chest, were completely bandaged in thick layers of gauze. None of her fingers were visible.

"You can stay a few minutes, but she won't make much sense, or remember what you say tomorrow. The anesthetic is still wearing off."

"Thank you. I will only stay a moment."

" Selena. Sei tu?" Maria's voice was slurred.

" Sicuramente, cara Maria." Yes, my darling Maria, I'm here. Selena responded, leaning over to kiss her brow.

"E Carla..?" Maria persisted.

"Tutto va bene." All is well with her and the shop.

"Ah, si. Benissimo. Sono contenta" Good, good. I am content. The last words were barely audible as she drifted off under the influence of the general anesthetic she had had.

Selena rose, left the room silently. All that could be,

had been done for now.

Chapter: 5

The next weeks were a blur of unceasing activity for Selena. During the day the beauty salon where business seemed if anything to have increased, in the evenings the hospital, where Maria had already undergone several more debridement operations. The prognosis for her hands, remained poor, Whenever Selena visited, she always left brokenhearted with the image of almost motionless hands under the surgical dressings, and the offensive antiseptic smell of the sulfa ointments used to treat the burn.

As for Maria, she understood that her livelihood was threatened, and that simple every day activities might not be within her grasp. But her spirit and practical advice sustained them both. Selena thought she was a miracle of a person. And brought and fed her the tiny pastries baked by the pasticerria, or the little pizzettas from the pizzeria, or freshened her forehead and neck with special scented pochets sent by the farmacia.

Word of Selena's skill spread through little Italy with incredible rapidity. She couldn't handle the numbers of customers who came asking for appointments, until one day Carla Silvestri turned up, young niece in hand, and presented her to Selena. Selena hired her on the spot, was grateful for the assistance, and still could barely manage even working from eight in the morning until after eight in the evening.

There were often so many clients awaiting her attention, that she and Carla's niece actually tripped over each other. And when several weeks later, Maria, newly discharged from the hospital, came to the shop, and was visited by virtually every woman and many of the men in the neighborhood, each of whom came bearing one or more 'gifts', things became impossible.

They talked about the situation over dinner at Rocco's. Selena exhausted by the weeks of dawn to dusk schedule, not thinking too straight, suggested if they took on another assistant, perhaps they could manage. Maria laughed so hard, that other diners, turned around to see if they had missed something funny. Still laughing she waved their attention back to their own tables.

"Cara", she said to Selena, "there is not one more ant to be added to the ant hill. It cannot be done. But a larger ant hill and the problem is solved." Then added triumphantly, " I, Maria, have found the hill and it is just to the side of us. And it is ours."

Selena had no idea when Maria could have managed this, but she did recall that the store immediately to their left, at 165 Mott Street, which had been a notions shop, seemed dark most days.

"And now, since I cannot help with the women", she went on, Lifting the hands now lightly bandaged, but still only able to perform the simplest of tasks, to emphasize her point, "I have the time to supervise the workers who will make the growth of our shop into the next store."

Selena realized that here indeed was the solution to their problem. Especially as when Maria continued, it was evident she had thought the matter out completely. " I have checked the moneys in my account, it will do. To get more help for you can be easily done We will go over what is the best way to use the space, and all will be well, se Dio vuole."

It was to be exactly as Maria had predicted. Six months later, Selena had two assistants. The new space permitted them to treble their business, and contained the latest equipment. Gone forever were the permanent wave machines in favor of the new 'Cold Wave' permanents which were done sparingly.

Selena designed the coiffure of all new clients, took personal care of some of the oldest customers, but turned much of the routine over to her two assistants who had carefully studied her techniques.

Maria insisted on sharing the profits equally. "Cara, it is your hands and your skill which has made the salon what it is. And that is an end to any argument."

Both women were content with what had happened.When Selena told John of the new arrangement he said he couldn't have been happier for them both.

Now too, instead of eating out, Maria insisted Selena come to 'mia casa' for their weekly dinners. Given the pain and stiffness of her hands, Selena knew it took Maria hours to prepare the Verdura or insalata, the vegetables and salads and the 'contorni', the side dishes that graced the meals she served. The chopping and peeling alone had to begin in the mornings.

Selena couldn't imagine how she got the veal scallops thin as pancakes, or made the home-made pastas, hand cut 'capeletti', little hats, or how she created and stuffed the ravioli.

These dinners gave meaning to a phrase which Selena had heard, but failed to appreciate before-'a labor of love.'

At table, she and Maria spoke always of things that were important to the salon, and then of things meaningful to Mother and Daughter.

Maria never spoke of her hands, nor of the painful struggle she was still undergoing with the physical therapists to try to regain increased use. She simply got on with what she could do. More and more at the salon, it became a matter of customer relations, or keeping the assistants functioning happily and efficiently. It gave Selena some breathing room.

An old valued client came in one day, sat down in 'Selena's chair', looked pleadingly in the long mirror.

"My son, he is marrying wit' a girl. The famiglia it is living in Long Island. Vera important, the famiglia. Next week he is marrying. Is a big ceremonia. I mus' not disgrace. I mus' look the best-capisci? Bella, bellisma."

Selena could have finished the rest of her thought, but waited with patience for her customer to express her ideas, as she analyzed what she could accomplish for this middle aged Sicilo-American.

"Tutto. Voglio Tutto", I want you to do everything, the hair, la face, "La prossima settimano". The wedding was to take place next week.

Selena went to the neighborhood drugstore, chose cosmetics which would best go with the swarthy Sicilian complexion and dark eyes of her client, and brought them to the shop.

Late Saturday morning of the afternoon wedding, Selena did a soft wave and light frosting, followed by a complete make-up. Then explained what she had done, so the client could do it for herself, with a couple of rehearsals.

"Grazie, Grazie infinissimo". The client was thrilled with her new appearance, which she felt would serve her well at the wedding festivities.

The customers in the salon were to a woman fascinated, and in some cases incredulous, when the final results were to be seen.

It was the first of the new aspect of what was to become the basis of her business. That night she wrote Fatimah telling her what had happened, and received six weeks later, a letter containing but one line.

" And so it begins, Cherie."

Chapter: 6

As weeks turned into months, Selena worked out a routine which satisfied her clients as well as her own time demands. After talking with a new customer for a few minutes, she would design the hair style to be done, explain the technicalities to one of her assistants, and return for a final inspection or adjustment when it was completed. For the older customers, a couple of supervisory touches or a look sufficed. Which left her free for her cosmetics.

The girls in the shop when booking referred to Selena's make-overs or as doing a 'Look'. When Maria first heard one of them using the term, she called it to Selena's attention. Both thought it was good- unpretentious, uncorrecting, and descriptive of what Selena was trying to do.

Maria's presence each day, provided a sense of continuity and Italian character-however the reputation of the salon was beginning to draw customers from the Village, that area to the north of Little Italy, where many artists and writers, as well as old time Manhattan residents lived. It was these new customers as much as anything which prompted her to suggest that Selena become licensed. And attend the graduation with pride later that year.

Selena spent time when not at the shop, or the beautician school, searching locally for the best national brand cosmetic products for use on her customers. She was unhappy with the quality, the nature of many of them. And often longed for the choice of ingredients of Fatimah's tiny shop. But nothing even remotely like them was available. She looked in vain for accurate description of the contents in lotions and ointments, liquid and cake bases, or lipsticks.

On one occasion, a very pretty new client came in for a 'look'. Her face had an odd, almost pasty appearance. When her own cosmetics were removed in preparation for a new 'look', Selena was shocked by the underlying dry redness, the noticeable swelling around her eyes and mouth. She adjusted the clear spot light she used while working, sat down behind the client on the swivel chair that let her see her subject clearly from all sides, then met the client's eyes in the mirror. She saw an expression there, which could only be described as fearful, even desperate. She knew only one way to handle it.

"Signora, do you have this about the eyes and mouth, always?" Selena asked as she gently but deliberately touched the areas. Her tone was as matter of fact as she could manage.

"I must use steroids if I want to use any of the normal cosmetics, and I've tried them all. There is something in them that I react to."

The client's words came out rapidly, almost as if she wanted to hurry through an often-repeated story with an ugly ending.

"The exact contents don't seem to be listed, so the allergists can't do more than tell me not to use certain products. It's true I have allergies to many things, foods, soaps, even fabrics."

The slump of her body in the chair telegraphed despair. "My dermatologist, finally suggested the hypo-allergenic products which I've been using daily. They're not very good, but I cannot keep on with steroids."

Not very good was a considerable understatement, but Selena said only, "I understand."

"I am often ashamed to go out, looking as I do."

Selena didn't offer false reassurance, or even hope. But settled for what she felt was possible for her client.

She suggested she clean her skin with diluted lemon juice, use virgin olive oils with the purest aloe for a night cream, and do away with any 'base' for the moment. Use the lightest touch of lipstick for rouging the cheeks, and an application to the lips for evening only. A touch of the same aloe to darken lashes and brow.

"I can't tell you how grateful I am" the client said turning her head this way and that.

"We really haven't solved the problem." Selena wasn't satisfied with what she'd accomplished.

"But I look a thousand percent better."

And the client left with a better appearance, maintenance routine, and trust.

Selena knew she couldn't accept the defeat inherent in the situation It went against everything she wanted to do, everything she had learned from Fatimah, somehow she would have to change things for this young client. And too she knew, although this reaction was extreme, there were many others like her.

The cosmetic products she had collected widely were impure, inaccurately labeled, sometimes inflammatory to the skin, and even more often, false looking, and making the face unappealing to touch. She had no idea where to start, but somehow she would have to find a way.

She began leaving the salon late afternoon on Fridays, hunting for beauty supplies wherever they were listed. Sometimes she would go as far away as an outlet in Queens, or a supply house in the Bronx, sometimes nearer, in lower Manhattan. She searched small drugstores in remote, even rough neighborhoods.

She spent hours, driven by image of the misery and embarrassment of the pretty young customer, haunted by the abuse meted her complexion by impure ingredients or preservatives. And frustrated because she couldn't really get a grasp on how to solve the problem, other than searching for a better 'substrate', as her uptown clients were wont to say.

When her search took her to Harlem one evening, first Maria, then John, when he heard of it came down with both feet.

"Selena", Maria said at once exasperated, and worried, " You cannot go in these places. They are not safe. And you will not find your answer in this way. What you are seeking, Cara, does not exist."

"But it must, and I must find it."

John pointed out how fruitless her attempts had been in places which were on the one hand uninviting, and on the other, now she had ventured into Harlem, risk-filled, even downright dangerous.

Selena hoped against hope they were wrong. But she could see that for the nonce there was little point in continuing. Still her failure nagged unmercifully.

John decided to see what he could do about distracting her. And so began to invite her uptown to theater or Opera. Once a week, Selena would join him.

At the Metropolitan they could hear Maria Callas and Di Stefano in works by Puccini; or the Americans Dorothy Kirsten and James McCracken in Verdi; Kirsten Flagstad or Helen Traubel and Lawrence Melchior in Wagner-their choice was rich. It was an extraordinary time for Opera.

The New York Symphony Orchestra boasted Dimitri Metropolis as its maestro or occasionally was led by its young assistant conductor, Leonard Bernstein. Selena was enchanted by these evenings. She loved it that she was able to explain to John many subtleties and the poetry of the libretti which made the outlandish stories less fustian. As to the music, she said every Neapolitan sang before they talked And knew intimately either the piquant and sunny native songs, or the operatic arias of Bellini, even Donizetti and of course the soaring melodies of Giuseppi Verdi.

Then John expanded their attendance to include theater, which were giving the plays of Tennessee William, or Inge, or Albee, or the sophisticated annual selections of the Theater Guild-the best of the new playwrights. Her language difficulties with these, prompted Selena to ask if he knew where she could go to improve her comprehension of English. She wanted to learn as much as she could about its idiomatic or literary use.

John thought for a moment about the possibilities, then suggested The New School in Greenwich Village. He knew the night courses offered there to be taught by an extraordinary faculty.

Shortly after World War II, much of Europe lay devastated by the economic and physical destruction of the conflict. So, many distinguished European academicians immigrated to America. Dozens of its most prominent pre-war teachers, who survived the holocaust, or other extreme conditions, either wouldn't or couldn't return to their old posts-most particularly those in Germany, and countries consumed by the Soviet Union.

They immigrated-often to the teaching centers of New York, or California seeking posts, to be met by stiff American teaching tenure. The New School was opened in New York by a confederacy of charitable foundations to provide these scholars with a teaching venue and young students a mini-fee but the best of education.

New Yorkers were enriched by The New School's presence. Even teachers from other universities or colleges came to hear lectures given by the extraordinary staff assemnbled at the New School.

The fly in the ointment, if any, was that the school

was not accredited by other universities and colleges. In essence, one could learn at the feet of the experts, but would receive no academic credit for so doing. This didn't deter those whose aim was knowledge alone.

John suggested a course in American poetry. Selena enrolled almost at once, and on the nights she had previously spent roving was to be found at the New School.

Chapter: 7

The New school served as Selena's introduction to Greenwich Village. She used both school and neighborhood to enlarge her horizons, and to become more a part of her chosen city.

In the beginning it was tentative, requiring concentration. But after awhile she became aware of the vibrant, restless, absorbing activities, most of which centered about the Arts.

Within 'The Village', the American version of La Vie Boheme, as it was lived in the Latin Quarter of Paris at the turn of the century, played out. It was not so much that the arts were important, they were the only thing. They were all of life. Money, society, business had no place in the irregular warren of 'the village' streets. Tiny art galleries devoted to avant guard painters, bookstores where the books of unknown poets lay open to the hands of passionate browsers, twelve-table polyglot restaurants invited the young, and not so young to linger over cheap food, and talk

Visually there was color everywhere, in the outlandish clothing of the flower children, as the young generation was known, in the psychedelic paints used to identify 'head shops', in the exotic signage used to identify small stores.

Foreignness was not a liability in this mix, but rather like drops of tint in a bucket of paint that was constantly changing, constantly agitated. Imagination was the coin of the realm. Newcomers from everywhere sought out the village to re-invent and express themselves.

In the Whitehorse bar, she found a Welsh poet singing and discoursing for drinks; a Mid-West artist who would later become famous for abstract expressionism, designed menus in exchange for a few meals; jazz musicians 'jammed in tiny cellar clubs, reeking of marijuana and cheap beer until five in the morning for avid buffs; actors who either went on to great careers, burned out, or turned to whoring in a year or two, were found as barely adequate waiters in the local restaurants. Art wasn't a subject, it was a language spoken here almost exclusively. It made little difference if one was native-born New Yorker, or for that matter what native tongue you spoke.

Selena grasped and was able to enjoy the spirit and tides that washed around her, often swept up into its currents. So that one Sunday, drawn to the Lafayette French Bakery, a village must for weekend mornings; seduced into a sort of sensual laze on a sunny morning by the smell of fresh-baked European bread, and the waking sights and sounds of the diverse crowd seated in front of its doors; seeing the easy exchange of sections of the Sunday papers, purchased by those with money and shared by those without, she stopped for a croissant and coffee.

The summer day was bright and warm. As she sat at one of the small sidewalk tables, semi-blinded by the sun's mid-summer glare, and reached for a proffered theater section of the Times, her hand met that of a young Chinese she hadn't noticed before seated just to her left. Both relinquished their hold at the same time. The paper dropped to the sidewalk, their eyes met, and they laughed.

" Please. Go ahead. I can start on the business section", he said politely, with an accent completely American.

Living so near the ghetto that was China-town, she was aware that few of its residents ventured out except to work as waiters in the uptown Oriental restaurants.

This young man was obviously Chinese, but had an open American air.

Selena was puzzled, and made impulsive by curiosity asked him where he was from.

He looked at her as if to decide how much to tell her, then attracted to something in this dark-haired vibrant girl answered, "I was born in China, but I've been in this country for a long time, if you call living in Chinatown living in this country."

His voice was absolutely flat as he spoke the last phrases, but Selena caught a wry smile crossing his lips. She wondered what else he would say.

"Actually, I work there and come to the Village to get away."

Selena found his voice soft, made melodious by the faintest hint of sing-song orientalism, melodious, despite expressing dissatisfaction. She wondered at the range and ease of his vocabulary.

His tall thin frame draped gracefully over a sidewalk chair turned backwards. His shoulders were narrow, but power was evident in the sculpted muscles of his forearms. She saw that they lacked bodyhair. It seemed to go with the lack of bearding on chin and cheeks. But, she thought, taking in the firm line of jaw, and brow, it was a masculine face, made interesting by the acanthic folds about brilliant black eyes, eyes that darted with intensity from object to object as his interest was caught first by one thing then another. And just now he was focused on Selena.

Seeing she had finished the last drops of her Café filtre, he said, "My name is Chen. May I buy you another?"

She found herself nodding consent to this young intriguing Oriental who he might be anywhere between the early twenties to the mid-thirties. Age had left no stigmata of any kind on his smooth face. No lines to be seen, not even in the cruel light of a midday sun. His hair was thick black and combed straight back from his face, emphasizing its contours, giving it strength and cleanliness.

She thought him graceful, fascinating and wanted to know more about him and his life and why he came to be in this place, the haunt of area students and village denizens.

When they finished coffee, they strolled west toward Washington Square park. Children were throwing and catching Frisbees, dogs were romping about socializing with each other much as their masters did with whatever was of interest, a guitarist was practicing riffs and snatches of songs, the city traffic was heard only as a soft background note to the sounds of children and dogs and people at play.

Chen and Selena found a corner bench. The rest of the morning passed quickly. They talked of the village and what they liked about it, they talked a little of what each did, and what they liked and didn't like about that. They shared what they knew of business on a small scale-and found that a traditional Chinese apothecary and an busy Italian beauty salon had little in common except it took up so much of their lives, and could provide frustrating problems with customers and stocking.

Finally they discovered that they were both taking courses two nights a week at the New School-Chen in American History. Selena in American poetry.

"It's really made a difference in my English," she said with her musical Neapolitan accent.

"I can hear that", Chen tried not to laugh aloud.

"Oh I don't mean that'" Selena said referring to her accent, " It's the words, it's the language. I've improved so much this last year."

Chen, having spoken English since a teenager, and

with the patience of someone who had also had to learn, stood ready to help and correct her.

In the weeks after they met, he was so gentle that she never minded and hardly even noticed. In turn she took him to places where Italian was spoken often over espresso, and Chen to his pleasure, heard her speak musically and fluidly in her native tongue.

Many weekends they spent wandering about the legendary streets and haunts of the village, or having Chinese food in a no-name restaurant deep in lower New York, or riding the Staten Island ferry across to St. George, where the view of all of lower Manhattan was at its best, or to Ellis Island where so many immigrants had their first taste of the new World.

As they got to know each other better Selena perceived that Chen felt excluded from many of America's opportunities. He was expected and required to maintain and protect his family's business.

He had been given an opportunity when he was sent to America from China as a youngster, but it was the opportunity to fulfill a pre-ordained destiny. His problem was that he didn't fit this small destiny. He was educated and trained by Stanford University in modern chemistry, he had honed laboratory techniques and skills which were totally useless in his present setting-a traditional Chinese pharmacy. It was as if a Tennessee pacer was hitched to a plow. And yet his sense of family obligation, of debt to those who had rescued him from the hardship of communist China, made this life inevitable.

"Sometimes", Chen told Selena, "I experiment a little in the laboratory we have. It's perfectly equipped. I try to find ways of making our Chinese products better. It's very controversial with my relatives, who think I must be mad to try to change cures and drugs thousands of years old."

Selena looked at him sympathetically. He was frustrated, unable to use the skills he had acquired at great effort, Jianhua, which translated to Jimmy, had been given travel money, and a little towards his books by the Chen family, his degree came by dint of full scholarship and a night job as a cleaner.

"There must be new ways of applying our talent for curing..." his voice trailed off. " And then he added something in a low almost bitter tone of voice, " and using our talent to make money."

Listening to him Selena experienced a visceral stab of excitement-a feeling she had had at every turn when her instinct told her that a door was about to open. She heard the echo of his words as if they were formed in her own brain.. There must be new ways of applying our talent for curing...!"

The idea of this capable young man laboring behind the counter of a Chinatown apothecary of rigid tradition, unable to do anything but accept the burden, struck her as the essence of waste. Even more, although she didn't want to tell him yet, she wondered if fate had not sent her someone with a knowledge of chemistry and physics to help her in her search for the products she had been seeking these many months for her clients.

With barely suppressed excitement she asked Jimmy whether he would show her where he lived and worked. Again she could see that his desire to show her and that odd oriental reluctance to reveal much that was personal warred in his face. But in the end he said yes, perhaps it was time. And they agreed to meet where Mott Street crossed Canal.

Chapter: 8

Canal Street was a broad, garish downtown artery which ran from the East River to the Hudson. Littered with discarded papers and wrappers, with city detritus of every imaginable type, and above all with seething Oriental humanity. Old and young, many of them with no certain discernable sex dressed as they were in a virtual uniform of dark blue or black worn cotton pants, flat slipper shoes, and long sleeved collarless shirts. All hurrying in the streets, all burdened with large sacks or heavy boxes and packages. But like an anthill with underlying purpose in their ceaseless movement, purpose that they seemed to understand perfectly, however unreadable to an outsider.

As Selena made the turn onto Canal, the change from the neighborhood just to the north was abrupt even violent.

Oriental stores and businesses lined the street packed one against another, along with Chinese benevolent and social organizations whose names revealed nothing of their actual function, and five-story buildings that sported names written in lurid geometric hieroglyphs.

Jimmy later told her many of the signs were in Cantonese. Although, the most universal of the fortyChinese dialects in the orient was Mandarin, which was also the official written language. Despite the glare and flash, they had a secretive look.

She felt most decidedly out of place. To be fair about it, she thought, hers was one of the few non-oriental faces to be seen on the entire street. What was it Jimmy said she would be considered?...an 'occidental white devil'!

As she went along the street there was none of the gaiety, or bonhomie of her home blocks. Rather a quality she couldn't put her finger on it, but 'inward-looking' would be close enough, or perhaps unwelcoming even somehow 'threatening'. Certainly to her and anyone cinsidered an outsider. No one lounged or gossiped in the street.

The feeling grew making her uncharacteristically on edge. Mentally she gave herself a shake and told herself not to be a child. It was just a street in the city, she'd been in many worse.

She knew that Jimmy wanted to ease some of the 'cultural shock', and take her to one of the better restaurants before showing her the Apothecary.

As they were walking toward the restaurant, he explained, that the Chinese rarely decided things on an empty stomach. Hunger contributed to unbalanced decisions. And life was all about balanced decisions. Yin and Yang had to be brought into harmony.

Selena listened fascinated by this glimpse into a foreign world. "It's such a different perspective. Westerners so often admire unthinking headlong passion."

"I know, both in affairs of love and politics." Chen stopped cautiously at a yellow light before a cross street, catching Selena as she was about to dash across to beat the red.

She laughed, "and that", taking back the arm which he had grasped, "must be a balanced and sane answer to risk."

"Impetuosity is not a way of life" he answered half joking.

Both caught up in thought, they arrived at the Peking Duck House, and there had the specialty for which it was known, Bok Choy and countless side dishes. Selena thoroughly enjoyed the unaccustomed flavors and voluptuousness, the glimpse into the Chinese genius for combinations which gave rise to unique tastes and sensations. When Selena could eat no more, not sweet nor sour, Jimmy paid the bill and they left.

It wasn't far to the Chen pharmacy, which was in one of the typical shuttered-looking buildings of the neighborhood. Through two large windows framed with heavy wooden beams, she could see a small dimly lit and dusty room with ancient glass display cabinets containing jars of all sizes with handwritten labels in Chinese. On wall to floor shelves rested packaged creams, lotions, medicines, products for health, beauty and longevity, brought from the Far East.

"Come." Jimmy led her into the Apothecary. Directly in the back was a counter-intricate stories carved in its dark wood. Above the counter, where a middle-aged man sat with an abacus and a cash box, were two formal life sized portraits painted on glass. Wedding portraits of the paternal Grandparents of his cousins, Jimmy explained. A man and woman dressed in traditional robes looked unblinkingly and soberly at posterity. They had come to this country to escape a China ravaged by a century of oppression, flood, famine, and civil war.

Selena was entranced. She examined and made Chen tell her about the exotic materials she found on the shelves. He sighed, knowing from experience when Selena became curious there was absolutely no way she was going to stop until she had answers. And so he described and explained patiently the use of each jar and box.

They contained traditional Chinese medicine.

"Many of these dispensing containers", Chen said turning over a box covered with bright orange wrapping paper and calligraphic Chinese characters, "hold what are considered illegal substances. Forbidden to be imported into this country."

"Why do you sell them? I mean if you're caught you can be prosecuted." Selena was at once curious, and surprised that cautious and balanced Chen would not be more uneasy with these substances some in full display on the shelves.

"I grant you it's a slight gamble. But the wrappers carry the label of everyday medications. We only give them to very old and trusted buyers. If by chance they were to be opened very few would guess they were anything beyond a homeopathic simple-a brown or grey powdered remedy."

For Chen this was a lengthy explanation. Selena still found this practice at odds with much the Jimmy she knew, but figured it was a family enterprise and not under his control. Still she recognized a degree of discomfort.

"Some sales are under the counter", she said grasping the essence of the illicit dispensation.

"I suppose so. Let me show you some of the oddities."

She saw rhinoceros horn and tiger paws imported surreptitiously from Burma. Selena hesitated to ask by what means they had arrived in America-she knew many to be on the endangered species list. Less endangered creatures-snakes, frogs and lizards-had also been deployed to make liquids and powders guaranteed to ameliorate most human problems.

Tiger balm and acupuncture needles were stacked on shelves full of jars of herbs and spices sold by the ounce in brilliant paper packets. Selena saw clearly the extreme contradiction of the new with the ancient, that whirled around Jimmy in this place of tradition, and had to torment his sense of being a contemporary scientist, in a world that prized ancient methods and practices..

" So you see, now", he said, a certain animus in his voice, "my past and future."

Selena reached out and touched his arm, "Not necessarily, Jimmy. I have an idea that..."

At this point two Chinese men suddenly appeared in the doorway, blocking any possible entrance or exit-men dressed head to toe in black except for a brilliant scarlet emblem blazing out on their chests. Both smacked the doorframe several times with thick Bamboo sticks to call attention to their presence. It was loud and terrifying.

Chen turned, saw them, and froze. Each raised his stick directly in front him to mid-chest, placing each foot in a wide based stance. They addressed him in hissing Chinese as if no one else existed. Their voices seemed to whip around the shop. As they neared him foot by foot, their postures became more and more menacing, the sticks rising to shoulder height.

Selena stared at them with fear. She looked to see if the cashier could help. He had vanished as if never there.

Suddenly, to her surprise and horror, Chen began shouting violently, flailing his arms in a show of anger. At a certain point he pointed to her. The argument stopped as suddenly as it had begun. Nothing indicated why, and she could detect no sign of resolution.

One of the men made some sort of gesture at Chen, then without another word the two men left as abruptly as they came. Chen was flushed, with an expression which seemed part frustration and part hysteria, shaking badly. She didn't think he'd gotten the upper hand even when the halt had been called. It was more like an interruption-certainly not any kind of resolution, that much she understood.

She looked at him, waiting for some explanation.

None was forthcoming. She knew she couldn't ask or even comment. She had to let it go.

Chen disappeared behind the counter, and returned in a moment swallowing a cup of water as he crumpled one of the bright paper packets in a free hand that still shook.

They stepped out into the street into a light rain. It was filled with vegetable and fish stands, variety stores and bakeries, vendors hawking their wares. In the front of each store, or just outside on the street on a stool was a tiny old woman watching with hooded and knowing eyes the street, the customers, the comings and goings.

Chen finally spoke-indicating the women, he said "They know everything that happens. Nothing escapes them. It has always been this way in Chinese life, the old women watch the street, watch the family, watch the neighbors. They know everything that happens or even may sometime happen" he spoke with bitterness and anger.

Selena sensed he somehow intended to explain the just-finished incident as well as the women dogging their steps in silence with hooded, knowing eyes.

" It's as it is in Italy. Le None, the Grandmothers, watch the goings on of the young." she laughed trying to lift the shadow that had fallen between them. She knew in her heart that these Italian watchers were often light-hearted, playing a spicy well-understood game. But here on this street, the watching had a powerful brooding accountability to it. She shivered remembering her earlier reaction to the neighborhood. Thinking her Papa would have made the sign of the Malocchio, to ward off evil.

" They'll be talking about the beautiful woman who wasn't Chinese who came here with number two Chen son", Jimmy said recovering his composure. The compliment was so unaccustomed that it seemed to transgress an unspoken barrier between them. Seconds later that feeling had passed without fruition. Just a fleeting intensely personal moment.

They walked away from this quarter where he breathed as a Chinese but clearly suffocated as well, back to the Village. Chen obviously wanted to say something. And so, rather than explain the shocking scene she had witnessed, he began to tell her the story of his family.

Chapter: 9

China, at the turn of the century, was a land which had fallen from the splendors of the Ching dynasty into regions of ruinous anarchy. Poverty and famine ruled the land. Rice paddies and tiny indigo farms serviced by rib-wracked water buffalo were raided cruelly over and over, and made to render most of their product to local war lords in exchange for permission to survive for yet another day of tribute.

The cities were centers of degradation, where workers earned pennies a day for back-breaking work in factories, children were sold into slavery of one kind or another, starvation was a rice bowl away, and opium reigned as king.

It was into this world that Mei Lee, Chen's Grandmother was born to a poor farmer in Yanchow his tenth child. Unwanted. Another mouth. A girl. Worth in trade at best a few yen, or perhaps two or three fowl.

When the proprietor of a shabby traveling theater company came through the poor village, and spotted the eight year old girl curled between the feet of a pair of huge horned oxen without fear or self-consciousness, he bought her on the spot from her father in exchange for a ticket to the performance to be given that night.

Once delivered to his wagon, and washed, he inspected his get-a graceful thin-shanked child, made stoic by the hardships of her eight years of existence. He took off his robe, and showed her what the divine rod was for, and how he expected her to service it. When this was accomplished to his satisfaction, he beat her, indicated she should see to the bedding, floors and food, and locked her in.

After several days of travel, she no longer had any idea where they were, and did not try to flee when the manager let her out.

The company moved on eking out a living through the muddy villages of the mountain provinces, staying a day or two in one, then moving to the next.

Days became weeks. The manager was content. She had learned her duties well and he no longer beat her. As she learned how to please, the child was rewarded by being given enough to eat for the first time in her short life.

Once having taken care of the manager, Mei Lee was set to sweep the portable stage, to help repair rents in the painted canvas backdrops, to clean and care for the company's costumes.

It was an odd existence, on the one hand grounded in the grossest realities of the physical wants of the old body of the proprietor, on the other immersed in the fantasy, brilliant colors, of the scenes and times depicted in the theater. On one hand the magic of the traditional heroic epics told night after night, on the other assisting at their shoddy, inept presentation.

By watching she began to learn the arts of the troupe, although if truth be known, they didn't have to be very skillful. The country audiences they played to didn't require excellence.

Still she watched the black-clad scene changers who did their best to be invisible as they shifted scenery and props, the application of bright face paints as actors created the grotesque, time-honored 'masks' of the traditional roles they were assigned, the gymnastics and juggling the actors used to keep bodies supple and graceful, and the 'singers' as they rehearsed and practiced their dances and roles. At least the most conscientious members of the troupe.

Mei Lee was quick to learn. Both the good and the

bad. She watched the audiences by night noticing how they responded-to whom and what.

When she passed her tenth birthday she knew the manager's appetites were growing jaded. He would soon seek a fresh server for his wand. For what she planned, she must control the selection. And so, when they passed a tiny village, and she saw a suitable child, she had a scene shifter take her up and secrete her in the wagon as the troupe moved on. This time Mei Lee saw to the washing and beating.

That night she served dinner. When the manager was liberally supplied with wine, she began for the first time to sing in a low voice some of the romantic songs she'd learned from the troupe. And when his senses were so fed and lulled, she introduced his wand to double ministrations.

It was a performance the manager wished repeated many times. The new 'server' was so delicate and her openings so small, the sensations she could evoke were exquisite, especially as abetted by the schooling of Mei Lee and accompanied by the singing..

One of these nights, before he could gainsay her, she also showed him how much she had learned of the actor's art. She had a low, perfectly pitched voice, and it gave the long, vowel filled phrases of the Chinese Theater, an appealing twist and sound. To which she added an original dance which she called the Sighing of the Willow for the Brook.

It was an enchanting performance. The manager listened and watched. She had indeed learned well.

It was also from his view fortuitous as he needed to replace the second female lead, who was quite untalented and frequently forgetful as a consequence of a craving for strong drink. Mei Lee was fully aware of all that went on with the troupe. Unaware of her astute manipulation of events, the manager was to congratulate himself time and again for his perception and subsequent use of the talent she displayed.

Mei Lee was able to give the ritualized movements of the plays the group performed a unique and imaginative grace and character. And her voice was a marvel of reed and smoke, seducing the ear as her body, with the smallest movements, seduced the eye.

As months went by, Mei lee's performances began to be noticed, and more and more evoked the applause of their audiences.

The manager moved her into lead roles, as his coffers swelled, and the company began to become well-known in the provinces. Venues became more stable and important. Often they could count on one week of full houses in one location. A blessing for the company, the traveling wagons, and the beasts who drew them.

Mei Lee was fifteen, at the height of her beauty and skill, when she made the decision to leave the stage. She had gone as far as she could performing with a theatrical troupe. One day the audiences would tire of her. And although she had put aside almost all she had earned, the money that could be made was small. It was a difficult life, offering little security. No. She had a better idea.

She proposed to the manager that the troupe present their play to a wealthy patron, or the lord of a new area, a private performance before the first public performance. So doing would undoubtedly lessen the tribute and taxes to be exacted, and smooth things for the troupe in countless other ways.

The manager would never reveal in anyway he thought the idea brilliant, but put it into effect at the next stop they made. And so it went, that the troupe would first perform for the local mandarin or lord, and only then the local populace.

Mei Lee found her patron one night at such a private showing. He was an elderly merchant, not a mandarin, but one who lived in an even more sumptuous style in a richly appointed manor. His wives, equally elderly, were formally seated in the front row beside him. His eyes and theirs equally, told her that here was her opportunity.

After her performance she begged, and was granted audience with the number one wife. A bargain was struck.

That evening she became the mistress of the merchant with a substantial first night dowry, a number of silk robes, a hand servant, and a promise of more to come should she suit the merchant, and of course remain subservient to the number one wife.

It was a pleasant, peaceful existence. The demands of the number one wife for small domestic services greatly outweighed the demands of the merchant, who was often more concerned to produce a strong stream of urine on demand, than to play flute with his organ. The wives taught Mei Lee to read and write, and much of the ancient history and philosophy of China.

But in the world outside the manor, life had become revolutionized. Chiang Kai Chek, Mao Tse Dung as well as regional warlords, began to fight for control of the country. What little centralized government from Peking there had been, collapsed. And finally The Japanese invaded. The country was torn apart, ravaged and re-ravaged by whatever force passed through the province seizing temporary power.

Mei Lee, visiting the village of the manor one day, saw a band of soldiers, enter the offices of the merchant, haul him out, kill him, then without further ceremony, loot his warehouses, and burn what they could not carry away.

She fled immediately back to the manor, quickly

sewed all her jewelry and money into an old robe, and
went to the stables.

There with expertise left from her childhood, she
picked out two of the oldest, sturdiest horses, and the
strongest, tallest 'boy' she could find. Most of the
servants had fled already hearing of what was
happening in the village. Certainly the 'boy' who
looked at her knowingly knew about it.

"The mistress will need help, to flee the Ta-phung?"
It was a question which held threat at its bottom. Mei
Lee with her usual quickness arrived at its heart, and
the few choices open to her. She knew she must leave
at once, and that on any road she would need whatever
protection she could gather.Without hesitation, she
bought his escort with several gems.

After several weeks on the road, passing village
after village in ruins, they saw their best chance for
survival lay in the anonymity of the city. The 'Boy' had
brought them passage through roughness and danger.
But had exacted a further price. By day he protected
her and cared for the horses. By night he required that
she see to all of his bodily wants. She had no choice.

However when they arrived in Shanghai, she
arranged to buy a small apothecary shop in one of the
lesser neighborhoods, with some of the jewels sewn in
her robe. She also persuaded the proprietor, as part of
the purchase price, to retain his assistant, a deaf mute,
who in turn would rid her of the 'Boy'.

As she was the first to acknowledge him as more
than an animal to serve or be whipped if he failed to
respond immediately, the mute did her bidding with a
glad but silent garotte.

It was this assistant, unable to hear her shrieks of
pain, who delivered her child ignoring the blood and
excrement, in the back room of the shop eight months
later.

A girl. The year was 1939.

Pu-Yi, the grandson of Theu-sze the last Empress to reside in the forbidden city stripped of any real power, was shipped off as a puppet to 'rule' his token kingdom-the province of Manchuko. Mao and Chou en Lai were everywhere seizing the power structure of the sleeping giant that was China. Enveloping all officialdom into their tight control. Nothing and no one escaped their hands.

Over the next years Mei Lee kept a low profile but prospered not so much because of the apothecary, although she and the assistant made a show of long hours, but because she was a bold gambler, who kept a small illegal den in the back room for those few in the neighborhood with an inveterate habit and a few silver coins to play.

Fortunately, for Mei Lee and her child, one of the constant Mah Jongg players in a China turned more and more rigid and puritanical by Mao, was a highly placed Military officer stationed in Shanghai. He was a man well into his late sixties-pock-marked, huge, and obtuse as only those with absolute power can be, His grey rumpled uniform chest littered with bright-ribboned medals. He ressembled nothing so much as a scarred toad, whose eyes were hooded and nearly hidden by rolls of fat. As a General who'd risen through the ranks his power locally was total.

He became her new protector, taking for his trouble half her profits, and her body, as the fancy took him. His desire for profit was steady, however past dissipation made other desires transient, for which Mei Lee thanked her household Gods faithfully each evening.

Life was difficult for her as for so many under the regime of the Peoples Republic. She had little time for her daughter, who grew up very much a part of the streets-a believer in Mao and his teachings which promised such a sterling future for the proletariat, and who became the willing partner of any male who showed her the least attention, or gave her views any importance.

At fifteen she too bore a child to a promising subaltern in Mao's youth cadre, delivered just as she had been, in the back room of the shop.

At sixteen she disappeared, to an unpromising future as the camp follower of a lieutenant in the army-leaving behind her a son. Jianhua.

Regulations regarding newborn children were rigid and rigidly enforced. Mei Lee had to avert the child's destruction. She had her protector buy the papers of another, a dying child to legitimize the existence of Jianhua.

As time passed, she taught her Grandson all she had learned in the household of the merchant-of the Tao, Confucius, and the great epics of Chinese history. She taught him the beauty of calligraphy-the Number One wife, grateful for Mei Lee's obedience had been generous with her knowledge. She taught him to cook and count in his head faster than she could click on an abacus. She loved the child passionately and was loved in return by the little boy who knew no other parent.

Mei Lee was herself a gifted and shrewd gambler. Her 'association' played Mah Jongg in the back room separated by a curtain from the apothecary. She took a small but consistent 'house gift' of every game played. The small boy fell asleep to the sounds of tiles being slapped on the wooden tables, and calls of "Crack", "Bam", "West Wind" and "Dragon". He knew what the 'Great wall' was, and the meaning of the square enameled metal coins slotted on the end posts of each player's rack before he could run to the end of the street.

Perhaps her most successful operation was a pool for betting on the horse racing in South China and Hong Kong. The results of the races always seemed to arrive daily no matter the difficulty of conveyance and no matter what catastrophe visited the city. She kept the betting always small, and beneath the notice of officials.

Like any practical Chinese she'invested'much of her cash under the floorboards of her house. But the rest, no small amount, she sent through intermediaries to Hong Kong, and on to New York, where a son of her merchant had immigrated. Times were too precarious to do otherwise. Mistrust was survival.

When her Grandson was eight, she sent him to an old survivor of a House of Flowers to be taught the poetry of the physical, the truth of Yin and Yang. It was forbidden. All the houses of favor had been eradicated in Mao's China. But nevertheless, Mei Lee felt compelled to complete his traditional education

In Shanghai, life was no longer a matter of cash or gold. Famine was the currency of the realm. Sickness, death and regulations its return. And at just this most unfortunate of time, her gamblers melting away into the attempt to survive, her protector suffered a long overdue stroke and died.

The junior officer in charge of the district immediately raided her shop, with a troop of soldiers, and took what he wished of her medicines-asked and received from her a protection pay-off, then closed her shop, and the gambling room as a den of immorality. He found the three beds she kept for those of her clients seeking the oblivion of the poppy after a loss. These too he 'closed'. Mei Lee feared for her life.

However, though closure of the 'Den of iniquity', assured the regime that immorality in this quarter had been arrested, but the officer informed Mei Lee, she would have to come to his headquarters to arrange for payment of penalty fines.

Jianhua was left for weeks with no word of his Grandmother. Desperate and frightened, he finished what was left in the house for food, then went out with the deaf-mute to beg on the streets, and fight for rotten fruit from the discard baskets of the shops, or steal at night from others less strong than he.

When Mei Lee lurched to the front door supported by improvised crutches, and in rags at the end of the eighth week, he barely recognized her.

 She who had prided herself on her cleanliness and grace, was running with sores and indescribably filthy. She coughed incessantly, and rubbed at her back as if in pain. Her gait was that of an old, old woman. She was unable to stand upright..

She said nothing, but slid into the back room, beckoning her assistant. When Jianhua tried to go to her, the deaf-mute held him back, mouthing words he could not utter. The door locked behind them. And shortly, Jianhua smelled the sweet odor of opium.

After four days Mei Lee came out. She was broken in health, and had just enough presence of mind left to perceive her current situation. The government had taken her gambling, her 'Den', and closed even the apothecary shop. Her savings might suffice to take care of her and the deaf-mute for a time, but a young teen-age boy? No. Arrangements had to be made to get her grandson away

She went to the last of her silk robes, from it got the few remaining jewels and the address of the son of the merchant who had gone to America in the thirties. It would have to be enough...

She arranged passage on a ship, that specialized in smuggling people who had to escape, put the name and address of the son in a waterproof pouch hung from a steel chain around Jianhua's neck, sewed the last of her jewels in his trouser seams, kissed him four times in blessing, and sent him off before he could see the tears stream down her cheeks and grief double her over.

Jianhua, too was in tears. He loved his Grandmother deeply. But he had been taught, respect and obedience to one's elder was a principle never to be questioned, never to be disobeyed. Not even for desolation. And so he went, ultimately to be reared conscientiously but with little love, in America by the family of the old merchant, bound and obliged to them by indissoluble bonds.

A week later Mei Lee died. The deaf-mute, made sure that an overdose of the purest opium, would ablate all pain and carry her out in a sleep from which she would never awake.

As he finished the story, Selena's heart went out to him. It was amazing that such a turbulent story lay behind the cool exterior Jimmy presented to the world. " Thank you for telling me", she said. And then added with a deliberate change of subject, "Jimmy, I want to tell you about a project I want you to take on. If it works out, it may provide an answer to some ...", She searched for the right word, "to some of your difficulties."

He looked at her with skepticism in his eyes. But mixed with the skepticism was, she thought, just the smallest glimmer of something that could only be called hope.

It was really a huge gamble she had in mind. But she knew, somehow, that his Grandmother, Mei Lee, would have approved.

Chapter: 10

Several weeks elapsed after the visit to the apothecary shop. Selena was particularly busy, everyone seemed to want a new hairstyle or 'look' for the Spring season. She hadn't seen nor heard from Chen. But one day, when the morning post arrived, It brought a sealed package wrapped in layers of brown paper. When she saw the return address, she realized he'd sent it.

It gave her a sense of anticipation that was almost sexual. She opened the tidily wrapped package. It contained a single Jar. When she opened it, she knew that here was the cream she had asked him to make, the cream based on the ideas they had captured in their talks.

A delicate and original smell wafted from the jar as she undid the top. It was incredibly fresh, like an ocean breeze with a smooth and sensual texture and a light green color which recalled a springtime sea.

Trying it first on herself, as she would do all her products always, Selena was excited to note an immediate effect. Her skin felt alive and soothed. She stroked it in delight and disbelief.

After a week she could see a rejuvenating effect. She knew what she had to do next. She gave a few samples to old trusted clients.

" Try this", she said, " I don't want to say anything about it. Take a week. No, take two, then tell me what you think."

The next two weeks were an agony of anticipation. How would they react? What would they say?

When the customers came back to rave without exception that the cream was superb, all they hoped for and more, she wept, overjoyed with their reaction and her own.

She reached Chen and told him what had happened. And at the same time asked when another batch would be ready. Her first customers were already insistent on replenishing their supply.

"Wow!" he said. "Tell them ten weeks. The process takes that long. By the way, have you thought of a name. You can't keep calling it 'Cream'.

Selena had dreamed of this moment. "No, we can't keep calling it 'cream'. How about Creme del Mare Verde. Cream of the Green Sea".

"Yes. It has a ring, Selena. but use your name with it as well. And find someone to do labels."

Selena realized he was right. For the moment it was circulating in plain white apothecary jars, but they should be labeled.

Word of the product spread among her customers like wildfire. When Selena next saw him, she asked Chen for a hundred jars. He looked at her with disbelief.

"Selena, I gave you thirty a couple of weeks ago, You can't mean you've given them all away?"

"No!", She said, unable to suppress a wide grin. "I gave the first dozen away. The last fifteen were repeat orders and I charged for them."

"My God!" he said in awe. Then after a moment's reflection," Good. I need some money for supplies."

Selena gave him the money the cream had earned. "Tell your clients as soon as I can do a batch, they'll have it."

Selena's first response to his statement, which she knew to be based in reality was impatience. She worried about keeping interest in the cream alive when she had to disappoint some of the women waiting for their jar of cream.

Then it struck her. Inadvertently, by not being able to fulfill the demand immediately it would create anticipation, which would fire still more demand not less. It was to take several major companies years to come to the same conclusion, and deliberately use this marketing technique.

"Jimmy...," she said slowly, thinking as she spoke, "On second thought, can you make two hundred? I mean can you do that many with the equipment you have?"

"Yes. I think I can handle a batch of two hundred. But that's about the limit."

"Va bene. Make two hundred. I'm going to set the price at double."

"Double the price already?"

In Chen's voice, doubt and admiration warred.

"Double", said Selena firmly. "There is nothing remotely like the cream to be found, nothing like it being made, or as far as I can tell being dreamed of. So..."

"Okay. You must know what you're doing."

It was not the last time Chen's inner conflict between risk and conservatism would make him worry if she was doing the right thing.

Selena realized that he needed an explanation.

" Jimmy", her voice gentle, "We have something which is top quality, healthy, enticing, safe-in a word unique. And for unique there is no price. No competition. For the moment we'll keep production small, within our means. I'll take orders for more, then we'll see."

Selena's strategy worked perfectly. So perfectly, that Maria informed her they were inundated with orders. Chen worked furiously to try to keep up as word of mouth created an ever-increasing demand.

"Selena", he begged one day, exhausted " either we

set up to manufacture this cream, get enough supplies and enough manpower, or you're going to kill me off. " She knew he was right, and found herself in the kind of mood which felt dangerous, and productive, and fast. First they needed a proper manufactory.

Exiting Chen's laboratory one day, she happened upon a 'for lease' sign on a neighboring building, and signed for it the same day.

Having a building was only the beginning. The cream's formula called for a slow melding process, and then elctrolytic hyper-oxygenation. That could be handled in the new facility they would set up, but above all they needed a flow of Pacific kelp-an essential base ingredient.

Chen's family had sent him kelp from California. Originally it was for medicinal uses-but it was the ingredient which made this cream unlike anything else on the market, and gave it the nutritious properties and almost edible consistency that produced such a miraculous effect on Selena's clientele.

Having a continuous supply of this material would require some doing. Chen suggested that his family in California, all of them involved in one way or other with the sea, and already set up for shipping and distribution, would be ideal suppliers.

In this step, as in every other, Selena insisted on being personally involved. She needed to understand intimately every stage of development, and know first-hand all of the origins of her products. She needed to see with her own eyes where things came from, and exactly how they were used.

She thought then of Fatimah and her understanding of the workings of natural ingredients on the outer and inner self. How she would have loved all this. But the last letter she had written, had come back with large stamped letters. The Egyptian authorities informed the sender that their letter was 'Undeliverable. Recipient deceased'. And another stamp appended '20 July 1966'. Selena was shocked by the brevity and administrative finality of the cold printed words. She went to church, and arranged for a candle to be lit in perpetuity each day in one of the side chapels devoted to Mary Magdalen. She mourned her friend and vowed one day to find a personal way to memorialize her.

Having rented space, signed for the redesign of it, ordered the major equipment Chen needed, and now undertaking to ensure a constant large flow of the ingredients, the next order of the day was money.

Maria had insisted on paying for the design and printing of the labels. She had saved quite a bit but most of it had gone into the new plant. Now again she needed money.

As so often in her life, Selena thought of John. They had continued to talk to each other at least once a week although the times when she was able to see him were infrequent these days. She knew he was working on yet another biography, but sensed she remained the 'woman in his life. Yet she hesitated to trade on his good nature, feeling slightly guilty knowing no matter what, he would never refuse her . He would always be there for her.

They met for tea at the Plaza. Amidst the potted palms, gold-painted chairs, violin-piano duo playing refined 'tea music'. After their finger sandwiches and Lapsoong Suchow arrived and been tasted, John looked over and asked her, "What's the latest? Where are you? And by the way, I think Crème del Mare Verde is a sensational name."

"Grazie, tesoro mio."

He smiled, his eyes as well as his voice expressing interest and perhaps something more like admiration for her latest project.

She told him all that had happened in the last weeks. Then spoke of her need for money.

Having some idea of how much she and Maria generated at the shop, he was at once impressed and worried.

"Selena, how much do you have in mind?"

" One hundred and fifty thousand. It should carry us through until our income stream catches up."

Without further questioning, John wrote out a check for the full amount, as an investment in the new product, and laughed heartily to hear that the some money would be spent on an expedition to California in search of kelp.

" Good hunting," he said, and then added with a certain wryness, "I hope Chen will keep you out of trouble."

What could that   mean? Selena mused briefly. John seemed almost jealous, but that couldn't be right, she thought. Chen was her trusted lieutenant, what kind of trouble could there be?

Chapter: 11

As they waited in the lounge at Butler airfield for the flight, already more than two hours delayed, Selena looked at her traveling companion as if for the first time. She was about to fling herself all the way across the continent and probably into the deep Pacific as well with someone she didn't really know-for all the hours they had spent working together and talking.

He had told her the story of his Grandmother, and something of his immediate relatives, but other than knowing he had graduated with honors in pharmacology from UCLA, had then taken an advanced degree in chemistry, and was highly ambivalent about his present, she knew almost nothing about his private life. He hadn't volunteered anything. When she stopped to think about she had never asked.

But this, this adventure with so many unknowns awaiting her in California, had still another unknown-Chen.

As if to reassure herself, she went over what she did know. She knew the dedicated scientist in him, she knew the man who wanted to learn poetry and history, she knew the clever hands and skilled way in a laboratory but the man himself? What was the cant phrase used? Inscrutable. Non-confrontational. To which she would add, oblique. He seemed to approach life obliquely.

Despite his prodigious intellectual energy and drive, he was capable of a hypnotic stillness-a quality he now manifested as they waited for the ever-later departure. She envied him. She had to pace and have the occasional cigarette while they seemed to wait, and wait, and wait.

Finally strapped into the cramped economy seats they took off.

Jimmy was soothing, stimulating and helpful on the long trip. The idea of sharing one room in Half Moon Bay to save money gave her no pause at all. She thought of him as she thought of a casual friend-no flirting, no tension, no insinuation. It was purely a working relationship containing nothing of the Male-Female element.

His stoicism and their shared sense of humor as well as their excitement about what lay before them were what was needed to endure.

It was a travel nightmare ending in arrival in San Francisco at one a.m. after what seemed purposeless stops in Chicago and Denver.

"Let's get rich so that we will never have to do this again," Chen proposed, as they sank into the sprung seats of a Rent-a-wreck Corvair.

"Agreed." Selena resigned herself to another hour or two of endurance.

As they drove, the moonlight was reflected on the near black Pacific water-almost too picturesque to be true. The ocean stretched on until it met the curved horizon, the austere cliffs dropped dramatically off from Highway One. Monterey cypresses silhouetted in the moonlight gave this coast an overwhelming air of mystery and a haunted quality to its shadows.

Exhausted and quiet, they checked into the Seabird Motel on Half Moon Bay at three, barely speaking as they took turns in the bathroom and collapsed into their waiting beds.

An impeccable Northern California day dawned with a cloudless sky, huge gulls swooping and cawing overhead, and the potent smell of the ocean - discernibly different from the Atlantic, somehow more tangy.

Selena took her first deep breath of pacific air, becoming intoxicated by the combined aromas of ocean, Eucalyptus, and Broome particular to this part of California.

Like many Chinese in America, Jimmy had an extended family which reached from Coast to Coast but the largest part resided in California.

They carried on a fishing tradition which went back to the nineteenth century when Chinese fishermen lived lives of poverty, isolated in small camps up and down the California coast. Making a bare living harvesting and processing shrimp to send back to China.

Now the original family was prosperous, owning a small fleet of fishing boats, warehouses, refrigeration and distribution plants-well able to help successive generations as they arrived in the New World.

A cousin met them on the dock with the diving gear for their exploration of the kelp beds. Selena had to laugh at the once over he gave her after they were introduced, it hinted he was more attuned to American mores than Jimmy.

He took them down to the dock. A skiff with an outboard motor was tied up together with a second boat. Dockside another cousin waited with the scuba equipment they would need.

"How many will we be?" The cousin asked not sure if Jimmy was diving.

"Three, assuming you're diving this morning", Chen joked with a poker face.

His cousin laughed and asked Selena, "You're sure?"

Selena's defiant look brooked no further discussion. She began to struggle into the wet suit he provided, refusing his help to do a final 'fit adjustment.' especially after his wolf whistle.

However, once they were all suited, he became dead serious and all business. The boat took them out a hundred yards from shore.

"We'll do the pre-dive check, then get going while the light will help us see", referring to the angle of the sun which permitted light to penetrate the first twenty feet of the deep green waters.

The boat rocked slowly in the off-shore swells. As they bobbed up and down in the early morning tide, he proceeded to examine the valves, connections and supply hoses of the scuba tanks. He tested the clasps of the counter-buoyancy weight belts to make sure they broke open at a finger's touch. Then the fit of the face masks. A leak underwater in the air supply or facemask could be compromising, even dangerous. The failure to loosen the weight belt, in an emergency a potential hazard to be avoided.

It was not so long ago that Jacques Cousteau had helped bring scuba equipment to the commercial market. Each year that followed saw improvements in the gear but still professional users always checked.

Chen's cousin explained to Selena "Even experienced divers go down in pairs. We use the 'Buddy' system. Constant contact with your partner underwater."

"I see".

Selena understood the commonsense involved. These instructions were essential. Jimmy was an old hand at diving, but still listened with attention.

When both men were 'suited up' She said she now understood the term Frogmen, as indeed both looked like overgrown amphibians, in the sleek rubber wet-suits, webbed flippers, masks and mouthpieces.

She felt as ungainly as she ever had, and traveled the short distance to the gunwale of the boat where the two men were waiting with awkward, high stepping moves. Based on this utterly alien feeling, she wondered if she would be able to carry this through. Perhaps for once she had been too bold.

Before she could think, Chen's cousin grasped her hand, and indicated with a thumbs up gesture, they were about to go over board. When she nodded, he flipped them backward into the sea.

For a moment Selena was totally disoriented. Then she realized that the strange brightness above, was sky seen through twenty feet of water. She was suspended under the waves, weightless. She later learned scuba divers called this being 'neutral.' She could rise or descend, with a flick of her flippers or hands at will.

Exhaling trains of bubbles in the deep silence of the water, she followed the pointing hand of her partner. There about ten feet below them, she saw the kelp, undulating sensuously in the ocean current.

Selena was deeply moved by its silent beauty. She was an intruder. She felt honored to take a place in this enormous chain of life. To use it for the well being of the earth's human creatures was a sacred trust.

Floating weightless in time warped continuity with the sea around her, she felt as one with the water surrounding and supporting her, and the life within it.

As she slowly turned her head and she appreciated the deep green of the kelp bed arising from a coral-colored sea floor. She knew that these mysterious and beautiful colors would be the colors for her products, in this she would render homage to nature and its nurturing powers.

They cut and collected kelp in over-sized nets for the next hour, changed tanks and worked for another three hours. The harvest was enough to fill both boats. Emerging shivering from the ocean, she felt Chen's smooth sinuous, almost feminine hands helping her into the boat. He had taken from the ocean a sea cucumber which he had put into a plastic bucket filled with water and now carried with them.

"It was so beautiful and so..." Selena was at a loss for words.

Chen, now out of his suit, and into jeans and a heavy pullover, handed her a towel, said "Man and his ways are only a patch on this world we see and so much less on the world we don't often get to visit."

He was right.

They sat in silence, weaving with the motion of the harvest boat. One of the Chen cousins offered them each a glass of plum brandy, as Selena dried off in the chill of afternoon.

Thanking everyone, and pleased with the almost endless beds of the seaweed they'd seen, they got back into the rental car, stopped for a quick meal at a local diner, and exhausted, returned to the motel to sleep.

The next day, they met with the family to discuss the methods by which they could supply Selena with enough kelp to meet her demands. Thanks to the cohesiveness and influence of Chen's California family, negotiations were simple and relied on gentleman's agreements rather than complicated contracts.

To Selena's surprise they were finished that day.

" What shall we do now?", she asked Chen, wondering if indeed they could manage a few days of leisure.

" I have a cousin who is a marine biologist." It seemed an abrupt change of subject. But by now Selena knew that although there were many things about him she didn't know, she did know there would be a purpose in the seeming irrelevancy.

" He has a cottage a little farther south. I know he's not there now, but he won't mind if we use it. Shall we go?"

The sudden direct gaze of his brown eyes prompted

in Selena a flicker of something she couldn't quite identify, almost an intimacy. Dismissing this feeling for the moment, she responded positively to the idea of a few more days off.

Waiting for him in the car as he emerged from the Chinese grocery store in Half Moon Bay, she began to look at him for the first time. Nothing about his movement or his attire had ever called her attention to his body, which she now realized was tall, thin, lithe and graceful. He looked eighteen or thirty-eight, only the history he had given her, and a certain fully-grown maleness gave his age away. A shock of thick black hair, through which he had the habit of running his right hand, fell over a wide and intelligent brow. She remarked his eyes, set in high and wide cheekbones. They were beautiful, she realized. And they gave little away. Perhaps the next few days would supply some of the answers.

Chapter: 12

Going back along the coast from Monterey they took the seventeen mile drive along miles of protected sea shore, white sand beaches, cypresses, and barking sea lions, symbols of the beauty of the California coastline. Past Carmel the coast road narrowed, threading along the cliffs dropping to the ocean and hills rising up opposite.

The car turned up a steep dirt road, which seemed to lead nowhere. There were no houses in sight. Half a mile later, they drew up in front of an attractive but unprepossessing redwood A-frame.

One arm full of groceries and a bunch of chrysanthemums, Jimmy steered her gently with his other arm into the house. What she saw took her breath.

A front wall entirely of plate glass looking over the ocean, invited all of the outdoors in. A large low double bed faced this window. Behind it and up two steps was a kitchen with a cooking island, a complete set of woks, clay pots, and utensils suspended from the walls. An aged and polished wooden floor, flax carpets, and natural redwood walls created perfect harmony. The smell of sandalwood hung lightly in the air. The room was sparsely decorated with few objects. A Chinese flute made of jade mounted on a pedestal held a prominent place, a coiling dragon in rosewood another.

"I propose that you have a bath," said Chen, "While I cook us dinner. It won't take long. And my cousin's tub is a must."

Selena saw the rest of the house behind the kitchen consisted of two rooms, a study hung with marine maps of the California coastline, and a bathroom dominated by a sunken tub-spa looking out a window onto a small garden of succulents.

Chen came in, knelt down, ceremoniously started the water running, and added sandalwood oil to its roiling surface.

Luxuriating in the tub, Selena contemplated the garden through the tall windows. It was as if she were bathing outdoors but safe, protected from the elements. Aware only of the hot water caressing her breasts, inhaling the scent rising from the water, she was no longer aware of time, only of a kind of tranquillity she did not often experience. Wind chimes in the garden tinkled distantly.

The sizzling of oil in the wok, the rhythmic percussion of a metal knife chopping on a wood block unleashed delectable smells.

"You'll find a robe in there, I think," Jimmy called out softly.

Indeed a long dark red silk gown hung beside the door, a pair of embroidered slippers on a shelf beside it. " Where did you learn to cook?" she asked, positioning herself on a stool to watch his expert hands chopping, slicing, preparing. A fragrant soup simmered on the gas flame.

" My grandmother taught me. She taught me everything she knew, the way of Chinese life, how to be a good Confucian son", he said rolling his eyes, "but also a lot about food and love." His eyes rested on the food he was preparing. His words hung on the air a moment, then he went on.

" It was perhaps not the usual relationship of a boy and his granny, but our circumstances were not usual." And then almost reluctantly, "I loved her you see, I'll always be grateful to her." And more strongly, "she taught me a lot about women." Selena was startled by this turn of conversation, suddenly so intimate.

He handed her a small ceramic cup filled with a strong-smelling liquid. " Gambe," he toasted. Warmth soon spread through her mouth, down her throat, and continued down, until it seemed to reach her toes.

"What is it?", she asked.

" Ginseng marinated in rice wine. Drink it slowly," he cautioned.

Seated on her stool next to the cooking island, she took small slow sips of the wine and looked out at the approaching fog and the rain now blowing in large drops against the windows. The temperamental Northern California climate was building up to a dramatic demonstration. Now she saw that the bed was ringed with heads of chrysanthemums, candles on both sides. It seemed to float like a boat heading confidently into the storm.

" We're ready to eat." Chen indicated a small wooden table set with blue Chinese porcelain and chopsticks. "I'll be there in a minute."

The potent wine had relaxed her. Despite her languor she was intensely aware of the silk robe where it touched her nipples, her thighs, her buttocks.

Chen reappeared. In spite of her self she felt a twinge, more potent for being unexpected.

He was wearing a long silk mandarin robe in the deep blue of the night sky. The slippery cloth clung to his body as he moved towards the table, revealing clearly he was naked underneath it.

Whether this had been his plan all along, she had no way of knowing. If he had always been attracted to her, she had been unaware. What was certain was, that unless she protested, they would make love.

The sensual warmth aroused by the wine, the silk clinging to her body, and the spicy perfume of the waiting food disarmed her. She would not protest. Still the inner voice which never ceased to observe and record, even as she fell under the spell of his concentration and thoroughness, asked faintly. "What do I know of this man? What do I know of his desires, his needs?"

Selena had never tasted food as subtle and seductive in texture, taste and smell. Food which aroused all of her senses.

First, a fragrant soup - the sea cucumber from Monterey Bay in a bouillon of rice flavored with dill and ginger. As she finished her soup, she felt increasingly heated.

Chen went to the stove. He beat four eggs in a bowl, deftly adding diced scallions, soy sauce and a little red pepper. Peanut oil warming in the pan added its earthy odor to the air. The eggs cooked quickly in the pan and came steaming to the table.

" I'm sorry this is so simple, he said, perhaps it isn't very good." It was the mandatory Chinese cook's disclaimer Her look stopped what could be a litany of further excuses. She devoured the eggs with unabashed hunger.

To complete the meal, he peeled fresh Lychees, forcing their rough outer skin open to give up the firm and slippery white fruit.

After two cups of the rice wine, he had ceased to pour it. She realized that any more would have been too much.

Jimmy looked at her persistently, a question in his penetrating eyes. Seeming to find the answer in hers, he arose wordlessly and knelt beside her. Removing a slipper he encased her foot in his smooth hands, stroking slowly and softly, and blowing on it lightly.

When he bent his head to take her toes in his mouth, she felt her heartbeat quicken, her nipples harden, goose bumps rise on her skin, and then a sudden moistening between her legs. The approach was

208

so deliberate, so slow.

For what seemed an eternity he sucked and stroked her feet, refusing gently all her attempts to caress him in return. Replacing the slipper, and helping her to her feet, he took her hand and led her to the bed.

As she turned, wondering if he would kiss her, she saw his penis coming to sword-like life under the silken robe. She had yet to touch him. She abandoned herself to his choreography - so measured and intense and inevitable.

A bottle of oil was warming beside a candle. Slipping her robe off her shoulders, and letting it slide down her body to the floor, he moistened his hands and lightly caressed her nipples.

One after the other they responded to his touch. His hands moving with aching slowness, and the heat of the oil, suffused her breasts with a delicious heat. To a measured rhythm he massaged them with a perfectly calibrated touch.

Letting his own robe drop to the floor, he revealed an androgynous body, slim and hairless, a long and thin cock in erection arching upwards, its lotus like head glistening with a drop of liquid.

She couldn't conceal her astonishment when she saw a gold ring nestled at its base amongst the sparse hairs. He answered her unspoken question, .."For thousands of years.." was what he said. She had crossed into an unknown country.

Now she yearned to quicken the pace as her body cried out. Again firmly refusing her touch, he flicked his oiled fingers over the insides of her thighs and her clitoris. The hold his eyes had on her was as arousing as the deep kiss she longed for. She was more than ready. He lowered her onto her back, arranging her legs apart, and kneeled between them sitting back on his haunches. He was motionless except for his penis which swayed and urged itself higher. Reaching between her legs with both hands, he gently parted her lips and pulled them sideways, letting the air penetrate the entrance to her vagina. Her need to be filled was now almost unbearable. But she matched his calm gaze at the open flower of her sex with an equally intense regard of his organ, her hips thrusting towards him, inviting, awaiting.

Behind him she could see the rain flinging itself violently on the glass window, hear the pine branches roughly caressing the roof, and the constant but irregular percussion of the distant wind chimes. No man-made music could have provided such an accompaniment.

Finally he lowered himself towards her, supporting his body on his arms. Lightly and quickly at first, his penis prodded between her legs, on the sensitive skin of her upper thighs, on her clitoris now again concealed. Her desire was unbearable, and her hips no longer controllable, thrust more and more urgently.

Deep inside she felt an incipient inundation preparing. Finally he started his cock on a slow and effortless slide into her. Once out of sight, it seemed to glide for a long time, so smoothly that she felt its every movement exploring the widening passageway, prodding gently as it made its way, seeming as if it would never stop. She knew it so well by now, that she could even visualize its delicate head making its way into the wide-open cavern.

He withdrew for an instant. Lifting up one of her legs and turning her on her side. In a fluid movement he penetrated her again from behind, their bodies curling together cradling and thrusting at the same time.

So long and intense had been the prelude, and so like silk unwinding was the feeling of him inside her, that only several moments passed before she felt a

210

profound shudder begin inside her and spread to every outpost of her body. She moaned, a low sound like the wind, tuned to the temperament of their lovemaking. A flood of liquid escaped her and spread onto the sheets. Chen lay for sometime inside her, still erect, until she urged him out with her inner muscles and turned on her back, looking up.

The ceiling directly above was made up of two large cantilevered panes of glass. Pouring out of the mist, half illuminated by an outdoor floodlight the rain streamed down the glass, directly towards them.

" Clouds and Rain", he said. She looked at him quizzically.

" Love is the play of Clouds and Rain", he said.

His whispered narrative guided her into a new world - familiar sensations defined by poetry thousands of years old. He was again kneeling between her legs.

Her precious door, was opened wide, as if to invite the rain and wind beating on the glass above to merge with her own wetness. His organ was still fully erect, and she realized that there was no evidence of his orgasm. He sat calmly, in complete control.

He lowered his mouth to her sex and licked, obviously savoring the flavor of the copious liquid. Grasping his abundant hair with one hand she raised his head, reaching to take his cock in the other.

" Don't you want?..." she whispered.

" The Tao teaches us", he said half smiling, "that if we spend our precious fluid as little as possible, and if we drink at the jade door we will remain young and beautiful. And also that if we make love to ninety-three women without ever coming, we will live forever."

" And do you expect to live forever"?, she asked.

" I doubt it." He laughed.

He placed her legs on his shoulders, looking all the while into her eyes, and entered her. Soon again the sensation of his sleek organ slipping so easily back and forth, gave her an intense pleasure, this time unexpectedly explosive. This time she screamed aloud.

After a series of small aftershocks she lay motionless. When eventually her quiescence indicated that the cycle of her pleasure was complete, he removed the gold cock ring and allowed her to suck him until he shot strong and hard and almost silently. The taste left on her lips was faintly spicy.

The rain tapered off slowly as they slipped into a sated sleep, lulled by the distant sound of the long Pacific rollers spending themselves over and over again on the deserted shore-arrived exhausted from the other side of the world.

Chapter: 13

Waking, as if after being drugged, so profoundly and dreamlessly had she slept, Selena looked curiously at the willowy supine body next to her, intimate now and yet... Although she was used to the unexpected in her life, and had always welcomed it, she could never have imagined her genius apothecary beside her in bed, nor the revelations he had offered her.

Leaving on their planned flight this evening was inconceivable now. They needed to see through what they had started, despite the cost of changing tickets.

In the days that followed, Chen showed her that legendary stretch of California from Cannery Row in Monterey to the Missions at Carmel, and San Juan Bautista to Point Lobos-the place beloved of Ansel Adams who lived nearby. They saw otters and seals cavorting out of harm's way in seas plangent with kelp, and all manner of sea birds and plant life.

Driving further south on a small road shaded at times by enormous redwoods, the biggest trees Selena had ever seen, they broke out into the massive landscape of Big Sur. Selena stared dreamily through the open window, inhaling the pungent ocean breeze, while Chen negotiated the hair-raising twists of the Coastal Highway.

This coastline, so rugged but so fragile, imprinted itself in Selena's visual memory, taking its place alongside the harshly beautiful deserts of Egypt, and the savage hills of southern Italy.

As she had thought while diving into the kelp beds, these colors which she would use for her own packaging of Creme del Mare Verde, would serve to remind her of the passionate oneness with nature that she had experienced for the first time. And this she would always owe to California and to Jimmy Chen.

Their nights had a rhythmic ritual. Jimmy's ability to delay her orgasm and his for the sake of indulging every sense was astounding, and his gentle instruction in the positions of love insistent-as if he wanted her to understand everything in these few days.

The love-making words which passed between them were from an immemorial catalogue - the jumping white tiger, the bamboos near the altar, the coiled dragon-attended by the redolent aromas of allspice, and chive, ginger and cinnabar.

Three days later when Chen had gone for a walk, she took up her diary, capturing the scenes, sensations, and smells of this particular time and this particular space. Her ceiling was the cross beams of the redwood A-frame overhead, the immense blue of the California sky seen through the slanted window panes, a glimpse into an unending space which sheltered this wild coast, the shores of the orient, and the oceans between.

Finding herself using the past tense, she sensed that this chapter might be closing even if there were more positions, more words, more food that could be explored.

Selena had the distinct feeling Chen felt, despite their intense physical intimacy, that she lived in a different world, in which he would always be a stranger, an oriental oddity in an occidental world. She would never force him to choose worlds or adapt to something innately alien.

His strength, she had learned over these last days, lay in his sensitivity as hers lay in the desire for challenge, to meet and conquer the new. They were very East-West in differences.

Then too, Selena thought of the 'grandmothers' sitting like so many malevolent crows staring out at the streets of Chinatown. The 'second son' would have to render account, to bear unendurable pressure if he were to return with a 'White devil' girl. She was almost certain it was beyond Jimmy's ability to handle. She would not ask it of him.

She knew, that they would always be bonded as colleagues. But with no need to acknowledge what had passed between them and no compulsion to continue. The future was open for them to define.

After an outdoor lunch at Nepenthe, haunt of Henry Miller and many of his artist friends, perched high over the Pacific on an infinite and cloudless day, they knew without ceremony or explanation, that it was time to return. There was so much work to do.

If Chen had thought that this might be more than a passing moment, he never let on, maintaining the familial courtesy and restraint with which he had always treated her when they came back in New York.

CEILINGS IV

Chapter 1: New York

Only the French would combine the chic and the perverse in just this way. Selena caught an image of herself in a street window as she walked toward her rendezvous with Chen and his young cousin Fat, whom she was to meet for the first time.

Moving easily in a pair of Yves St Laurent 'Jeans', she had to admit that it was amusing that one of the brightest young French couturiers had spotted, chosen, and then re-invented the tough work-a-day pants made for generations of cowhands by Levi-Strauss-and presented them to his haute couture clients. His obvious success made 'jeans', 'le dernier cri'-the latest, as the French would have it.

The sales girl had explained just how St Laurent proposed the pants be conformed-again a technique based on how the ranchmen used to break down the tough fabric. And the image of herself naked save for the jeans, in a warm running shower came back to her. The sales girl also explained the second step-that pants be permitted to dry on the body, assuring custom fit. The result outlined her hips and long legs like the proverbial second skin. With high heels and an over-size hand-knit fisherman's turtle neck, it definitely made a fashion statement in a world in which New Yorkers tended to long skirts and matching cashmere sweaters for casual wear.

Chen had to have help. Of that there was no doubt in Selena's mind. If the increased and daily increasing demand for Creme del Mare, which they had encountered in the months after their return was not enough, the lotion in development made it a necessity. They already had taken on floor helpers, who could see to the filling and packaging, but what Chen needed was scientific aid.

When he mentioned a distant cousin, who had just graduated from his old alma mater in chemical engineering, Selena's first reaction was Chemical Engineering?! Did they really need that kind of advanced technical help? But she so respected Jimmy's opinion that she felt the least she could do was meet the young man, and listen to what he had to say. She would do her best not to pre-judge the matter, although she could not help being skeptical.

She made her way up a flight of rickety linoleum covered stairs, entered a room redolent of herbs, and cooking oils, to find seated next to Chen and behind a huge mound of Dim Sum dumplings, disappearing at a rapid rate, a stout bespectacled smiling young Oriental. The contrast with Chen's lanky elegance could not have been more extreme. Froglike came immediately to her mind. He definitely looked as if he needed a princess to kiss him.

Both men rose as she came to the table, Fat quickly swallowing the last of a dumpling. She later found him to be devoted to his older cousin, with a relish for American slang, baseball, and fast cars. He stated frankly his other interest-money. But in his heart of hearts he lived for his specialty, the interface between the new field of computers and chemical engineering.

Selena and Fat hit it off immediately. There was something about his smile, and his ways of explaining complex matters in the simplest terms, without the least condescension of the scientist for the non-scientist, that was at once appealing, and she somehow knew, genuinely authoritative. It was quite apparent that he was thoroughly familiar with his field and the cutting edge of a new tool just coming into play for manufacturing-the computer.

Fat spoke casually " They're developing more power, more memory capacity. Hard drives of megabytes, speed in mega-hertz", his voice contained growing enthusiasm, his eyes, snapped with excitement. Selena , thoroughly lost, laughed. "You might as well be speaking Chinese." It was a gentle pun, meant as a joke. Chen stiffened becoming noticeably quiet, but Fat burst into his jolly laugh and told her it would not be Chinese for long. Then proceeded in a few simple sentences to explain how a computer worked.

"The central unit is really thousands of off/on switches' miniaturized and put in tandem and series. The stuff you feed into the keyboard gets translated for the digestion of the computer into a series of yes/no, off/on options. Get it?"

"As a matter of fact I do."

"Great! But remember there is a major glitch for all computers. As we 'hackers' like to say, garbage in garbage out".

"Your computer is only as good as what you feed it?" Selena with her open mind grasped immediately the problem and potential.

"Give the little lady a cigar"-Fat quoted a popular comedian as he wiggled his eyebrows, tapped the ash off an imaginary cigar, and giggled helplessly at his own wit. So did Selena.

Then he said, turning serious,"Actually within the next years, we should be able to link it to automation. It will revolutionize the mechanical part of manufacturing processes, including Selena products."

His statement was that of an expert, visualizing a reality of the near future,with unmistakable sureness and accuracy. Selena was impressed, and then pleased as he went on, explaining specifically how they could take advantage of these new techniques to guarantee consistency and accuracy of formulae. Selena listened with increasing appreciation of his insight into the world she wanted to create.

And it was Fat who perceived that the base which she and Chen had created, would serve as the base for all the products she had in mind-explaining that the base would never change, but the adjunctives would turn the end product into astringent, or shampoo or, cleanser or soap, or even a make-up base.

Selena was thrilled. In his thinking Fat simply assumed the long-term vision of her products. And his assumption lent the validity of scientific approach to her creative ideas and imagination.

"That's terrific, Fat!" Selena was thrilled. His vision of the future matched hers. She had the feeling that Chen and Fat would prove a fantastic alliance of abilities.

She was fascinated to see Chen defer to his young cousin in the area of manufacturing and development, and pleased that Fat in turn was so impressed with what Chen had already achieved. It was clear they would work well together.

The discussion then turned to when she could anticipate the lotion. A cleansing cream was ready to test out with clients. They were talking of no more than a few months at best, Chen assured her. Selena was happy with what was happening. She tucked into her Dim Sum w0ith a will.

Over desert, She turned to Fat " When can you begin with us?"

"Now, ma'am," the young man answered without hesitation

"Monday? "

"Yes."

They were both sure of their decisions. Fat thought Selena astonishing in her quickness and understanding. He approved of her ambition, liked her and wanted to

220

be a part of things.

All in all, lunch proved a miracle of accomplishment. Selena could hardly wait to tell Maria about all it promised.

If they had been Italian, the two men would have left the restaurant arm in arm. Being Chinese as they rose to leave, they bowed slightly to one another, then turned and bowed low to her.

Later when Chen phoned to thank her for her trust in his cousin, she told him she felt they were lucky to get him.

Over the years, the quick judgment to take on the odd young man was to prove right over and over again.

Chapter: 2

1967 had come by the time the riots taking place in Los Angeles gave a section called Watts lurid headlines in East Coast Newspapers and produced one of Warhol's famous fifteen minutes of fame as far as recalled American history was concerned.

Manhattan women, along with hundreds across the country, reading the titillating details of designer drug abuse in the world of films and modeling, made Jacqueline Susanne a household name.

John somehow managed tickets for the Opening night for the New Metropolitan Opera Home at Lincoln Center. Where Leontyne Price sang the lead role in the premier of Samuel Barber's Anthony and Cleopatra under thousands of priceless chandeliers from Switzerland's Nestle company, gigantic murals by the Russian artist Chagall, and a white-tie and tails, haute couture long evening dress assembly of New York's most chic.

On Monday Maria came bursting into the salon, breathless. She pounced before Selena could get started on her first customer, pulling her into the back room, and almost pushed her into the nearest chair. Selena was unable to protest, or get a word in edgewise.

"Cara, we must do something!", her tone was a command, "Subito!" She insisted steam-rolling ahead. "But just look at this!"

She thrust one page after another of the appointment calendar before Selena's eyes, forcing her to look at the scrawled names, erasures, and write-overs that blurred the pages without interruption from top to bottom.

Selena stared at the sheets, wondering how she

would get through this schedule, even with the help of her full time assistant. It was almost laughable. Do I have a worst enemy I could wish this on, she thought.

She looked again at the schedule, then at Maria, and sighed.

"Well, let me think..." she began, only to be forestalled from saying anything more by Maria, who flipped the pages of the weeks to come in front of her young friend's eyes.

" Basta!" Maria said, taking back the limp pages. "Selena, These you see, eh?... What you do not see", she added, "is all those I must refuse. There is no room, there is no time, there is no help. "Che cosa dici!". What can one say?!

"So.." Selena responded at a loss for a helpful answer.

"So. We must do two things. Uno-you must train other assistants. Due-we must make another salon, e Tre- we must provide for you to sell your cream and lotions without interrupting your work."

Selena knew Maria was right. Lack of time and space had caught up with her, and she must take steps. Chen wanted her to work out a testing scheme for the new astringent. He and Fat had just completed work on its prototype. Fat wanted her to see a trade exposition demonstrating a computer driven small manufacturing process.

Maria knew she was being pulled here and there with demands on her time. And couldn't help worrying. Selena took the older woman in her arms, noting the increasing gray in her hair, and the careful way Maria disguised the misery of her hands. Mornings especially they were painful, stiff and swollen-a source of embarrassment which she was able to hide from the world but not her protégé.

"Tesoro mio, You count beautifully and know best."

"And so today I will begin to look for a good place for us."

"Si. And Maria...I think no longer here in the Quartiere", she added.

It was as if Maria had read her mind. " D'accordo. I thought perhaps the beginning of Fifth Avenue."
She referred to the first few blocks above Washington Square, a prestigious and prosperous residential area of large well-kept apartment buildings, interspersed with small shops and specialty stores.

Within weeks Maria found a promising location with semi-frosted windows fronting both Fifth Avenue and an attractive side street. Ideal to display Selena's products, and give a glimpse of the activities going on within without affording actual vision.

'Privacy and promise', Selena said when she saw it. Perfect! She took a long-term lease on the space immediately.

Over dinner, the two women decided the space layout and equipment needed, giving special attention to the lighting. Selena's colors, sea green and coral, would be used exclusively through out.

The front of the salon would be given over to products, the back would serve as a treatment center. There was even a small space overlooking an interior courtyard garden which Maria insisted Selena needed for her own. Maria would see to the hiring of young assistants, Selena to their training,

Earlier Selena had earlier gone to a sign makers studio, and there overseen the design she wanted applied to the store windows in colors matching the interior-The name written large in her own hand.

She also went to a printer who refined the signature for use on all her labels. He'd used a word with which she was unfamiliar-Logo, and explained it would go on everything and identify them as hers.

He did a sample business card. On the face was Selena Ltd in her hand, and under it the word in conventional print "Botanica", which stated boldly what gave all her products their distinctive character. The printer indicated the bottom of the card where the address and telephone number would go.

Selena looked directly at him and said simply, "No. Not like this. I want whoever handles this card to have to turn it over to see how to reach Selena Ltd. It will help impress the address and telephone number on their minds."

"But," he said. That is not the way it's ..."

"No buts", Selena interrupted, a little impatient with him for not seeing the strength of the idea, "this is the way I want it, and this is the way it will be."

The printer perforce, had to give in. After all she was the one paying for the job.

Over the years, it was one of those instinctive choices which was to prove absolutely right.

As to the name, Selena had given it a lot of thought. Inferred in the name was a business organization behind it, implied was a certain exclusivity.

The word Botanica signified to Selena, and she hoped it would come to do so for her customers, that her products were based on the organic, on natural biota. But it was also a word meant to tantalize. It was meant to pique curiosity. It was not, after all, a commonly used word.

As to that business organization, she knew she would have to do something about it, and soon. It's future was now. It's demands pressed today. She must answer them.

That night she called John and brought him up to date. He listened and agreed whole-heartedly.

"Selena, you have two shops, a factory and lab. It's time you put the whole thing on a professional basis.

It's way beyond what you, Maria , Chen, and yes, even Fat, with his computer can manage."

Selena felt an unfamiliar one step behind. With John, she felt safe even though vulnerable because she trusted him. Fat and she had started a primitive accounting system. In his spare time he produced sheets which she hoped would satisfy the tax people. Now she was aware of an area of inadequcy and need that had to be tended.

"You are quite right, John. I'm getting into waters I know nothing about."

"I want you to meet Noah van Vloeck. He's my legal and business advisor, and an old friend. If he agrees to take you on, I think he's the man for you. I'll set a meeting up here. Next week good?"

"Yes. Almost any night except Tuesday. I promised Fat I would go look at the latest toy he's drooling over. It's a little too soon to be useful to us, but I think he wants to get me used to the idea. Rob the future of shock." She sighed. "I think he's probably right."

She knew Fat would grin if he heard her talking. And would give her the successful boxer's hands over head congratulations gesture.

Chapter: 3

"Noah, this is Selena."

She turned from the blaze in John's fireplace to face a large figure standing absolutely still in the middle of the room as if awaiting what she would do or say once she saw him.

He's like a giant sea otter, impossibly large, impossibly sleek, she thought. He was easily John's height but had twice the heft with powerful broad shoulders. His hair grey but darkened by faintly perfumed brilliantine, and slicked straight back off a high forehead. There were deep lines across his forehead and around his eyes. She guessed his age in the mid fifties. His eyes were hazel, a green flecked with brown, framing a long straight nose. A wide mobile mouth with faintly mocking upturned corners completed the image.

"Piacere." he said in a light baritone. The Italian accent flawless. He crossed the room to where she was standing, his gait slow, almost ponderous which puzzled her as she knew John played squash with the man twice a week, and complained that he consistently lost to him. She wondered whether her first physical impression was right. Otters were quick and graceful. Noah was almost hulking and measured in movement. But then she remembered two other things which made her smile. Otters were at their most graceful when actually in water, and on land they loved to play games of misdirection, of feint and pop.

He wore hand made shoes, an old tweed jacket, an impeccable tailored shirt pulled loose at the neck but still held by a quiet tie, sartorial contradictions but the whole worked.

In the European way, he raised her hand toward his lips without making actual contact. That she knew could only be learned in a Latin country, it was so fluid and unself-conscious. And on further thought added, learned a long time ago, long enough to be second nature.

"Shall we sit?" Noah asked, as if he were the host. John smiled, used to Noah's ways and not bothered in the least.

"I'll get some wine, shall I", was all he said and disappeared in the direction of the kitchen.

Not releasing Selena's hand, Noah led her to a sofa, seated her, turned found a large wing chair, and settled himself down crossing an ankle over his knee.

"I like to smoke," he stated. And took a case from an inner pocket, extracted a large Cuban cigar, and looked inquiringly at Selena. She simply nodded assent, wondering what would have happened if she'd indicated she did mind.

Noah went through the ritual of lighting the cigar with complete equanimity. When she knew him much better, Selena would have known he would have refrained from smoking with the same calmness and acceptance had she objected. He continued to look at her with interest but made no effort at conversation.

Selena thought, he looked out of scale as he sat smoking contentedly, too large for the intimacy of John's simple wood and leather living room. It was as if he belonged in a framework of skyscrapers gracing an enormous corner-view office or even in the huge formality of a federal courtroom. She learned later she was absolutely right in this perception.

Selena let her thoughts drift in an easy silence. John adapted to his surroundings wherever he found himself, without fuss or problem. In many settings, especially the unfamiliar, Chen simply folded up inside himself, out of touch and almost invisible. This man seemed to overwhelm his surroundings.

She couldn't help but continue her thoughts, as John hadn't returned from the kitchen, and Noah showed no inclination to open conversation yet. If I proceed with this man, get to know his skills and knowledge, I wonder what I will think of him then.

Noah saw a stunning young woman, seated entirely at ease. Her feather-cut shining hair molded the strong features of her face. She wore little make up or more accurately the little she wore complemented the sharp cheekbones and brilliant eyes that needed little enhancement. She called to mind the image of a young Grecian autocrat he had once seen profiled on a coin from the Hellenic period.

He felt attracted. She was different. Novel. And it pulled him like the first day of a trial, or the first words of a book. He wanted to know her better.

John returned. Selena watched him as he poured out two glasses from an old, dust-encrusted bottle, Swirled the wine in both glasses and handed one to Selena, the other to Noah.

"What a lovely wine", Noah said after a sip. Then raised a eyebrow inquiringly.

" A 55 Terrefort Quancard" John had chosen a medium bodied Bordeaux from a very small vineyard. Noah toasted his selection in the only way for true wine lovers, a silent appreciation of smell, look and taste. John had told Selena that Noah might have been a Tastevin in another life, he was certainly what the French called a 'top amateur" which really meant a real expert, and lover.

When they had consumed most of their first glasses, Noah turned to Selena addressing her quietly, his vowels prolonged in a sound usually heard on Philadelphia's Mainline.

"Tell me where you are now...."

"Where I am..." For a moment Selena was thrown by the form of the question, then understood that John had supplied enough background that Noah felt he could ask a totally open-ended question, letting her start wherever and however she wished.

"History first." She responded.

Noah nodded.

"Over the last three years, I have created, with the help of my pharmacist, a face cream, lotion, and astringent. They are made in a laboratory on Canal Street, sold in my salon on Mott Street, and I have just opened a store on lower Fifth Avenue.

""And the present..."

"Now we are working on a cleanser and a tonic. I think we're near ready to start on a line of cosmetics. Fat thinks within the next year or two."

"You mean lipstick, rouge, base, and eye products? All?"

Selena appreciated Noah's comprehension.

"And then next...?"

"More like at the same time, I'm almost sure I will want to open on Madison Avenue."

"Why not upper Fifth avenue?" Noah asked with a note of challenge in his voice. In the late sixties, Fifth Avenue in its middle reaches, encompassed all the smart department stores, Tailored Woman, Best's, Altmans, Lord and Taylor, Saks Fifth Avenue and Bergdorf Goodman higher up.

"Fifth Avenue is the present, but Madison Avenue is the future especially for small chic salons and boutiques. And the future for me I think."

"Why?"

"The beautiful stores of Fifth Avenue are large. Splendid sometimes, but large. Women and makeup is not about large, It's about intimate. It's very focused.

Their selection is intensely personal. These large settings are not right for it. They are too impersonal, too dispersed, too public."

"John, how long did you say Selena has spoken English?"

John chuckled. " Don't be such an elitist Noah. Even someone not born and bred on the East Coast can acquire a good command of the language."

Secretly he was thrilled that his former pupil had become so fluent.

Selena simply cocked an eyebrow at the man who posed such a question. Before she could form a rejoinder however, Noah unfolded his large frame, rose and began to walk slowly back and forth in front of the fire. She recognized it was what she often did when thinking.

Noah paused, and asked," And how have you financed all this?"

"In the beginning, John loaned me money. This has been repaid. Now money from Mott Street has paid for most of the laboratory and lower Fifth Avenue. Maria, my original patron, and the bank where I deposit my money, have made up the rest. To date the bank is almost paid off. They told me they will consider money for Madison Avenue.

"The Bank will 'consider'... is that what they told you?" Noah asked in the softest tone he had yet used.

"Yes."

John looked up at the face of his friend and was satisfied with what he saw. He knew Noah well enough to know he was impressed. Selena had done this with just a few words and ideas.

"And the future...?"

For the first time there was some uncertainty in the response. "I'm not entirely clear." The emphasis was on 'entirely'

"You know where you've been. You know how you got from there to here, and are open about the future. Would you say that sums it up?"

"Yes", Selena waited to see what would follow.

"Fine. That's all I need for today." Noah settled his jacket, straightened his tie, and prepared to leave. "We'll talk together at the end of the week if that's convenient."

John rose. Got his coat and shook hands warmly.

"Arriverderla", Noah said, again bending over her hand. He turned and left swiftly without another word.

"My God, John," Selena said, her mouth open, "What was that all about? What happened?"

"Translation, my love.... First, you just saw what his colleagues call the quickest business mind in semi-captivity in action. And I know from experience also legally he's as tough and aggressive as they come. Second, He wants to take you on as a client."

"How do you know?'

"He would have said 'no' before he left. My reading is-he wants to give his advice some thought, form a business plan, work out your next steps.

"How does he know that I want to take him on", she asked with some severity.

"I don't think it ever entered his mind that you wouldn't", John's expression was mock judicious. "But you will decide at the end of the week how you feel about that after you see what he proposes."

"Vediamo", Selena said with a laugh, "We will wait to see what the Otter has in mind."

She got up and went towards the kitchen, " And now caro mio, I think I shall make us a pasta and salad. You bought all I told you? Pomodori, basilico, Parmigano? "

"Certamente."

"Benissimo!" Selena gave him a quick kiss on her

way to the kitchen.

After she passed, without thinking, John put a hand to the spot she'd kissed for a moment. It was a gesture she would have understood better than he.

They had dinner. Afterwards they sat comfortably in the living room on either side of the fire. John replenished the oak logs.

"You know, I never did ask you how much trouble you got into in California." It was as near as John would ever get to possessiveness. Selena realized he was a little anxious.

"We were able to set up the kelp supply, which is working well. Fat has smoothed out the process of hyper-oxygenation. At this point we're really set."

John realized that for Selena this was an answer. A small sigh escaped him, and a momentary regret for the young girl he had met, now replaced by what had become a formidable independent and subtle young woman.

"And now, John. Tell me about the Otter."

"As I've already told you, he's brilliant, ruthless, eccentric even egregious."

She smiled at him, "And now I know many of those many syllable words you so love".

"John, he reminds me of a light switch or as Fat explained to me the other day one of those tiny units which make up the computer-it's either off or on, there's no in between. With Noah you feel his presence full force or not at all, almost as if he's absent from the room."

"Yes. I think that's pretty accurate." John responded, and Selena knew she would have to be satisfied with that statement. But still she wanted to know something more of this man who might become important to her future.

It was an odd history. John knew parts of it, but only Noah knew it all.

Chapter: 4

The van Vloecks were a contentious, artistic, opinonated, and idiosyncratic Dutch family from Hoek of Holland.

For generations they had been sought after as designers and makers of the fine Siberian fur coats which protected the more discerning burger wives against the bitter Lowland winters. But it was this first characteristic which ultimately caused them to emigrate from Holland in a fit of religious pique.

Among the earliest settlers to arrive in the Americas, they arrived in the era of the Minuits, the Dyckmans, and the Van Dykes. With them, they settled New Amsterdam.

It was the second characteristic that was useless in the raw new country to which they'd come. Sophisticated design and creation of stylish furs being superfluous to the life style they found there.

This forced them to analyze their position, and decide, that the chevron branch of the family would go into fur trapping.

The successful Astor family had shown the profitability of this endeavor. The elder branch would see to the financing of not only of their own expeditions, but naturally, those of Astor's competitors-entirely compatible with the primary family characteristic.

At that time New York deferred to the Astors in all spheres. The Van Vloecks, were unwilling to defer to the dominance of a family they perceived as financial peers but social inferiors.

They moved to Philadelphia, arguably the most sophisticated and cultured community in the new world. And there, despite their character, they thrived since the city was very much the purview of the Quakers, who did not acknowledge contentiousness, but did appreciate acumen and style. They settled down in tandem if not harmony, and prospered.

Several decades later, the American Colonies rebelled, declaring war against the English Empire. Perhaps more specifically Germanically rigid over-taxation by a poorly advised and often quite mad British Monarch.

Most of the old Dutch families and Patroons sided with England, a matter of temperament and tradition, against the loose confederacy and rag-tag antics of continental troops lead by an American part-time military leader. A home-grown jumped-up general.

The Van Vloecks recognized as fundamental that which was as true of the 'American revolution' as it was to be of a much later twentieth century war 'the conflict in Vietnam', that war cannot be won at a distance. Local supply and turf-familiarity falling to the native side would always win out in the end. And so, they supported outwardly, and more to the point monetarily the cause of the rebels.

The result of most choices put many prominent old Dutch families into financial decline, when the 'wrong side' won. Not so the Van Vloecks. Post war left them as important financiers and bankers in the new capitol of the United States. Both they and their colleagues the Quakers survived and prospered.

Changes in manufacturing and farming in the nineteenth century provided great opportunities for advancement. Especially if one were in the business of financing these changes. And the Van Vloecks were.

And then came the 'War between the States'. They came down firmly on the side of the industrial North, although their natural sensibilities might have led to emotional support of the great estates and lifestyle of the more prosperous of the South.

The fortunes made during this war were immense compared to what had gone before.

Having amassed enormous moneys, which re-investment increased exponentially, there then seemed a lack of challenge in the fiduciary world, at least to the males of the family, who turned to more overt conflicts. The Spanish War, World War I, the Loyalist struggle in Spain, and finally the Second World War, which effectively decimated the family. Leaving his Father, and in turn Noah as sole surviving Van Vloeck men.

Noah's mother was a Delano, ethereal, blonde beyond blonde, educated entirely at home, spoiled and unworldly. Her universe was limited to the view from the thousands of family acres overlooking the Hudson River, and the world seen and interpreted by carefully screened tutors. She was given in marriage at the age of seventeen to van Vloeck.

Noah's Father was a world class sportsman and hunter. His presence and activities dictated by the seasons of prey-deer, grouse, duck, fox along with lion and tiger. His skill on a horse elicited a bid to become a member of the Olympic team in 1938, the year 'the American negroe', an 'ubermensch,' Jessie Owens made a mockery of the vaunted German athletic superiority. He turned the offer down. He was to be married that year.

He thought his bride and wife would accompany him to the estates and manors around the world to which he was invited, at least that was what he envisaged.

So much was public history.

The rest was familiar only to Noah and much of it seen through a glass darkly, as one poet described his vision of his own life.

One year after they were married Noah was born. It was a difficult pregnancy, and an even more difficult delivery. The fine Delano bones and framework made child-bearing a hell from which his mother would never completely recover, and which she would never repeat. Even had she wanted, the birth effectively destroyed her uterus as a functioning organ.

With no inner resources, and no self-reliance as an individual, Noah's mother withdrew from her household, her son, and of course her husband, plunging into a world of prescriptive drugs, drink, and finally protracted 'visits' to relatives many of which covered bizarre, ill-considered sexual escapades, all the result of schizophrenia-unrecognized at the time, and in any case untreatable.

Appearances were kept up. The household was run impeccably by a housekeeper and large staff. Her absences went unremarked, her well-bred husband continued his rounds of hunting, but her son haunted the hallways of the mansion awaiting permission to visit his mother when she was in residence.

To Noah, his mother was a distant, fairy-tale creature who was seen never before noon, and then perfumed and peignored. She existed for him as a dream, a figure of fantasy. For the rest of his life the scent of the her hair, the roses she always kept fresh in her boudoir, the Guerlain perfumes she wore, evoked the yearning for closeness with this delicate and unattainable icon of a woman.

Living with this unfilled longing was a wound so deeply hidden he did recognize it until he grew up, and then could do little but endure it.

The elder Van Vloeck tended to maintenance of his son, and the family fortune as a matter of duty or perhaps conscience. His heart was in the sporting life he led in many corners of the world. But he visited the mansion on Philadelphia's Mainline every few months, to make sure the boy was being well looked after, his agents were keeping things up to snuff financially, and his wife's indiscretions were adequately blanketed. He was fully aware of the nature and frequency of them.

One day, the nine-year-old Noah came home early from school, with a minor ailment. Deposited by the chauffeur in the front entry way, he paused as always, and searched the air for the fresh scent of l'Heure Bleu that would tell him that his mother was at home, and which held the promise of a deliciously fragrant embrace.

Quietly climbing the main staircase, past the formal sitting rooms, the study, and the huge dining room, not wanting to wake her in case she was, as often, 'sleeping', he paused at the top of the landing leading to the family quarters.

Strange cries greeted his ears. Frightened lest something had happened to her, he rushed towards her bedroom door and flung it open.

Over the footboard of the ornate bed, he was face to face with his mother's naked torso, gyrating, bathed in sweat, a horribly unfamiliar grimace on her face, as she uttered animal moans.

Lurching a few steps into the darkened room, uncomprehending, he saw that his mother was astride a man, whose face was hidden. Only his legs and feet were visible. It was ridiculous and horrible.

" Noah...Darling.." his mother gasped out, reaching for him. The man, a stranger, peered around from behind her, annoyed at the interruption.

Noah froze for what seemed an eternity, then ran to his room, where he burrowed into darkness and silence. His mother came in. It was a first. She took him in her arms smelling heavily of newly applied perfume, liquor and the sex she had just had. Without explanation, she kissed his mouth almost as if now he knew, he were to be her preferred lover.

He was sickened, repelled. He shoved her roughly away. She staggered, her robe, came partly open. He stared fascinated by the white flesh it revealed. Then gestured wildly for her to get out. She smiled crookedly, in a parody of appeasement and seduction. But when he repeated the violent gesture, she had to leave.

After he watched her stagger out, he knew he had been wildly attracted. He couldn't hate her, but his adulation had turned to the need for distance. He left the next week for boarding school.

Within a month, without once leaving her bedroom, unwashed, and unattended-offers of meals always refused, she managed a lethal overdose of drugs, vanishing from the face of the earth as if she had never existed.

Noah, standing at her graveside grieved. His father perfectly attired in conventional mourning, felt nothing but relief.

Matters concerning his wife and son suitably arranged, he parted several days later for a trek in Mongolia, to be followed by return to his habitual peripetic existance.

For Noah, St. Paul's was followed by Princeton, an M.B.A. at Wharton and a Law degree from the University of Pennsylvania. All before the age of 26. And then an incredible work schedule.

His father was shocked. None of the Van Vloecks had been geniuses or scholars, and certainly none slaves to work of any kind. He himself managed a life of complete avocation, and died at ninety having never experienced anything other than its indulgence.

The summer of his graduation from law school, as if sleepwalking, Noah, bowing to the expected and the thought of children, went into engagement and marriage with a Mainline debutante from a prominent family.

It was a disaster from the outset. After the first night of his honeymoon, having drunken far too much to have a clear recollection of the "first night" or the actual deflowering of his new wife, he fled. He was panic- stricken, even claustrophobic at the idea of lockstep marriage with this well bred, conventional girl, of bondage in a marriage as unhappy as his Father's.

The upshot was a scandalous divorce, and a son Paul, with whom he was permitted visitation rights on neutral grounds.

In New York, to which he moved, he became the much-prized perpetually eligible and secretive bachelor. He received numberless invitations, and accepted those which were for engagements which interested him, rejecting those which were merely "useful" or "socially desirable". He was a loner.

His sartorial perfection and informed conversation gave no clue as to his inner thoughts, or for that matter his shark-like legal success. He never discussed business out of business hours, and he never discussed his personal life altogether.

His physical energy was spent in ferocious squash games, and his mental energy went into his work. Rejecting the harness, and case confines of a partnership offered him by an old-line firm, he struck out into the world of corporate start-ups and corporate starters, of speculative investments, and investors.

The conventional, established or accepted, held little interest. Money in and of itself was not an end- but the thrill of fighting and winning over great odds was. He became the lawyer to have for those who needed, or perhaps had to have, a strategist, and cutthroat if push came to shove.

He was an old friend and attorney to John Harvey. He chose now to take on Selena.

With this in mind, he called her, asked for a meeting at Café des Artistes, one of the places frequented by the quiet movers and shakers of the city for lunch, and told how he wanted her to dress for the meeting.

Chapter: 5

Seated side by side, Noah and John watched the progress of the slim figure of Selena as she was ushered towards them by the Maitre d, clearly happy to escort such an attractive woman to her table. Her breathless haste so added to her allure, that they simultaneously forgave her lateness.

John was astounded, Noah pleased that she had understood and executed his intention to a fare-thee-well. No one, neither male nor female lunching on this particular day in the Café des Artistes, would soon forget Selena Di Angelo.

She was dressed in a bias-cut fuschia Rucci-Chado wool suit which set off her naturally beautiful skin. She was dressed for success. The color of her suit being a powerful statement, she was sparingly adorned apart from a pair of heavy gold earrings in an original Fulco di Vedure design.

The combination of taste, unabashed and Latin sensuality was not to be ignored. Her cleavage was understated, but framed by the vivid color and texture of the outfit. Heads turned.

She sat down quickly, a waft of enticing scent lifted, from the back of her neck exposed by a French twist. Neither man recognized the charm of Diorissimo, but each resolved to find out its name.

Both were silent as Selena apologized for being late explaining briefly a problem at the new salon. What she did not say was when she left, she saw two Chinese men dressed in out of date business suits, engaged in prolonged conversation at the corner of Fifth Avenue. Something about their presence on this corner nagged at her. Without really thinking why, she walked several blocks until she no longer saw them and only then took a cab. Having gotten a slightly late start, the traffic heading uptown compounded her lateness.

Finally caught in a real snarl, she asked her cab to let her off on Central Park West, two blocks from the restaurant. Again she thought she glimpsed two Orientals in the block behind her. Could they have possibly followed her?

She was not normally paranoid or fearful, but these areas were not places where one would expect to see Orientals. Perhaps she should talk to Chen about it. Other than that there was little to be done. But she dismissed the whole thing the minute she stepped into the restaurant excited by what the lunch meeting might bring.

John drank in the familiar husky sound of her lightly accented voice, her smell, the wisps of hair which escaped the twist, at the nape of her neck.

Noah had already filed away her sensational entrance, and began to use his flair for promotion to contemplate the possibilities. He saw a naturally gifted businesswoman, perhaps too much guided by instinct and emotion, a little too confident of them, ferociously ambitious and in need of business advice.

He must explain to her that the world's money and power was, in principle spoken for. She would have a share only if she fought for it. Noah had drawn this conclusion long ago, and it fueled the aggression for which his clients paid him handsomely.

As they ordered and ate, Noah explained that a limited partnership was the form he felt best for her business at this stage of its development. The investors would share equally with her in the profits but all decisions and responsibility would reside with her, the general partner.

Selena looked at him for a moment frowning.

"What is it," Noah asked, "have you some objection?"

"I want Maria and Chen to be a part of the general partnership."

"No, Selena. Give them a small part of the limited partners share if you must, but never any part of control." He was absolutely adamant.

Unshaken, and meeting his eyes calmly Selena gave her reasons. She would reward those who helped her, there was no question about it. Noah found her attitude foolhardy but charming. In the end he was almost sure he would bring her around to giving monetary rewards not part control, to her helpers, with perhaps a small number of shares in the company to be set up.

Still he was impressed. And intrigued. She was the polar opposite of most of the women at whose right he habitually sat at the smart New York dinners he had to attend.

Noah went to the next topic he wanted to cover. Chen must assign any and all rights or patents to the new company. The rights to Selena products and processes must inhere in the company. It was what gave fundamental and objective value. Ownership of the rights together with the thriving salons would enable them to raise appropriate capital.

"Can we get Chen to a face to face meeting?

"I think so."

"I find it's much easier to explain this sort of thing with all people involved present."

Selena felt he was right. She for one would be more comfortable explaining to Chen in person. She hadn't seen as much of him as she would have liked to recently, and didn't trust communication with him on paper with something this important.

Noah asked that a meeting be set up in his office a week hence when he'd lay out the position, and Chen could sign the requisite releases. Only then could the products be adequately trademarked.

He would have his son Paul, an attorney whose specialty was trademarking and patents, draw the necessary papers and see to the registration.

John following the course of the conversation, said when he saw doubt on her face, "Selena, Noah is absolutely right. Not only for what you've developed so far, but think of all the potential products. You must establish clear ownership and rights and now as well as a clear business entity which you and you only control." After several moments of thought Selena nodded reluctantly, seeing the wisdom of what both men were saying.

"Now" said Noah, somewhere around the time espresso was served, "there are two other matters I want to go over today. If you agree, I can get the paper work done and over to you for signature within the next few days."

Selena again nodded.

"The first is, I would like your consent to approach Nieman Marcus to set up a Selena Botanica boutique in their Dallas store."

It was a choice based on his knowledge of their balance sheets, and expansion plans through out the United States, the high visibility and quality of their catalogue, and a personal relationship with the President of the company which permitted him to pick up a phone and complete a deal with a simple conversation.

"You will have virtual control of the outlet. It will give you branches, without having to capitalize and create them entirely on your own. I would think that their share of the costs of set-up should be in the range of 60% and of net profits about 30% "

Selena saw his idea had validity, and would give her a good base outside of New York. And again nodded her approval.

"Lastly, you need capital. You must never rely on a bank as the sole source of money. They have an odd way of ending up making all your business decisions for you, especially if you let them do the exclusive financing. Here is a list of possible investment sources."

He handed Selena a list of twenty names, at the bottom of which were two which were familiar. Opposite them Noah had noted- Harvey, $1,000,000 and van Vloeck $2,500,000, which he had also marked down opposite the name of the Hanover Bank. Selena stared open mouthed. Noah chuckled.

"You have mastered making an entrance and first impression, now you must learn the art of 'whatever you offer is no less than I expected' ."

Selena shut her mouth, and again nodded acknowledgment of what he was saying.

As lunch finished, Selena thought, things had changed for her, never to return to how they had been. It was a change not of degree, but of kind, an enormous challenge. She saw that Noah was entirely convinced she was up to it. Now she had to prove him right.

Chapter: 6

From her vantage point Annie Karol Katz was able to observe Selena as she in turn inspected her corner store-across the street, from a distance, passing by, and finally close up. And saw her nod as if in satisfaction.

"It's really eye-catching don't you think?" Annie asked in a voice that was nearly baritone. It was the result of years of chain smoking. Often, hearing its tones, people looked to see who other than the rail-thin woman might have been speaking, but soon learned there was only Annie.

Selena started. She was so wrapped up in considering whether the name of the salon was visible from all vantage points, she was jolted when someone spoke to her. She turned around.

"I'm sorry," Annie apologized, raising her hands in the universal gesture of good will, "I didn't mean to startle you." Then as Selena caught her breath, she introduced herself.

"My name is Annie Karol Katz. I'm a features reporter with the Village Voice. And if by any chance you don't recognize that name-It's the local rag, or if you care to dignify it-Newspaper. I am what is loosely called one of its feature writers."

Annie referred to a local newspaper, esteemed, supported, and bought religiously by 'Villagers' as their own journal.

This spate of information, coming from a stranger in the middle of her thoughts made for a certain amount of disorientation. Things didn't get much clearer when the ebullient young woman went on with what seemed like a non-sequitur.

"I noticed the paint is practically still wet on your

sign." She grinned.

Selena was still puzzled, but responded, "Actually we've been open a week, and thankfully we've been relatively busy."

Annie picked up on the contradiction-a charming foreign accent, and a sophisticated syntax and phrasing. She also noted that Selena's statement was backed by seeing several customers arriving while another left.

Actually, she had been watching the comings and goings long enough to know that the traffic was brisk for a small newly opened Village salon.

"Let me try again. I'm a nice Jewish girl from Rockaway Beach, currently employed, if that's the word to use for the pittance they pay me, by the 'Voice'. And you are the Selena of Selena Ltd., are you not?"

Selena nodded.

Actually Annie had long since concluded that the inspection she had just witnessed had to be that of a proprietor.

"We've been doing a series on interesting new shops opening downtown. I think you and your salon should be included."

Selena was pleased with the idea, and said so.

"That, is a refreshing reaction"

Annie referrd to what was common knowledge. The attitudes of the editorial and feature columns of The Voice were inclined toward the critical, tending to favor exposé. It gave the paper much of its color and interest, but made for wariness, even reluctance in some interviewees.

Selena invited her into the Salon. Showed her the Creme del Mare products, had her see a 'look' being created, and took her back into the tiny back room office.

"As an executive suite, it qualifies as a broom closet", was Annie's comment. They both laughed.

Over espresso, Selena answered the reporter's questions. They ranged over the beginnings and growth of Selena Ltd. She explained the significance of Botanica. And talked of future plans and products. But never anything about her personal history.

Annie was redheaded, freckled, and homely as a mud fence-as the expression went. Her habitual dress was the nearest thing to hand as she dashed out of her walk-up flat in the mornings. Things matched or they didn't. It was of no particular importance. However, she had charm to spare. Her lively wit, and intelligence, made her an ideal feature writer. Her subjects responded to her questions recognizing that her interest was genuine. Her editors trusted that she would bring them a well-founded story.

If she uncovered weakness, or even ill-intent in one of her subjects, it would be reported-framed in wryly understated but devastating prose.

Annie understood precisely what a weapon humor and irony could be leveled on the subjects she thought deserving of its deadly effect.

If her subject showed imagination, or creativity no matter if flawed, it would be treated with respect and honor. Her readers knew they would get a fair, informative article written with style and perception.

When Annie brought up Selena's origins, the subject was subtly dismissed. The reporter perceived it was a sensitive area but since it didn't affect the heart of the story in any substantial way, didn't pursue it. Another time, perhaps.

She liked what she saw of the energy, the ambition, and honesty of this young Italian imigree.

After they had covered most of the information she needed for the article, Annie brought out a clipping from the day's N.Y. Post.

"Did you see Cholly Knickerbocker today?"

Selena took the clipping , looking at it puzzled.

"Don't tell me", Annie chortled, "It wasn't a plant after all."

Selena was really at sea, and Annie recognized the reaction as genuine.

"Selena, Cholly Knickerbocker, and page 6 of the Post, is where everyone who wants mention or notoriety, wants to be 'seen'."

"See here", she said pointing to a small paragraph and reading aloud, "What luscious young dark-haired companion dressed head to toe in Schiaparelli, was seen last week with Wall Street shark Noah Van Vloeck, and Bio-author John Harvey at Café des Artistes, lunching tête á tête? "

In a flash of understanding, Selena knew why Noah had asked her to dress for the occasion. It was to be the beginning of notice which would help build recognition of Selena Ltd.

She explained, how it had come about. Annie, again refreshed by the directness, advised her to heed Noah and nurture what he had started.

"You can't buy publicity more valuable than this kind.

Their meeting resulted in immediate liking and respect. They were kindred spirits and became fast friends from this encounter on.

Many years later, after she had become editor-in-chief of Vanity Fair, and had written several books, Annie was always available to Selena when she needed the best advice in the area of publicity and effect on public money couldn't buy.

Spontaneously, Selena asked if Annie would permit her to do a 'Look' for her. The result was so striking, that Annie never again used anything but Selena's cosmetics, applied as she had been taught in the salon on lower Fifth Avenue.

Selena had to drag her in, and personally modify the look when ten years had passed, and Annie's face was no longer that of a thirty year old. For Annie it was a trauma to be endured and undergone only because her friend insisted, that some changes had to be made. But again the look that Selena created met with her whole-hearted approval.

As she left the boutique, Annie promised to send over a preview of her article.

Still later that day, Paul van Vloeck, Noah's son, arrived with a briefcase full of documents. Noah had written out in full a projected business plan based on their discussions, with detailed explanations as to the legal and technical aspects. All figures were annotated clearly and concisely.

Selena had the feeling that the potential sources of investors he had proposed would be a fait accompli, virtually predictable.

The capital to be raised, 15,000,000 dollars seemed an astronomical non-specific funding at first look, but in Noah's projection and budget sheets, it all made sense.

"My Father wants you to take your time and study these papers. If you need any help with the language, one of the secretaries in our office is bi-lingual Italian-English," Paul said.

In one sentence he managed to imply that much of their contents would prove difficult if not beyond her comprehension, and that he assumed her command of English to be lacking. Before she had a chance to respond he continued.

"I will be preparing the patent applications in the name of Selena Ltd. I will need to speak to your Chinese pharmacist, so I can protect a range of variation."

He evidently meant that he would try to protect

their products against those who would alter one or two minor ingredients and thus not violate their granted patent.

The further implication was that she would probably not be sufficiently informed about the technical aspects of the products to answer detailed questions.

She looked for the first time more closely at Paul. And saw now why he had not caught her attention when he first stepped into her office. He was a very pale, shorter immitation of his father, with nothing of Noah's prepossession or charm about his manner. On the contrary, there was a condension a stuffiness and snobbery about him that was hard to take.

"Thank you", Selena said with careful politeness. Then added, " I'll call for an appointment in the morning."

Paul seemed skeptical that she would have digested the bulk of papers he had brought by then, but figured that was her worry not his.

"I'll tell him to expect your call."

There was something about this young man... antipatico was the Italian phrase for which there was really no English equivalent, unlikeable was the closest translation. Well, it was of little importance. It was Noah with whom she would deal.

Chapter: 7

Having read in bed until three in the morning with an occasional trip to the kitchen for Verveine tea, Selena felt tired, but at the same time excited by the contents of the mass of papers Noah had sent her. She had studied each one, and marked those parts she thought she needed to review with him, or with which she had some question or disagreement. She looked forward to seeing his office, the quarters from which he had produced this work.

At eleven-thirty she arrived downtown, to the address he'd given her-48 Water Street. It was a tall building, in the heart of what had been New Amsterdam. A van Vloeck had come full circle.

The building exuded power. It was a handsome deco structure of Granite. The massive front doors framed in brass, reflected the midday sun. It stood out against some of it's conspicuously maintained 'older' establishments. Knowing and sophistication showed in the deliberate lines and geometric façade of the thirties architecture.

As she entered, she saw at the back of the marbled lobby a statue, larger than life of two graphically carved monolithic male figures each struggling under an oversized globe.

Dio, what monstrosities! Well, they have the weight of the world on their shoulders. She laughed to herself. In spite of the gravity of the coming meeting, and its significance to her future, she couldn't repress her sense of humor.

She took her surroundings exactly for what they were worth-no more or less. Meant to catch the eye, and interest some beholders with the capacity to impress others. All thought out and above all intended. It was a facet of Noah that was of a piece with the Lunch he'd arranged.

She gathered her thoughts as she turned to find just to her right a burled maple elevator operated by a uniformed attendant, who took her to the 40th floor.

She exited the elevator into a lushly carpeted hallway, which held at either end a high wooden doorway framed by columns and a pediment.

A large reception desk occupied the center of the room, manned by a male receptionist in a dark Brooks Brothers suit. A modern day Cerberus, she thought.

She gave her name. He rose immediately, offering to help her carry her briefcase. After she indicated she felt she could manage it, he escorted her through one of the tall doorways into Noah's office.

A cross between a gentleman's club, and a library she decided as she entered. It was furnished in massive leather armchairs, and low, sturdy coffee tables. On two walls she saw floor to ceiling shelves filled with deep red and blue bound law books. The exception being one shelf which held old athletic cups and trophys- obviously Noah's. One day she would ask him to tell her about them.

On the wall behind a grouping of chairs was an antique map of New York State. Opposite this, a huge plate glass window gave onto an expanse of the roofs and spires of skyscraping buildings that housed people who ran New York, as well as much of the rest of the country. Beyond this a view of the harbor.

Noah's desk, was a simple walnut top, empty of any indication of work, other than a phone/intercom system. He rose from a swivel chair as she entered, and indicated they could sit where it was convenient for her to spread out her papers.

"Selena, I've scheduled an hour and a half for us to

go over the partnership and possibly Neiman-Marcus proposal. Then lunch. I ordered cold roast beef sandwiches and a nicoise salad-you can have your pick."

"Paul will review the patent applications at one-thirty. A half-hour should do for him. Chen, I've asked in at two. I really want that situation clarified, and signed off before we do anything else."

Selena was not surprised by the scheduling. It had been obvious from the beginning that Noah was accustomed to organizing the affairs of his clients down to the least detail. She liked his thoroughness, and the obvious attention that went into it.

She sat, opened the papers, and indicated the places needing discussion. She laughed. "I have more than a few questions."

Noah looked at her, questioning for a moment her intent. But when he read the seriousness in her eyes, realized she had studied every paragraph and word he'd sent her, and was simply lightening the moment, he decided that for this woman, if it took hours he would go over anything she had the smallest question about.

Actually, Selena was a quick study, and had familiarized herself so thoroughly with the material, that they were able to cover everything by the time lunch was brought in by still another male assistant.

Selena wondered how many companies or law offices were still served exclusively by men. This must be one of the last, she decided. John had mentioned he thought it Dickensian. Now she had read some of the Victorian writer's work, she considered the description suited. Actually there was something Edwardian about Noah himself, although his work was irrefutably au courant.

"Noah", Selena asked as she ate her lunch with good appetite," Will Nieman agree to place us on the ground floor, near the store entrance?"

"Yes." He was pleased. As they went through the paperwork she made no fuss about minor points, grasping the essential point behind some pretty formal legal wording.

"And do we have the right to select our own sales staff?"

"Absolutely".

"I will have approval of material for the catalogue?"

"Yes. We will share all local advertising costs. The catalogue exposure is a 'thrown in' ."

Selena looked at him, realized the hours of work that had gone into the material presented, she was really pleased and wanted him to know it.

"I think you've worked out a marvelous arrangement for Selena Ltd. What does Neiman Marcus get out of it?"

"Association with a first class, unique series of products, a new field of activity, and thirty percent of your profits. Good for them and good for you. By the bye, as they open branches across the country, you will have the right to go into them or not, as you see fit."

Selena was more than content with what he had worked out. He had been tough, but never enough to break the agreement. She thought him an extraordinary combination of smart, aggressive and creative. Many years later she would realize just how rare this combination was in an attorney.

When Paul came in they were able to go over the technicalities quickly. She understood what he would ask the government to grant. It took exactly half an hour.

Chen arrived promptly at two, formally attired in a grey pin-stipe suit Selena had never seen him in, with a pale blue shirt of fine cotton.The only unconventional touch was his tie, which hinted of the Orient in its bold colors and design of chinese glyphs.

He seemed somewhat subdued by the setting, and official nature of the appointment. Noah seated him with the best view from the windows. Selena greeted him as he came over. He bowed slightly but said nothing. Selena indicated he should sit beside her.

Tea was brought in and served immediately in thin handle-less porcelain cups. That it was a rare personalized blend of Chinese teas served in the Chinese manner, was typical of Noah. Chen was impressed but said nothing, choosing to wait behind neutrality. But Selena knew he was also pleased by the attention.

When tea was done, Noah explained that the rights to what he and Selena had developed, and would develop in the future had to belong without stint or reservation to the partnership. And he, Chen, was being asked to sign off, and quit claim any rights to the products.

He would also be asked to agree to a noncompetitive clause, should he stop working for Selena Ltd. In return he would be given a five-percent share of the limited partnership, and 500,000 dollars. A fortune.

Noah saw a repressed anger in his eyes, especially after hearing the phrases involving the conditions of working 'for'. It alerted him to possible trouble, made him uneasy. He had modified Selena's desire to share everything as much as he could. It had been a battle. He knew she would give no less.

However with little hesitation and without comment Chen did sign all the papers, he was asked to. And was pleased when a cheque for the cash settlement was ready and given over without delay at the moment of his signature.

"Selena", he said as he left. "Fat wants to deliver samples of shampoo to both salons today. If you call me, I'll set up a convenient delivery time. I want to check the containers before they go out."

Selena knew there was no need for him to do so. She'd seen the simple plastic containers and they were fine. She also knew Chen was establishing 'face' with Noah, and that in his eyes, his importance in Selena Ltd, had been lessened. Later she would have to be sure that he understood how important he remained to her and to the company.

After he left, Noah voiced his suspicions to Selena. " I know Chen well. We're close friends, it will be fine," she reassured him.

As usual, Noah had the last word. "Friend is an elastic word in my opinion. You must learn, Selena. Business is business, and must not be built on friendship. It's not that they don't mix well, sometimes they do. But one should never seriously depend upon the other."

He took the signed papers to his desk, put them in a folder, and stretched hugely. "Friendship is a plastic, changeable relationship made up of occasions, and mutuality. Doing business is a matter of purpose, and definition and above all specific and written agreements. Not at all the same thing, wouldn't you agree?"

"Noah, you sound stuffy", Selena teased.

"So be it. But keep an eye out Signorina Di Angelo, Eh? And remember what I've said."

"All right" . Selena had little intention of doing that. She knew Jimmy. After all they had shared those wonderful nights in Montecito. And Noah could not know him the way she did.

Later that day she telephoned the Laboratory. Fat answered. When she asked for Chen, he said he'd not seen him since early afternoon. But he couldn't wait to tell her.

"Ma'am, you've got to come down tomorrow morning. I have a B-A-S-E, the Momma and Daddy of bases ready for you to try on your beautiful Faccia! Hotcha, hotcha!"

Selena couldn't help bursting into laughter Hotcha Hotcha and the Italian Faccia was just too much in one sentence.

But she was delighted with his progress, and said she'd be there at eight. After that there were only the salons to close and she would be through for the day. Almost as an afterthought, she wondered briefly why it was Fat who announced the base to her, when it had always been done with a semi-formality by Chen.

Chapter: 8

Over the next three years it seemed events, activities, and interviews ran one into the other in a blur. She was nearly always tired as were Maria, Chen, Noah, and even Fat who was often at a loss for the latest 'hep' word to describe it all.

A hither to unknown Air Force officer was to take the 'first giant step for mankind' after a miraculous landing on the moon, and be seen by millions watching in their homes on television in the act of so doing.

In a little known Cape Cod village, Edward Kennedy, the last Crown Prince of that 'royal American political family', involved himself in a drunken vehicular accident which with one blow permitted the death of his female passenger and insured he would never be able to run for President.

And perhaps most astounding of all in October, The New York Mets, who were the joke team of both baseball leagues won the World Series of that sport, and won it with style.

Neiman Marcus had opened branches in Chicago, Los Angeles, and Palm Beach. In each of the boutiques Selena had spent hours training representatives, showing and teaching how to create a 'look'. And then there were the endless personal appearances, media interviews, and the travel from place to place.

The Lab had to keep up with increasing demands for all the product line. More factory space was needed. Noah had negotiated for an abandoned mill in New Jersey, which was now set up and running full time.

Fat had started automating the measuring phase of ingredients with the aid of a computer. Selena Botanica now included a full line of lotions and creams and saponics-soap, shampoo and conditioner. As John pointed out it was a staggering achievement in such a short time.

Since   the meeting in Noah's office, when his reaction was so formal and angry, she had seen very little of Chen. She had tried to get him to come to dinner, or one of their Dim Sum Sunday lunches, but he always seemed unable to make it for one reason or another.

Their contact was frequently indirect, through the intermediary of Fat. And it was through him accidentally that she discovered Jimmy was spending long hours playing Mahjongg.

Mahjongg, a four person gambling game calling for the use of 136 brilliantly colored tiles, had been called the second curse of China after opium. Exquisite ivory pictograph tiles bearing symbols called by such names as West or East Wind, Flower, hid the ugliness of addiction to playing long hours to win or lose huge sums.

At the Third Dragon club, the player always gambled with an action cut to the house. The house took a fee from every player and percentage of the 'pot' at every table for each game-so the winners won less than they should, but the losers were doubly penalized. If the loser was a regular, who gambled significant sums, the house would carry him on credit for a time. And the 'house' was the property of a Tong, one of the underworld gangs which controlled Chinatown.

Fat had let the name of a gambling den slip when she asked to speak to Chen one day. Although Occidentals were allowed nowhere near the stairs leading to the cellar rooms, even she had heard of the infamous Third Dragon Club.

However she didn't have the time to deal with Chen's Mahjongg afternoons, and in any case was sure as an experienced player together with his balanced view of life, and with the Tao, he would have it in control when needed. She gave it no more thought other than to hope he enjoyed himself.

Two weeks after Annie Karol Katz interviewed Selena, a long article had appeared in the Village Voice detailing the concept incorporated by the Creme and cosmetics, and describing the salons where they were sold. It had created a series of other articles and interviews, and a surge in business that became permanent making continued expansion a necessity.

Selena thanked Annie Karol and opened the Madison Avenue Selena Boutique. The publicity also served the Neiman-Marcus boutiques, now six in number.

Noah found and bought space in the low 70's on Madison. With Maria's help the store was staffed and functioning within the year, freeing Selena to do yet more out of town work.

At that point two things happened almost simultaneously that were to affect her deeply.

Maria prepared her favorite dinner-osso buco, insalata di rugola e pomodoro, and for desert a zuppa Inglese. After both were replete she said,

"I think it is time you have a better home. And so once again I have found for you a wonderful place. It is just above Mott Street. They are making a wonderful new area. There are art galleries, and many of the old food stores have moved there.

"You mean where the loft conversions are being made, in Soho.

"Si. I have put a deposit on one for you. If you like it, Annie Katz has said if we go to the Wannamaker furniture department, there they have very good home consultors. They can show you everything, even anticitá. I will watch after you choose. We will make you a new home."

Maria knew Selena had no time to do this for herself, but with the aid of a decorator to facilitate ordering and delivery, she could do it for her.

Selena didn't know how to thank her. She had wished to move for a long time, but simply couldn't find the hours to do it. Maria's offer was a Godsend.

"Si, sarebbe meraviglioso". That would be marvelous, I accept.

The two began to discuss how to make the loft into a home. At the end of the evening, Maria brought up the second part of the subject.

"Cara, once I have seen you into your new place, voglio tornare in Italia", after I settle you, I wish to go back to live in Italy.

It came as a shock, but Maria was telling Selena, she wanted to retire to Puglia.

She explained she felt the time had come for quite a while, but knew Selena could hardly spare her. But lately mornings brought pain, evening exhaustion. She wished to return to her old village where the everyday sun warmed the body and life was gentler, slower. She had cousins waiting for her to come 'home'.

"Oh Maria, veramente? Sei sicura?" must you! Are you sure? Selena gasped heart-broken at the thought of not being able to see her cheerful face, nor feel her constancy, her support, her love. But when she stopped to consider Maria's needs, she knew it was best for her dearest friend and surrogate Mother that she go back to Italy.

"Devo, carissima", I must my darling, Maria responded kissing her over and over, assuring her of her love, but of her tiredness, and wish for rest.

Wanting her to have every thing she could provide, Selena insisted on a retirement settlement which included large monthly pension cheques. This together with the partnership share, would keep Maria in comfort.

Both women were in tears when Selena came to the harbor to put Maria and mounds of luggage, flowers, and candy on the steamship for Italy. But both knew it was for the best. Maria promised to send first pressings from the olive groves of southern Italy. You are to take the best of care of yourself, Selena instructed.

"Che Dio ti benedice, mia figlia", God bless you my only child , Maria murmured to Selena.

Selena overcome could only embrace her a last time, and let her go onto the gangway. Maria disappeared in a sea of boarding passengers at last call, and didn't come to the railing. Selena knew it was to spare her, but still had to watch until the ship's churning wake flattened into the ordinary surface swell of harbor waters, and the ship could no longer be seen.

Empty weeks followed Maria's departure. Noah saw to it that Selena was alone only if she wanted to be. John was out of town on an extensive book tour. Work was if anything more onerous, but helped numb the ache of missing.

Late one day, not long after this, when Selena was seated doing paperwork in her fifth avenue office, one of the assistants came in saying that a Principessa Nicoletta San Lorenzo asked whether she would agree to see her.

The name struck her as familiar. She hesitated, then it came to her that San Lorenzo was the surname of an ancient titled family, who had once owned and ruled miles of rolling Tuscan hilled countryside. Time had eroded their fortunes, lands, and numbers. She learned later that there was left only Nicoletta and her Mother, who still lived in one of the old castellos on the few hectares of land left in family possession.

Curious as to what this Principessa might want of

her, Selena asked that she be shown in.

The presence and looks of the bone-slim woman who entered her office was striking. Nicoletta San Lorenzo could never be mistaken for anything but what she was. Her bearing and grace spoke of generations of inherent aristocracy. On a subway, in a ballpark, in a supermarket, there would be no mistaking her lineage. Selena wondered what the individual person within would be like.

Small, dark-haired with brilliant green eyes in a delicately sculpted face, Nicoletta San Lorenzo was in her late forties. She wore an all black Armani suit from several seasons back, which set off her coloring, and focused attention on her face. The effect was remarkable-deliberate, yet somehow not competitive. She crossed the room to Selena, extending her hand to the younger woman who rose to meet her.

"Buon giorno, Principessa," Selena said.

"Nicoletta, if you please." The Principessa corrected gently. Selena sensed the security of old title in the suggestion to ignore it.

"Won't you sit?"

Nicoletta folded smoothly into the one free chair in the office.

"What may I do for you?"

"A great deal, if it's possible", was the quiet answer. Selena let her curiosity show .

" I have followed and read of the progress of Selena Ltd. I have personally tried all the products and found them everything that was claimed. You have now three New York salons." She paused.

Selena waited, pleased but knowing there must be more. She saw the other woman brace herself to go on. "I must tell you, I have no formal training of any sort. No profession, No business experience. Yet I find now I must earn some money. I thought of your Selena Ltd, because the one thing that I thought the salons lacked was a consistent style of seeing to clients. And I thought it needs only this to be complete."

When she saw the interest in Selena's face, she went on. "I have lived among the kind of women you want as clients, I know they would respond to, how shall I say it, a kind of upper class approach. I think I could handle and sell your products to your satisfaction. And so I would like to apply for a position as a saleswoman."

Of all the things that Selena might have anticipated, this was the last. She was astonished that a woman of this quality would consider working in sales. At the same time, she knew that if she could handle the day to day servicing, and had the stamina demanded by the job, Nicoletta San Lorenzo would make a superb saleswoman for Selena Ltd.

" Have you thought of the physical energy and patience needed to sell?"

"Actually," Nicoletta smiled reflectively for the first time, "I have. I know that to be good you have to keep a kind of positive energy. I'm in very good physical condition. I suppose it's partly a matter of genes, but I hope part of it comes from exercise and walking the city everyday."

Selena knew that behind this response lay the need to save expense of traveling. She also admired the ingenuous in Nicoletta's frank acknowledgment of her heritage. And knew it was for her ears only.

She also felt that Nicoletta had a combination of dignity, warmth and freshness that would serve her well. She made the decision to take her on, explained the hours and salary, and decided to start her immediately in the new Madison Avenue salon.

Nicoletta began the next day. She was amazing. Within weeks she had 'See you' returning customers, and others referred specifically to her by satisfied clients.

Selena, who reviewed the break down of salon sales figures weekly, was astounded. Nicoletta's book showed almost twice the sales of the other personnel. After still a few more weeks, she noticed that all the sales books in the Madison Avenue salon had gone up substantially. She wondered why until she spent several hours in the salon. She saw Nicoletta, helping her fellow sales people.

They had come to rely on her help and guidance with customers, not that they imitated how she handled her own customers, but something of her elegance and graciousness carried over into their manner with clients. They came to Nicoletta, freely and easily. It could be seen she was a natural leader and a superb teacher.

The next day she called her down to her office. "You're an absolute waste as a salesperson, no matter what your book shows!"

Nicoletta was dumbfounded, unable to utter a word. "As of this moment, you are in charge of supervising all Selena Ltd. personnel, not only here in New York but all over. I hope you're prepared to travel. I want you to develop as a constant the customer approach, you've developed for the staff uptown. I think it can be caught and taught to everyone I will employ from now on."

Nicoletta was thrilled. She would never be able to express to Selena, what her confidence meant to her, but she would be endlessly grateful.

"Signorina Di Angelo, we will try to create a Selena Ltd. salesperson who represents all that is unique and priceless in the products. A client should want to return for the services as well as the things they are able to buy."

"Selena." Selena smiled.

"Selena," Nicoletta agreed.

And so it was that Nicoletta was able to build on what Maria had started. But she gave a special imprint to Selena's people, and ultimately the look and design of the existing salons and the new ones as they came along.

Noah was not only the single heaviest investor, but ceaseless in his help and availability. She'd gotten used to his odd silences, which were more than made up for by the brilliance of his ideas, and their execution.

On her behalf, her 'Otter' had all lived up to his other sobriquet. They met at least twice a week, when both were in town.

Although no one could have guessed, Noah anticipated these meetings with Selena with the excitement of a schoolboy, thinking over his wardrobe in advance to enhance his patrician good looks and impressive physique.

In fact, Selena occupied a dual role in his life. She was a client he saw for business meetings, to whose calls for advice he readily responded. At the same time she was an increasingly frequent subject of his fantasies. These fantasies were so persistent that they sometimes spilled into his nighttime dreams.

Through a natural professionalism and the lifelong habit of controlling his feelings, he was able to separate the Selena who appeared in his fantasies by a steel door of will from the Selena for whom he did business.

They were two different Selenas. Each vivid. Each magnetizing. After their first meeting, he had kept a bottle of Diorissimo by his bedside with which he occasionally sprayed his pillow before going to bed. He would have been mortified had she found out. As he had no intention ever of inviting her to his house, she never would

Nevertheless, as she gave him a familial kiss on the check and slid smoothly into the booth at the New

York Athletic Club next to him, he felt a twinge of excitement.

And as she bent to get into the booth, her suit parted at her cleavage revealing the top of a rounded breast before closing again as she sat. The glimpse of breast and ivory lace tantalized him in spite of himself, so that he felt the first stirrings of an erection pressing into his trousers.

Determined to ignore it, but knocked a little off kilter, he heard his voice break as he greeted her. He didn't dare look at her in case his eyes gave him away. Finally in control enough to look at her, he saw a fatigue and a sadness around her eyes that shocked him. The balance sheets were brilliant, but she was clearly exhausted.

" Selena", he said after they had finished up their business, " you need a vacation."

Unbidden tears filled her eyes. "You've done very well by me, in fact by all your investors. It's time you…"

Then an idea occurred to him. He leaned toward her.

"I've plans to go to London by boat next week," he lied, "it would be my pleasure to invite you, if I can get another cabin." This last was more than truthful.

Selena heard his words, and to her surprise found herself thinking that as a matter of fact everyone needed a break.

"My God, but you're right. All of us have been snapping a little recently. I didn't recognize that we're all tired."

Chen and Fat, she knew, would love to get off to California.

Nicoletta, had been receiving an inordinate amount of calls from Tuscany. Annie Karol had asked over one of their recent lunches whether Nicoletta was being 'importuned' by her family. Selena had to smile at the delicate wording Annie Karol chose.

" There is some kind of financial scam, involving prominent old Italian families, and the use of their name. It's prompted official investigation and demands for restitution. The innocent may be swept up with the guilty"

Thinking about it, Selena was pretty sure Nicoletta's mother, the old Principessa may well have been taken in, would need her help and support.

It was time the 'second in command' at the various salons got a chance to try their wings. She knew the product supply was well in hand. There was no perfect time to take a break, but now was as good as time as any.

Noah held his breath, amazed that he had dared ask her.

With the same spontaneity with which he had invented the trip, she accepted it.

Chapter: 9

It was a five-day voyage on Cunard's Queen Mary. The crossing filled with the eternal beauty and remoteness that only a vast ocean seems to bring, was outwardly uneventful.

Some times they dined formally in the sway of the ship's grand dining room. Subdued dinners served with impeccable style by waiters whose short white jackets and braid had been worn by their fathers and grandfathers before them.

At those times-Alone in the ebb and flow of tuxedos and formal gowns, of brilliant white napery set with special export china, and gleaming heavy cutlery, lapped by conversation never loud enough to interfere with their isolation, never distinct enough to become more than background susurration, they talked of small diurnal things, never in any way referring to professional matters or business.

Sometimes Selena dined alone in her cabin, tended by a steward who came and went laying her place and clearing it in perfect silence and respect for her desire for solitude. Pouring wine or lighting her cigarette without need of request.

She hadn't realized how close to exhaustion she was. Nor how much she needed the restorative of an ocean crossing. Noah did, and made sure she had everything she needed including solitude. He allowed her this time happily, pleased to see the lines of fatigue and anxiety around her eyes disappear, and the color return to her face.

In the first days, she passed many hours in a deck chair mindlessly watching the passing seas, letting the swells rock her. Isolated from past and future as well.

Then she began to take stock of her life. This reverse journey to Europe was her first chance to think. Things had happened so fast over the years and there seemed almost no time to reflect.

She wasn't sure why, but she'd packed her Ceilings in with her gowns. Now in one of the middays of the crossing, she opened their pages, and allowed the past to wash over her- John, Hussein, Fatimah, Chen and his cousins, and Maria. People and events came bidden to her mind. She let the flavors and days of the past swirl into the present. And learned through her own words, that the girl she had been before John and America, and the woman she had become were one. Fundamentally the Selena of Egypt and California were one and the same, and the acknowledgment released a tension, an uncertainty she'd not recognized before, involved as she'd become in being the head and icon of Selena Ltd.

Considering the beginning she could scarcely have imagined the present. This perception freed her from speculation as to what the future would hold. Let it be a surprise when it came.

She tucked a rug, more securely around her legs, as she sat in the deck chair sipping the strong Bovril the steward had brought, listening to the moan of the ships horn sounded out over a moving mist-shrouded morning.

The strength she had gained from the past and all who had helped shape it would let her deal with whatever might come, she thought as she closed the last ledger book And rang for the steward to clear her table. It was a brave thought but neither adequate nor accurate as it turned out.

The fifth day dawned, the ocean lay behind them, the ship eased into the harbor at Southampton, nosed and nudged into its place by cheerfully hooting tugs.

As they passed through passport control and customs, Selena emerged from her cocoon. She was suddenly and strongly re-aware of Noah's presence, and felt a burst of affection for the gift of time he had given her.

It had been a long since she had let herself depend on anyone for any kind of personal care and attention. She knew she'd missed it, now that it had been offered with such open-handed generosity.

On the way up to London, they stopped for lunch at a sleepy Kentish village, eating a the hard-rined local cheese, and heavy brown country bread washed down by local cider, then drove on leisurely through rolling countryside. Through fields divided by hedgerows of hawthorne, often as not dotted with sheep who grazed on their bright green expanse, and small hamlets under the soft afternoon light of an early English summer.

"Noah, I don't know how to thank you. The peace and quiet of the crossing, have done wonders for me."

"It was no problem. I could see you needed some time and distance."

"It's the first time I've had to myself in many years. I had the chance to think about many things. Again, I have to thank you."

Then wanting to change topics, "Look at the color of those fields. I've never seen such intense gold."

"Those are fields of rape seed. They'll cut them soon. The seeds are crushed into oil in commercial foods, and the rest of the plant is fed to sheep ."

Their Rolls Royce arrived at the Hyde Park Hotel in the heart of Knightsbridge. Originally a Victorian men's club, the turreted and flamboyant brick building exuded confident masculinity, the proprietary certitude of a ruling class, the very sense of superiority she loved in Noah.

Inside the door a short flight of steps led to a

landing in four kinds of marble. Under the subtle lighting of huge crystal chandeliers, massive bright-colored bouquets in marble urns stood on pilasters and banisters. Tail-coated functionaries with pearl gray vests and high gloss ebony shoes covered with spats of grey, moved noiselessly about their duties. It was unmistakably in the tradition of the Grand British hotel.

Almost as if it were an afterthought, the reception desk was tucked off to one side of the reception hall. There a discrete transaction of only minutes, produced an exchange-passports for room keys.

The elevator stopped at the third floor. They were ushered into a vast high ceilinged hotel suite-a large sitting room flanked by two oversized bedroom suites. The porter put her suitcases in one bedroom, Noah's in the other, Then opened the windows onto a balcony overlooking Hyde Park. Selena crossed to them. The view has of Hyde Park in full early bloom. Plane trees shaded a broad well-kept bridal path. Somewhere in the distance a lake glimmered.

She turned to look at Noah and saw an unusual expression on his face. He seemed almost nervous. She thought perhaps it was their accommodations. She was happy to reassure him with a light embrace from which he released himself quickly.

" I propose dinner here, if you would like," he said in his courteous fashion. This was obviously what he wanted and she agreed without second thought.

" Of course. It's too beautiful to leave."

" I'll arrange it," he said, a pleased smile breaking out on his unusually grave face.

Selena took a short nap and a bath in her room. Puzzling about what to wear for dinner in the suite, she followed her instinct and dressed as if for dinner on the ship, in a black silk Chanel cocktail suit, black stockings, delicate black evening sandals, and her favorite Van Cleef diamond drop earrings. She twisted her hair into the French knot which bared the back of her neck and perfumed the cleft between her breasts, her elbows, wrists, and just behind each ear.

Emerging from her quarters, she saw that she had made the right decision- Noah was in tuxedo.

For the first time, she really looked at the suite.The sitting room where they now stood was both elegant and casual. A typical English combination. Light-tinted William Morris wallpaper on the walls; fauteuils and sofas in classic Singerie chintz: thick piled rose carpeting underfoot, and overhead a high ceiling bordered with twining fruit and vine relief cast perfectly in gesso. It all seemed in harmony, all of a piece.

There were large candelabras set on high on the mantelpiece, outside light was shed by street lamps. All enhanced by the faint perfume coming from pink Cabbage roses in shallow bowls resting on scattered walnut side tables.

" It's lovely," Selena said. Noah said nothing, but his eyes didn't leave her as she crossed the room to him. " Thank you again. Thank you for everything Noah. You've no idea what this trip has done for me"

" I think I might," he said, avoiding her eyes while adjusting his cuffs. It was an odd thing for him to say. She didn't know what to do with the response, and so let it slide.

He was a complicated man, a fascinating man to whom she owed much, including her new found serenity. She was touched by him, by his sensitivity and generosity.

Their business relationship was far away, and with it his dominance of her. Which seemed to lead to tonight. She had the feeling he'd choreographed the evening.They would each play roles in what it would bring. But not yet.

Strawberries, fresh cream and coffee-dinner came to an end, and the table was taken away. By now darkness had fallen. Candles high on the mantle, sent flickers of soft light through the room. A warm breeze entered through the windows moving the drapes almost imperceptibly. Small tongues of reflected light licked at the ceiling.

The slow clop of horses hooves drew Selena to the window to watch a troop of mounted Queens Guards in mufti returning along the elegance of Rotten Row to the palace stables.

She felt Noah come to stand close behind her. She leaned backwards, resting her head on his chest, inviting him to press his body into hers. They stood together, leaning against one another, silent except for the sound of his breathing against her neck. Her earring brushed against his cheek.

She waited for some other gesture from him, but there was none. She understood instinctively that from here on whatever might happen was in her hands. The timing, the movements, hers. She sensed his growing excitement and felt slow subtle palpitations beginning in her own groin.

She turned toward him, and stepped slightly back so that she was framed in the doorway of the balcony. Holding his eyes with hers, she began to unbutton her jacket. It parted to reveal the curves of her breasts, cupped and rounded by the La Perla bustier she wore underneath.

The top button once open, she continued pulling the lapels of her suit wide apart, opening more of the warmth of the globes in their lace cover to his gaze. Her earrings flashed in the candlelight, caressing the sides of her neck as she moved.

Still he was motionless. Waiting. Her every gesture reflected in his eyes. Time stretched out seamlessly. She released the rest of the buttons. The jacket parted to reveal the whole of her lingerie and all the top of her generous breasts.

A pulse visibly beating was rapid at the base of her throat, her skin smooth and flawless.

Once again she paused for any signal from him. There was none other than his expression, one of appreciation and hunger, devouring her body, penetrating her eyes. Her own excitement grew.

Except for the leaning contact at the window, they had yet to touch.

She knew that over her shoulder through the balcony door he could see the passersby, the mounted riders, and that perhaps they in turn could see her silhouetted in the window, undressed to the waist. It didn't matter.

When she could no longer delay, she took his hand. Singling out his index finger she inserted it between the lace brassiere and her naked flesh, inviting him to touch, to explore. She ran his finger lightly along under the soft globe of her breast and into her cleavage. The moisture gathered in between her breasts released an odor of her perfume now mixed just faintly with light perspiration.

Opening her bustier she let his finger feel the soft weight of her fullness, and stroke her with exquisite languor. Her nipples hardened.

She put her hands behind her back to open her breasts to his touch. She could feel the warm breeze on her back. Still seeing the intensity in his eyes and imagining eyes of the passersby on her. She became excited.

Control was becoming difficult, but she felt she had to arouse him to an equal pitch. Her breath came irregularly, and she started feeling the involuntary secretion which she knew would moisten her.

The waiting and watching had to end. She knew it was time. She began to remove her bustier. Noah shook his head slightly. She understood that he wished her to keep it on. But when she lowered her hands to undo her skirt. He made no objection.

Letting the silk skirt fall to the floor, she stepped out of it, leaving on her high heels. His eyes widened taking in her black lace pants and the garter belt holding her filmy dark stockings molded to her long slim legs. The flesh gleamed through their transparent length.

He took a step towards her, and again stopped, as if something were holding him, but his eyes now showed her that he wanted her overwhelmingly.

Dropping his hand, she released her stockings, one by one, deliberately caressing her legs in his vision, and then removed the stockings, and with studied grace the lacy garter belt and panties.

He watched as she let them slide to the floor.

Nude save for her high heels and open bustier she approached him, her skin glowing in the candlelight. She stood for a moment, letting her excitement and the sense of her readiness envelope him as she slowly removed his tie and his studs, then his jacket and finally the starched evening shirt itself. She let them drop to the floor.

He stood before her a living statue-motionless, naked to the waist. His broad chest moving quickly with the pace of his breathing.

She let her fingernails scrape lightly across the skin of his chest standing close enough so that he could feel her breath move the pattern of fine hair that lay across his broadness. Bathing at sea had turned him the color of bronze. His nipples came erect under her touch

Finally liberated from his trance he moved, almost startling her. He dropped to his knees and buried his face in her soft-haired moist triangle, inhaling the odor of her increasingly wet sex.

By now her own breath was coming in gasps.

She cradled his head, pressing it to her, stroking his hair, his cheeks, massaging his head. She leant over and kissed his ears-lingering. He moaned.

Then straightening for a moment, holding and controlling his body, she pushed him insistently from his knees backwards onto the floor. He groaned, his eyes closed and expression on his face of painfully intense longing.

She leaned over, him and slowly unbuttoned his fly, reaching in to his trousers to find him fully excited. She drew his penis out, still hovering over him. She looked alternately at his erection and into his eyes.

His cock throbbed in front of her, as it sprung from the black tuxedo pants. It was large, long and clean-looking, suffused, in a full arousement.

Slowly she straddled his body so that his penis strained straight up towards her. He looked unabashedly her at full black bush now glistening with moisture. She let him look at the lips of her vagina swollen with desire. He threw his head back moaning her name over and over.

She could no longer bear this slow dance into nudity. Bending over she removed all his trousers. She was so aroused she was almost rough in her haste, then removed his shorts, freeing his cock completely. She grasped it, guided it as she lowered herself down onto it, taking it in to the root.

Her knees sank to the floor on either side of him . She began to move up and down along the length of his rock-hard shaft. Deeply, violently she took him into herself again and again.

The sensation of his cock filling her, as she plumbed him was almost unbearable and she came quickly. He followed seconds later with a shout of relief.

Through the open window their sexual cries could be heard on the street below.

Finally, lifting herself up just enough to reach around, she took herself completely out of her lace cage, and put her breast to his lips. His mouth opened automatically. He began to suck at her nipple.

She felt him stiffen immediately within her and come again into orgasm, never once stopping to suck like a starving child at her breast.

When he finished the peace on his face brought her to tears. He murmured something so softly she wasn't sure what he said until he repeated it.

"I love you Selena." His words asked no response, no answer, but as a wave of tenderness towards him welled up in her, she pulled a rose from a vase just within her reach, and scattered the fragrant petals on his chest, one by one.

She kept him inside her for several minutes, stroking his body with her hands, and feeling their combined liquids draining out of her and onto him.

Gently lifting herself off him she lay down on the carpet beside him. Convulsively he took her in his arms and held her as tightly and gratefully as she had ever been held.

She looked up at the ceiling. A glow from a street lamp suffused the balcony and crept into the room, where the light from guttering candles superimposed complicated patterns onto the swags and cornices atop moldings and walls, so it seemed as if the ceiling were a vast moving pastoral scene. That the intertwined vines and flowers belonged to a live wood forever caught in sculpted plaster of Paris.

They were in their own cosmos. Their own Eden.

Sounds of their breathing mingled with the night sounds from the street-formal and fluid, private and public, the contrasts melted together in this night that held them.

The Noah she knew had disappeared and would never return. The careful, proud appearance lost in his need, and her desire to fill it.

This man so invulnerable in his world, so needful in the one they had created, would not be easily understood. But she accepted that he trusted her and had put himself in her hands. That he trusted her with his desire and the truth of her response.

" I needed to be sure you wanted me", he whispered, "at least for this night."

As she lay against his chest, she responded in a husky whisper, partly in English, party in Italian ,

"Ti voglio bene. Sei il mio grand'amore", I want you, be sure of it my love-convincing him of her regard for him, of his capacity to excite her, of her pleasure in making love to him.

"You make it all wonderful". His words were simple but uttered with such intensity that she knew Noah had never known love before.

Then they lay together simply, without words in the calm that followed satiation.

It was the first of many nights. Nights of passion and tenderness. He had given her the hidden keys to his pleasure. She came to know that he needed to see and, take her half-dressed half-nude, even in the act of disrobing as he waited passive until aroused to a longing which could only be quenched by orgasm after orgasm.

It seemed almost as if he had stored up his passion over the years and now she was able to release it.

In the mornings, Noah usually went out to ride after they breakfasted. She watch him go in a casual Harris tweed jacket he wore over a shirt and ascot. The fit of his jacket set off the breadth of his shoulders. Hotel staff had his black boots cleaned and polished each morning, and his velvet hard hat brushed and gleaming. It was as if the hotel wouldn't permit him to ride in 'Rotten Row", the best horsed and equiped bridal path in London, unless he was perfectly turned out.

Noah told her of his love of riding, and she knew that whenever he could he rode in the early hours of morning. It was evident to her in the grace and ease with which he managed his horse, that he was a superb horseman.

When he went out, it gave her time write in her journal. She found that she wanted to write of objects and times which captivated each of them, of her feeling for Noah, and his daily gifts of small and large things, the silly or the sublime, often a particular piece of clothing or jewelry she had admired.

She was learning to be careful how she expressed her liking or appreciation, because oddly, Noah had the penchant of the Arab host-if you saw and admired one of his possessions no matter the cost or uniqueness, it would be taken off the back or off the shelf and given to you on the spot. For him that was normal host behavior. Selena had no idea where or how Noah had picked up this characteristic, but it was a constant.

Wheeler's St. James was a particular favorite for lunches. The seafood served was of a supreme quality. Selena tasted for the first time Dover sole as a local fish, and smoked Irish salmon, as a regional specialty.

One time, Noah took them to the Cheshire Cheese for steak and kidney pudding, the house specialty. It was an old, age-blackened pub known to have been frequented by Dickens, Lamb and Walpole among other nineteenth century authors and journalists.

"Noah, I can't believe it. I've always understood

English cuisine to be somewhere between awful and awful, but I'm crazy about these dishes, heavy as they are." At which point Simpson's for roast beef, Yorkshire pudding, and English brewed ale, was put on the list of musts.

Afternoons, they went to the National Portrait gallery, where the works of the great English portraitists were hung, or the Tate museum, or one of the marvelous churches by Christopher Wren.

They did the houses of Parliament, and the Tower of London, perennially attractive to tourist and cognoscenti alike.

They shopped for his clothing on Jermyn street, or Bond. Sometimes wandering off into the area around Charing Cross where incredibly well-stocked second hand bookstores were to be found.

Selena bought one of the numbered aftershave lotions, and shaving soaps of Chzech and Speake for John. Noah bought Paul a dozen shirts from Heydritch and Heydritch. Selena thought the imprimature of these famous shirtiers would please his name-conscious son. She noticed that for himelf Noah used a much less known firm, an old shirtmaking firm. They knew his taste in shirting, and made him update his measurements each time he came to London. Lobb had done his shoes since he was a boy. Noah explained almost apologetically that this was really the most efficient way to dress for men who were in the public eye and didn't have the the time to shop.

At Sotheby's auction house, Noah found, bid on, and got an early Stubbs to add to his collection of horse paintings. As to her, Noah would have bought everything on offer at Harold Nicholson's endless collections, had she permitted.

By day, whatever they did, they found they loved being in each other's company.

In Ceilings, Selena described the peignoirs in mauve and tea rose he bought her-which she took care to wear in the long summer twilight when dusk fell. Noel told her she looked as if the dusk were a mantle, created especially for her at twilight, folding and holding her beauty.

He loved to watch her doing small things about the suite-arranging flowers, or cutting a piece of fruit for them dressed in chiffon or silk she wore in their quarters. The half-light itself heightened sensuality and appetite for him. He found her movements were miraculously graceful.

And then there was the profound passion brought by unrelieved midnight black lingerie, and the deepest shadows of night, by pleasure in the delicate chiaroscuro of moonlight on lace from Antwerp or Chantilly.

Often, although theater or dinner out was planned, they found themselves canceling to stay in the suite making love, delighted with their newfound relationship. Caressing each other, learning each other's ways, what pleased, what excited, what could delay and then satisfy.

For Selena, she was enchanted with the man by day, the last of the Patroons of unchallengeable heritage. By night she sought shadow and nuance to unleash his sexuality. Her desire to understand it all, to capture it, flowed from her pen to the pages of Ceilings.

While she could never heal his wounds, she had the feeling she had helped. She thought she might have gone further had he let her. But the time was not quite yet. If it happened it could only be with infinite patience on her part.

That the wounds of his past never totally scarred over would remain their secret after life in New York re-imposed normal social facades.

That she loved him would remain her secret.
Except when she wrote of their time together in
England in Ceilings.

Chapter: 10

They flew back to New York On BOAC's overnight
flight. Noah was unable to fit his large frame into the
berth which had been made up with Porteau linens, so
he settled for the comfort of his first class seat knowing
Selena was sleeping like a child curled up in her berth.
It had been three weeks in which they'd found renewal
and they'd found each other.

He'd learned a lot about her during their stay in
London- Not the distractions of museums full of period
portraits of monarchs and princes; not mornings on
horseback in Rotten row, not leisurely high teas at
Browns or The Ritz; not the lush Cotswold countryside,
and faded regency elegance of Bath, distracted him
from caring more and more deeply.

He was truly in love for the first time in his life, and
what a difference it made. Selena was what he'd
dreamed of finding in a woman, and yet as real as flesh,
with faults and foibles that made the dream a poor
intimation of the reality. His mini-magnate! He had
teased, and Selena laughed in agreement, saying and
who indeed helped create the mini-magnate?

Nevertheless, he thought that in New York, their
liaison, should be kept completely discrete, from his
firm for the time being, even from Paul. Selena knew he
would handle John with care and tact. For her part,
Nicoletta, she felt would know instinctively but say
nothing to anyone about it. And their relationship had
nothing to do with Jimmy or Fat.

After a 'full English breakfast' aboard the flight,

they arranged that they would spend their first evening in New York together, after they had each tended to affairs accumulated in their absence.

When Selena saw Nicoletta in her office, she looked like a different woman. She'd cut her hair short, and it clung about the extraordinary beauty of her face in a way portraitists idealized but rarely found in their live subjects. She was bronzed from her stay in her beloved Tuscan hills, and full of energy.

She told Selena that she was able to order repairs begun on the castello, so that her Mother's quarters at least, would be warm and weather-tight for the coming winter. Pride and relief shone in her eyes. Selena knew without words that the financial imbroglio involving the old Principessa had also been resolved.

In turn, Nicoletta caught the happiness on Selena's face. And said simply, "Amica mia, sono felice per te", my friend I'm so happy for you. She had no way of knowing she repeated words Selena had heard once before from a dear person. She was moved to tears. Nicoletta had become a true friend. They began catching up on Selena Ltd.

Fat called to say he'd returned from California by way of Port St. Lucie Florida and that he was sure after a great Spring training the '69 Mets were a miracle team that would 'go all the way'! Selena laughed hearing the excitement in his voice, and even agreed to attend a game with him that season.

Then he went into detail about what was occurring at the lab. He told her Jimmy was content with the way things had gone in their absence. He also told her of his visit to Silicon Valley. An area in Southern California which was becoming home to small company after company specializing in what Fat called software development. Some of what he told her in addition to being unfamiliar, sounded actually garbled, almost muffled. She was puzzled for a moment. Then understood and asked him,

"Fat, What are you eating?"

He answered as if it were the most natural thing in the world that she should assume, he was stuffing himself with fast-food.

"I was trying to make up my mind, Howard Johnson or this new Macdonald's. The hamburgers looked about the same. So I'm testing a range from each."

She had to laugh. She was glad for this adorable funny scientist with his wild enthusiasms, and even more glad that it was clear, he always seemed to keep an eye out for what was best for Selena Ltd. Somehow she knew he always would.

"The first warm evening we both have free, we will go out to Shea Stadium. In fact we can go to one of those, uh, what do you call it when they do two games instead of one?"

"Wowee! You mean you're up for a double-header! Boy! You've got a date!"

Selena called John. She had phoned him before she left to tell him she was going to London with Noah. He knew that in all probability they had become lovers, but it was clear he didn't want to hear about it just yet. So instead they talked of the progress on his latest work. It was a departure for John. Something he had never tried, never wanted to try before. It was a book about a woman. And not just any woman, but the mulatto slave-mistress of Thomas Jefferson. She was well educated, and served as the mistress of his house-a well-known, but well-kept bitter-sweet 'secret' in that genius president's life.

Selena she wasn't sure of the direct connection, but knew with certainty that their affair, and their relationship since, lay behind this new turn of events, She thought it might turn out to his advantage as a

writer.   Carla's niece now in full charge at
Mott Street, called to suggest that it was time for a
complete refurbishing . She'd also found out that space
immediately adjacent to the salon was coming free and
wanted Selena to see it, and approve the plans she had
formulated for expansion. Selena was pleased with her
initiative and ambition. It was a good idea. A time was
set. Selena would meet her the next day.

Annie Karol showed up unannounced late in the
day.

"My dear, or perhaps considering what's happened,
ma chere, as we say on the Right Bank..." She squinted
through the smoke of the inevitable cigarette bobbing
up and down in the corner of her mouth. Selena caught
an odd odor, then realized her friend had taken to
Gitanes cigarettes-beloved of soccer players, and
indispensable in any self-respecting cabaret. She simply
waited for Annie to deliver the denouement.

"I, Moi, Yours truly, have just become associate
editor of Vanity Fair! I'll cover France and Italy."

"Oh Annie! Congratulations.! That's wonderful
news!" Selena was delighted for the recognition she felt
Annie more than deserved.

"Well, it will be a welcome change to be able to pay
ALL my bills on a regular basis, I must say."

The comment was typical Annie, humorous,
understated, but oddly to the point. It said nothing of
the professional leap upwards, and the
acknowledgment of her ability implicit in the new
position.

Noticing a decided glow about Selena, she asked
"And was London all you hoped?"

"Yes, it was. Noah was wonderful." Selena knew this
was an understatement of what she felt and what had
happened, but they'd agreed to keep a low profile for

the time being.

"I'm glad. And you really needed the break" Annie was delighted for her. "And, by the way, I think it may be time for an uptown article on Selena Ltd. What do you think?"

"For us the timing couldn't be better. I just got off the phone with Noah. Neiman wants us to open in San Antonio, St. Louis, and Atlanta."

"How bout using Coast to Coasting as a title ?"

Annie opened a battered filo-fax, and took out a Pentel fountain pen. It was an old friend she used to longhand her articles. Cards and papers fell out of its overstuffed covers, had to be retrieved, and stuffed back in.

"Next week good? I'll start the photography. Won't need you for that right away, but I want to do an exclusive 'V.F.' head shot of you."

She was taking notes rapidly as she talked.

"Annie." Selena raised her voice slightly to interrupt this ongoing rush. "You'll have to give me a couple of weeks. I have a pile of things to do, including some out of town commitments, I can't get out of."

"Okay. To be sure lets make it definite. Three weeks from today."

"Fine." Selena got up and got her coat. "Are you going up town?" Annie nodded." Shall we share a cab?"

"Great.

They left together, neither noticing the middle aged Chinese ostensibly picking out a magazine at a nearby kiosk.

Selena and Noah spent the evening quietly in his apartment. He'd ordered in Suchi and steamed vegetables from a neighborhood Japanese restaurant. They talked of the future.

For the first time Selena used the word love,

speaking with him. She'd wanted Noah to know of her past, to know how special he was. So she told him of Naples, and then of John, and her brief affair with Chen.

Noah took her in his arms, murmuring and kissing her in understanding of what she wanted him to know and feel. He'd found his 'person' in her.

Selena wanted days and weeks and years with him. They made tender, passionate, joyous love.

Still later, sitting side by side in bed, a thick down duvet covered in satin, bathed in the silk shaded light of Noah's large bedroom, they sipped fifty year-old Armagnac, as they reviewed their separate days. They spoke of the new branches to be opened, and the proposed enlargement of what Noah called her Flagship store, the Mott Street salon. He asked when she was going down to see it and offered to make time in his schedule to meet her there if she wished. She did.

They both were at once glad and sorry to be back, considering all they both had to do separately, but still mostly glad. The future, was not without problems or what Selena told him the Italians called 'contra tempi" the arrival of unanticipated obstacles . But it also held for them both, a wonderful promise. A future with one another.

Noah turned off the lights, so the room was bathed only in the moonlight coming from the french windows of the balcony. They turned as one to reach for one another. And so slept the night in each other's arms.

Chapter: 11

Virtually every one had gone by the time Selena and Carla's niece returned from their tour of inspection. One last client was just having her hair blown, and two assistants were gossiping idly as they changed to leave when the door burst open.

A sudden crash, the sound of glass splintering, and high-pitched Kwon screams filled the shop.

Selena spun around. The front window was viciously smashed by a nightmare figure-head to toe in black except for the scarlet symbol blazoned on back and chest. She'd seen them once before!

Two other men, leaped in the door, she knew instantly they were Tong! But why were they here!?

In a flash they assumed martial stance. Feet akimbo, knees bent, clubs held rigidly shoulder height in front of them. They were trained!

The leader pointed quickly. He wanted everything smashed. Crushed. All around her, shattering began.

Counters and equipment erupted in showers of glass under the attack of heavy bats. The noise became incredible-the women shrieking, the sound of breaking metal, the heavy blows of clubs hitting, destroying, gauging out the salon. Violence filled the shop.

For seconds Selena was paralyzed. Too stunned to move.

Then she saw she stood in total wreckage. The shop was destroyed. Gone. But the women had seen it all. They would remember. They would be next.

No! She couldn't let that happen. In a flash she knew the only thing she could do.

She ran for the nearest closet. She had always kept the gun John gave her on the top shelf at the back. She had to defend the few left in the store. There was no choice.

Selena found the gun, grabbed it, and turned.

At just this moment Noah appeared at the door, Grasped the situation in seconds, and without stopping went for the leader.

She saw the flash of a knife, heard a sickening thud. Noah gasped then crumpled against the leader even as he attacked.

A second knife appeared magically, in the Oriental's hand to sink home into Noah's flank.

Without thought, she aimed and fired.

Explosion ricocheted around the small space.

The leader's head disintegrated. He collapsed instantly carrying Noah with him impaled on the knife buried in his side.

Blood from both men began to pour onto the floor.

With the sound of the gun, the other Chinese stopped. Saw what had happened. The gun still smoked in Selena's hand.

They bolted, leaping over the wreckage and the bodies of Noah and their leader.

Selena ran to Noah's side, the gun still rigid in her grasp.

The effort to breathe was becoming torture for him. But he knew he must get her to release it to him.

"Selena. Give me the gun!" He could barely whisper. "I must have it in my hand. The Police...Give me the gun!" He managed to reach his hand toward her. It was slippery with blood.

Without thought she fell to her knees beside him and let him take it, freeing her hands to cradle his head. His blood was pooling rapidly in the glass and debris.

"Noah", she screamed. She took him in her arms, clasping him tight against her breast. His mouth gaped open. A gush of blood came. It frothed as he panted for air. She struggled to breathe for him. She felt him try to once more to inhale, gasp, then shudder. The weight of his body fell against her.

"Noah!" she screamed again. But it was to ears that could no longer hear her. He was dead.

She was seated on the floor, surrounded by shards of glass and metal, rocking his motionless body when the police came.

To them the picture was clear, backed by the witness of the employees, and a customer. The Tong had entered seeking to destroy. Noah was stabbed to death defending, but managed to kill in turn.

The investigation that followed was perfunctory-solved immediately by the open and shut nature of the case.

Selena was numb. It was John who took charge, making arrangements for Noah, with some help from Paul who felt he had to take up the slack at the office immediately, as well as arrange for his father's disposition.

Nicoletta and Annie, did the best they could to comfort her, but she went through the days that followed as an automaton.

Fat figured the Tong, tired of promises, had come to show Chen the consequence of unpaid debts. Gambling debts he owed the Third Dragon Club. Gambling! He thought. An instant of high-a life time of payment. Fat figured, but he had no proof.

Only Chen knew. He was overcome with remorse, then anger, and then again remorse. When he turned to the Tai for aid, it was silent in these matters. His days he folded into silence and absence. Nights when he relived history were broken and haunted by images which when they spoke, spoke harshly in his ears and to his heart.

The police were powerless to identify three Tong

members in a sea of Orientals, and in a protective society, which closed against the foreign devils when official trouble came.

Nothing would ever be quite the same again. They were all scarified by what had happened.

Selena had no sooner found Noah and his love, then they were gone. She overwhelmed by loss.

CEILINGS V

Chapter 1: New York

The great, the near great, and the coat-tail riders; the giants and giantesses of New York and Philadelphia society; the moguls and power brokers as well as the arrivées of business and politics; in short anybody who was anybody or thought they were, were gathered outside Campbells Funeral Home on Madison Avenue one week after Noah's shocking death.

For Campbells, it was the memorial service of the season. They had managed the dozens who wanted to 'view' the deceased, curb-handled the limousines of those paying their respects, and managed to log each visitor meticulously in the 'visitors book'.

Now the large chapel over-fragrant with masses of lilies spiked artistically with the brilliance of the traditional chrysanthemums of mourning, and wreathed with garlands of arbor vitae harbored more than a hundred gathered for the service itself.

Professional grooms in mourning frocks, ushered the invited to their seats. The funerary home had had to augment their normal quota of red plush seating with gold-painted caned folding chairs in the side aisles to handle lesser celebrities, and late arrivals.

The bier which bore Noah's satin-lined ornamented casket was set at the foot of the center aisle, the focal point of perfect sight lines for the attendees.

In point of fact, it had all the earmarks of a state occasion.

Paul Van Vloeck was seated in the front row with a middle-aged woman in a Givenchy version of mourning black, which had not overlooked a heavy widow's veil. It was his mother, Noah's ex-wife, who was either told or felt it incumbent to be present.

Paul had orchestrated the reception in the antechamber prior to the service so that he was able to 'press the flesh' of important 'mourners'. He'd asked John to give the eulogy for his father, bearing in mind Harvey's caliber as a writer of fine words.

Selena was seated near the back of the chapel, drawn and white-faced with grief.

John left the recitation of Noah's many accomplishments and the other landmarks of his life to the Reverend who preceded him. He looked over the sea of faces, and realized despite any quality of 'de riqeur' to the occasion, many were here because it mattered to them, or they admired Noah.

When it came his turn he spoke few words- those of a dear friend to a dear friend-those which echoed Keat's Ode to an athlete dying young-those which he hoped would assuage the pain of those who cared for Noah the man.

Noah was to be cremated. In his will he asked that his ashes be scattered in the upper reaches of the Hudson River, in the heart of the old Dutch Patroon country now mostly desolate. John would see it was done.

Immediately after the service, Paul hired one of Manhattan's eminent caterers for a buffet to be set up in Noah's apartment. They had been engaged to see to important clients and friends who wanted to 'pay their respects' to the family in this most conventional of condolence visits.

Selena wanted simply to sit alone in her apartment as she had for many nights with the lights off, and the music Noah had loved playing softly on the phonograph. He'd especially liked Albinioni's Adagio. Its soaring melodies carried on the strings of the London Philharmonic repeated as she let it go on.

Profound grief was an emotion Selena had so far been spared. For Fatimah she had felt nostalgia and regret. The pain she felt now had no precedent in her life.

She had loved him, and had put him in danger. The vulnerability he had shown only to her, played and replayed in her mind every night until sleeping pills took effect.

If she were just left alone, if there were no demands made on her, if she sat very still, the raw wound that was his death might quiet, stop tearing at her. But she knew as a gesture of respect she had to attend the buffet. It was a must. She was Selena Ltd, a significant client of the firm, and as such she felt she had to put in an appearance.

She rang the buzzer and entered the apartment. In the boiserie of the foyer, a rent-a-maid in black uniform with white apron offered to 'hang her wrap' on a portable coat rack. The uniform barely fit the buxom form of the 'maid', the rented rack could barely contain the Minks and cashmere overcoats crammed one next to the other on rented wire hangers that sagged with the unaccustomed weight. It tipped her off to what she might find inside.

Smoke spiraled up from cigarettes, conversation was muted but an unending tide which flowed around guests, the odor of the caterer pervaded the large living room where a bar and buffet table steadily dispensed mixed drinks and finger food.

Nobody seemed to notice how uneasily all this fit into the antique oak-paneled living room with its Stubbs, Landseers, and Fernleys-18th century horse paintings in their hand carved frames, and the leather bound first editions reposing in sculpted shelves. The indignity of the occasion mocked its surroundings.

As she looked around, it tore at her, this sham

celebration. The last time she'd stood here, it had been in Noah's arms. Then she saw John across the room and started toward him. Just as she got to his side, Paul appeared.

"Selena. Thank you for coming. Father would have been pleased. Won't you have something to drink?"

For a moment Selena thought she'd be sick. The words were so unctuous, so loaded with empty bonhomie. She turned pale with anger and disgust. Dio! What am I to say, she thought.

John broke in, "Paul, just the man I was looking for. I was looking for you to tell you Selena and I have an appointment this evening. I'm so sorry. I tried to break it, but I couldn't. We have to leave shortly." He put his arm lightly around her shoulders, fending for her.

Thank God for John. She found herself just able to nod and smile.

"Of course. I understand." Paul had to accede.

Then he went on, "Selena, perhaps you can give me a call in the morning. There are some strings that Dad left undone. We really need to pull them together."

She had no idea what he meant. But doubted its importance. Noah never left strings.

"I'll call tomorrow," She answered.

John put his arm through hers, and turned towards the door. As he helped her on with her coat, he saw she looked almost ill. In the elevator down he asked, "Tea?"

"Please", was all she could manage.

They stopped at the nearest luncheonette. Got a booth. John ordered then remained silent, realizing that nothing he nor anyone could say would be of comfort at this time-between the devastation of her loss, and the appalling gathering they had just attended.

"Thank you, I don't think I could have borne it for a minute more."

Selena's courtesy and gratitude offered as they were under such stress, were heartbreaking.

Tea and toast arrived. She sipped her tea, but pushed the plate of toast away. Her eyes focused down on the table. She toyed with the plate, absently.

John thought she must have lost pounds in the last week. He knew Annie Karol dropped by each evening with delicacies from Zabar, a renowned purveyor, or one of the Carneighie Delicatessen's specials. Selena was undoubtedly grateful for her presence, but he was equally sure, unable to eat the things she brought.

"You must eat something, Selena." Not only did his heart go out to her, but he was really worried about her appearance and manner.

"It doesn't seem very important right now."

John knew he absolutely must do something about her apathy, and so chose his words deliberately,

" Noah would not appreciate this."

It was a shocking thing to say under the circumstances.

Selena's head snapped up. He saw anger flare in the dark circled eyes.

"How would you know what Noah..." she started only to stop, knowing how well John did know him.

Then in an instant she knew. Not only was John right, but she realized what he was trying to do.

"You are right". She acknowledged.The faintest trace of a smile reached her eyes.

He had succeeded in breaking the chain of inertia which sorrow had clamped on her. After that she pulled the plate of toast toward her and began to eat. It was a symbolic gesture, a promise to get on with her life. Gallantly she went even further in her effort.

"I'll call Paul in the morning. I must tell him as soon as possible, that I have to look for another firm for the company. We don't see things at all alike. Never have and never will. It won't work for me to go on there

The fact that she had used Noah's name was a positive sign.

John was sensitive enough to say nothing more as he escorted her home. And smart enough to know she was on the mend.

Chapter: 2

Nicoletta saved all the obituaries from the papers as they appeared. In addition to the local, national and even international newspapers carried obituaries. She didn't show them to Selena, it wouldn't serve now, but she knew in time she would want to read the tributes to Noah.

She was delighted that her young friend had begun to work again. In addition to its therapeutic value, there was so much that needed the attention only she could give.

They had been able to clean up the wreckage at Mott Street, but exactly what should be done with the shop and its redecoration rested with Selena.

And so, a two weeks after the funeral, Selena went to Mott Street to survey and decide what had to be done to restore the salon. She noted all the traces of violence had been assiduously removed.

She held wallpaper samples in one hand, fabric swatches in the other when the phone rang. She thought it would be either John or Annie Karol calling about dinner plans.

When she heard the sing-song voice and the short brutal message, she knew the Tong had not finished their mission.

She was terrified. The terrible moments when Noah's Body lay crumpled on the floor flashed back. She was helpless. Those cold, nasal sounds in her ear! Meting out punishment.

'Selena Ltd would immediately hire guards to protect every store-now, and in the future. And there would be an additional protection fee. Her linens would be done in their laundries. All deliveries would be carried in their vans. In one week a second call would be placed to give exact instructions as to implementation and coordination.'

She was stunned. Her world falling apart. What on earth am I to do? These people are not to be denied. Such was her shock that for an instant she thought, I must call Noah, he'll know how to handle this ... only to be jerked back into the present by the emptiness of the salon, by the scars and scratches on walls and floor-agonizing reminders of how absurd this reaction was.

She thought for a moment of calling Chen. But in the same moment realized he couldn't help her. She, like Fat knew he gambled and felt more than likely the Tong demands were connected. But what could he say? What could he do? What could he do? One of them had been killed. He had no power to allay or stop these men.

And the police? They would be less than useless. If they couldn't find a murderer, how would they locate the source of an anonymous threat.

The Tong would exact its blood money. For as long as she lived. For as long as Selena Ltd. existed, it would be under a merciless hand demanding pay-off for the life of one of its members.

She knew then the full meaning of the saying 'Revenge is a dish best eaten cold'. It was a cold, endless revenge they would take.

"Hang up!" A deep voice ordered. She looked up to see framed in the doorway a short, dark-haired powerful man. Her instant impression was-he's Sicilian.

"What?...Who are you?", she managed.

In two strides, he was at her side. He was rugged, athletic, and his manner suggested that he wasted little time with niceties. He took the receiver from her hand, and banged it down.

Her confusion and terror were compounded by the

suddenness of his appearance. Something of this must have come across to him. He took her by the arm, and settled her in the nearest available chair.

"The name is Marchetti. Dino Marchetti. And no, you would have no way of knowing who, or what I am. But," he paused for effect, "I am the solution to your problems. I'm pretty sure I could tell you exactly who called you, and what they are asking." He detailed almost exactly what the Chinese demanded.

Selena was bowled over. She had no idea what to make of this man and his uncanny knowledge. Clinging to the arms of the chair, shock set in. Her teeth began to chatter.

"That's no good." Dino said and pulled a silver flask from his hip pocket. "Brandy. You'd better take a slug." She didn't move or seem to understand.

"Beve!" Drink, he said succinctly.

Selena in spite of her terror had several swallows.

"Now a deep breath." She did as she was told.

"Better Now?" he demanded. Surprisingly she was. "The whole of the Quartiere knew the Chinks would attack."

His allusion to the Quartiere told her that he was a denizen of Little Italy.

" This salon was Maria Gemignani's, now yours-Selena Ltd. Yes?"

It wasn't a question although his voice inflected it as a type of inquiry requiring some response.

"Yes. Exactly."

He smiled. She was aware of strong approval in his look. "It is always good, to remember who helps you start." She was aware of approbation.

Then in a swift mood shift he said somberly, "But I must tell you, in my experience, what the Tongs start, they finish. Why smash and trash your salon and let it go at that? Especially as you managed to rob them of the services of one of their senior soldiers."

And in the same mode he went on "And, you have just lost your Consiliere." Now Selena knew that likely he was not only Sicilian and of the Quartiere, but mostprobably Mafioso.

This dynamo of a man was not yet finished. " In a nut shell- you've lost your business manager, and are now threatened with an untenable yoke."

The last phrase startled her. It was a sophisticated metaphor. Not at all what you would expect from a member of Cosa Nostra. It had nothing of the street in it.

In a mercurial change Dino laughed uproariously. "Got you, didn't I?! Come let me take you somewhere where we can sit and talk with calm. I think I can make some sense out of all this for you, but this is not the place. You need to get away from here for a while." His tone combined the authoritative and polite. She agreed. She had to get out of the salon for now.

He took her to a neighborhood Trattoria-dark, refulgent of tomato, basil and garlic. The owner came over, patted Dino on the back, with familiar affection, and recited several choices of pizza del giorno, flavors of the day. Selena felt she couldn't make any decisions not even as to what to eat, and indicated he should choose.

"Bad as that, eh?", he chuckled. When she started to take umbrage, he added quickly, "I don't really find the situation funny. It's just not being able to choose from the suggestions here which are limited to three choices of pizza is funny. And by the way, It's the real thing here done in a wood fire oven."

As Selena had still not chosen, he said to the owner, " La Signora prenda Pizza Margarita, e una birra Azzuro."

To her surprise, Selena was able to finish her meal.

And was thirsty enough for two beers.

Over expresso Dino told her just who he was and what he thought should be done about her situation. She understood clearly a number of points which helped .

The first was that the Tong attack represented an intolerable incursion into his territory for Don Salvatore, Capo of the area's Mafia. The family's power was at her disposal, and Dino had been sent as representative to tell her so.

Until the problem raised by the Tong was dealt with, and dealt with permanently, nothing else counted. He made it clear that the attack seemed like the first moves of a major turf war. It was not her war, and so she would incur no obligation in accepting their help. But a meeting with the men controlling the Tong was set for within the week.

Selena believed him. She was aware of the incendiary nature of the territorial feud which had been growing for years. She knew of the power of Cosa Nostra. And Dino made it clear that he was a lieutenant speaking for the Don in this matter. Although he told her she would not be trading one master for another, she was not entirely convinced.

However, It looked as if she had no options. This man offered the only feasible solution, and so she said with wry humor, "When you have a choice of one, two through ten don't seem to count."

Dino laughed. He sensed that this small figure of a woman, who'd been struck with so much trouble and sadness, was a survivor. So, he went on to the second subject he had in mind.

" My usual work is as an independent business consultant." He handed her a business card. "I know your company. In fact I have a small participation in the limited partnership. I find it has an enormous potential, which hasn't been fully exploited, and I would like to help see that potential become a reality."

Again Selena was taken by surprise. This is my day for shake-ups she thought. But one shake up I cannot permit, is to have my business an offshoot of Cosa Nostra. Would there be strings or subtle ties if she let Marchetti become a part of Selena Ltd.?

Dino was pretty sure what she was thinking. "I am the Don's friend, but I have been independent of the famiglia, with his blessing for many years. It's a long story, but you can easily check it out. The Don sent me through college and business school, so that I could help with this 'outside training' the Famiglia's, need to get into legitimate business postures, and refocus the intent and efficiency of their organization. Crime has become more and more targeted, and risky these last decades. And that is as long a curriculum Vitae, as I've ever given anyone."

Selena wanted to hear all of what he would propose. Mocking gently, she still wanted to be reassured that this was not a ploy of the Famiglia.

"Go on, independent Business consultant," was her way of encouraging , and distancing without agreeing.

"After we deal with the Tong, I propose we sit down again. You let me tell you about my experience and the companies I've handled. If you like what you hear, you take me on as business manager. I'm not Van Vloeck. But I have my own ways, and they usually work."

The words had a braggadocio but nevertheless seemed to come from a man who knew who he was. Certainly it was not the statement of an underling, or one who was obligated.

Selena was not sure how she knew, but understood, that this, a man who usually took what he wanted or made it happen, was asking for once.

If he could truly deal with the Tong, she would listen

with care to his proposal.

Chapter: 3

Nothing would have it but Dino would escort her home. She recognized the elaborate Italian male formality in the gesture, however this once was grateful for the protectiveness involved, and there was something truly genuine in his concern.

The customized Lincoln Continental seemed to have everything except hot and cold running water. She asked for and got an ice cold ginger ale on the way. And was gently handed out when she arrived at her curb.

Once home she made a beeline for her bathroom, and a luxurious bath. She'd had a sunken tub fitted out with a Jacuzzi in a mood of self-indulgence when she had earned enough to buy the modest co-op on lower Broadway.

The rest of the apartment consisted of a living room, bedroom, and well appointed kitchen. It was her first real home, and she loved it.

Exposed brick walls, bookshelves, a good stereo, and lots of plants was the way she described it. She remembered to thank Maria once again for the gem she had made for her in her weekly letter. The letters kept contact, but she missed the smile, the love, and the care of her 'carissima Mama' every day.

Once bathed and more relaxed, she took stock of the events of her day. For once she thought she'd really like to get the reaction of her team.

She called Nicoletta first. After listening to Selena describe what happened, and hearing that her voice was calm, her thoughts orderly, Nicoletta felt they should go along with Dino.

"Cara mia, if there is to be a long future, there must be a short one, don't you think?"

Selena had to agree.

"And if this Dino can give it to us, we must accept, no?"

"Lei a raggione", you are right, my wise Nicoletta. You will be there when he presents his plans for us?"

"Certamente! Senz' altro!" There is no way I would miss it.

Annie Karol had more specific information. She said that Marchetti was known throughout Little Italy, as a square-shooter, who didn't have to kow-tow to the Don. He was also the Don's illegitimate grandson, which may have had something to do with his original sponsorship, his education, and subsequent freedom.

However, she said, it was believed that Dino had 'made his bones', that was the term for a ritual murder usually in revenge for an injury or betrayal on behalf of the famiglia. He was not the man to be trifled with or taken lightly as a caricature Sicilo-American.

"I'd go with it, but watch yourself kid" was her conclusion.

Fat had to admit that he felt they needed help, and that the most effective help would be of the kind Dino offered. For once he sounded subdued, and used complex sentences to render his opinion. She knew he felt miserable about his cousin's probable involvement.

She didn't call Chen. It would have been too painful for her to have her suspicions confirmed, and would have so robbed him of face, that he would have had to do something drastic about distancing himself from her and Selena Ltd. And this she didn't want.

Although as the sole personal beneficiary of Noah's will he had become a major stockholder in Selena Ltd., she also didn't bother to call Paul. She was certain he would tell her to call the police-an exercise in futility. She hadn't yet told him of her decision to use another firm for future work.

Finally she called Dino, and told him to go ahead.

Chapter: 4

Even the Police picked up that Canal Street was preternaturally calm just after midnight two days after Dino and Selena spoke. It was so arranged by the two negotiating parties.

The meeting held in Lower Manhattan, lasted until three in the morning. An entente was worked out which would serve the immediate desires of both groups, and set the terms for avoidance of direct confrontation.

Included in the agreement as a rider, was a permanent hands-off on all Selena Ltd properties and business. The trade-off for this particular inclusion was some slight give on the Italian stranglehold on the wholesale fruit and produce markets, especially with regard to fruits classified by fruiterers as 'over ripe'.

Dino set an appointment to see Selena two days after this. He needed the time to check on two or three of the proposals he wanted to advance. With his call, she understood without asking that her problems with the Tong had been settled.

What Dino wanted for Selena Ltd. should have come as no shock, and yet she was startled by its scope and boldness. Nicoletta, present as she promised, found she was often in agreement on points that he made. Her desire for Selena Ltd to continue to grow was strong, and her grasp of the interface between customer and product complete, so she was able to appreciate his plans from her special point of view.

In essence Selena Ltd was to go international starting with Italy, Germany and England, to be followed in short or order by the rest of Europe including France, and then South America. Nicoletta smiled. When Selena asked about France being in the second group rather than the first, Nicoletta answered for Dino.

" Because, the French are aware that Italy, or more specifically Milano has begun to set the real fashion pace these days. Yet the French will not want to be left long on the shelf and will want the imprimature of Alta Moda Italiana. By giving it to Italy first, you create a 'must have' situation in France, cara. You will walk into Paris with a ready-made market just waiting for you. But Rio, and Buenos Aires still follow established French chic slavishly." She gave Dino full marks for smart promotion and marketing strategy.

"Then too", Marchetti said," we ought to open in some of the cities in the states where Nieman is not going to go. The publicity you've made here with every appearance and every advertisement in national publications-Vogue, Bazaar, Vanity Fair, should be maximized.

Even in Ocala Florida, or Duluth Michigan, or Tuscaloosa, the women read of Selena Ltd and her extraordinary owner. Why should they be less glamorous than their big city sisters?" This time Selena nodded seeing clearly where he was going.

Now, to do all this, and increase factory facilities, we need to do two things that require outside help. The first is to hire a law firm that specializes in international law. That means that we will be giving a substantial amount of business to a law firm other than Van Vloeck's.

But bear in mind, you don't want to create enemies whenever you can avoid it, certainly not of old friends, and remembering also that Paul van Vloeck is a large stock holder, we should let him suggest the bank to help capitalize us, and also let him set up the new Corporation. At least let him 'paper' it, I'll have it re-checked elsewhere."

"But why a new Corporation, Dino. We already have a company."

"Because we're talking big numbers. Much easier handled or raised using a Chapter-S Corporation. Also, I want you out from under the financial liability you have as general partner in a limited partnership."

Selena began to acquire a healthy respect and gratitude for the shrewdness and vision of this charged-up business sophisticate who had literally popped into her life.

Dino went with her to see Paul-whose first reaction to the plans was to be miffed at not remaining the sole legal firm to the new organization. But even he had to admit international law was one of the few weaknesses in his own firm.

Then he realized the advantage he would gain from bringing a large piece of business to his very close friends at Hanover Bank and Trust. It would put him in a strong position with a major financier especially as he himself wanted to continue with the initial capitalization of start-up firms, as his father had done so successfully.

" I think we can work with this. How much were you thinking of raising?"

"About thirty-five million. A total cap of fifty, puts us in the small but not insignificant corporate range, and will cover our immediate needs."

It was a symbol of Paul's recognition that he would not assume his Father's position in Selena Ltd, that he did not demand at this minute to know exactly what Selena had in mind.

When she got home that evening, Selena called Maria, to tell her what had been happening. It was too pressing and altogether too much to explain in the weekly letter.

Maria was startled but thrilled. But made it very

clear she did not need all the money Selena was sending her, and didn't want any shares in the new corporation. Her cousins were comfortably situated, and she didn't wish to leave a complicated estate.

Interestingly Fat said much the same. He had a thing for cash, and would accept with pleasure a raise or bonus, but didn't want shares in anything. This was a thoroughly traditional Chinese reaction, which she found surprising in him, but accepted. He would receive very generous compensation in the new set up.

John's reaction was more distressing. He had always distrusted Chen, his warning about California had gone unheeded. Now he had lost a very close friend, and there was quickly a new influence of obvious importance to Selena Ltd. making large-scale changes, that he was being asked to go along with.

His reaction was to withdraw entirely from the day to day doings of Selena and the company with some astringency, but to accept the transfer of his financial interest to the new company as she wished.

"I can only hope that you know what you're doing!"

"John, many things you are, but a businessman is not one of them!"

"Of course I'm not a businessman, but even I have heard of some of the things the Mafia is doing these days. And even I can worry about a scam." Even knowing it was concern for her that caused him to argue, Selena began to be angry with him.

"Have you checked him out?"

"When you have a choice of one, two through ten don't count, John! She reminded him as she reminded herself of the basic facts of her situation."

"I only hope you know what you're doing.!"

"You said that already. I can only hope that I do.!" And on this note they had to leave it.

As to Selena and Dino, it was soon clear that he was

a hands-on type of business manager. Their working relation was nearer a partnership than anything else, and that partnership was volatile.

Raised voices were often heard through the paneled doors of Selena's office. People were amazed that Selena could permit anyone to talk to her like that. And even more amazed to hear her responding in kind, in an English liberally sprinkled with Italian words, phrases, even whole sentences..

Necessary ritual in a combative combination of energies and egos, a natural Latin way of relating, or a defusing of tension between the female boss and her right hand man-whatever it was, they got used to it.

The squalls were usually over very shortly after they began. While she was often angry for a day, Dino was able to proceed within moments as if nothing had happened.

As for the plans laid out at the original meeting of these two dynamos, they came more and more into being with every day.

She was the head of the company, that was clear. Dino made no move to undermine her, he understood too well that Selena herself was the image of the company thanks to the promotion which had started in Vanity Fair. And that the instinctive genius behind the development of products and their marketing would always be hers. Without Selena herself and the special products she inspired, Selena Ltd. would be just another american cosmetics company which couldn't compete with the Europeans.

It was mutual. Selena Ltd needed Dino. He had extricated her from a frightening mess. His connections and his strategies were paving the way for the crucial phase of international development. If Noah had been the fund-raising wizard, Dino was a genius at making things happen.

She wondered about his life growing up. What must it have been like for him being the unacknowledged Grandson of such a notorious man as Don Salvatore.

Chapter: 5

The blow came out of nowhere. A rocket that dropped him to the canvas. The arena spun upside down. Dino had no idea of what happened. One in minute he was up, weaving and bobbing in spite of a rapidly closing eye. The next, a heavy hook to his temple exploded. It had to have come from his blind side.

Pain came along with the gush of blood from his nose. Right before his eyes he could count each grain of rosin and stitch of canvas. He had never seen them so clear. Beyond them, the expanse of ring, and beyond that a blur of screaming spectators. Many on their feet, their mouths open and working. He knew they were screaming for more blood and punishment, but he couldn't hear their cries, only the rush of his pulse loud in his ears.

Blood. They loved seeing blood. And they counted in cadence with the referee, 2-3-..he managed to get his head off the canvas. He knew he should not have lied about his age. A thirteen year-old had little chance against the heavier build of sixteen.

Pain pounded with his heart beat. The arena began to swim again...

4-5-6..

Then he caught the eyes of Don Salvatore sitting in the first row. The remote yellow eyes of a tiger which said, 'get up boy, Be a man. Get to your feet. And fight.' 7-8..

He knew he must do it. He could not win the fight, but he must not lose it here, down on the floor, like an animal. He rolled over and rose to his knees.

Approval gleamed in Don Salvatore's eyes, 9.. He

got to his feet, crouching, and waiting for his opponent. He had no clear recollection of the rest of the round. And then it was over.

He had been defeated, but left the ring on his own, a dirty blood-stained towel draped over him, shielding part of his eyes, and swollen mouth from those of avid prying fans.

Sometime in the last round he had lost his mouthpiece, unnoticed by the referee. The jabs of his opponent, had landed on his unprotected mouth. He spit out the accumulation of bloody saliva.

It was his first club fight, and he would get twenty dollars.

He had no clear memory of the walk to the locker room after the fight-couldn't remember putting one foot on front of the other.

What he did remember was the roughness of the filthy towel draped about his head and neck. It reeked of old sweat, liniment, and dirt.

It was over. He wasn't sure what he'd proved, but he'd done it. He was a man. He felt the rough wood of the scarred bench pressing against his bare shoulder blades. He was glad be able to lie down on the locker room bench.

After the glare of the overhead bulb stopped shifting and he was finally able to focus, he sat up and leaned his elbows on his knees, drawing his breath slowly in, and releasing it, as he rested for a moment.

Someone handed him a paper bag full of ice. 'Put it on and keep it on. Keep the swelling down', he was told. It smarted like hell, but...They were probably right. He closed his eyes briefly.

When he opened them again he was looking directly down at a pair of black mirror-bright wing-tipped shoes. Such small feet he remembered thinking. He heard a gravely old man's voice speak,

"Boy..." It was a command.

He had to look up and into the face of Don Salvatore Gobbia. The Don, known as one of the deadliest of Mafia Capos had a reputation as a dandy. This night, he wore his trademark black raw silk suit, with a dazzling shirt of the finest Lawn, with a silver repp four-in-hand tie.

Dino had no way of knowing about these things. But he did know exactly who this tiny figure in front of him was. It was simple-the dispenser of all the good things of this world if pleased, the dispenser of debt or even death if crossed.

"What age are you?"

Dino couldn't lie. "Thirteen."

"Thirteen," the deep voice repeated without inflection.

He felt a broad hand clear off the towel, and knew the Don was looking at the mess about his nose and mouth.

"On your way home, boy, you stop at Donatelli's Farmacia." It was a well-known drugstore in little Italy. A five-dollar bill drifted down onto his lap.

"You come to me tomorrow."

There was no need for the Don to say where or when. Everyone knew the Social club where he spent his afternoons playing cards, and administering the affairs of his famiglia.

Followed closely by a small entourage of muscle, Don Salvatore left.

Dino could make no sense of why he should have come for a local 'palooka' or 'virgin' fight card, especially in this broken down arena, but then this was not the time to try to make sense of anything. It was time to wash up as best he could, change, and get out of here. As to where he would spend the night...wherever he could with some degree of safety.

He left the arena, Dino broke the twenty he won, and ate a huge Pasta with 'scungil' chased with a bottle of 'Rosso Italiano', the cheapest red wine. As the weather was warm, no rain threatened, he slept out in a downtown pocket park. It was locked up at night but 'open' to anyone with his touch for a hasp and pin lock.

Squeezed in between the Roma Expresso bar, and a small printing press, the Grand Street Social Club could easily have been overlooked. Its windows were small and dusty, its doorway narrow, the whole building had a battered look. It was deliberate, a kind of veiling to all but the initiates. All three were owned by Don Salvatore's Famiglia.

The Don came every day to the Social club after lunch. In the early afternoon he tended to family matters-collections from numbers and betting, quarrels to be settled, promotions and plans to be reviewed, and intrafamily affairs to be considered. It was busy but entirely orderly and effective. In fact one eminent civil court judge, for years 'in the pocket' of Don Salvatore had been quoted as saying he wished his court room ran as efficiently. Later there would be the permanent on-going card game with cronies.

On each corner of the block, and across from the entrance heavy 'muscle' lounged casually. If one ignored the dead-cold eyes that never ceased to rove the block, and the bulge in the jacket coat to accommodate a shoulder holster, they might have been neighborhood louts simply hanging about.

"How long this time?" The question came without preamble of any sort as soon as he was led into the back room by a soldier with a wrestler's build.

Dino responded directly to the Don's question.

"She got a dime."

Both referred to the sentence just handed down to Dino's Mother for dealing drugs. It was her third conviction.

"Heavy. Was it a three time?"

"Yes."

"Ah." The Don expressed complete understanding. Actually he was pretty sure he had the picture before he summoned the boy. Ten years for a third time drug related felony was not an unusual sentence.

Dino's Mother was a full-time street dealer, and part-time whore. His Father had simply melted away a year or so after he was born. The first time she was caught, she was sent up for a year. The boy had been foisted on a cousin, who resented an active fresh-mouthed eight-year-old who was nothing but trouble. But the cousin was also a user glad to be paid off as soon as Dino's mother got out and got her hands on his drug of choice.

The second time involved three years in an upstate penitentiary. She had to make arrangements for him to stay with 'an Aunt' who'd slept days and worked nights. It didn't work. He was underfoot and present at awkward times. Once he was beaten badly by a 'friend' sleeping over for being the wrong person in the wrong place-at the wrong time, and to some extent just for the hell of it.

He'd run from the 'friend' into life on the street, and a series of street jobs, mostly 'errands'. Occasionally he'd get to stock goods for a neighborhood store.

In the streets he'd learned there'd better be no one and nothing on whom you depend. He'd learned not to expect but to take what came for all it was worth. He'd learned that to be hungry wasn't the worst that could happen.

Ultimately he found steady employment in the local gym as a spit boy. Working in the corner of the club fighters who trained there, and paid him out of their meager purses. He held the swabs of styptic and the buckets for the expectorated water in between rounds.

As to school, he was truant. But the system was such an anarchy of violence and inefficiency, over burdened with pupils, under-supervised, and only minimally dedicated to education, that one more truant was never missed.

Dino found there was much in the halls and yards of the inner city world of Education that made survival problematic. The street was actually safer, especially for one who's skin had no tint.

He'd fought on the streets, for street 'rights'-scraps and jobs. Watching the Hispanics go at it, he'd perfected techniques, with a shiv and the underhand tactics that went with them. The part which involved fists, he picked up from over-the-hill or no-hope boxers at the gym.

At thirteen, his education in hand to hand combat was advanced.

The Don guessed a great deal about the youngster he'd called in. Dino's Mother was the by-blow of an ill-considered affair the Don had had when he was young with a stunning young whore who'd not 'taken precautions'-figuring if she got impregnated, she had a sinecure for life. For the brief duration of her days she was right.

She'd borne a daughter, the Don knew to be his. He'd set up a small apartment and income for her. Within a few short years she'd drugged and drunken it all away.

Despite his attempts to have her cared for and educated, the daughter, predictably, had followed a sad but identical path.

The Don was determined that her son should not. And was pleased when he found Dino to be durable and smart. He now hoped with just a touch of ductility to go along.

The boy reminded him strongly of the toughness of his own hard youth. He knew what it took to live for long on the streets, it spoke of qualities he looked for only in himself and a few tried family soldiers.

As to Dino, he had no idea of a future, much less what next week or even tomorrow might bring. But remembering his Mother, there was one thing he would have nothing to do with, not now and not ever. Drugs. With this the Don was in complete accord.

" You're a street boy, Eh?"

" Si, Don Salvatore."

"I've seen your fists. What else do have?"

For answer, Dino whipped out his Shiv. Even faster he felt the cold steel of a gun pressed against his ear. It was totally unexpected and shocking. He felt a surge of adrenaline.

"First lesson-don't ever pull a weapon, you don't intend to use. And don't ever pull a pea-shooter when you can figure others around you got automatics. Capisci?"

For the Don, this was a sermon length speech. He waved the gunsel to back off.

Then added, " You come to work for me."

It might have been a statement or question. But for sure it was a one-chance offer. If Dino turned it down, it would not be repeated. If he accepted, it was a lifelong commitment. Dino accepted without a second thought.

"Tonight you sleep in the back room. Tomorrow you start St. Patrick's. Here."

The Don beckoned him over, poked a ten-dollar bill in his shirt pocket, and waved him away in the general direction of the furnace room. There were no further words. The Don turned back to his table, in anticipation of the card luck he would have this afternoon.

The next months brought fetch and carry chores for the Don and his soldiers, and school with endless home assignments handed out by the iron-willed demands of dedicated teaching Sisters. He found himself challenged in a new way, and was as he always would be, unable to resist responding.

Dino ate at the local pizzeria, and slept in the room next to the furnace. The Don was generous with money, but other than that seemed to take no further interest. As to the famiglia, no matter how low the rung, he was one of them annointed by the Capo. They accepted him. And sharing their street knowledge-taught him favored techniques of enforcement; how to calculate the vigorish on a bet; how to spot undercover police, and trouble in an instant; how to use the garrote, gun and muscle in controlled but punishing ways.

Word came to the Don that his daughter was killed in a fight started by an inmate in the penitentiary. The instigator was dispatched within the week-a single shot to the back of the head, the trademark Cosa Nostra execution.

The Don informed Dino, who listened to the events of his Mother's death without reaction. What was there to say? The inevitable arrived. Nothing new in that. His mother had danced on the knife-edge of trouble for years, and as always happened in the end, the blade turned on her.

During the days, the next years brought graduation from high school with high marks, to everyone's surprise except the Don's. The nights, brought another sort of high marks, from the ladies of the Famiglia's 'Houses' for his precocious sexual encounters.. And at the end an interview with the Don.

"I understand you're quite the man." His activities with the ladies had not escaped notice. Dino had sense enough not to answer.

"If you haven't fried your Cervello, your brain, from the night life and vino, and if your Cazzo doesn't fall off and leave you half a man, I have plans for you. Deh, but you need to clean yourself up, scabbo." Again here was a take it or leave it instruction. Dino chose to take it.

"Yes, Don Salvatore. It will be as you wish."

" Scabacchione! Don't butter. Listen. You are smart. Listen and learn."

Dino knew no one smarter than the Don himself. No one who better understood the world and how it worked, how to get and hold power. The Don called him over to his table for the first time and indicated he should sit.

"The days of the Pistol Petes are done. The days of smash and grab are over. The days when there was no one but us are finished. Now we got contenders-the chinks, and the spics and the melanzanos", he used the Sicilian slang for blacks. They're all grabbing a piece of power.

" The Narcs, and Feds have gotten smarter. They've been turned onto drugs by the press and the politicos. It's their Numero Uno. But gambling, and the supply business don't cut it on their list much anymore. So We, we're going to change, play where gli altri, those others, aren't strong or don't care as much. We'll stay with gambling-the public wants it, the cops turn an eye. The restaurant supply business, the garbage hauling, may they stay solid.

But what we really want to do is go legit. We got years of money to bank and convert, and more to come if we're smart. It won't happen tomorrow... maybe the day after. But we're going to need people who can handle it. More than anything. Smart people. Educated people. American business people. People we trust. Capisce?"

Dino understood completely the current

movements around him. Drug trafficking was surely going to bring major investigative forces down on an ongoing basis for the foreseeable future. Especially now when some of the greedier families had set up as dealers to the kiddie market. And others who were competing and killing for exclusivity in cocaine and heroin. The Feds would get hot after them. Then there were Gang vendettas and violence-more and more they brought arrests and court trials, and a public insisting that these not be tolerated. Labor Unions which had been in the Mafia pockets, were becoming independent, reform minded. The clout and control of Cosa Nostra was simply not what it had been, nor would it ever be again..

"You're going to College, and then business school. Then you'll be of some use", Don Salvatore told him.

It was as the Don said. He was sent to N.Y.U. and then on to graduate business school. Here he mastered other 'street' tactics-equally deadly or dirty, but not usually punished by imprisonment. Many sanctioned American business practices could only be described as cutthroat, rock-hard, or killer.

The Don knew something else. Going to college in this enclave North of Houston street, miles culturally from Little Italy, was a deliberate separation and seasoning. If he'd been a 19th Century scion of one of New York's golden Four Hundred families, he would have been sent off for two or three years to be finished, readied for a role in polite society by a 'Stay abroad' most particularly in the cultural centers of Europe.

As it was, being a student in the center of the Village did much the same, it gave him perspective. It gave him a chance to interact with students from a very different walk of life.

With his male colleagues, he discussed the problems raised by the subjects they studied, and the assignments of the professors who taught them. With his female colleagues, interchanges tended to be horizontal, and the subjects intensely interpersonal.

He bonded with no one. But was so vital, and so real that both took to him. He learned well the use of charm which could either maintain distance with the appearance of closeness, or attract those he wanted, or simply ease his way through life, gaining whatever he sought with the least expense, personal commitment or effort.

By the time he was twenty-five he was handsome, polished in a typically New York urban male way, and well on his way to fulfilling the Don's wishes.

At twenty-seven he had finished two degrees. Then as a 'Man' was given a gun. The Don had not abandoned all the old ways and traditions of Cosa Nostra.

One of the Famiglia's lesser bagmen, thinking small missing sums would never be noticed, was caught skimming the take from several numbers parlors by the Don, who knew what was owing to the penny. There would be no discussion. No warning. He would simply be disposed of.

At twenty-eight Dino was given the assignment. Without cavil or comment, he 'made his bones'. Then in the same manner, he returned the gun he'd used to the Don. Both men knew that it spelt the beginning of a different relationship. Dino would never be a soldier. He would be an associate, and a consultant when and because both men agreed.

At twenty-nine he had bought and sold two laundries, three 24-hour souvenir shops on 42nd street, and produced several popular porn videos. The profits were laundered in the Cayman Islands and then turned over into a chain of highly profitable electronics stores.

At thirty He had acquired a dress code, which

echoed the Don's, had a small penthouse uptown, and a cottage in Casa di Campo in Santa Domingo. And when at thirty-nine, with a sense of the watershed of forty, he counted, he had laid over a hundred women.

At forty-three he decided to rescue and become an integral part of Selena Ltd..

Chapter: 6

Over the next year, the curtain of grief for Noah lifted. Looking at Dino one day over a worktable littered with papers, after one of their frequent high voltage arguments, she was shocked to feel an ache of physical attraction.

There was an animal quality to the way he moved like a big cat, graceful and powerful. The dark suits he wore suggested more than they concealed of the powerful body underneath them. That he had charm was undeniable.

From time to time, she'd registered his appeal, it was always there, but resolutely ignored it. And if he felt anything beyond the casual for her, it wasn't apparent. They were a working team. They worked closely. There was so much to be achieved that without giving it undue thought, she hadn't considered her personal life. God knew, Selena Ltd provided enough excitement, demanded her full attention and energy each and every day.

But too Selena knew that many of the arguments over matters for Selena Ltd sprung out of intense strongly held opinions and feelings on matters. Neither she nor Dino were cool strategists, or number crunchers. Decisions were hammered out as the expression had it 'tooth and claw!' That was funny combined with her image of Dino as a big Cat. But the point was, she had to acknowledge, that when these kinds of fights were resolved, either it led the two combattants to the point of separation, or in resolution, much closer. All mano a mano combat took place in intimacy no matter what the weapon.

Now, as her numbness and guilt about Noah began

to wear off, and as some parts of the European development began to fall into place and function without hourly attention, her senses awakened. She could do little to stop it. Physical attraction brought into play by proximity-it was not unpleasant, even titillating, an edgy feeling of excitement. The thought had sometimes crossed her mind that she would never again feel this way.

She found herself staring at Dino's tanned, forearms rippling with beautifully articulated muscle, and covered with dark hair like a sleek animal pelt, as he rolled up his sleeves. Or catching the attractive scent of his aftershave, combined with slight perspiration after a day's work.

Catching her glance one day he looked back at her, briefly, quizzically. The aura of her desire was so strong, that he couldn't help but pick it up. Selena felt that it gave him a power over her she wasn't sure she liked.

She would ignore it except to permit herself the occasional fantasies that were delivering her whether she would or no from the memory of Noah, the dreams from which she awoke caressing herself, and could do nothing about. Dino would never know.

With an amazing tenacity and talent for cutting through red tape, he arranged for the registration of Selena International in Germany, Scandinavia, Holland, Belgium, and England.

Business in Europe being complicated and subject to a tangle of laws and restrictions particular to each country, Selena Ltd needed a team of international lawyers who worked endless hours to create an interlocked European enterprise of the individual national companies.

It seemed an overwhelming project. Enormous. She lived in the grip of a heady, unpredictable mix of damn-the-torpedoes excitement, and full-stop checks to be overcome. Always overcome, or surmounted or evaded-often with a Dino-patented solution.

Italy was complicated in its own particular fashion. The delicate and not so delicate, eternally intricate relationship of the legitimate and the illegitimate being more than familiar to him, Dino took charge of the establishment of Selena Italia personally, disappearing for any number of quick visits to Milan, Rome, and Genoa before announcing to Selena that it was time for the two of them to 'go home.'

She had to go. The other branches in many of the other countries had stabilized for the moment. And all of the Italian women's magazines awaited interviews with her. Photography sessions were scheduled. Her personal roller coaster feelings were irrelevant.

Another matter weighed on her. The tour was so tightly scheduled that it would allow no time for a side trip to Naples.

Naples which Dino had proposed but she had turned down as a possible Selena Ltd branch city. It was something she had thought about, but still didn't know entirely why she had decided no.

She had distanced the thought of her family, cold-storing feelings with sizable gifts of money sent-to which there'd never been any response nor acknowledgment.

The idea of her family reading about her in the newspapers stuck her as so bizarre, she had no way to deal with it. The idea of her success-much the same. Ah well, despite her ambivalence, it would have to wait, as would anything else personal until this Italian promotion was achieved.

She packed her suitcases with the best of her couture pieces. And thought ironically but fondly of Maria as she did so. One thing she had no doubts about, once she got work out of the way, she would make time to visit her, even if she had to get to the mountain village on mule's back.

Chapter: 7

Dino promised her a whirlwind, and he was as good as his promise. She was barely conscious of the greyness of Milano-its elegant shops, and gracious streets- Via Montenapoleone, Via Spiga, the soaring glass of the Victor Emanuelle arcade, and the elegance of La Scala; nor Venezia, glorious queen of the Adriatic, its canals crossed by arching small bridges, the ochre Palazzi whose intimate balconies overlooked the waters from which the dream city rose, and the space and beauty of St. Marks; nor Genova at the head of the Italian Riviera embraced by surrounding terraces of carnations, and visited by the top ships of every cruise line.

And then-Roma. The earth colors. The noise, the incessant movement, the sheer masculinity of the city made her blood race. Beautiful boys with smooth chests flew by on Vespas smiling irresistibly while dodging around flocks of fully habited nuns; the mass of the coliseum deserted by the Romans for so many years. but home to hundreds of wild stray cats, whose sinewy forms flitted in and about the ruined columns and stands, the Forum its walls chiseled with ancient Roman family names whose renown celebrated classical history; the grace of the curving descent of tree lined Via Veneto, Piazza Navone with its Bernini masterpieces, the beauty of sculptured fountains forever spouting from the centers of neighborhood squares, or the public squares beloved of Piranesi still caught in the magnificent perspective he etched; the smell of roast coffee wafting from corner bars; the exuberant noise and clamor the city spawned. Above all the sun baked languor within the furor that was Roma.

The city's insolent energy evoked her confidence. She approached it in a siege frame of mind. She would meet it head on and she would conquer. However, she couldn't deny it was a man's city, and she was not unhappy to have Dino at her side.

The Italian press took to Selena as its new celebrity. Her pictured adorned the covers of Oggi, Gente and of course, Italian Vogue whose edition was timed to appear during her visit. They loved the idea of the Italian girl having vanquished America and returning home.

Still she had to continue to seduce and conquer at the never-ending rounds of meetings, and cocktails, and press briefings. Day after day went by, as Italian fashion dictated, into the small hours of the morning. But the coverage was gratifying, the openings successfully achieved, Selena Ltd. well and truly launched in her native country.

Accustomed by now to Dino's scheduling and trusting that his timing was good, she agreed when he suggested they steal a couple of days in the hills of Umbria to celebrate the successful launch .

The drive north was broken when they stopped for a merenda-simple local bread covered with garlic and tomatoes. Caciotta cheese washed down by a bottle of Lambrusco in the generous Umbrian sunshine.

"Well, Selena, wonderful as it is to get away, I've got to tell you how great you were with the Press. I've been around a lot of pros, but you're a natural."

"Grazie. I seem to remember you saying we were under-using our publicity."

"Yes, I think I did." Dino's lack of false modesty made her smile.

"Let's forget about business, relax and enjoy this fabulous countryside."

Dino was quick to accept the suggestion, "Good

idea!"

Looking at his perfect physique encased in immaculately tailored tight khakis, the warm olive of his skin, the flashing eyes which showed no signs of fatigue, the thick slicked-back hair, feeling the sun warm her own skin, smelling the freshness of ripening grape wines, and field of grain waiting to be scythed, it felt good to be alive. And as the sensuality of the countryside filled her she reflected partly with guilt, partly with hope that if she was beginning to feel something of happiness, Noah would have been glad for her. It was time.

The country was magnificent. Tiled roofs sheltered low Umbrian farmhouses that dotted the valley, blending with the earth, covered with vines, surrounded by flowers and blessed by the warmth of a sunshine belonging only to the Mediterranean, perhaps only to Italy, perhaps only to this day.

Native poets celebrated in terza rima hundreds of years ago what she could still see before her-the working of the rich volcanic soil, or long convivial wine filled meals on shaded terrazzi with old friends, family , even strangers, under the skies brilliant overhead.

"The Olive surely must be the most beautiful tree God ever made", Selena mused aloud, as she watched the play of sunlight on the silver undersides of the pointed leaves dancing in the slight breeze.

The whole seemed eternal. And the man at her side belonged to this countryside.

"For me, this country is as close to heaven as you can get." It was an unusually poetic thought from Dino. Rough, tough, can-do Dino, she thought. But after this one statement, he seemed to clam up, as if his mind was on something else.

Selena was in a kind of lambent sensuality, even she had to admit to herself ready sexuality that seemed to wash over the years alone without Noah. She thought briefly of John and perversely in this moment of incipient desire hoped he had not forgotten the magic of their days in Egypt. The gave herself a little shake as she returned to the present.

The big Mercedes eased up the country road lined with trees towards a set of gates. The chauffeur stopped the car and got out, first looking around carefully. Outside the gates a peasant sat on a stool, rifle cradled in his arms, regarding the distance. Then focusing on the car as a long silent look passed between him and the chauffeur. The peasant rose to see to the gate.

Alone with Selena in the car, both of them sated with sun and wine and fatigue, Dino turned his magnificent eyes on her, his look intent, boring into hers. Raising her hand to his lips, he kissed the inside of her wrist, then the palm of her hand. And before she could respond nonchalantly turned her hand over and placed it on his inner thigh.

Taken by surprise she failed for an instant to realize that her hand rested on a warm mound of gabardine. She felt it stir and quicken. With a start she came out of her reverie. She let her hand remain for a moment, then exerted the slightest pressure. It was a signal she knew Dino wouldn't miss.

"He's been waiting for you", Dino murmured, all Italian theatricality, his smile charming away any possible awkwardness. But setting a definite stamp on a shift in their relationship.

Now, he thought, now she would see. She would find out many things he had to teach and show.

Selena felt very sought-after, female, and vulnerable. At the same time she resolved that he not have her all on his own terms on his own turf. Why this thought asserted itself, especially now she wasn't certain, and so dismissed it.

When the wooden doors slid aside automatically, it was obvious to her that this was no simple Umbrian farm nor farmhouse. The peasant outside had all the earmarks of a guard on duty. She heard heavy gates shut behind them as they entered a courtyard.

'Dio. I don't know whether I feel more sheltered or captive', she thought. But the nascent concern was muted by her desire.

The massive wooden front door clanged shut with a suspiciously metallic sound. The woman who had ushered them in disappeared quickly. Dino and Selena faced each other in the entry hall.

She was unprepared for the dramatic change in attitude. Even in the expression which came over his face. Something arrogant even brutal seemed to emanate from his being.

Abruptly he grabbed her by one wrist as he directed her other hand to the huge protrusion at his groin.

Pushing her up against the wall in one violent movement, he pressed his body against hers so that she was trapped, unable to move. Rubbing against her, thrusting. She could scarcely breathe. She was trapped by his powerful body.

Suddenly a reciprocal violence rose up in her. As he tore at the buttons of the linen jacket she wore, she tore at his trousers. He unleashed her breasts, apparently not caring that he was ripping and destroying her brassiere, shredding her silk blouse. Her hair tumbled down with his violence.

Even now with warnings screaming in her head she was desperate to see, to touch and taste the monstrous member that had obsessed her. She used both her hands to plunge into his pants, seeking it and found a wide thick cock, as powerful looking as she imagined but huge. Especially now in its tumescent state. This living pulsing object in her hands excited her beyond reason.

He pulled her hands away, and holding onto his pants, yanked her out of the hallway, up a half flight of stairs into a room, and slammed the door shut. He tore off the damask cover of a oversized canopied bed. And half threw her across the room onto its sheets.

Abandoning herself to the need of her sex to have him inside her, she reached again for his cock. Cursing under his breath, he swept her hands aside. His powerful chest and shoulders loomed over her. His knee pushed her legs open. She was captive to his strength.

Desire and fear fought each other. She wanted to command his member to her service, even as in her furor she began to know why she had avoided this. Her wrists hurt, where he'd clenched them, she was shoved rudely against the bed. Her back scraped against the rough linen. For a moment the nightmare image of her attic room in Napoli flashed before her. She was torn hopelessly between her desire and the physical memory.

"Lasciami!" she pleaded, twisting and trying to free her hands. He held them so hard, they burned. "You have me. I want you. But let me go."

He didn't respond, so intent he didn't hear her words. He spread her knees wide apart with his own iron thighs. Loosening the grip of one hand to grasp his shaft, he aimed his enormous erection into the space between her legs, and like an expert marksman rammed it directly into her.

A loud, involuntary gasp escaped her. That her excitement had lubricated her was fortunate. The width of his cock and its force would otherwise have hurt her badly.

Still holding her down, he thrust hard and quickly, deep into her, grunting with effort and excitement. She felt like an object. Used. As if she were simply a receptacle for his penile drive. He had no interest in her response or reaction. No interest in anything other than his own gratification.

"Let me go!" She had to repeat several times before he seemed to be able to hear.

"Why? It's what you wanted, wasn't it?"

He finally grated out in answer. Then without pause covered her mouth with his, biting down hard on her lower lip bringing tears to her eyes. He gripped her wrists even harder, excited.

He growled, a long low sound. Still pinned under him, she felt him begin to harden. As he burrowed down onto her again ready to penetrate her, her eyes slid over his shoulder seeking some means of escape. Looking up over his shoulder, she suddenly found she was looking directly into a distant reflection of her own eyes. Eyes full of humiliation and pain.

It was a mirror. She was shocked. A mirror set in the ceiling of an Umbrian farmhouse? It had no business there. No way could it be for decoration. It was meant to function. But as what? Then it came to her, it was probably a two-way- a thought which made her blood run cold. There was no doubt left. This was a Mafia stronghold. A very private and guarded set-up for the pleasures of the men of the famiglia. What else For the convenience and servicing of its members, to arouse avid audiences, to...

Hypnotized by the image above her, mentally, she shouted at herself.

"Idiota! What are you doing?"

Her own eyes looking back seemed those of a stranger on whom sex was being perpetrated, and gave back no immediate response. She should have known better.

And yet this man 'of many women' how could she

have guessed at the crudeness, the quality of what? Almost anger in his love making. Where had he learned it? Did the women he'd known really want this? This bestiality? This one-way sexual possession?

Again she looked up into the reflection of her own eyes, now angry, under the violently moving bulk pinning her down. Perhaps this was normal for him. But now it set off something in her she could suppress no more than she had suppressed her desire. Pure flaming anger. Anger at him for submitting her to this parody of love-making, anger even more at her shaming response to it.

She screamed his name aloud. He stopped, looking at her as if stunned by the sound of it- startled by the voice shouting his name. He looked at her uncomprehending as again she screamed as loud as she could.

"Maiale! Porco!", you animal, you pig! The lowest of insults. "You think women want this?! You think this is love? Lovemaking? What?! You think women are objects? If you think at all."

He stopped, raising his body so he could look into her eyes. What he saw there appalled him.

"Or maybe you can only fuck objects! Maybe a woman feels softer than a cornhole, maybe she smells better than a sheep!"

Shocked he eased up. His eyes widening. This was not going the way he anticipated. She accorded him no mastery, nothing of dominance. Wasn't this what she sought?

Out of the corner of her eye she had seen her stockings in the chaos of clothes by the bed. Grabbing them, she turned and rubbed them in his face as roughly as she could. They caught on his heavy beard, and scraped across his eyes. Taking advantage of his shock and passivity, she whip-tied the nylons quickly around his wrists and then secured them to the bedpost. He was lost.

With one concerted move he could have freed himself. But stunned by the unexpected, he became flaccid, and then totally immobile. Only his eyes had life. And they darted around the room as if he had forgotten something, or was trying to get oriented.

The way his eyes shifted about the room called her attention to the walls. They seemed to be of solid carved wood, containing nothing save the bed with the two-way mirror over it. She was missing something. Something...

She rose. Walked over to the walls and looked closely. They weren't walls at all, but the fronts of a series of armoires-carefully built in.

She reached out to one of them. The catch was spring-loaded, and opened immediately to the slight pressure she applied.

Ranked by size and shape were dozens of devices. An army of whips- braided. Light chain. Leather Cat-o-nine-tails. Shackles, metal hooks large and small, long handled pincers. Every type of whip or crop she had ever seen and some she couldn't have imagined. Chains, with complicated clasps and locks. Probes, ropes, and bars. Cuffs and collars, leather vests and helmets. And some things she could only guess the purpose of. A cornucopia of Sado-masocism. All precisely arranged and secured, awaiting only the hand and intent of an adept.

She looked back once more at Dino still motionless tied to the bedpost. And knew that the violent sex he had visited on her was the least that could have happened in this room, and possibly prologue to the use of some of the devices in the armoires. Briefly she wondered again about all the other women in his life. My God! She knew what these devices said about Dino, but what did they say about them. For every sadist, there was an equal and opposite masochist?

The sex she had had was on an edge that pain dominated. Whether this could ever produce the heights of pleasure was something she would never know. But-if she hadn't known before, she knew now she wanted nothing of the dramatic and romantic portrayals of the   dominator-dominee, captor-captive sexual roles. It had nothing to do with life, and nothing to do with love. Nothing at all. She completed tying Dino with some thin braided leather strapping. He watched her but saying nothing. Hers was the mastery of the scene.

She gathered her clothes, left the room and found one down the corridor which looked like it might have been prepared for a guest. She found an adjoining bathroom, bathed, then robed herself and went to sit in silence at a window.

Outside was all unchanging beauty. The hillside fortress towns she could see in the distance rose as if mysteriously thrust up by the fecund shimmering flat wheat fields and vinyards between. Gentle rolling hill shimmered under a crescent moon with evening mist sitting on their crests. Deserted of toil and toilers the land seemed to still for the full darkness to come.

She thought about what had just passed and why. For Dino's part it seemed clear. He wanted to take her in just that animal way. It was his way. For her part, she had wanted him, knowing that he was Latin, and macho. This alone dictated that he dominate, but it had been far overdone and purely self-seeking pleasure for him. Perhaps both of them had overreacted to their interdependence, perhaps their sex had been about who was really top dog.

She knew somehow that Dino would not bother her again this night or ever. Once he saw himself in the two-way mirror, trussed and imaged as the potential subject of the objects in the closet, he would never recover his machismo with her. At the moment she had reversed sexual roles with him, she had put finis to all that. And in spite of this fortress-like house she knew would be free to go where and when the wish took her.

In evidence of that, a quiet dinner was brought to her room that evening. She dined alone, still obsessed with what had happened between them. Not seeking to know where he was or caring what he might be doing, using the utter quiet of the countryside to gather herself, collect the thoughts or shards of thoughts as she contemplated the afternoon.

She wished that she felt as inviolate and certain as before she'd come. Dino's roughness brought back memories of Napoli, desperate, frightened memories that she'd thought beyond the power to hurt her. Remembered violence-would it never disappear for good. Certainly not so easily after the souvenir of the afternoon. She was far from proud of her evocation and, she had to face it, her participation, however unwitting.

She could speculate endlessly, but thought the best she could do would be to get her thoughts down in Ceilings. There perhaps, she could sort it. But not now. Sometime at a calmer moment when she could reflect just what she'd felt at the moment she spotted the mirror on the ceiling.

The next day, Dino knocked softly at her door. He appeared as he always had to her-Dino, the enabler, her talented business manager. Selena wanted to forestall anything he might say.

"Dino, I don't want to repeat or continue what happened. I don't think it's good for you, and certainly not for me."

His dark eyes showed complete acceptance of her

words and all they implied. He too knew that as creative as their business relationship was, the personal had all the earmarks of total destruction- nothing good could come of it.

Dino needed to restore his poise and prove his worth to Selena. To regain his balance and purpose. And to put this Umbrian experience behind them.

"I have an idea. Why don't you go to Paris. We have to open there shortly anyway. Take a good look around, get a feel for the city. See what we should modify or change for the French launch."

"Good", she responded, pleased that he understood, and was making the effort to return to business.

"Try the Plaza Athenee. I think the hotel will suit you."

"I'm sure it will." Then Selena added, " There's one thing I want to make time for before I go."

"Family?"

"Yes my family. My very own, very dear family." Dino had no way of knowing that she was speaking of Maria. And no way of knowing that his single worded assumption triggered off in her the sure knowledge that blood was not always thicker than water. She would not revisit the past. She would not visit Napoli.

CEILINGS VI

Chapter: 1

Selena Passed through the douane at Charles de Gaulle airport with no challenge, except for the casual and automatic male/female 'coup d'oeil', once-overlook, the customs officer cast. Her air of self-possession and chic virtually guaranteed that her Vuiton luggage would pass through stamped without inspection.

To the official's disappointment, she paid scant attention to his para-military splendor. The deep reds and blues, the gold braiding and stiff army kepi , which he wore with an air of importance went by barely noticed. She also missed the typically Gallic shrug as he turned sternly to the next passenger in line for customs inspection, and gestured for him to open all his cases.

She paused on the way to the 'sortie' at a kiosk to buy cigarettes and a selection of the amazing profusion of French and Italian fashion magazines on offer. She was to learn that the French, all the French from the travailleurs to the litterati, were avid readers of 'Revues et Journaux', magazines and newspapers. The bold colors and illustrations were taken for granted. Print media seemed virtually a national 'Fix'-monthly, weekly or daily.

She watched her bags being arranged in the 'coffre' by her porter, the size of her tip got her cheerfully installed, and sat back in the box-like taxi for the trip in to the city. A small no-breed dog was curled up in the front passenger seat. Later she found that she been taken to the Plaza in a quintessentially Parisien cab.

As she rode, her thoughts drifted back to the exquisite Italian countryside she'd just left behind.

The contrast between its serene beauty and the

unappealing physical experience with Dino ran again in her mind. She was disgusted, mostly with herself for expecting an extension of his friendship, his protective and inventive business persona to play over into the physical. It was an unreasonable and unimaginative expectation on her part. To use an Americanism 'sloppy thinking', and a wasted time. Her fault, not Dino's. He was as he was, and that was an end to it. She smiled wryly, reached into her large Fendi pocketbook, took out a cigarette and lit it.

The smell of a Gauloise bleu filled the cab. Her driver looked up in his rearview mirror, startled by the aroma. Mon Dieu! Quel monde! What on earth had the world come to when this elegant woman with her expensive luggage and clothing, smoked the 'worker's friend' cigarette-the cheapest, strongest made in France? Then it came to him as it was always to come to people who met Selena, that she was unique, she set her own standards and ways, and was never to be trapped by other peoples rules or expectations. It was at times conscious, at others totally unconscious, but as much as anything else it had made Selena Ltd. possible, and would always nurture it.

Dawn lit the sky as the banlieus, the suburbs, passed with their new built massive residences or multi-national high-rise industrial headquarters, with twenty foot neons blaring Sony, Citroyenne, or Blaupunkt. The white dome of Sacre Coeur could be seen in the distance, and in the foreground the beginnings of the huge modern structure to be called La Defense. Finally, as the cab entered the 'centre de Paris', she looked out to see the Tour Eiffel.

No question of where I am, she thought. Anyone the world over could identify its improbable geometry. Just amazing. The lacework iron structure piercing the sky of the city.

She remembered a bit of history. It had been commissioned then erected as a disposable structure to confound, even provoke the masses attending the last World's Fair of the nineteenth century. Intended to flash to the international visitors France's 'Twentieth century Modernity'. Temporary and controversial. But it continued to astonish Parisians and foreigners alike one century later, defying the susceptibility of iron to the elements, and the structure to its intense use.

The welcome in the vast Brabantine marble reception area of the Plaza Athénée was all Dino said it would be.

She was shown to a spacious room, whose floor to ceiling windows overlooked the manicured garden and vine-hung walls of an inner courtyard. She looked gratefully at the huge bed with its profusion of pillows and then the mirrored bathroom furnished with double-sink, Swiss manufactured shower, bath, countless snowy towels of all sizes, warmed and precisely stacked. She relaxed as the gouvernante brought her petite dejeuner of Café, croissant et confiture de fraises de bois-wild strawberry jam.

Tired, she asked that the 'do not disturb' sign be hung on her door, showered, dropped into bed and slept until noon Then rose, dressed in a lightweight Cardin pantsuit, and went down to the concierge to get advise about a light lunch.

She was directed across the street to the busy Bar de Theatre, an upscale bistro. She had no way of knowing that this small restaurant was the bistro 'normale' of the television studios next door.

As she was seated eyes went to her as if she were a stage or film personalty that should be recognized. Her posture, self-possession, and striking looks called forth this reaction. But no one actually approached her, so surrounded by the buzz of rapid jargon and shoptalk of producers and actors, she ate, then left the bistro and began to walk.

She strolled at an uncharacteristic ambling pace. She had leisure on her hands for the first time in many years. There was no pressure, no rush. She and Dino had left things in good shape before they had taken off. Fat and Nicoletta would be be able to handle day to day affairs.

Passing along Avenue Montaigne, she saw the haute mode clothing salons-Chanel, Dior, Louis Scherer, Celine, Nina Ricci-so many small stores carrying heavy-weight fashion names, and glanced at their windows without concentration, still in a drifting mood.

She crossed the Champs Élysée, pausing to take in the spectacular purview intended by its architect-up towards the Étoile, with its Arc de Triomphe and eternal flame, then down towards the Place de la Concorde surrounded by giant Art Nouvaux torcheres, Cleopatra's 'Needle' the cynosure. The sky over the fountains on either side was an amazing shade of palest blue-grey. It gave a clear luminance to the grey buildings, bastions of the finest 19th century architecture. She'd always heard of Paris as the city of light, but always thought the phrase belonged to the infinite variety of street lamps, some designed by Gaudet, but many pre-dating that art nouveau genius. In their beauty and variety they were as much objets d'art as many paintings in the Louvre. But she hadn't reckoned on this radiance cast by the skies over the city and all in it, lighting the space above this queen of cities.

Its beauty moved her to tears.

If she'd sought an anodyne to all that had been ugly or depriving in the past few years, she couldn't have found anything more perfect.

She continued walking till she reached the Rue

Faubourg St Honore-the street world-renown for its numbers of chic boutiques and specialty shops. She stopped and window-shopped when anything caught her eye or interest just as any first time tourist might. Turning in the direction of the Palais Royale, she began to realize that this street...

She began to realize that this street of exclusive shops was in reality extended by cross streets where slightly less costly, but prestigious boutiques could also be found.

She noticed that as the street continued on it was called simply St. Honoré, and the shops looked simpler, and more given to shops of as antique jewelry and objets. She was about to retrace her steps when down St Roche, one of the small cross streets, she noticed a striking tall blonde in the deep blue pants of the French oeuvrier, the rough workers, and an open shirt of white silk, scrutinizing a display in a small shop window behind her.

The blonde draped one arm across her body to use as support for the other, and in its turn as support for her chin as she continued to inspect the window, head cocked to one side. Selena recognized suddenly and with surprise that she too used this stance as she studied a display.

Drawn to see what fascinated the other woman, she approached her. She was aware of long slim legs, a slender figure, intense concentration, and a waft of smoky perfume as she neared. It was the quality of that focus and attention which drew her to the side of the other.

Her arrival was so quiet the young woman didn't notice Selena standing slightly behind, looking at the same display in the window, until she said softly, "I don't know if that is what you intended, but the effect is to recall the blue of the sea of the Riviera."

The young woman started.

"Oh please. I didn't mean to interrupt, but I couldn't resist."

Selena was met with a wide, warm smile, a light laugh, and heavily accented English. "How silly I must look, standing here in my street, looking at my window, as if it were a serious work of art."

She held out her hand, " Je m'appelle Jacqueline Bleu, et Voila", she indicated her tiny boutique, "Chez Jacqueline."

Selena took the proffered hand. " And I am Selena, and I think we may be in the same business." She took a longer look at the tiny store given over to cosmetics.

"Won't you come in." Jacqueline welcomed her.

The odors and the enchanting display of the limited amount of merchandise captivated the visitor. Selena appreciated the professionalism, and the creative element of choice behind what she was seeing. It spoke of talent, enterprise, and to her especially, remembering her Mott street shop, an imaginative use of limited capital and space.

"All this is yours? I mean these cosmetics, you created them?"

" Mais oui." But of course.

Selena reached for one of the Lipsticks, "May I?"

Jacqueline started behind the small glass and wood counter, nodding as she went. And seeing Selena's interest, began opening testers of rouge and base.

Professionally, Selena felt, smelled and applied many to the skin of her wrists and inner arms, as Jacqueline watched.

"I try always to use the most natural of ingredients. The dyes of the colors are vegetable, the base the purest lanolin I can find. I do not make much of each, because the 'application' must be the freshest."

Selena understood immediately, that Jacqueline was

not apologizing, but merely explaining the prices, which were high for basic cosmetics. And that the approach of this young French woman was amazingly like her own. She wanted to know more about her, and what she planned for the tiny cross street boutique.

They went through the color range of each product. Jacqueline explaining the purpose and desired effect of each. They talked duration, and removal, composition and combinations, even allergies.

Jacqueline said that to the best of her knowledge, her clients had not experienced allergic reactions, nor intolerance. She was sure, as was Selena that purity, and all natural product, lay at the heart of this history. And as they talked, Selena became aware that Jaqueline, had heard of Selena Ltd, although it had not yet come to Paris.

Both women were startled after a time to see that it was well after seven in the evening.

" Where on earth did the time go?" Selena asked the younger woman as she prepared to leave. The French woman merely shrugged, then after a beat asked,

" Selena, have you plans this evening for dinner?" Because if you haven't, and if you would like, there is a small bistro in my quartier. It would be my pleasure to invite you."

"As a matter of fact, I have no plans."

"Bon. Let me close the shop. I will meet you at Chez Catherine in two hours." She wrote an address on Rue de Provence. "C'est bien?" Again Jacqueline offered her hand in the common French manner of farewell and greeting.

"I'll be there." Selena shook her hand made aware of the warmth and firm grip, then left the little shop. There were some things she wanted to think over.

Chapter: 2

Selena walked into Chez Catherine to be welcomed by an atmosphere that was pure neighborhood bistro. No one except native Parisians, and not many of those, would have known of this tiny restaurant in the unfashionable 9th arrondissement Its decor was simplicity itself, a solid wood bar with a lead top to the left as you entered, faded leather banquettes surrounding spotless white table cloths-many darned, and the plainest utilitarion silver + plates. Those who knew of it ate there regularly once a week.

Catherine served only the freshest of what was in season, prepared simply, because it needed nothing else. Catherine's friends from Normandy, Brittany, and sometimes much further south in the Midi were possessed of fermes, or vineyards, or orchards whose products found their way to the few tables.

The 'Cave', held a surprising group of 'no-name' vintage wines which were superb. Often these were 'Cadets' of renowned premier crus.

Jacqueline had arrived a quarter of an hour earlier to consult with Catherine as to what she 'proposed' to serve, and was seated at a small table next to the bar. She rose as Selena spotted her and came over to the table, and stood until she was seated and unfolded her napkin.

"I took a chance and ordered our dinner this evening , after I spoke with Catherine. I hope that's good for you."

"Wonderful. It seems my life consists of making decisions for myself and others. It's nice to have someone else do it for a change."

She saw Jacqueline had changed into all black. A

Black linen shirt and pants. And wore not a trace of jewelry. The black set off the long blonde straight hair and the deep blue eyes.

Selena wore a light forest green St Laurent 'overall', wore a heavy gold chain that supported an old Roman coin and had put her hair up in French twist which was easiest right after a quick shower.

She'd been unable to resist phoning New York. And although Nicoletta had reassured her that all was well, had fussed over a few details, until the older woman had said "Basta, Selena.Tutto va benissimo." Stop now, my child. All is well here. After which she'd had to hurry her toilette.

They began with Oursins de Bretagne, the delicate sea urchins in their shells presented on a bed of seaweed so fresh the small air bladders which suspended them in the sea were still full, followed by Riz de veau, sweet breads prepared with a light mustard sauce, and a salade of wild roquette vinaigrette. Their bread came from the neighboring boulangerie artisan, which meant it was baked there fresh that morning. One of fromageries had sent in a special Conté from Haute Savoie, the mountain region of southern France. Catherine served with it an aged Calvados, then came over to be sure all had gone well.

Selena praised the chef. "Dinner was absolutely superb, but I can scarcely breath."

Jacqueline smiled. "Coffee and a little more Calvados will do the trick."

As the meal became less a focus of attention, Selena pursued her curiosity about her dinner companion, with a calculated open-ended question.

"Tell me your ideas, for the future for your shop", Selena invited Jacqueline to talk. And as she did so, the most amazing thing emerged. Both women had arrived independently at a brand new concept, at once an approach, and product line, a concept and market.

Selena wasn't sure how it had happened, but she knew it was a bold new thrust in cosmetics. No one to date had thought to design cosmetics specifically for the "Femme d'un certain age"-usually a typical Gallic way of referring to a woman, a chic woman who would not see fifty-five again. It was a charming expression, but normally carried the stigma of the departure of youth.

It absolutely must not be an acceptance of despair and the onset of 'old age', Jacqueline insisted, using both hands for emphasis.

Exactly, Selena added, D'un Certain Age must capture sophistication and wonderfully attractive worldliness. The products, the colors must say this to the woman who wears them and to the world who sees them. And we must do away with the cruelty that so many products on the market today visit on older women.

Both women paused as they thought over what each had suggested. No one had dared even use the word age in descriptions, or promotional material, or title. It was considered absolutely not to be done-except perhaps to be denied or like a disease to be treated and perhaps cured.

Then Jacqueline reminded Selena, there was yet another use of the phrase, more gentle and flattering to the object of the expression which and occurred when the phrase was used for the truly older woman-seventy plus. It implied they still had a place in the world of glamour, and glamorous women. And this group of women too had to be remembered.

"I don't know what to say", Selena murmured. "You see just recently I have spent hours thinking of products for exactly this group of people. It is incredible that you here in France, and I in America should have come to the same point at the same time."

"Oh yes. But I have so far to go before I could dream to develop it. As you see, I've just begun to establish my shop."

"I understand completely. It is as I started."

In a sudden change of subject, Selena asked Jacqueline about her background. She introduced the thought by saying, "Jacqueline, I've been so curious since I met you. French women are small, and dark, but you must be five feet ten and are as blonde as any young Californian.

Jacqueline looked at her, to pick up on why she was being asked, and whether what she answered would have some bearing or impact on their future association. Then decided she couldn't guess, and even if she did, had to go straight on.

" The short version, then? I was born in the Midi. Many of us are quite blonde. Naturally", she added with a twinkle. Selena laughed aloud in response to the insider quality of the comment.

" My parents died when I was no age, and there was no other family, so I was reared by Ursuline nuns in their orphanage.

The Ursulines are self-supporting and have been for generations. They are known far and wide for the delicacy and beauty of their hand painted porcelain. The small output is valued by connoisseurs of china and collected avidly. It takes care of all their basic needs, and permits their charity to the poor. I learned about colors, and combinations of colors from them.

When I got older, I was required to assist in the infirmary, and there I learned something of the properties of lotions and ointments, especially those which healed and those which inflamed."

"Inflamed?... Selena looked at her questioningly, and then before Jacqueline could say anything further, a recollection came to her. From ancient times many country people thought when you had an illness with fever or 'inflammation', you fought it with another, a benign inflammation. There were ointments which produced healing by healthy counter-inflammation, which inevitably produced a natural rouging of the cheeks.

"Now, of course," Jacqueline said with a grin, We moderns know that you must run to seek an 'anti-inflammatory', which comes neatly packaged from a pharmaceutical giant in an appropriate container. Counter inflammation is far too radical an idea."

Selena understood the inference. D'un certain age was also in its way, counter inflammatory to the ordinary ideas of how to cosmese age.

They both appreciated the irony and history.

Jacqueline continued, "I came to Paris when I was eighteen, started to work for a small cosmetic shop. Spent several years with Guerlain, saved my money and opened my own boutique. And there you have it." Selena picked up on the isolation that lay concealed beneath the quick story. Her heart went out to the younger woman, and yet she knew if she said anything directly, it would not go well. She suspected that Jacqueline in her way might be one of the loneliest of loners, but would not want sympathy or friendship on that account.

Then she did something characteristic, something instinctive, and seemingly non sequitur- she said in response to the younger woman's story, "Jacqueline, I want you to join Selena Ltd, and develop the 'D'un Certain Age' with me. We will work out some kind of participation and partnership in the corporation, and compensation for the new products we develop together that will please you. But I want you as a part of my company."

The offer startled Jacqueline. Although it seemed as if they had known each other for a longer time, they'd met only hours before. She looked deep into Selena's eyes, seeking to read all that was being offered and all it meant.

" Mon dieu, what an offer!' she responded, overwhelmed by the magnitude of the proposition. Then with characteristic Gallic caution, " May I take a little time to think it over?" Selena nodded her assent.

With a smile, Jacqueline reached across the table, put her hand over Selena's and added " Perhaps you will give me forty-eight hours?"

" But of course" . Selena responded warmly. Instinct told her that despite reservations and native caution, despite the habit of independence, Jacqueline would not only accept, but would make more of it than either could imagine at this moment.

I would have handled this very differently ten years ago she thought. I'd have sold and resold the idea, I'd have charmed or enticed. But I want Jacqueline to come to the decision freely and with enthusiasm not because I induce her. I know it will be good for both of us.

The bill was not presented at the table. When the two women rose to go, it was approaching midnight.

Chapter: 3

Selena had leisure. She woke at nine, a late morning hour for someone habitually dressed and out by seven thirty. And had 'petit dejeuner' at La durée where the petits croissants aux amandes were not to be found elsewhere and the café filtre had a hint of chicory as the French preferred.

She saw the museums, she'd read of, the Louvre and the D'orsay of course, and then explored some of the small extrordinary collections, the Guimet, the Rodin, the Monet. At night she attended the Palais Garnier, the old Opera de Paris, and the new Bastille.

She had her hair done at Alexandre, a busman's holiday for a stylist of her caliber. Then went to Balmain, Jaques Fath, and Givenchy for clothes for formal occasions. As to Coco Chanels suits, she really preferred the look and feel of the younger Italian designers for casual wear. Their names had not yet become the household words that still remained the claim of the older French couturiers just now turning to pret-a-porter or ready to wear.

Evenings she dined at Taillevent and the oldest of Parisien restaurants Le Voltaire. She lunched at one of the small bistros to be found scattered like pebbles on the stony Normandy beaches in the Quartier Latin or St. Germain on the left bank.

After two days, Jacqueline called to accept the offer. They met, ironed out the business part of the entente, and over the next days worked on just what the project would entail.

Often their conversations were most productive during long walks on which Jacqueline also showed Selena the Paris she knew so well. Not just the Paris of the Tour Eiffel and the National Congrés, or Deux Maggot and Café Flore but exotic markets, intimate museums in 'hotels particuliers', hidden gardens where lovers embraced unobserved and unremarked.

One walk took them from the Seine through the Jardin des Plantes. They came upon a domed building with a small terrasse.

"Let's stop for a cup of tea," said Jacqueline with a look of fun in her eyes, "this is a place I want to you to see."

It was the café of the Grand Mosque, serving Arabic sweets and small glasses of tea.

"Am I still in Paris" Selena marveled, as memories of John and Egypt flooded over her, with the sweet minted tea in the cool air giving her a warm and sensual glow.

"Oui, et non." said Jacqueline, bright-eyed, "Let's see." She took Selena's arm and started into an odd mostly hidden door nearby.

If you had not known it led somewhere, you would never have tried it.

"Why is it that I'm so ready to let you take charge?" Selena joked, delighted to have such an imaginative guide. It was the second time she had been conscious of this unusual feeling.

Jacqueline didn't respond directly, but opened the small door patterned with Arabic fretwork. They descended a circular stairway of ancient scuffed stone. There, abruptly, they were in a timeless world of women-the Hammam.

Naked and half-naked women of all sizes, shapes, ages, and degrees of beauty reclined on mattresses, being massaged, talking to each other or simply dozing- a scene from another time and a more, much more exotic place.

A group of Arab women in one corner sang a lively

song, using plastic tubs or their breasts to percuss its eastern rhythm. It was clear many were passing the whole day, freed from care, catering to themselves and each other.

"I feel as if I've left one country and gone to another," Selena laughed, marveling at the exotic ambiance in which she found herself.

"You have," responded Jacqueline.

The two disrobed, each remarking silently the other's splendid physique. Wrapped in towels they proceeded through the enveloping steam from the first large misty steam room to the second-hotter, where still other women lazed, doused themselves with cool water from giant Persian urns, washed each other, relaxed, silently surrendering world cares to the pure sensuous, isolated-somehow totally protected for the moment by the billowing heat.

After a brief exposure to this slightly claustrophobic humidity, they retreated to the mattresses in the front room to talk.

Looking at the women arranged around the room, they found themselves particularly observing the older ones-the lack of self-consciousness with which they cared for their bodies in the presence of other women-deprived of all outward indications of wealth or social class.

" These are among the women we want to know about 'D'un Certain Age', remarked Jacqueline excitedly, "These women should feel so at ease in our shops. If they could feel so pampered and their age so cherished, we would have done something good, non?"

Selena realized again, in this moment, that the genius of Jacqueline, in addition to her powerful aesthetic sense, and imagination, lay in her heart. This was what she had always tried to give Selena, Ltd. and now she had an ally, no more than an ally, a real peer.

The more they talked, the more the gestalt, the total concept and package that would become 'D'un Certain Age' was emerging full and exciting. Selena was increasingly aware of the synchrony of ideas. It was something she had never experienced before. An intellectual and creative partner sharing, urging on and re-sharing ideas.

When the Hammam announced its closure for the night, the two were still drinking tea and talking animatedly. Reluctant to leave the warmth of the Hammam and exit into the winter evening, they dressed. Taking a last look at the seductive setting they were about to leave, Selena remarked the beautiful tiles decorating the bath - many an arresting velvety blue - the colour of a night sky in Egypt. She laughed with delight.

'I've got it. I want to use this colour for an eyeshadow, and I want to call the color Selena Bleu. Will you let me use your name?"

"Of course," said Jacqueline, "and you saw the flacons of attar the women use to perfume themselves after the steam? I used the shape for a container for a night cream, I'll show it to you later."

Chapter: 4

The following day they telephoned New York from Selena's room at the Plaza Athenee to share the news with Chen, Nicoletta, and Dino all of whom instantly recognized its appeal.

They made plans to put the line into immediate research and development. Selena announced that her confidence in this initiative was so firm she was giving Jacqueline 5% of the company shares. Nicoletta, Chen and Dino already had the same percentage.

It was the feeling on both sides of the Atlantic, that this was not only fair but desirable, in view of the major contribution Jacqueline brought. And actually bonded in a celebratory feeling of progress to come fitting into past achievement.

Nicoletta said she would start looking for just the right personel to handle the new line. Chen for his part said it was pointless to try to explain the mechanics Fat and he would work on, when one look at a proto-type would make it immediately clear.

"We might want to think of separate boutiques for d'un Certain Age, or at the very least a special section in the shops." Dino's mind was already working on the implementation of the concept.

"He has a point. The more importance, the more special feeling we can give these customers, the better", Nicoletta added.

Selena smiled broadly, feeling the support and enthusiasm coming over the phone

" I suppose I'd better get back to New York one of these days," Selena said with ambivalence, after the call-torn between wanting to get at the new project and a curious regret at the thought of leaving Paris.

"Anyway, I think we should celebrate, somewhere special. What do you propose?"

"I think, for us, nothing is too good, ' laughed Jacqueline, 'let's go to the Le Grand Vefour in the Palais Royale. I'll call a taxi."

As the taxi passed the Pont de l'Alma Selena sensed something in the air. The scent of Detchema to be sure, but something else. The intoxication of speeding along the Seine, illuminated by the spotlights of the bateaux mouches, relaxed and excited her at the same time. She attributed her agitation to the thrill of a new business chapter unfolding-almost like a new love story.

As the light from the Eiffel Tower momentarily illuminated the taxi Jacqueline, who had been silently looking out the window towards the river turned, an expression in her eyes which Selena had never seen-at once authoritative, tender, and provocative.

In one very natural movement she slid her hand under Selena's skirt, to rest on her inner thigh above the knee. Turning Selena's head towards her with her other hand, Jacqueline kissed her. At first so lightly that Selena wondered what it meant. She found herself breathless.

With no time to think, her mouth completely taken by Jacqueline's, she surrendered to the tenderness, the force, the softness, the delicious feminine smell .

A look in the rear view mirror confirmed that the driver had observed this moment. True Parisian that he was, his eyes gave nothing away as they arrived at the restaurant and paid the fare and got out.

The two made their way into what was arguably the most elegant restaurant in Paris. If its painted ceilings framed in gold leaf applique, huge enameled fruit-bearing figures gracing its walls, and tables carrying plaques of legendary figures of history and the arts who habitually used them were not enough to satisfy the esthete; its menu, wine list and food would certainly content any gourmet.

They made no reference to what had just happened, but for the first time in their long series of dinners together, they talked no business. Their eyes met insistently, penetratingly. Without knowing that in French the look which cannot be refused has a name-le regard assassin-Selena was under its spell.

When Jacqueline went to make a phone call Selena had her first moment of reflection. Perhaps, she thought smiling, this was 'la femme eternelle', 'la femme française' who had charmed so many generations of men.

"Ne me regarde pas comme cela." Don't look at me like that, it melts me", she murmured when Jacqueline returned. By way of response Jacqueline, suddenly more business-like, said "If you're really free tonight, I'd like to show you something I love-I think it will do us good."

There were few moments in her life when she had put her destiny, financial and emotional, in the hands of others, but her response was immediate and visceral.

"C'est toi qui decides," she responded.

They finished tiny scarlet berries and intense small cups of coffee. Selena paid the bill, as Jacqueline went for their coats.

Outside the voiturier brought up a Citroyen D.S. sedan with its unique fluid suspension system. Jacqueline's phone call had been to summon the car. Selena found herself ensconced next to her.

Jacqueline drove towards the newly built peripherique, the highway, avoiding the center of the city. Selena had no idea where they were. What she did know was that the woman at the wheel was someone she knew, respected, and admired as a colleague, but whose mystery was just beginning to unfold.

The Citroyen sped along the autoroute. Selena felt fatigue and relaxation overtake the stimulation of dinner and the exhilaration of taking the road. The music Jacqueline chose was romantic and nostalgic.

Selena was surprised and moved to hear the voice of Milva-an Italian singer she had always loved with a voice which bespoke pain and survival as well as joy and life. It was so like Jacqueline to play something in Italian-for her. Charles Trenet sang of love in the French style' 'tu qui passes sans me voir'. Selena fell asleep to the rhythm of their sounds and those of the whispering car wheels.

Chapter: 5

As the car turned off the autoroute at Avignon into the spectacular countryside of Provence Selena awoke, unaware that she had slept off and on for six hours. The dawn light illuminated the immaculate fields of grapevines graceful with neat lines in full leaf, punctuated by neat Ficus hedges and gnarled olive trees. The white stucco Mas were still closed for the night.

After Paris, it was good to see so much sky, blue and lightly punctuated with pure white clouds. She was delighted by the resemblance to her native Italy, she was reminded of Bergamo-a landscape also austere, but seductive nonetheless. In the distance were Les Alpilles, small mountains protecting the tranquil vineyards and fields of lavender just beginning to come to flowering life.

"Where are we ?", she asked as Jacqueline smiled at her, fatigue from the long drive showing in her eyes.

"You see the cliffs over there?" Jacqueline pointed out a strange vertical smoky blue mass in the early light. "They're 'Les Baux de Provence.' An enormous and mysterious cliff rode over the landscape on which could just be made out the structures of an ancient fortress. " We're almost there." With Les Baux still in view, they went deeper into the countryside until at the village of Le Paradu they slowed and turned.

The car wheels crunched on the gravel driveway, a sound that Selena had always adored. A large square white house greeted them silent and shuttered, the wall facing them bathed in early morning sunlight. A pergola of climbing roses protected the big wooden doors from the light. Under a fig tree, and surrounded by lavender plants, was a wooden table which spoke of languid summer lunches and all the colours of Provence which would come with the summer.

With an old key left under the mat by the caretaker, they entered the house by the kitchen where an impressive modern stove, next to the original fireplace, gave evidence of residents who liked to cook. A rustic candelabra hung over the wooden table, copper cooking utensils and bundles of dried flowers, and herbs completed the decor.

"How beautiful it all is", Selena said in wonder.

"There are many times I can hardly bear to leave it. But as you've seen, my work lies in Paris."

Jacqueline explained that the house had once been a blacksmith shop One could actually drive the car in where the carriages had once arrived just off the living room which was the original workshop. It was a heritage from her parents.

Selena looked in wonder at this enormous two-story room. In the absence of Jacqueline and her family the house had been occupied until his death by the painter and frequented by his friends, many well-known artists and musicians. Four music stands and chairs in the corner still awaited these visitors. Huge paintings and wall hangings recalled those who had passed, stayed, created there. Jacqueline had left it as it was when she took it back.

There are rooms which vibrate with memories and presences, and this was one. You could almost hear chordings, and tunings, themes of quartets and trios, and smell opened tubes of oil paints spread on palettes, paints being layered on seized canvases in this glorious space. But the 'Blacksmith's' room was too cold to use. They climbed well-trodden wooden stairs to a bedroom. Jacqueline led Selena gently to the welcoming double bed from which the magnificent landscape could be seen through the window. Jacqueline fell asleep almost immediately. Selena too despite her sleep in the car.

Later that afternoon, both being refreshed, Selena put herself in Jacqueline's hands. As if by meticulous planning the afternoon unfolded. The quiet, small village actually boasted a renowned restaurant - Le Bistro du Paradu- where Jacqueline was greeted as a lost relative by the proprietor.

They ate slowly, in the warmth of the late sun, pistou, and a salad of local greens.

"What is the wine?" Selena wanted to know. It was an odd combination of piquant and smoothness caught in a color that was deeper than the usual Rose'.

"It is a vin du pays, a wine grown and made from the local vineyards. It has no name, and never travels out of the district. You like it?"

"Mais oui. C'est enchantant".

"And the pistou?," Jacqueline was inquiring about the rich vegetable soup, larded with garlic.

"Considering the amount of garlic in it, it's a good thing we both had the same dish." Selena grinned.

The dessert was a carmelized apple tarte, Tarte tatin, as only superb French cooks can provide.

Well fed and relaxed they strolled to the Cooperative Oleicole des Baux to buy what Jacqueline said was undisputedly the best olive oil in France. Then in the car they wound upwards towards Les Baux. At the top amidst the ruins of the Roman fortress town, and the mediaeval chapel, a high blue sky reigned over the most spectacular 360 degree view in Provence.

They explored the ruins marveling at the weight and size of the stones somehow hauled by man and beast up the sheer vertical rise. Late in the day, they found a small terrasse looking out towards the Luberon. They ordered mouresque-a potent mixture of the local pastis and sirop d'orgeat.

"D'un Certain Age", toasted Selena.

"A nous deux," replied Jacqueline.

"A nous deux", Selena could not resist the response she evoked.

The burnished light of sunset suffusing the landscape, and the power of the mouresque making itself felt, they drove in a comfortable silence back to the house.

Closing the large kitchen door behind them, Jacqueline took Selena in her arms and leaned her against the door. Very gently and questioningly she began to kiss her, caressing her as she did so. light strokes of her tongue soon engaged Selena's. Her lips softly began on Selena's cheeks and eyes, then downwards to where a pulse beat in her throat. Jacqueline's hands seeking Selena's nipples through her shirt left no doubt as to her desire.

Once again this beautiful French woman had taken her breath away, as if she had jumped off a cliff but landed safely in a pool of warm oil. And yet it felt so natural, as if this was something she had known about forever.

Regaining her breath slightly, she began to respond easily to the increasingly insistent caresses. Selena found herself more and more aroused. Finding her knee, Jacqueline's hand traced a light path directly up her inner thigh, moving slowly towards her palpitating sex.

"You will have to show me what to do," Selena whispered.

" You'll know what to do, you'll see," came the answer.

Jacqueline's fingers began to caress her sex through her lingerie. Selena began to want more closeness, more intimacy more of Jacquelines hand and mouth.

She took Selena's hand and led her up the stairs and to the bed. Shedding clothes as they went, but never losing contact with one another, pausing over and over to kiss and caress. They lay down, full length to full length, each wanting more shared contact, more shared warmth.

Insistently Jacqueline claimed Selena's mouth again and again, as she gently parted her legs.

Wrapping themselves together, each opened her legs to the other's thigh.

As they rocked together rhythmically, their caresses became less tender and more forceful, with an innate sense of the other's timing. Their moans of excitement mingled.

Rather abruptly and forcefully turning her on her side, Jacqueline removed Selena's panties, and began to explore her wetness with her tongue. Although she was shocked by this sudden profound intimacy, Selena's body gave her no choice but to accept and encourage it. "Prends-moi, take me, she whispered .

She heard Jacqueline gasp at the lake of liquid which greeted her fingers. Jacqueline kissed her mouth, then her sex, and again her mouth, bringing the smell of sex into vivid play between them.

Selena felt it totally unfamiliar, but overwhelming in its excitement. She could never have imagined lovemaking so imaginative, so evocative. She wanted more and more of Jacqueline. More and more of her love-making.

Overcome by the sensuality of the soft female flesh pressed against her own, and freed from considering the needs of an erection, Selena soon abandoned herself to the spasms provoked by Jacqueline's fingers. To her surprise she came with loud sobs of pleasure and emotion. Incredible as it seemed, Jacqueline stirred a sexual response as profound as she'd ever felt.

More than once in the night they reached for each other. Selena tentatively at first, but with increasing confidence found the keys to Jacqueline's pleasure - turning her on her stomach to penetrate her sex from behind, simultaneously nuzzling, and sucking at her neck, then biting her at first gently, then with more force as she caressed full young breasts.

Jacqueline in her turn came to tears of pleasure. 'C'est si bon,' she whispered.

Selena didn't deliberately compare what she felt and did with other times- but she was aware of a pervasive sinuous quality that hadn't been there with others. Somehow everything between them was curved or curving, even the fit of their bodies back to front, or top to bottom. The movement of body against body was more fluid, fit and even somehow instinctive. Hollow went to hollow, sensation matched sensation, communication seemed instant and full.

Selena had not thought that sex , especially between two women, could be so powerful, nor satisfaction so complete and achieved in so many ways. The word consensual came to mind in its full sexual meaning.

It was not until morning when they lay naked on their backs, smelling the residual scent of their lovemaking, and lightly caressing each other's breasts, that Selena looked at the ceiling.

Painted on the white stucco, a gift of the artist to the family, was a larger than life-size floating figure. Rather in the style of Picasso, she resembled at once a woman, and a goddess suspended in the sky. Her eyes, gazing from a geometric head with streams of blue-black hair running behind her, seemed to take in the scene beneath her and offer a benediction.

I must remember this wondrous creature floating overhead as I am floating here beneath-here, earth-bound, heaven-bound, real or imagined-my Goddess of the Mas.

Then while Jacqueline fell back to sleep in the deep feathered bed, Selena rose quietly so as not to disturb her, found her diary and in it wrote of the ceiling above her head with its incredible deep blues and greens, the unmistakable mother earth figure so skillfully created by the artist- an odd shape from an odd perspective.

In the days that followed, they walked hand in hand through the Roman ruins at Glanum, and the museum of its treasures at St. Remy en Provence. They tasted wine, and bought dried lavender. They drove to the Luberon to see the red hill-town of Roussillon. The colors of the earth there, famous for the tints they produce in the equally famous pottery, began to fill Selena's eyes. She couldn't help but comment to Jacqueline that they must not forget some of these colors as potential for their line. Then had to giggle as Jacqueline stroking her arm said that the only workaholic she knew worse than herself was sitting beside her.

" All too true", she sighed. Then deliberately cut off all thoughts of work. Actually in none of these enchanted locations were they able to restrain from intimate caresses-under the table at lunch, in a deserted museum room, in the car parked at a scene Cézanne had painted. They gave themselves anywhere to the pleasure they knew awaited. Their profound kisses were a nourishment that was never enough in the Summer sun and enchanting moonlit paysage of Provence.

The countryside would always be colored with the hues of their love and closeness, with the sounds of quiet intimate talk of everything and nothing typical of young lovers.

The nights were full of love-tender and savage, both, but always joyous and full of Jacqueline's imagination. Selena knew she would never forget the sensation of their breasts slipping against one another - lubricated by 'the best olive oil in France', and the deep understanding she got of the rhythms, the desires and needs of her own body which served as well with slight but fascinating variations for Jacqueline because they were each women.

After two weeks, they reluctantly admitted that their colleagues needed their help to launch the new line.

They shared a bittersweet recognition that the end of their affair was written in its beginning. No matter how enchanted by what had happened and would be forever between them, each had a life firmly rooted in their country of choice. Although the future would hold much back and forth traveling and planning, not to mention profound understanding and warmth, there was no question of where each had to be based. Their relationship would be one of interruptions and fragility imposed by distance, and all the other commitments each had to honor.

The decision to return to Paris was only a matter of mtutally decided date.

Lying in bed on their last night in Provence, Selena permitted herself to wonder about their love aloud.

Jacqueline put her fingers, lightly perfumed with the precious nectar of the night, over Selena's lips. 'If une histoire d'amour finds you,' she said, 'il faut le vivre', you must live it, all the way-but you must let it stop where it has to stop."

Jacqueline intuited, that the woman to woman relationship they had developed, was marvelous, never to be denied, or minimized, but probably not for Selena the final one.

Selena brushed the corners of her lips in the lightest most affectionate of kisses. "But remembered l'amitié is forever, n'est pas cherie?"

Jacqueline looked at her deeply, silently, as if memorizing her face, her touch, her closeness, then responded, "Oui. Amitié est pour toujour et puis toujours, mon amour", the love of a dear, dear friend once given, is forever.

It was to be as the deepest, trusted and most close friends that they were to go forward with their future.

One night remained before Selena's departure for New York, a night they knew would be the proper end of this chapter.

" I want to spend this last night of your love in luxury" said Jacqueline, always inspired in choosing the perfect surroundings.

The Plaza Athénée where Selena was by now a valued long-time client received them, the expert receptionist discreetly ignoring the obvious heat between them. There was no pretending and no wanting to pretend after the bliss of the preceding few days.

Passing through the lobby, Selena greeted some of the regular tea customers-a charming and beautifully dressed Countess from New York who was her client, with her an American doctor turned mystery writer, a music promoter whose Pierre Cardin wardrobe, Selena observed, didn't conceal the anxiety of the older woman for whom D'un Certain Age was going to be created. She wished she could share her excitement about the new products with all three. But that would have to wait.

" J'ai envie de toi." Jacqueline whispered as they got into the elevator. A huge suite, decorated in shades of yellow awaited.

"Encore?" laughed Selena. The bed was enormous and canopied. They sank into it, tired and a little subdued. Both of them knew that their histoire d'amour had been lived to its fullest, and now must now have its denouement.

"I miss the Goddess looking over us in Provence. I was in seventh heaven," Selena said.

Jacqueline turned on her elbow to look intently at her. "You know, the ceiling of this bed-the canopy-is called in French, le ciel, and so the same expression in French le septieme ciel- the seventh heaven, has a particular nuance for us which has to do with love."

Selena smiled tenderly at her and was moved to hear her say softly but with utter conviction, " I know that you will find your real septieme ciel one day." She wasn't sure that she shared Jacqueline's belief.

But the following morning Selena returned to New York.

CEILING VII

Chapter: 1

Nicoletta came to the airport to meet Selena as she arrived from Paris. The two women caught each other up on the last few weeks. Nationally, Selena Ltd. continued well. Nicoletta detailed parts of the training program she had started up. Both thought that it was promising. She said Fat and Chen were waiting in the office to go over some ideas. She wouldn't preview their information but was excited about it.

Selena went over the highlights of her European introduction. And then to her surprise was able to tell Nicoletta of some of the personal experiences she had gone through.

Nicoletta told her Dino had already returned and was hard at work to integrate all that had happened in Europe with the American organization. Very much his old self, he seemed unaffected by what had happened in Italy.

Despite the personal turmoil of the last few weeks in Europe, Selena Ltd. was still a productive entity. And now with the support and enthusiasm of both Dino and Jacqueline active ingredients in the mix, there was much excitement in the air.

The New York skyline was always amazing, Selena thought as they entered the city on the upper level of the Queensboro Bridge. The large advertising billboards cleverly perched at the foot of lesser buildings the old Wonder Bread Bakery, Wrigley's Chewing Gum plant, the Eagle Electric factory, all leading like some many advertising foothills to the soaring landmark skyscrapers spawned by fabled names in American architecture and justifiably depicted so often on souvenir postal cards.

Not a beautiful, not always a safe city, but always exciting for first time tourist or returning denizen alike. For the first time she felt as if she truly belonged.

"Tell me more about D'un Certain Age", Nicoletta encouraged, as the taxi took them downtown.

"It's based on several ideas- the basic one is obvious, at fifty-five you're not through as an attractive or glamorous woman. Not on the shelf. But you can't achieve the effect you would when you are twenty, nor should you."

"Absolutely right." Nicoletta spoke from obvious experience. " Actually as a woman who fits exactly into this category, I know I can be far more sophisticated and probably more glamorous than a twenty year old."
"Exactly! So-softer colors, and lighter base, to de-emphasize lines and wrinkles. The kind of base drier older skin can handle. So-no beading or accretions by the end of the evening. No harsh colors. All muted to give a glow not contrast. Light oil in water base. Everything calculated to keep moisture in middle aged skin ." The ideas came in a stream with her enthusiam.

"And shades which will go with gray, or blondined hair."

"Yes."

"Then we thought about a two stage base. Under toner, to help with contour and the base to finish and emphasize planes."

" So a real new look for the older woman."

"Yes."

"It's a really exciting project, Selena."

"We thought so, we talked about it for hours. Jacqueline is a marvel."

"A wonderful way to finish your tour."

"Yes." Selena said quietly. Thinking of all that had passed with Jacqueline.

When they arrived at the office, Dino was waiting

for her.

"Selena!" He greeted her enthusiastically. "Before Chen and Fat tie you up I want your okay on the idea of a corporate headquarters. We really need something more than 'my office or yours' at this point. I've found space in the Mansard building. Upscale but not pretentious. About 3,000 square feet. Should do well."

"Can we afford it Dino?" Selena asked, more than a little concerned.

"We can't not afford it, Selena. We need it now for administrative and display functions. In fact we needed it yesterday. We've got the funds in hand so..."

Selena had to laugh. The way he put it in four short sentences was typical. But even more she trusted his conclusions.

"Then do it. But I'll want a hand in the design."

"What else?" He laughed in turn. "Okay. I'm gone. Speak to you later." As he started out of the salon, Dino turned back for an instant, and said softly, "Welcome home."

Selena responded only with a smile, but it was enough.

"Boss Ma'am," Fat greeted her as she stepped into her tiny office.

"Look what we have for you!" He opened a box lined with applicators.

"Hello Chen", Selena said as she finally seated herself behind the desk. "Hello Fat. You've not wasted time!"

"Selena, we had a number of prototypes done. We think they're what you had in mind." Chen handed them one by one to Selena who marveled at the execution in metal and brush of what she had only been able to describe roughly in words.

She looked at a lipstick tube with a square base almost an inch across, a mascara wand with a large rectangular grip, both with a mechanical advantage built in to the torque, so that turning was liquid easy.

Then Fat showed her a small leather case with slots for lipstick, mascara, and a container of base refresher, all fastened with Velcro. The top contained a magnifying mirror as did the side of the ipstick case, making application of the contents visually a cinch for older eyes.

Selena turned them over, and tried each, then handed them to Nicoletta who did much the same.

"They're a marvel!" Selena exclaimed with pleasure.

"I think they'll be easy to show, easy to use, and easy to sell", Nicoletta added.

"Not too hard to manufacture", Fat said handing her the cost estimates.

"How soon could we get it up and running?"

"Fat estimates within a matter of months", Chen said.

Selena guessed that most of what she saw before her was really Fat's work, but appreciated that he had presented it as the mutual accomplishment of them both.

There was a feeling of anticipation and excitement in the room that day. As the months went by, it was an accurate harbinger of success.

When Jacqueline came over just prior to the launch, she was delighted with what had been realized, and even more delighted that Selena had referred openly to age, and even used the word older in promotional literature. The colors and apliers were all right from her point of view, incorporating as they did all Selena and she had talked about.

She watched the beginnings of the campaign in the States, but couldn't wait to get back to France and introduce it in her own country.

Annie Karol was glad of the excuse to do yet another article on the development of Selena Ltd. The two women smoked up a storm over the proofs of the article just before it went to print.

The timing on Selena's new headquarters was helpful. It was designed, up and running almost at the same time that D'un Certain Age was introduced to the American woman.

It was hard to know where the time had gone, Selena thought late one night when she had come back to the office to finish up some work. She looked out of the window down at the scurrying miniature figures from the window on the thirtieth floor of the Mansard building. Tours, and interviews and openings seemed to pass in a flash, and yet she knew from the date at the top of the balance sheet that 1979 had come and gone.

She had received a note from the Hanover, congratulating her on paying off the notes of the past, and offering her virtual carte blanche on any loans or financing she might want or require in the future. It was gratifying, considering their initial skepticism, no matter how politely disguised.

She hadn't spoken to Chen in several weeks. He'd been in California, Fat had said, checking on the kelp supply. So she called him. He reviewed the problem he'd just solved with the help of his cousins.

"You sound well, Chen. I'm glad it went smoothly." Selena knew how important this credit would be to him, and was glad to offer it.

Selena", his voice came back with a casual idea, "Being out here gave me a thought. What about Asia. Have you ever thought about doing anything in China or Japan."

"No. But it's certainly an idea." She answered equally casual. "Will you be back soon?"

"Next week."

"See you then?"

"Yes," he answered, but she wasn't sure he would. He seemed so often 'out' when she telephoned. But the lab was functioning unbelieveably well considering the demands of the last few years.

As she hung up, For some reason the sheer numbers of the ant like figures still active below her caught her eye , and triggered off an image of Japan with its teeming population and healthy economy.

She noticed that more and more there seemed to be a vogue for things American. American food, and clothing, American films and TV programs in the Far East. And ...Why not? Why not Selena Ltd. Oriental. She could have Jacqueline create a whole new line. European style adapted for the look of the oriental face. Fat and Chen could research the differences in skin. Dino would study the market and possible outlets. It was two in the morning. But all of a sudden she couldn't wait to discuss the idea.

"Do you have any idea what hour this is?" Dino said when she called him. "But it's a great idea! We'll have to dig up some R&D money. Let me work on potential market figures. Fat has a new computer whiz, I'll borrow for a few weeks. We should be able to get you some usable figures."

Nicoletta and Jacqueline when she reached them were wild for the project. Nicoletta especially as much of her young days had been spent in Japan, where her Father had been the Italian Ambassador.

"You speak Japanese, Nicoletta?"

"Yes."

"Any Korean or Chinese?"

"Well, I'm reasonably fluent in Cantonese."

"Wonderful. How do you feel about spending time in the orient? I'll need you with me to set up in the East."

"I'd love it." Nicoletta didn't give a second thought to the possible disruption of her personal life. For her as well as Jacqueline, Selena Ltd. had become a center around which everything else revolved.

Several days later when he arrived East, she spoke to Chen. His response was positive. And then he rocked her.

"Selena, I think I'd like to head it up. I mean think of it. I am after all Oriental. I know the products very well, I think when all is said and done, it would be a good move".

Selena didn't know how to respond. Chen had seemed to distance himself the last year or two from the affairs of Selena Ltd. And although he knew the products inside and out, he knew next to nothing about marketing, or customer relations or promotion.

His request was unrealistic. She had no idea what occasioned it, until she remembered an odd conversation with Fat several months ago. He'd asked Selena if Chen had mentioned the possibility of going back to China to live. She hadn't given it much thought. She always felt Chen was American by conviction and desire, Oriental only by birth.

Now she wondered whether her careful distancing, and his diminished role in Selena Ltd was finally coming home to roost in this odd request.

It was totally out of the question. He had no experience or flare for this part of the business.

As gently as she could she said, " Chen I can't offer you the position. I don't honestly think you're qualified, and there is so much that needs your attention here, don't you think?"

There was a pause. His voice was cool and calm, as he accepted her decision. "I guess you're right. Maybe I wouldn't be much a good as a manager."

Selena felt overwhelming sadness hearing his

words. There was something so defeated in their tone. She knew that with her refusal she had somehow shut a door once and for all.

But during the next year, once the idea was sounded, its realization   seemed to take on a demanding, exciting life of its own for all of them claiming their time and energies. The planning was a nightmare, complicated as it was with cultural and practical differences, but was slowly was taking on reality.

Chapter: 2

"A plenary board meeting? I'm sorry Paul I don't fully understand." Paul's voice sounded cold and mechanical in the earpiece of her telephone as he explained the obligatory board meeting. It was written into the articles of incorporation that such a meeting could be convoked at any time a large portion of the board thought it exigent.

It had been weeks since she had last spoken with him. He'd called her several days after he received his packet of figures for Selena Ltd Oriental, and voiced some reservations, especially at the amount of new capital that they would have to raise. But a plenary board meeting?!

Selena was aware, as he must also be, that the Asian development would raise their corporate profile, possibly evoking competition or opposition from companies that previously hadn't been challenged by their special niche within the cosmetics industry. She was willing as always, even eager for challenge, but she wondered if a 'businessman' would be as keen. It gave her pause for a moment until she thought about Dino's solid business sense, his shrewdness and positive judgment on the project.

"Will next Tuesday do?"

"Perfectly. At the Mansard. Five o'clock," Paul stipulated.

She had a feeling, from his tone, that this meeting might be about more than the details of the Asian proposal. Or even its funding. The Asian project spoke to some real fundamentals- her vision, her judgement, and her leadership of the company.

For the first time in years she felt anxious. Balance

sheets were good. Year after year, despite expenses the growth was there. And out of the blue this questioning. She'd notified everyone about the meeting.

Dino and Nicoletta, no problem, she reached in the city.

Chen she reached in California through his answering service.

She phoned John. His answering service referred her to a hotel in Cleveland. He was on a signing tour for his latest. When she reached him she asked how things were going. He told her, fine with a tone of voice that told her as usual he would rather be somewhere writing, but felt obligated to his editor to 'be in Cleveland'.
When she told him about the meeting, he listened, but she could tell from the background voices someone was urging him to 'hurry up we can't be late', with a good deal of distraction. However, he said he would make a point to be back in time.

Jacqueline when reached in a small hour of the morning, responded with her usual energy "Ne t'inquiete pas cherie. Je suis la avec toi le mardi" don't worry, I'll be there on Tuesday.

So they would all come

Now in the last hour before the meeting, the past swept over her. The memory of moments and years, of people and times, the landmarks of her life. All seemed to lead to this moment, this meeting in this place at this time.

Noah had taught her to meet adversity with a calm outward look no matter what the inner turmoil, Dino had shown her how to fight when odds seemed insurmountable, Fatimah to trust her own taste and judgment, Jacqueline to welcome the new, and John, bless him, the virtue of loyalty. But still all her people gathering today depended in the end on her and her alone.

Looking at the hands of the clock sweeping the last minutes before five, she had a last cigarette, checked her appearance, and put down her notes on Selena Ltd. Oriental. She breathed slowly and deliberately using the image of kelp waving beneath the Pacific Ocean almost a mantra to give her calm and strength. She would walk into the meeting with nothing in her hands, and a smile on her lips.

As she entered the boardroom her eyes swept the table, There were her friends and allies. Three of them had been lovers. Nicoletta gave her a smile, Jacqueline fresh from her flight blew a miniature kiss of encouragement and approval. Dino was concentrated on his notes. John had phoned he would be a few minutes late, but she would not delay beginning for the presence of the smallest shareholder. Nor she thought should she dilute the impetus of her entrance.

Her bankers had been more than supportive. They had done well for each other. So it had to be Paul. If there were an adversarial spearhead it would be he.

Leaving a faint trail of Diorissimo, she went directly to the head of the table, and stood.

Her hands gracefully placed on the back of her chair. She paused, and looked once more around.

Paul was at the foot of the table facing her, with two senior vice presidents from the Hanover on either side of him-the three identically dressed in navy pin-striped suits with hand tied bow ties. She had often found this uniformity amusing. Suddenly it was sinister.

Jacqueline and Nicoletta sat side by side, next to an empty chair which awaited John. Facing the windows were Chen, and two representatives from Selena LTD's current law offices. To her right Dino. Another meeting would have found them all chatting amiably . This time there was only silence. The air was charged.

"Good afternoon", she said softly, her inimitable husky voice miraculously steady. "Shall we begin?" The question as she put it was a command, and with it she took charge of the meeting for all the world as if she had called it. At the end of the table she saw one of the Hanover men restraining Paul with his hand.

"I hope you have all had occasion to study the figures for our expansion into Asia. I will ask Mr. Marchetti to talk them through for you, and I hope by the end of this meeting we can agree that this is a logical step for Selena Ltd. and clear up any questions you may have."

Dino started. "As you can see from the marketing research, we have done extensive exploration of the Selena Ltd. potential of this territory. While it is true Asia has its own approach to beauty and beauty products, we have also extremely positive indications that prestigious up-scale name-brand European products for Eastern women have gained an important foothold. We are, if anything, even a little late entering the field. But I think we can all agree it was necessary to establish a solid hold in Europe before venturing elsewhere."

"It will be the European Selena Ltd. going into Japan and the other Asian markets which will fetch top dollar, as do other Produits d'excellence from Europe. The marketing perforce will be expensive matching that of the top French and Italian marques. But the moneys we have already expended in investigation of just what products, and where they should be offered, will in the end pay off and provide us enormous savings. Perhaps we can take a look at the breakdown now."

Giving them a minute to turn to the budgeting pages as she sat for the first time, Selena caught a look passing between Paul and one of the Hanover VPs. The only word for it was snide and it made her uneasy.

She wondered-just how and when will they attack ? It has to come just as sure as 'night must fall'.

She looked again at the foot of the table, neither of the Hanover men nor Paul had touched their papers.

She counted again in her head. Together they held 46% of the voting stock. Conceivably they could make funding difficult, even refuse to underwrite the project, but they didn't have the power to stop her. At least not on paper.

They would have to control more shares, which simply wasn't possible. Dino, Jacqueline, Nicoletta, Chen and John together had 22%, she had 32%. They'd all worked incredible hours on the project singly or together. They were all enthusiastically for it. Although Chen had been in California the last month, she had talked with him extensively and couldn't imagine he would disagree. He was in a very real sense the originator of the Oriental idea. John never involved himself in strategic decisions. His shares she could count on.

Jacqueline and Nicoletta followed Dino's walk-through explanation of the figures attentively.

As her eyes turned to Chen she wondered why he seemed to stare blankly into the distance. Why are you so uncomfortable Chen? What is bothering you. I know money matters are not your thing, but now is not the time to be here only in absentia! And why have you too not touched the papers?

Selena was still worrying about Chen, when she heard the two bankers exchange sotto voce remarks, and simultaneously draw sharp deleting lines across the last few summation pages as she heard Dino say..

"And to recapitulate, short term potential losses will be covered by..."His sentence remained unfinished.

Rising to his feet the Hanover representative interrupted abruptly.

"It's not necessary to continue", he said "We can all see this is an under-researched and inadvisable fantasy."

It was a shocking statement. The emotional temper of the room exploded. Jacqueline, Nicoletta looked at her stunned, by the manner and discourtesy of the man. Dino flushed a violent shade of red. " What the hell are you talking about. I'm not finished. We have important decisions to complete here" And then nearly shouting,. "I'm not interested in some 'back office', off-the-cuff commentary at this point."

With the last word he slammed his palm down on the table. Selena was glad it was only the table he hit, she knew his temper and this was the kind of thing that evoked it.

Incredibly, still leaning forward on the table, the banker went on sarcastically, "We, that is to say the majority of stockholders, will not permit this expansion. We feel that the very existence of this proposition demonstrates a lack of responsible direction. Not only will we have nothing to do with it, we insist that the leadership which proposed the plan be changed, and forthwith."

And here it was. Out in the open. Not the project-the projector. Selena caught her breath. But the banker continued, louder and with even less courtesy.

"Clearly the present director is susceptible to very bad advice, or arguably on her own, has initiated this injudicious corporate project. The Hanover bank will have nothing to do with it, nor the policy which spawned it.

I do not wish to speak directly for Mr. Van Vloeck, but I believe his sentiments are the same."

A caustic smile crossed his face as he turned to Paul. "I couldn't agree more", said Paul on cue, looking angrily at Selena. "Father would have counseled against this, and so do I."

Dino's face was contorted, his eyes blazed. Selena recognized he was moments from physical action. She stood up, moved behind him, and placed her hands gently on his shoulders.

"Forgive me for saying so," she intervened with icy politeness barely concealing her own anger, "But I've never been convinced that you knew anything about what your Father thought or wanted."

And in that instant she recognized that Paul wanted 'his heritage' back. He wanted her company for his own. He wanted control. The rest was mere ploy.

He rose, so that they faced each other standing, as she said flatly,

"We can certainly put my leadership to a vote of confidence, if you wish before going further. But I believe that 54% of the voting power is behind the move which we were discussing. And I now move that we verify that statement with an immediate vote."

She sat down. Fury at what had occurred made her tremble. But she thought, Noah would have approved her actions. Paul's next words hit as if he had actually struck her.

"I believe, Signora, that you are mistaken."

Years of resentment and hatred oozed out with the words. Vengeance on the unacceptable Italian whore his Father had thought he loved was in his hands. To acquire his Father's power, and prestige, the son had to humiliate Selena Di Angelo, as she had once rejected and humiliated him, and for good measure destroy her creation.

" Mr. Chen will vote with us, I believe", he spat with increasing mockery in his voice.

Selena looked swiftly at Chen, aghast. He refused her eyes. Then glancing only at Paul, rose quickly, and quit the boardroom, indicating proxy forms sitting on the table in front of Paul, as he went.

My God! He's actually left! What is happening?! The words tumbled through her mind. Actually she said nothing aloud. Until her head could clear.

Nicoletta and Jacqueline remained stunned. Dino paralyzed by the turn of events.

A lightning calculation told her that without Chen's shares she could gather only 49%. If Van Vloeck was right she'd lost her company. Selena Ltd. would belong to these men.

Laying her glasses very deliberately on the table in front of her, she folded her arms across her chest so that her hands could grasp her rigid shoulders. Then said the only thing she could, "I will have to hear this from Mr. Chen himself." Indicating to Dino to go after him.
Paul shook his head in denial, picking up the papers, and starting to address the meeting.

At this point the door to the boardroom opened. All eyes turned towards it. It was not Chen they saw, but John arriving impossibly late, the rumpled artist incarnate, a large manila envelope under his arm.

What an impossible time for him to arrive, Selena thought, he's probably been with his agent. Even though his 2% gave him no leverage, she found she had wanted his support, his presence at this meeting.

"I'm sorry to be so late, ladies and gentlemen." He delivered a courtly bow in the direction of Jacqueline and Nicoletta as if he were entering into a social occasion instead of the havoc of a hostile take-over.

"I crossed Chen in the lobby on my way in. I presume he's no longer a part of this meeting."

"Quite right." Paul answered him. "But then you've missed quite a lot. We…"

He paused for effect, then went on with overt pleasure in the iteration, "We," indicating the bankers to his right, "are vetoing the Asian expansion, and furthermore are demanding the election of a new chief executive officer of this company, as we now hold 51% of the voting stock."

The rest of the room received these words in silence.

"And how is that?" asked John in a calm. Almost condescending manner, addressing Paul as if he were still a naughty child who should have known better, still at the knee of his old friend Noah.

Paul caught it, and was furious at the lack of respect. Even Selena flashed John a dark look. His behavior seemed almost ludicrous in this time and place. Damn him for coming late. Damn him for his casualness. He didn't seem to know what was going on was deadly serious.

"Chen has transferred his voting rights to us. He has plans to leave and set up his own company in Taiwan. We feel we will be able to find him the backing he needs. He will retain his shares but has ceded us permanent voting rights."

Paul grasped the proxy papers.

" He wishes to retain a financial interest in the company, but in light of his potential status as a competitor, and out of respect for his old 'friend' Signore di Angelo he will not vote", Paul announced to John. "His non-vote gives us effectively a share majority." A fifty-one percent equivalent.

It was clear to Selena he had gone to the pains of finding out about Selena's brief affair with Chen. And possibly used his bitterness and rejection to induce the transfer. It hardly mattered that Paul had always thought of her a whore. She had never cared, but she could hardly encompass her misjudgment about Chen's real feelings and the disaster that misjudgment had visited on Selena Ltd.

"And he left rather than giving Signora Di Angelo

and the rest of us the respect of telling us to our faces of his actions, is that it?" John asked.

"Let us say, that Mr. Chen felt that his presence was no longer required", Paul crowed.

The support she'd always had from Nicoletta and Jacqueline was neutralized by the sudden, drastic turn of events. Chen had made her a wide-open target. John seemed intent on making a fool of himself and her. She'd lost control of her beloved company. All she had was her dignity, and this she would hold on to if hell froze over. But My God how hard it was. Selena fought back tears.

"So now", Paul continued addressing Selena with mock civility, enjoying how long he could spin out the moment, "shall we take that vote you suggested?"

Selena didn't respond.

But John, in the jocular manner he had used since entering the room said, "Yes indeed."

He sat down in the seat Chen had abandoned, and produced a blue legal folder from the crumpled manila envelope he had carried in.

"Of course you can give us some documentation of the transfer of Chen's voting rights to you or your group, since they seem to be the critical ones", he added.

Selena thought, she could not stand anymore of this charade.

"Yes, of course we can."

"And those rights would be contingent upon his owning the stock?"

Paul enjoying his own arrogance and sadism didn't catch the irony.

"Of course. Now let's get on with it."

"Well then," John replied, still utterly dispassionate, " 'We' should take a look at this document which I have just come from having notarized. I think you will find that as of this morning Chen no longer owns shares in Selena Ltd."

He had riveted the attention of everyone in the room. Selena dizzy with emotion gripped the table in front of her.

"He sold his entire bloc this day".. John paused to let Paul squirm as he had suffered others to do, "to me. Now shall we go on with the vote?"

Selena's disbelief turned the corner to incipient hysteria. She wanted to laugh, or cry-she didn't know which.

John in his quiet way had saved her, as he seemed to have done over and over throughout the years. She couldn't help it, tears coursed down her face even as she smiled.

After a hurried and angry perusal of the documents, a demand for a copy, which John laconically supplied from the envelope. The Bank's Vice President took Paul's arm, indicating they no longer had any business in this meeting. So shocked was he by the complete reversal neither he nor they were able to say anything as they went.

"A retreat then gentlemen? Until another time?" Selena needed the lift of a parting shot.

Through her tears she knew full well there would never be another day with this group. She rose with an exquisite show of politeness and saw them to the door. "Do you think it would be safe to have some champagne?" She said returning and sitting abruptly in her chair.

"Not only safe, cherie, mais obligatoire", Jacqueline responded. Kissing her twice on each cheek, wiping her tears with a snowy handkerchief, then kissing her once firmly on the lips. Selena blushed. But squeezed Jacqueline's shoulder briefly in return.

" Most likely they'll want to sell their shares, John

said. "We can think about that tomorrow. Dino will have to come up with a new bank, and some kind of stock re-purchase plan."

Selena wanted to kiss him. Decided she would. Then did. The warmth and length of their embrace seemed only appropriate to the moment.

When she looked for him, Selena saw that Dino had left the room. She found him in his office, angrily examining the back of his signet ring, which had cracked with the blow to the table.

"Dino, come celebrate."

As he looked up she saw he was ashamed.

"Why didn't I know? I should have paid more attention to Chen." His voice broke, "I should have known all of this. I've let you down, Selena." He rubbed his hands through his hair, in frustration. It stood up in ringlets.

"You couldn't" She said softly, " Nobody, not even I, has ever really understood Chen or what he wanted.."
"Come", she whispered, taking his hand and kissing it gently, " have some champagne. We've all earned it after this morning's battle."

And so the toast by them all, "To Selena Ltd., and to Selena Ltd. Orient."

"To absent friends" Selena toasted in her turn remembering Fatimah, and Maria, and Noah.

CEILINGS VII

Chapter: 1

Selena walked with John out into the quiet blocks surrounding the Mansard in the after-work period that brought dormancy to Fifth Avenue. They saw a few weary leftover window shoppers, a policeman finishing his beat, a bag woman closing her pitch, a yellow taxi stopping for one last fare from the closing neighborhood. John stopped to light his pipe.

Selena didn't want to let him go. There were things that had to be said. And so she asked whether he would have a drink with her in the Bar of the nearby Gotham Hotel.

The bar was dark, relaxed. Comfortable padded leather seats, banquettes and heavy mahogany tables whose highly polished surfaces shined even in the subdued lighting, were discretely distanced one from the other. The service was attentive but didn't intrude.

When their drinks arrived they sat for a while without speaking. Each lost in their own thoughts. Each reviewing what had happened this afternoon.

John felt, he was glad he had been able to hear about what was going down in order to get hold of the critical shares. And even more glad that his beloved Selena was once again on her feet.

Selena thought-how am I ever going to repay John for what he's done, and done so casually. There's no way. He had read the situation correctly, she, who should have known better had not.

But that was not the heart and soul of it. He's loved and watched over me all these years. He's known about what I've done, what I've tried to do. And about my lovers. And through it all he's been there. Quietly, steadily there, just there. Seeing what's needed, and doing it. And that is what love is. Not the pounding excitement, not the fascination, not the physical gratification of the moment. Why have I not understood.?

And suddenly she did. I haven't looked with eyes that wanted to see, or a heart that wanted to understand. Did I not have the time? Was I too busy? Perhaps? Did I not want commitment? Perhaps.

He had been a marvelous friend, and a sort of Dutch uncle, but now she wanted him to be more. She wanted him at the center of her life, she wanted to share all that she had done, all that she had been, and all that she could be with him. But first she knew she had to tell him what she felt. It would not come easily, but it had to be spoken aloud.

And so, in the quiet darkness of the bar she told him about the part of her life she had not shared before, and about what she had come to understand. It took quite a time.

John simply listened. Then said, " You're tired Selena. Let me take you home."

Selena knew he deliberately didn't specify where. And so chose gladly. "To the Beresford?"

A smile passed over his lips, his eyes shone with pleasure. "The Beresford", he agreed.

As they entered his apartment, Selena asked him if he would mind if she showered, it had been such a long day, she felt she needed to refresh. But then had to pause until he showed her where to go. She'd never been in that part of his apartment.

She returned, enveloped in one of the large Terry-cloth robes she had found. John had prepared some sandwiches and coffee. They ate peacefully looking out over the park as the last of the sun's glow faded against its trees and lakes.

When coffee was finished, Selena rose, simply held

out her hand, and lead John into the bedroom.

He took her in his arms, breathing in the faint scent of his own toilet water from the softness of her neck and shoulders. He touched the tender skin of her temples with his lips, then both eyes and her cheeks. Then her glorious dark hair.

Warmth and hunger swelled within her, as she returned the caresses, feeling the faint roughness of beard on his chin and face. She traced the lines around his mouth and eyes, soothing with the warmth of her hands those touches of past suffering.

And now she knew she felt hunger for this affectionate contact with its strong sexual undertow which rose minute by minute, urging satisfaction.

John kissed her mouth, his was soft, so soft and trembling just slightly in his desire for her, so long denied. His lips moved sensuously over hers, gentle, but needing her taste, like food or drink.

Selena opened her mouth under his, seeking his tongue. Slowly he skimmed the inner softness of her lower lip with the tip of his tongue. Then sensing her desire, her welcome went deeper into the satiny warmth of her mouth.

With one hand he cradled the back of her head, with the other he half caressed, half supported her back.

He let her body accustom itself to the length of his, feeling her defined female curves and hollows.

And she knew that as a lover he had changed. His body, his smell, the feel of him against her was familiar, comforting, but the sensuality of his love making was new and, she had no other thought, exciting, enchanting her senses.

His need for her swelled against her. She was completely ready, when he took her into the bedroom, undressed her fully, leaving her in the wrapping and warmth of the robe.

He mounted, entered her and unhurried and sure, brought them both to climax in long, probing strokes.
Selena knew she had come home, in every sense of that word.

They made love again and yet again-gloriously, generously, reveling in the pleasure they gave one another.
John fell asleep in her arms.

Finally, she looked up to see the simple transparent cloth draped over the top of the four-poster bed and thought, it looked like what had been suggested- a seventh ceiling, but somehow felt more, no matter how sentimental it sounded, more like a seventh heaven.

Still later, just as dawn came rose-tinting the diaphanous tester above her head, she got up, went to her carry-all, and took from it the current Ceilings journal.

She opened it, paged through it musing. Pausing here and there briefly, then shut it, went to the bookshelf next to the bed, found the shelf holding all of John's published work, and tucked it in, just at the end, he might not notice, but she would know it was there. And if he ever wanted to read it, well... it was there.
Without waking him, she returned to bed, as if she had never left.

She had come home.

Lucienne Countess von Doz has lived in New York, and Italy, She now resides in Paris.

She is the founder of The Singers Development Foundation, a non-profit organization benefiting young opera singers world wide.

She also lends her time and image to Crème de la Mer in memory of her longtime friend Dr. Max Huber, its creator.

Countess von Doz is currently at work on her second novel *Folies Bergère.*

Dr. M.E. Hecht is an orthopedic surgeon and graduate of Yale Drama School. She has written several books and screenplays.